Starling
Nightcastle

Table of Contents

Starling Nightcastle

BOOK ONE

Deals With Demons

By Ubriel Bryne

Copyright

Starling Nightcastle

Book One

Deals With Demons

First Edition

Copyright © 2023 Amy Norton, Jami Lee Montgomery, and UbrielBryneBooks.com

ISBN-13: 979-8-9864469-1-2

Credit acknowledgement to:

Clarissa Kezen of CK Book Cover Designs for the beautiful cover of this book.

Connect with Clarissa at https://ckbookcoverdesigns.com/.

Madam Stephanie Ann Norton; cover model and all-around wonderful person.

Mademoiselle Josie Cheyenne Norton; freelance photographer and free spirit.

Connect with Stephanie or Josie (or both!) through email at mmes@ubrielbrynebooks.com.

---

1. https://ubrielbrynebooks-my.sharepoint.com/personal/admin_ubrielbrynebooks_com/Documents/

   Documents/C%20WRITING/A%20STARLING%20NIGHTCASTLE/

   Book%201%20Deals%20With%20Demons/C%20Scheduled%20to%20Publish/

   www.ubrielbrynebooks.com

Prologue

I was twenty-nine when I met Crow. That's when my life veered into the realm of fantasy. It took me a few years to recognize the nightmare it would become. Finding a way out took many years more.

I had just been released from an eight-month stay with the kindly sadists on staff at the Central Regional Mental Health and Wellness Center in southern Nebraska. I remember, it was so cold my nose went numb before I could fish my scarf out of the paper shopping bag full of my personals. The tail end of winter had brought freezing rain and sleet to turn the snow to sludge.

There I was, teeth chattering, knees getting soggy, paper bag clutched in one arm and my other arm elbow deep in my effects. A young man, probably a college student working as a process server to pay tuition, squatted down beside me and offered to hold the bag for me. I thought it was a kind gesture. I still do, honestly. He took the bag and stood beside me, patiently holding it open until I found my mismatched gloves and old Doctor Who scarf. You know the one. Tom Baker-style, wrapped triple around my neck and shoulders and still hanging to my knees. He waited until I had both gloves on and was breathing hot, moist air into the scarf to defrost my nose. When he handed my bag back to me, he stuck out his hand, told me a name, probably not his real one, and waited.

I've always been a sucker. To the best of my knowledge, that trick would probably still work on me. I took the offered hand and gave my name, and he pulled a thick envelope from inside his coat. I was still staring, gape-mouthed, at the envelope he'd dropped on top of my bag with a quick, "You've been served," as he walked away. I probably still had my hand stuck out, too.

I peeked inside the envelope on the off chance it had been filled with cash and discovered I was officially alone in the world. I remember staring blankly at the divorce papers in the envelope and thinking strange things like how we had planned to visit his family at Easter and wondering if we were still going to do that. I started to wonder where I would go and what I would do. I couldn't have been standing there too long, but I don't remember seeing the guy, or his car, as I crossed the empty visitor's parking lot to the bus stop.

I don't know if you've ever been in Chester City, and I don't recommend it if you haven't, but there are more hills than people. I slipped and slid and fell more than once. By the time I bustled myself under the bus shelter, it didn't matter if the bench was wet. The ass of my jeans was soaked and trying to freeze against my skin. I wrapped the scarf higher over my face and began to have serious thoughts about how pleasant and warm it would be to just quietly drift off to sleep and die.

Oddly, I don't think I actually cried. I have no idea how long he had been there before he made a noise and I looked up. He startled me, standing there, shuffling from foot to foot, turning his head this way and that, and his close-set, black eyes always on me. I don't remember if I said hello or just scooted my ice-butt farther down the bench, but he sat next to me, a little too close, and held his hands up to his narrow face, covered his mouth and nose and made a show of blowing into them.

He said, "I'm Crow Corvus," smiled and stuck his hand out.

I remember thinking his parents had a warped sense of humor. I also remember thinking that the last nice guy with a handshake had served me divorce papers. Remember what I said about being a sucker?

I shook his hand. "Star. Short for Starling."

The wind and sleet and even the freezing drizzle, sort of, stopped. The sun didn't come out, but I felt warmer. He tilted his head at me, still holding my hand, and asked, "What's wrong, Little Bird?"

Now, I know it's odd. Who just tells her life story to some random weird guy at the bus stop? But, apparently, I did. Bad marriage. Sad circumstances. Devastating loss. A diagnosis and, finally, a stay in the looney bin. There I was, one hand imprisoned in his and the other clutching those vile papers.

"Would you like the pain to stop?"

He was really much too close, but I can't remember thinking much of anything before I heard myself saying, whimpering really, "Yes, please, for fuck's sake, I really want it to stop."

Then, it did.

Chapter 1. Coffee

My name is Starling Nightcastle. I often wake from dreams about living someone else's nightmare. For most of my life, I've been stuck in my own nightmare, looking for a way out. One day, I'd find one. Until then, I needed coffee.

The Holy Grounds Café is open 24/7, except on Christmas Day. Then, it's only open after noon. That works for me. I don't usually wake up until a couple of hours before dark. Jacob, never Jake, the owner and worst short order cook ever, doesn't like it when I come in through the back. So, I do almost every night.

The heavy, metal door at the top of the stairs to my basement apartment effectively cut off sound, light, heat and smells from the kitchen. As I pushed it open, using the insubstantial force of my entire upper body, my senses were flooded with scraping sounds of metal spatulas on the metal griddle, glaring white brightness, warm and humid air, and the scents of greasy fries, searing meat, mystery soup and toasting burger buns. I inhaled deep and slow. *'There it is.'* Coffee, fresh, black and unfailingly strong.

"Hi, Jacob." I waved and snagged a mug from the top of a rack and kept walking toward the swinging half-door.

"Star! You can't come through here." I am still, to this day, surprised by the vehemence in his voice even after years of my nightly intrusions.

"I know. I'm going." I stopped at the server station and poured a generous serving of coffee into the mug.

Genia, Jacob's wife, came through the swinging doors, carrying a tray piled high with dirty dishes. "Hey, Star. How are you this evening?" Genia didn't bother trying to get me out of the kitchen. She just greeted me like another regular customer at the counter, set down her tray, and reached up to pull a pen out of her cap of strawberry blond curls. "You want breakfast or supper?"

I sipped my coffee and hummed as the scalding liquid traveled down my gullet. "Hey, Genia. A little of both, maybe? How about a short stack and a basket of chicken strips?"

"You got it, Hun. You go on and sit down out there and I'll bring it to you shortly." She never bothered to ask if I wanted anything other than coffee to drink anymore.

I waved again at Jacob. He waved his spatula over his head already turning back to his griddle. I usually took that as a hello or goodbye, whichever seemed more relevant.

My coffee and I wandered out into the dining area, leaving Genia to call out my order. I heard Jacob calling back. "She was right here, Gee-gee. I got it." That made me snort and I almost choked on my coffee.

There was always a newspaper on the counter beside the cash register. I didn't have any idea who bought it, but the funny pages, the legal notices and the obits were always missing. That's fine with me. I'd see who died in town when the sun went down.

I picked up the sales and coupons section and took it to the far end of the bar. I still like looking at what people are being convinced to buy. I don't know why. There is always something ridiculous to make me grin. I don't need any motivation other than that.

The AGA, Allied Grocers' Association, was running a sale on pig's feet. I scanned the rest of their ads but didn't see any equally discounted deals on chops, hams, loins, or bacon. There was, however, a competitive offer on jowls. "Gross."

"Have you ever even tried any?"

I still didn't choke on my coffee, although the ads caught a light spray when I sputtered. "Jesus, Crow!"

"Please, Little Bird," he held up a hand and turned his face from me. "Watch your language in my presence."

I snatched a few napkins from the countertop dispenser and wiped my face. I didn't actually need to, but a simple glare didn't convey the necessary emphasis that came with the glare combined with indignant blotting. "You're here early. I haven't even eaten yet."

"Oh! Excellent." He slipped his long, woolen trench coat off and picked up the plastic menu that served as a place mat. "I want to try Jacob's chili."

Genia came through the kitchen door carrying my food. She slowed not quite to a standstill when she saw Crow. "Mr. Corvus. Will you be dining with us tonight?" Her typically ebullient smile was propped up by sheer force of will as she deposited my food in front of me.

"Hello, Ms. Genia." Crow smiled so broadly I thought his teeth might begin to fall out. He had a lot of them. Too big and too pointy for his mouth, when he smiled that big, it gave me the creeps, and I'm used to him. "Do you have chili?"

"Sure do, Mr. Corvus."

Genia always called him Mr. Corvus. I asked her once about why she was so formal with him. She had said, "You keep things formal with the devil's minions and they can't catch you in a moment of weakness." I have no idea how Genia found out about Crow's true nature. I didn't tell her. But, it happened now and then.

"Then, I would like to have a bowl of chili, please."

"You're going to want something to wash it down with. It's spicy." Genia pulled the pen out of her hair, again, and scribbled on her order pad.

"Oh, what flavors of milkshake do you have?"

I, quietly minding my own business from behind the coffee-bespeckled newspaper, groaned. I crumpled the newspaper out of my way and goggled at him. I know he saw me. He could literally see out of the back of his head, and the sides. He ignored me, smiled at Genia, and listened to the options.

"I have vanilla ice cream and a bunch of sundae syrups. Caramel, chocolate, strawberry, buttersc..."

"Strawberry. A bowl of chili and a big strawberry milkshake with extra whipped cream, please, Ms. Genia." He smiled again. With fewer teeth this time, his smile almost managed to be as smooth as his voice. He was never much to look at, but when he wanted to, he could calm traffic with his voice.

Genia nodded and jotted down his order. She glanced up before scurrying away and I swear I could see her beginning to blush. I waited till she'd gone, then smacked Crow on the shoulder with my newspaper. "Bad demon."

Crow lifted one hand to fend off the next wallop and my newspaper crumbled to ash. I sighed, watching the ash flutter to the floor, and wiped my hands together to brush away any errant smudges before I touched my food. "I was reading that."

"In point of fact, Little Bird, you were wielding it as a weapon." Crow's hand shot out and stole a chicken strip.

"I was eating that."

His beady eyes squinted above his rounded cheeks as a genuine smile, not the creepy, toothy, or sexy ones, lifted the corners of his too broad mouth around the chicken strip. It looked almost obscene if it hadn't been so silly.

After more than a decade together, I could mostly see through his glamour. He wasn't ugly or deformed or anything like that. Really, just plain, scrawny, and pale enough to look anemic. If he'd been a real man, I could probably have snapped him in two. He had a boyish face, a little crooked, and all his features seemed a little under-done. He employed his glamour just enough to discourage anyone uninvited from looking too closely. Except, maybe Genia.

"Don't fuss. I'll be handing off that milkshake to you, I'm sure." He bit off another chunk of my chicken strip and turned to look around the dining room.

The diner was never very full. Well, there was that one time when Jacob's tiny generator had made Holy Grounds the only restaurant in the neighborhood still open for business for almost three days. But, otherwise, there were usually only a dozen patrons at any given time. The food was lousy, but the service was fast, and the coffee was excellent. So, they did okay.

"Well, now, you have obliterated my entertainment. You'll just have to talk to me." I stood on the footrest of my bar stool and leaned over the bar in search of syrup.

Crow turned just as I plopped back into my seat, still syrup-less. He shifted my chicken strip to his other hand and snapped his fingers. Warm syrup not only appeared, it materialized just above my pancakes in a golf ball-sized orb and oozed in a trickling line from its airy container to run down the sides of the stack.

"Thank you." I picked up my fork and watched the last of the syrup bubble drip from the air.

"Mhmm." He turned back to the other diners and nibbled the chicken.

Genia brought a pot of coffee with Crow's order and refilled my cup. When she had gone, leaving an enormous milkshake and a bowl of chili about half its size, Crow said, "I think I've found our next client."

I frowned and shook my head. "I don't hunt in the diner, Crow."

He scooped a spoonful of chili and sniffed it. With a small noise of approval, he popped the spoon in his mouth and closed his eyes to relish his treat.

He liked to make me wait. Once, he made a little old lady's grocery bag keep falling over inside a cab that I was waiting for. I stood there, holding the door and seething, for a full five minutes before the little old lady gave up and told me to keep the groceries.

When he'd swallowed the chili, he lifted the milkshake and sniffed it. He hummed and glanced at me before flicking his tongue out like a shovel to scoop whipped cream from the top. The grimace it produced was priceless. "That's worse than harpy shit." He shoved the milkshake at me.

I moved it to the other side of me just to get it out of his way. He used two paper napkins to scrub the remaining cream from his tongue before lifting another spoonful of chili. There he paused. "He isn't in the diner. He's outside."

I looked over my shoulder and through the plate glass windows. The darkening sky left long shadows on the sidewalk. In one of them, a grizzled man sat huddled against the wall of the building with a little cardboard sign resting against his legs.

I sighed and turned back to my pancakes. "Great." Using the side of my fork, I cut into the pancakes and stabbed them onto the tines, and into my mouth. The syrup, still warm and silky, provided the only real flavor to the bread. I chewed slowly, petulantly hoping to make Crow wait. I dropped my fork and picked up a chicken strip, dipping it unceremoniously into the whipped cream atop Crow's discarded milkshake, before turning my head to look back at the man-shaped huddle again.

A gust of wind rifled his greasy, lanky hair and made the thin material of his jacket sleeves whip around his thin arms. For Crow to have picked him out, his time was coming soon. Within four months.

It was always within four months. Well, one hundred and twenty days. It was a weird time allotment, and Crow was cryptic about why. I pestered him about it early on, until I got a very detailed, two-hour explanation of demon mathematics and something about the moon. I just kept nodding until he'd made his point and figured he probably didn't really know, either.

"So, what's in the folio?"

Crow lifted his napkin and dabbed greasy, red chili streaks from the corners of his mouth. "Not much. He was in the army in his youth but was discharged early for mental health. His pension-poor, single mother took care of him for a few years thereafter, until she died. His personal demons are the little, common ones, alcoholism and drug dependency. With the right treatment, he could have remained a productive member of society, but no one with the power to diagnose and treat him took the time to try." He turned a broad grin in my direction. "Ahh, when human kindness fails." He sighed wistfully and picked up his spoon. "That's my bread and butter."

I turned my narrow-eyed frown on him to convey my disapproval of both the apathy of humans and the delight he took in the suffering it caused. My narrow-eyed frown never bothered him. It occurred to me then, as it had before, that perhaps the look was just egging him on, but it's my only recourse for when he was being annoying. I wasn't giving it up.

"So, he's winning the fight against his own demons?" I looked over my shoulder out the window, dubious. He must be if Crow was interested in saving him from death.

Crow turned in his stool, leaning one elbow on the counter behind him. "He wasn't. But he's actually been completely sober for four days." Crow sighed. He reached into his inner coat pocket and pulled out a sheet of paper folded in half and with writing printed so that it could be read like a pamphlet. "That's when he began going here."

I took the paper in one hand and reached for a napkin with the other. "What is this? A church bulletin?" I turned around straight in my seat and lay the paper flat on the counter, reading the front while I wiped chicken grease from my fingers.

"Almost. It's a soup kitchen." Crow waved his hand in the air between us before flicking his fingers at the paper again. "Open it up. He's been getting a bowl of soup and a kind word." Crow twisted his mouth around the words with a grimace.

I chuckled at him and lifted the paper in my clean hands. The front cover was printed with the words, Fellowship Ministries. Inside, a daily menu listed a type of soup, a passage of scripture and an invitation to that day's volunteer event.

Some small voice in the back of my mind screamed. That little part of me knew how wrong what we did was. But it was as scared as the rest of me. Scared of what would happen to me if I refused to do my part. The chill of fear and dread tingled at the edges of my awareness.

I shoved the bulletin back at Crow and pushed away from the counter. "Time to go."

Chapter 2. Work

Crow walked with me, nattering about this demon or that news article. I pulled the collar of my long pee coat up over the scarf that enveloped my neck and winced at the feel of a sharp pebble through the sole of my shoe. "You destroyed the newspaper before I got to read about any of that, Crow."

"That's really too bad. Not really important, though. There's nothing really new in the news." He donned a self-satisfied grin and clasped his hands together behind his back. His straight-backed posture, clean shaven chin raised, thin lips slightly parted, and eyes half-lidded, was probably his most birdlike pose. I shoved my hands in my coat pockets.

It was full dark when we arrived at the city morgue. The big dark red brick building contained the vital statistics office and the county coroner's office, both accessible from the front. The morgue entrance was around back. The ambulance and hearse access from the street opened out into a wide parking area that would accommodate two of those clunky vehicles while still allowing a third to turn and maneuver. The small lot was empty, as usual.

The one small window in the red double door was covered with a white paper printout, backlit from the hallway inside, giving the hours the morgue was open to the public. I punched my access code into the keypad. Crow stood behind me patiently surveying the night. I cast a glance up the access drive to the empty staff parking lot as the lock buzzed and clicked, and I pulled the door open. Inside, my teeth took up a resonant hum in harmony with the soft buzzing of the white fluorescent lights.

Crow stepped in behind me and followed me to the morgue office. He took a seat on a stool in one corner and began thumbing through the day's reports, while I changed from my personal coat and scarf into my preferred lab coat and went about preparing for work. There were two overdoses and one car crash victim waiting for me to work them through the system. Four more had been worked in but the autopsies hadn't been scheduled yet. Three other completed autopsies needed their notes typed up and the cases closed out.

I glanced at Crow as I walked out to the exam room. He had joined his hands behind his head and leaned his head back with his eyes closed. He didn't usually just hang out with me in the morgue. He was waiting for something; probably our client. Asking would just give him a chance to tease me. I'd find out before long. I turned my back on him and stepped up to the first table. After checking the file number against the table chart, I unzipped the HRB, human remains bag, and sighed. This woman had definitely been in a car crash.

A couple of hours later, I had just finished the initial intake on the second new case when my phone buzzed in my back pocket. Break time. Crow hadn't moved a muscle when I walked back into the cramped office that served double duty as a breakroom. I pulled off one sterile glove, balling it up in the palm of the other, and pulled that one down over my fingers. As the wadded ball of discarded gloves hit the inside of the trash bin, Crow opened his eyes. A toothy grin, the predatory kind, spread on his face a breath before the CCTV security monitors flared to life.

Trained on the small parking lot, the motion sensor on the camera had been triggered by an ambulance pulling into the lot. I watched the bus maneuver into place with one eye as I changed the filter and spooned coffee grounds into the basket. Just as the reverse lights on the ambulance winked out and the doors began to open, I pulled the pot out of the machine and walked out to the water fountain in the hall.

Crow stood and clasped his hands behind his back to follow me as far as the hall. He was preparing his Boss Man façade. The light around him seemed to pull back. It actually dimmed behind him. With a sigh, I rolled my eyes at his display but kept my peace as I pushed the button on the wall. Hearing the click and buzz of the big double doors opening, I turned to the water fountain to fill the pot.

I didn't wait for the paramedics to push their gurney through the doors. As soon as the pot was full, I walked back into the office and started the coffee brewing. The demons would want a cup, too. In the ambulance, that would be Pete and Donna. They're alright as far as demons go. I've met a few less than alright ones. At least these two never broke anything on purpose. They even went so far as to try not to leak sulfur and brimstone around me. With the coffee brewing, I moved into the doorway and leaned my shoulder on the doorframe to watch them wrestle the gurney into the building, headfirst.

"Hey. Who do we have here?" It always rankled Crow just a little when I interrupted his displays of power, so I took every opportunity to do so. Pete and Donna, however, knew who kept their toast buttered and waited for Crow's lead.

Crow turned his toothiness on me, briefly. It was sweet of him to acknowledge my attempt to irritate him. Turning back to his two underlings, he spoke in a deep and reverberant voice. "Who comes?"

Pete and Donna bowed at the waist, still standing on either side of their gurney, and trained their eyes on their own feet. Pete said, "Madelyn Delaney, acute myocardial infarction, officially DOA, but we heard a little prayer..."

Pete and Donna stepped back to stand at the foot of the gurney as Crow stepped forward, the dimness following him. He reached out to lay a hand on the head of the dead woman. "Wake up, Madelyn."

I'd met Madelyn over two months ago, just after she'd celebrated her forty-ninth birthday. Poor health had been her life-long personal demon. It had brought with it a basket full of drugs and injuries and medical bills. She had been a nice lady, even after all of that. Crow's interest in her was a result of a new diet and exercise therapy that had been working for her for almost a year. The corpse on the gurney had lost half its girth in that time and its hair and skin looked healthier than it had two months earlier.

She had done it. She'd won against the demons she had been challenged with. If she turned Crow down, she could leave this life of pain and suffering, having earned the right to a blissful next existence. But, she hadn't quite shuffled off this mortal coil. Her eyes fluttered. No one ever turned Crow down.

Madelyn's eyes took a moment to clear as she focused on the ceiling. The glimmer of recognition sparked as she slowly shifted her eyes to look at Crow, not quite looming above her. She gave a start and sat bolt upright.

That brought Pete and Donna, still standing at the foot of the gurney, hands clasped behind their backs and heads bowed, into view. Confusion and shock began to give way to fear as she took in her surroundings.

The soft rattle of breath filtering through her dead lungs preceded a squeak and a clearing of her throat. "Where am I?" She looked down and gave a strangled cry at the sight of the open HRB and gurney beneath her. "Oh, God." That made all three demons wince. She lifted her hands to her pajama-covered chest. "You said it would happen. You said it was coming. Even with the dreams, I didn't really believe you." Her shoulders began to heave as her breaths quickened and her eyes grew wider, shifting this way and that in search of an escape.

I shifted my feet and held my tongue as Crow slowly stepped up beside her, judging it to be the right time to reel her in. He let the dimness fade, the lights coming back to full strength in the hall as he smiled. With measured movements, he reached out and took one of her hands between his own. His touch stilled the turmoil of her emotions so they could talk. I have no doubt he would have let her continue to panic if he could have conducted business with her in hysterics.

Her eyes locked on his and he asked, "Have you considered my offer?" For the last two months, she had been given dreams every night. Through them, she had been allowed to ride through the experiences of another woman's life. The other woman's demons were nothing like her own, but that woman was losing the fight. The choice was simple. She could choose to have her soul trade places with the soul of this other person, and live her life, with those demons, or she could die there and then.

Madelyn blinked. "Sonya had a big presentation at work today. She missed Lyla's soccer game preparing for it." Her brow creased. "She and Dan got into a huge fight over it. Do you know what happened to them?"

Crow's smile shifted with the smallest narrowing of his glittering eyes. He nodded. "Yes. But unless you accept my offer, that won't be any of your concern."

"Will I still be able to see my sister?" Madelyn had already made her choice. I knew it, Crow knew it, and by the way Pete and Donna's shoulders relaxed, they knew it too.

"No. Not as yourself. She wouldn't believe you anyway." Crow stood completely still.

Madelyn took one more deep breath. "I accept your offer."

I felt a chill run down my spine. That chill alone was enough to begin the fear. Unless something happened to make me pay attention, I never seemed to notice until that point. I cast through my memories of the evening as Crow helped Madelyn to lie back and relax. Had I laughed at Jacob and Genia? Had I enjoyed the warmth of the coffee at the diner? Had a bit of fear and dread accompanied the talk of a potential new client? Had I winced at a pebble poking through the sole of my shoe while walking here? *Was that pulsing ache a bruise forming on the bottom of my foot right now?*

I gave a little start when Crow called my name. "What?"

Crow tilted his head and looked at me from beneath his lashes. "Little Bird, if you would join us, please?"

I gave myself a mental shake as I stood straight. Of course, I could feel those things. Crow always found a new client just in time. I sighed again and could smell the faintest sulfur and brimstone in the air. I tossed a frown at Pete and Donna. They were excited but that wasn't really an excuse. I stepped forward and took one of Madelyn's hands in my own. My turn.

"Madelyn. Before we do this, it's important that we make sure you understand completely." I bent my head to look down into her eyes and tried to impress on her the seriousness of what I was saying.

The slightly older, dead woman nodded. Peevish, and in a hurry now that she knew what was happening, she said, "I remember what you said before. I will be relegating Sonya's soul to die. Tantamount to murder as well as preventing her from taking whatever opportunity she might have had to defeat her own demons, et cetera, et cetera." She made a wobbling motion with her head before meeting my eyes again. "I understand. I want to live. I want that fine and healthy new body. I want to take care of that sweet husband and those two adorable babies. I want to have those Christmases and birthdays surrounded by family that I never had."

A tear welled up and spilled out of the corner of one of her eyes. There might have been more if rigor mortis wasn't setting in. I nodded. I had tried. Not hard, but I'd tried. No one ever thought too hard about how exactly like murder this was. All they could see was the chance to live, to beat death. No one ever asked if there was a guarantee on how long their extension on life would be, either. I wasn't allowed to bring it up.

That was a stipulation of the deal I'd made in the beginning. Once we got them this far, I had five minutes to try to talk them out of it, but I wasn't allowed to mention warranties on the new body or guarantees for duration of the life extension. In exchange, Crow got his soul count, and I didn't have to feel. I didn't have to feel anything. I rarely took the whole five minutes anymore.

Chapter 3. Swap

Astral projection is weird. The ordinary sensations of being alive go wonky when you no longer have a body upon which such forces can act. Instead of gravity holding your feet to the floor and giving your inner ear a sense of balance, it feels more like an impression you might get when reading a compass rose on a map. It's just information; that way is down. Instead of a breeze rifling your hair, it passes through you, almost like a gas bubble traversing your intestines. It isn't unpleasant or anything, just weird.

Crow always appeared as an actual crow. At least to me, his black shadow flew while somehow surrounding my awareness. The client was carried along beneath us, a misty and faintly glowing cloud, sometimes in the vague outline of a person, but often just a roiling cloud. Madelyn kind of resembled a dough girl.

It is strange to me to think that it should take us any time at all to make that flight. Not nearly the amount of time it would take to walk or even to drive, but it did take a few minutes. I asked Crow about it a few times. He actually tried to explain, probably because he knew it would just confuse me more. I tried not to think about all the things he couldn't explain.

Eventually, we arrived in the bedroom of the sleeping, and completely clueless, Sonya and Dan. The woman sleeping in the tangle of sheets and blankets wasn't particularly beautiful or even very thin; her pudgy belly spilled out over the top of a pair of bikini style underwear. But she was alive and healthy and everything Madelyn thought she wanted to be. Madelyn's ghost hovered above her, a longing look on her ephemeral features.

Crow, in man-shape again, stood beside me holding my hand. I reached down to lightly touch the shoulder of the sleeping woman and closed my eyes. I didn't like to watch. I said a silent prayer for Sonya and Madelyn. She could still back out. Crow jostled me, as he always did, and my eyes popped open. I had to be an active participant, which meant I had to watch.

Crow laid one hand on Madelyn's ghost, and she slowly lowered into the sleeping body. At the same time, another form, Sonya's soul, seeped out of her body through every pore. Crow made a pulling motion, as if lifting a sheet, as we stepped back. Sonya's ghost coalesced in front of us, her face confused but not yet alarmed.

"Sonya?" Crow smiled as she focused on him. "My name is Crow Corvus. I have unfortunate news for you."

She began to look a little concerned at that. Before she could speak, another form appeared beside her. There was no pop or staticky crackle or any of that silliness. Only a slight stirring of otherwise calm air announced the reaper's arrival. Sonya turned and shied away a step. She bumped against the side of the bed and turned her head sharply toward it, toward her own sleeping body. *There it is. Now she's alarmed.*

The reapers didn't particularly like Crow's little venture. It cut into their schedule and caused last-minute changes in their assigned routes, but they're neutral parties. Professional courtesy, if nothing else, prevented them from interfering or putting their own strictures on him, but they wouldn't help him beyond the scope of their job either. This one was in the form of a young man, probably less than twenty years old at the time it was copied. There was no telling when that had been. The form wore the severe black suit with its hooded robe that was the uniform of the reapers rather than the clothes of any given era. But the hair was cut in a boy band style that spoke of the early nineties.

"Master Reaper." Crow gave a solemn and formal bow.

"Crow." The reaper groaned and turned to Sonya. "Sonya Melville Berkowitz?"

"Yeah? Who are you? Why are you here?" Sonya's strangled voice warbled, grasping at the common, while her eyes rolled toward her body and away again, fleeing the terrifying.

She was Jewish. They never asked about things like that. Everyone always assumed the new life would be the same as their own in all these little ways. I sighed again. *So much for Madelyn's Christmases.*

The reaper laid a hand on Sonya's shoulder and, in a voice that held a long-suffering note of boredom, said, "You are dead. Welcome to the afterlife." Before the ghost could work up a good protest, probably before she could wrap her thoughts around what the reaper had said, they were gone.

I turned to Crow and gave him the best withering look I could muster. He grinned, toothy and creepy, and reached down to touch the sleeping woman's hip. A tiny piece of soul material came away on his fingertips, like the dust from a nacho cheese flavored snack. He plucked his handkerchief from where it stuck out of his coat pocket and rubbed it between his soul-dusted fingers. Tucking the handkerchief back into his pocket, he shifted back into his crow form and flew us back to the morgue.

Pete and Donna had slumped a little on their feet but hadn't moved. They straightened sharply as Crow and I drew deep breaths upon reentering our own bodies. Well, I reentered my body. I'm not sure if Crow's body stayed or went during those trips. The soul dust on his handkerchief would seem to suggest that he went physically, but that's not definitive proof when it comes to a demon.

"How'd it go, Sir?" Donna chirped in a high and ringing voice.

Crow took my hand as he plucked the handkerchief from its pocket once more. "Excellent. Excellent. Thank you for asking, Donna." He shot Pete a significant glance, then turned to me. "How do you feel?"

The question was a trigger. All of the small sensations, all of the precursor feelings that warned of the avalanche to come, flooded into my awareness. The fear welled up in me and a silent sob shook my shoulders. All I could do was nod.

Crow squeezed my hand and held the handkerchief above Madelyn's corpse. With a little shake, soul dust fell from the handkerchief, scattering across the pajama-covered chest on the gurney. Tucking the handkerchief away, Crow lifted my hand to the corpse's forehead, and I felt the sensations flowing away. Like fog receding, the small pains and the fear flowed out of me through my hand and into the corpse. All of the small joys flowed out, too.

I told myself, as I did every time, that I wouldn't miss them. Who misses life's little happinesses in the absence of any pain and suffering? The grey and mottled miasma of feelings puddled around my hand like a dirty spill of water. Nothing like the inky oil slick that had been deposited into the divorce papers that first time. I watched it slowly soak into the corpse under my hand until it was all gone. With a deep cleansing breath, I lifted my hand and stepped back, letting Crow's hand go as well.

"Thank you." My voice was steady, and my mind was clear. *'Who needs to feel?'*

"You are very welcome. Thank you, Little Bird." Crow clapped his hands together and beamed at Pete and Donna. "Excellent. Shall we have a cup of coffee then?"

Pete and Donna followed me, pushing the gurney into the staging area of the exam room. We zipped Madelyn's bag up and left her and all my pain there, taking her paperwork back to the office with us. Crow had already helped himself to a cup of fresh black coffee and sat in his corner, waiting. I tossed the folder on the desk beside the other new arrivals. Pete lifted the coffee pot and began to fill cups as I passed them out.

"What does the rest of your shift look like?" I settled into my desk chair and started the light chit chat expected during a coffee break.

Donna sat on a short file cabinet beside Crow, crossing her long legs toward him. "Oh, you know. Trundle around a bit, find a quiet spot to park and wait. Avoid saving lives if we can."

I looked at Crow. "Do you know if they'll have any more deaths to bring in tonight?"

"No, Bird. I didn't check the schedule for that." Crow sipped his coffee and let his eyes flutter as he inhaled the steam. *'He's so weird.'*

Pete settled back in the third chair, a straight-backed wooden thing that looked less than comfortable. He stretched his long legs out in front of him and crossed his ankles. "We brought in the important one. How about you? Busy night?"

I shrugged one eyebrow. "Not terribly, but enough to occupy my time." Very dull chit chat. "Pete, weren't you trying to get some girl to go out with you tomorrow?"

That sparked his interest. He sat up straighter and pulled his feet back. "Denise. Yeah, and she agreed." He turned to Crow. "Thanks, Boss. Those tickets did the trick."

Crow nodded graciously; his eyes half closed. I studied him as Pete expounded on the physical virtues of Denise and what he hoped to do with her after the concert. Donna chortled here and there, adding her own suggestions and comments. Crow just sat there, letting Pete's voice roll by. I twisted in my chair to pull a bottom desk drawer out and lifted one foot to rest on its lip.

I could tell where the bruise was on the bottom of my foot and pressed the sole of my shoe into the side of the drawer, testing the sensation of the bruise. It wasn't like I couldn't tell when I touched things, if they were hot or cold, sharp or soft. I suppose I could, technically, feel them. It's just that there was no emotional response. I sipped my coffee, jabbing my foot against the hard metal side of the drawer, and pondered the sensation.

With a start, I realized I had been staring at Crow. He was staring right back, meeting my own unblinking gaze. He let the corners of his mouth lift in a subtle smile before lifting his cup to take a sip, never breaking his gaze away from mine.

Chapter 4. Paul

Four in the morning is an interesting time of day, no matter who you are or where in the world you are. Dozens of songs, poems, paintings and such have been dedicated to the essence of four in the morning. I even wrote a little haiku about it.

> What time be better,
> than cool four in the morning?
> Clock out now. Go home.

I didn't say it was a good haiku. It does get the point across.

Crow had gone when Pete and Donna had, off to tend some other nefarious business, no doubt. That was fine with me. My relationship with Crow was a little like what I'd had with my weed guy back in college. He had something I wanted. I paid him for it. We'd had fairly benign and superficial conversations in the course of that business, but there had been no emotional attachment to My Guy.

Sure, Crow and I spent more time hanging out together. We shared meals and physical encounters, but the only true emotions involved were the ones Crow helped me purge. Maybe I was more deluded than I realized at the time. If Crow and I were a little snarkier with each other than My Guy and I had been, well, he's a demon. He'd probably have shriveled up and cried about melting if I'd been too nice to him.

The day shift usually started arriving about two hours after I left each day. I always left the incoming, autopsy schedule, and to be filed baskets as empty as possible before I left a shift. I also tidied things a bit, consolidated bins, restocked the consumable supplies, and left a fresh and clean coffee pot ready for them to push the button. I poured the water into the top and replaced the pot, then stuck a little note to the side to assure them it was ready to brew.

I don't know why I bothered. I'd met the day staff a handful of times over my years there, but none of them ever seemed to make any effort to do any kindnesses for me. One Christmas, they had set up a pathetic little tree decorated with stockings with all their names on them. They hadn't even left me a blank to write my own name on. Still, I know I would appreciate someone leaving a fresh pot ready to brew, so I did it every night.

With my scarf around my neck and my coat buttoned and belted, I walked out into the dark. A chill gust lifted my hair as the heavy door thunked closed behind me. I pointed my feet toward home and my thoughts toward the homeless guy Crow had pointed out at the diner. Time to earn my keep.

The man wasn't there when I got to the diner. I walked inside and waved at Adrya, the nightshift waitress. She smiled back, her light pink lip gloss shining in the bright light, and walked up to the counter, order pad and pen in hand. I tossed my coat onto a stool and sat down atop it. "Good morning, Adrya. How has your night been?"

"Oh, you know. Pretty dull. There was a little excitement when the register drawer got stuck closed. We ended up giving about $300.00 worth of discounts before we could get the thing open again." The corners of her glinting brown eyes crinkled as she grinned. "How about you? Was tonight the night no one in town died?"

I chuckled. Most people avoid asking a coroner about work. Not Adrya. She had the best imagination and would sometimes tell me a completely imaginary tale of my night as a proposed scenario, as if she's guessing, and it was my solemn duty to reveal when she got it right.

"Not this time, unfortunately." I smiled up at her. The smile turned into a yawn. I clapped both hands over my mouth as my jaws cranked open wide. Adrya seemed to melt just a little in my sight as my vision blurred with yawn-induced tears. "Sorry." Adrya made a dismissive gesture as I wiped the tears from my eyes. "Could I just get one of those pull-apart coffee cakes and a couple of coffees to go?"

Adrya grinned and nodded, scratching the order onto the pad as she turned away. There was another copy of yesterday's paper on the counter, and I chuckled as I picked it up. Whoever left them seemed to take the responsibility a little more seriously than I would have expected. I flipped through it. There was the ad for jowls. "They're still gross." I lifted the paper and turned on my stool so I could rest one elbow on the counter while I read.

"You still haven't tried them." Crow's voice on the other side of my newspaper startled me, but I didn't even blink. I took advantage of the screen effect of the newspaper to arrange a properly scathing glare before bending down one corner and pointing the glare at him. He stood, leaning back against the counter, looking out the window.

I frowned and turned to follow his gaze. He was looking toward where the man had been sitting earlier. "He's not far, Little Bird. Are you ready to go meet him?"

Just as I opened my mouth to answer, Adrya stepped through the kitchen door with a brown paper sack and a little cardboard cradle with two white, insulated cups nestled beneath the handle. "Actually, just about." I smiled and stood, fishing my wallet out of my coat pocket as Adrya approached. She told me the price and I exchanged twice that amount of cash for the food. "You can keep it as a tip or put it toward the impromptu discounts from earlier."

Adrya winked at me and stuffed a couple of ones into her apron pocket before turning away. I grinned, pulled on my coat, and lifted the food and coffee. To Crow, I lifted both arms stiffly. "Well? I'm ready."

Crow led me out and down the nearly deserted sidewalks in the opposite direction from work. The shifting currents of air, warmed with the approaching dawn, whipped up a chill breeze that gusted in fits and starts. I rearranged the things in my hands to hold the food and coffee in one and pulled my coat closer with the other. "I should have buttoned up."

Crow tilted his head at me. With a quick jerk of his shoulders, he reached out and unburdened me of the coffee and pastry. "I should have offered to carry these things for you. I apologize."

I frowned at him. "Thanks." *'What is he up to?'*

'Not far,' according to Crow, was farther than I would have volunteered to walk if I had known. We walked almost ten blocks before I realized where we were headed. Alluvial Island Park wasn't very large and getting to it required walking across a berm jutting out into a lake. The sound of soft waves lapping on the mud reached my ears only moments before the smell of decay assaulted my nose and made it twitch.

"He's a smart guy." I muttered as I slumped along beside Crow, hands in my pockets.

"Indeed, Bird. He has several of these little hiding places around the city. The authorities don't like to get out of their cars to check the island during this time of year." Crow looked just a little bit ridiculous with the coffee carrier dangling from one hand and the bag of pastry in the other. He held both out before him like one might hold sacks of dog droppings.

I might have giggled, on a feeling day. The day after a purge, however, the emotion of amusement or humor translated into more of a mental note on what I might be expected to feel. So did every other emotion, for that matter. I faced forward again and sighed. "Isn't he cold?"

Crow nodded. "Very."

I paused as we stepped off the narrow path across the berm. Crow continued forward in a straight line. I followed and, after a few steps, I thought I could make out a mound on the ground, just an amorphous lump slightly darker than the ground around it. The dark spot didn't move as we approached.

Crow handed the coffee and pastry back to me. "Shall I go?"

I looked down at the sleeping man and began to nod. A thought occurred to me. "Wait. I need a writing marker, please."

Crow held his hand up, turned it over with a flourish and presented me with a black permanent marker on his palm. "Thanks." I took the marker and shuffled things in my hands a bit until I could write on one of the cups.

Psalm 145: 18-19: The Lord is near to all who call on him, to all who call on him in truth. He fulfills the desires of those who fear him; he hears their cry and saves them.

I handed the marker back to Crow. He made a disgusted face and waved the marker back into non-existence, or whatever happened to those things. "An apt choice, but I'm surprised you know it by wrote."

I shrugged. "Looney bins are full of Psalms." I looked at the cold, wet and muddy ground and lifted an eyebrow at Crow. "Would you mind fetching that blanket off my couch?"

He took a moment to study the ground before snapping his fingers. My densely woven fleece blanket appeared, not on the ground, but atop the bench of a small picnic table. At my questioning look, Crow shrugged and turned away. "Call if you want a ride home." He faded, quite literally, into the pre-dawn blackness. A moment later, I thought I heard wings flapping, and I was alone with a sleeping homeless guy.

I arranged the coffees and pastry on the tabletop and sat on one end of the bench facing the eastern horizon. The faint pink-orange glow of approaching dawn seeped into my awareness. Warm steam curled up around my chin and cheeks, as I held my coffee under my chin. Crow must have kept it hot with his infernal nature as we walked. Again, I thought it was funny but couldn't feel it.

I sat pondering the nature of my non-emotional state, watching the sun approach the finish line of night, and waiting for this dirty homeless guy to wake up. The wispy glow from the horizon wasn't enough to illuminate the darkness whole, but it caught on surfaces and reflected back brightly as if it pooled there and waited for reinforcements. My first good look at the man's face was in this light, an almost shining presence surrounded by darkness.

Finally, enough light must have gathered to filter through his eyelids, and he began to stir. He rolled onto his back and farted, loud and long. A moment later, he snored, a ripping sound from his throat that cut off with a snort as his breath caught. Thankfully, the few feet between us were enough to spare me the smells of either, but the sounds would have been enough to have put me off my breakfast, on a feeling day.

His eyes fluttered open, and he lay there, staring up into the empty branches of a sad, winter oak. Grunts and mutters, none intelligible, burbled out of his mouth as he shuffled into a sitting position.

I sipped my coffee, ignored him and watched the horizon. There was no use in trying to talk to anyone while they were trying to wake up. You'd just have to repeat yourself. He did see me eventually. He had just rolled over and pushed up on his hands and knees. As he sat back on his heels, his back to the rising sun, my table and I came into his field of vision.

I lifted one hand and waved. "Good morning."

With a little patience and the offer of hot coffee and food, I coaxed him up to the bench on the other side of the table. He sat, turning his head to study me and the lake around us, in turn. He stuffed coffee cake into his mouth, one hesitant piece at a time, while I calmly sipped my coffee. He lifted his cup of coffee and finally looked down to find the opening in the lid. Turning the cup brought the Psalm into view and he read it. A couple of times, based on the movement of his eyes.

I turned and smiled gently. "My name is Star." I held out my hand.

He sipped his coffee and studied my hand. Finally, he took it and squeezed. "Paul." He shifted his cup in an aborted saluting motion. "Thank you."

I reached out and pulled a piece of the coffee cake free. "You're welcome." I popped the cake into my mouth and grinned. "Tell me, Paul, what brings you to sleep in a park in the middle of January?"

Initial contact didn't usually provide much more information than what had been in the brief report Crow had given me. It was the contact, the expression of interest in him and his personal problems that was important tonight. This morning? Either way, I listened and nodded and nibbled and sipped while he talked. He started slowly with short sentences and no details. A turn of my head or a lift of my eyebrow was enough to encourage him to go on.

He spoke of his time in the military and the horrors he'd seen. He talked about his mother and how devastated he'd been when he lost her. Then, he started talking about his regrets. "I always thought my mom would be around forever. I still sometimes have dreams about her living with me and my family. I wish I could have given her a grandson. She had this way about her. If I ever had a son of my own, ..." He trailed off and looked down into his empty cup.

He tapped his cup on the table, fidgety and uncomfortable now that his flow of words had dried up. We sat a few moments more, not speaking. The sound of a crane of some kind broke the silence with a call almost like a warbling turkey. I stood. "It has been very interesting talking with you, Paul."

He watched me stand, looking confused, then scrambled to his feet as well. "Yes. Thank you for listening, uh..."

"Star. Starling actually, but most people call me Star." I began to gather the debris of our breakfast.

Paul sprang into action. He snatched up the shredded remains of the pastry bag and my empty cup along with his own. "I'll take these to the bin. I have to go that way now anyway." He shuffled from foot to foot.

"That's very thoughtful, Paul. Thank you. I think I'd like to sit a moment longer myself."

Paul nodded and began strafing around the side of the table, keeping me in front of him. "Yep." He nodded once more before hunching his shoulders and stepping quickly toward the waste bins lined up beside a small, cinder block building that housed the public restrooms.

The wind had stilled, for the most part, with the full sunrise. I stepped up on the bench and turned to sit on the tabletop. I threw my blanket around my shoulders and watched the sun as it rose almost fast enough to see it moving. "Crow?"

He stepped out from behind the winter oak. His head was bowed, and his hands were deep in the capacious pockets of his suit pants. "How did it go, Little Bird?"

I lifted one end of the blanket, inviting him to sit beside me. He gave a little shake of his head, without looking up. I pulled the blanket tight again and said, "It went fine, Crow. He told me almost everything we need to know, for now."

"Enough to begin screening for his match?"

I nodded. All we really needed was for him to express something he envied about other people's lives, or what he thought were other people's lives. "It's an easy one. He wants his own family. Particularly, he wants a son of his own." I stood on the bench and hopped down. "I'm tired, Crow. Will you take me home?"

Crow looked at me, finally. "Of course, Bird." He took one of my hands in his own and the world faded around us.

Chapter 5. Free Refills

Crow was busy following leads on a suitable swap for Paul, and I wouldn't normally expect to see him until he'd found one or I called for him. My time was free for whatever I wanted to do. The trouble with having no emotional value for anything in my life was that, during these downtimes, these periods of aloneness, there wasn't anything I found interesting enough to break routine for.

I woke up that evening and got ready for work, slumped up the stairs and waved at Jacob's waving spatula, just like the night before. Genia took my order in the kitchen and followed me as I carried my coffee into the dining room. My eyes flicked to the window once I'd sat at the counter. Paul was there, sitting outside the diner again, and I decided, on a whim, to buy him dinner.

"Genia?" The thin and patient proprietress looked up from where she stood at the register. "I'm going to invite an acquaintance inside. Can I have a menu at the corner booth?"

Genia looked where I pointed and a twist of her features, not quite a frown, preceded a slow nod. She was a good and lovely woman, but she had a business to look after. The other diner patrons might not be so understanding about a dirty and likely smelly man sharing their dining space. It was a reasonable concern.

"Thanks, Genia. I'll be right back." I moved my coffee to the corner table and crossed to the front door. A stiff wind gusted as I pushed against the door. The resistance was timed just right so I had to more than double my effort just to get it to crack open. Of course, when the wind died back, the door swung freely. I toppled out, only avoiding the windmilling dance of the clumsy by virtue of the death grip with which I clung to both the door and the doorframe. Paul didn't even look up.

I took a deep and fortifying breath as I released the door and stepped out. "Hey, Paul. How was your day?"

The sidewalk wasn't really clean. There is an interesting account of Benjamin Franklin convincing his neighborhood homeowners of the necessity of paying a local widow to keep their sidewalks and stoops swept. Obviously, the governing authority of Chester City had not read Franklin's argument. There was the normal dirt, pebbles, road and traffic grime, and even some dry and brown grassy weeds growing in the cracks, along with a black smear that ran down from the sides of the window frames. At least it wasn't mud.

He was still staring mutely at me when I sat down. "I work nights, so I only just woke up again about an hour or so ago." I folded my legs, crisscross-style, and arranged my coat to best cover my knees. "I went home and straight to bed right after you left this morning. Well, I read a couple of chapters of an old favorite and fell asleep on the couch." I turned my head to the side to look at him.

Paul's brow was so deeply furrowed, the creases almost looked like they'd been painted on with stage makeup. "Are you following me?"

I didn't expect the question and paused to consider my response before giving a quiet chuckle. "Sorry. No. Well, not quite. I actually live here, and I recognized you." Both true.

"This morning, the coffee with the verse on it..." One of Paul's shaggy eyebrows lifted.

It caught my attention for a moment. *'Why were homeless guys' eyebrows always shaggy? Did something about living in the elements make them bush out? Thinking about it, didn't Grizzly Adams have shaggy eyebrows, too?'* I tucked that away for pondering later and focused on the shaggy eyebrow being lifted at me, then.

"A friend of mine happened to know where you had bedded down, and I didn't want to have breakfast alone." I huffed a sigh and lifted my hands with a shrug of my shoulders. I turned my eyes away from him and pretended I didn't care what he thought. "Do you want some dinner? I'd like to hear more about your mom." I heard rustling beside me and turned back.

Paul had shuffled to his feet and stood looking down at me. "Inside?" He looked almost on the point of running.

I locked eyes with him and slowly got to my feet. "Not if you don't want to, but," all of my movements were slow as I pulled my coat tighter around me and bounced, bending my knees a little, playing up the chill of night coming on, "if we sit at that booth in the corner, we can see the whole place, both doors in and out, and the coffee refills are free."

Paul was a study in confliction. One of his feet was pointed at the street. The other was pointed at me and the diner's door behind me. He stayed tense, shifting his weight from one foot to the other. I honestly didn't know which way he was going to go. Finally, he glanced through the window toward the corner booth where we could both see Genia delivering my omelet and another cup of coffee. She waved at us, and Paul's shoulders relaxed. He nodded.

I cranked my enthusiasm up a notch and said, "Lovely." With a quick last bounce of my knees, I spun and walked back to the door. "I think, if you stay close and sort of hunch down, no one will be able to see you behind me." I put a hand on the door handle and turned a grin back to Paul.

He had taken a few steps to follow me and stopped to frown. He didn't realize I was kidding. That happened a lot when I was all flat and emotionless. Sometimes it was hard to mimic expected emotional affectations for other people. I tugged on the door and sighed. "I'm kidding, Paul. Come on. The strawberry blond waitress is Genia. She's actually the owner, and she said you are invited."

Paul glanced back through the window. Genia was laughing and talking with the people at another table. She saw us looking and waved again, a beckoning motion, before turning back to the kitchen. Paul inhaled, expanding his chest and lifting his shoulders. With his next step, I pulled the door wider and stepped back inside. I felt him pull the door further open behind me and relaxed.

I led the way to the table and peeled off my coat, tossing it into the booth seat ahead of me. The bench's warmth felt like a cushion under my concrete-cold butt, and my cup of coffee still steamed as I lifted it between both hands. Paul moved slower. His wide eyes darted back and forth as he shuffled into the seat across from me. He stared down at the black liquid in the 70s era white mug in front of him.

With a glance at the clock on the wall, I said, "I have about thirty minutes before I have to head to work. Forty-five if I call a cab. What sounds good?" I nodded toward the menu-placemat under his mug. Paul didn't blink. *'Did I break him?'* He sniffled and I realized he was on the verge of tears. I watched him like that for almost a full minute. I leaned back in my seat and reached over to fish my phone out of my coat pocket. "Let me just go ahead and order that cab."

It took another couple of minutes of coaxing before Paul finally sipped his coffee and looked at the menu. He ended up ordering a burger and fries and a cup of soup. Not very creative but there is a lot to be said for the old favorites. I nibbled my way through my omelet, Genia keeping our cups refilled and hot. He ate with the same deliberate focus that I remember some of the patients in the bin having. As if they were sure some monster was about to come take it all away, and this might be their last meal. Some dormant part of me registered that as heartbreaking.

Genia brought a couple of slices of Dutch Apple pie with ice cream on the side and a can of whipped cream, still half full. "On the house, but only 'cause I needed the rack for a fresh pie." She flashed that contagious smile and winked at Paul before she turned away. *'Bless that woman's giant heart.'*

Paul still hadn't spoken but his eating pace was slowing. I shoved my ice cream toward him. "I don't actually like ice cream." I picked up the whipped cream. "This, though..." I shook the can and turned it upside down to spray a generous dollop of the stuff atop my pie. "So good." I scooped a bit off with my finger, stuck it in my mouth, and turned a whipped cream smudged smile on him.

He half-smiled back. "When I was a small boy, before my dad died, we used to have summer parties. My mom had a special recipe for homemade ice cream, and everyone would take a turn cranking this old ice cream freezer while the grill was going." His eyes took on a faraway look. The creases and tension of worry faded from his face, replaced by wistful nostalgia. His eyes slowly lowered to the table, and he cleared his throat. "Thank you."

"Where are you sleeping tonight, if I may ask." I remembered making homemade ice cream as a child. Once. With my grandfather.

"I haven't decided yet." He shrugged as he scooped ice cream onto his pie. I watched him spray a little whipped cream into one of the empty bowls and give it a try with a spoon. I couldn't tell from his expression if he liked it, but he tucked into the pie and ice cream without adding the whipped cream.

I sipped my coffee and wondered if this was going to work. At the point of second contact, the client was typically more talkative. I usually had more to go on so I could bring up the swap. Crow didn't like it when I took too long to make the pitch. Once, the client had died before I got to second contact. There was that deadline to consider. Still, second contact was normally more than twenty-four hours after first contact. "How much longer do you think you will be awake? I mean, what is the deciding factor?"

Paul shrugged. "It depends on if I need a place, if the shelter has room or one of the guys is in with someone with a hotel room." He shrugged again, taking another bite. "Most nights, I just have to walk until one of my spots is available. The park is a good one, but so is the old warehouse. I just have to wait for everyone to leave wherever I want to stay."

I glanced at the clock. I didn't have much time left. "Paul, I have to leave for work soon; my cab will be here any minute." He started eating faster. I laid a hand on the tabletop between us. "No, you don't have to hurry. What I'm saying is, if you would like to come sit in the office for a while, you can come with me and ..." I cut off as his head came up, a look of panic in his eyes. "Only if you want somewhere out of the cold and wind to wait for later."

He glanced around the table at the remnants of food and looked back at me. "Where do you work?"

I picked up my coffee. "I work all alone on the nightshift at the morgue. I know it's creepy and most people avoid the morgue as long as they can, but it's safe and you are welcome."

Paul actually grunted a hoarse laugh. "The morgue don't bother me. The cemetery used to be one of my spots." He licked his fork and squinted at me. "Why are you being so nice to me?" He pointed the fork at my chest, half accusing and half brandishing. "You aren't going to steal my kidneys or my liver or something, are you?"

I coughed out a short, donkey-bray burst of surprise. "No, of course not. I'm a coroner, not a black-market saleswoman." *'No, I won't cut pieces of your body apart. I just want to convince you to trade your soul for someone else's.'* "I don't know. I just think you have a nice face and I want to know more about you. Maybe even be your friend. What do you say? If you come with me, Genia can pack us something for later and there is a coffee pot all to ourselves in the office."

He still looked dubious, but he agreed. I asked Genia to pack us up and smiled at Paul over my coffee. He got anxious waiting and walked outside. I watched him nervously, but he just bummed a cigarette and light from a patron walking in and sat in his spot to smoke. By the time my cab pulled up to the curb, Genia had packed our leftovers and two more burgers for later.

We had another moment of tension when he saw the keypad lock on the morgue door. With a little reassurance of his ability to get out again, he went in. I rolled my eyes at his back and followed. My shift hadn't even started, and I was already tired. It wasn't like I expected the clients to come to us with their souls all packaged and ready to trade. But, a little less reticence, a little more suspension of disbelief might have been very helpful.

I led Paul to the office. "Make yourself comfortable, if you can." The coffee pot had a little old coffee from the day shift still in the pot, cold and gross. I removed the basket and emptied the old, used grounds. Once I'd replaced the basket loaded with fresh grounds, I pulled the pot out and turned to Paul. He sat on a chair with wide eyes slowly taking in the clutter of the office. "Would you like a little tour?"

He nodded and followed me as I made my way back to the water fountain in the hall. I pointed out things as we passed by or through them. "This is the cold room. It's like a staging area and extra exam space. The full autopsy suites are behind the doors on the far wall and the freezer storage vault is on the other side." I nodded in the opposite direction as I turned toward the water fountain in the hall. "Restrooms are the blue door at the other end of the hall."

Paul turned his head toward the restrooms and back, pointing a questioning look at me. "Are they open? May I?"

I nodded, keeping an eye on the rising water level in the pot. He shuffled down the hall, and I frowned. Homeless clients presented a few more difficulties than our run of the mill clientele. A whole layer of small things we take for granted get in the way of having a businesslike conversation. Like the opportunity to make use of indoor plumbing with any privacy.

I set the coffee to brew and thumbed through the docket for the night. A groan hitched a ride on a sigh as I counted the initial intake cases. *Did they just leave all the incoming for me? Gee, thanks, guys.* I didn't really mind doing the initial intake procedures. It would have been nice, though, if the day shift did more than just stack them up. Typically, they were more conscientious with the homicide investigations, but the routine deaths by natural causes seemed to bore them.

I noticed Madelyn's body and all the feelings that went with it had already been transferred to a mortuary. *'Good.'*

With the sound of liquid slowly burbling through the coffee maker, I took the paper folder for my first case into the cold room and got to work. I was fully qualified to perform any level of autopsy that might be required, but the day shift didn't tend to leave many of the suspicious death cases. Those had to be handled more carefully in case an investigation was required. My cases tended to involve the very poor, homeless, or otherwise disenfranchised.

Imagine my surprise when my first case was a man found dead in his hotel room. Mr. Hotel Room would need a full work-up to determine cause of death. I donned my gloves, coat, goggles, face shield, and all the regalia of my office and stuck my ear buds in my ears. I turned on a podcast, then opened the HRB. I worked methodically through the initial photos, weights, and measures and almost forgot about Paul as I worked. I checked the file to determine what scans to take and wheeled him down the hall. Scans done, I had him cleaned up and laid out in an exam room, preparing to begin his autopsy, when Paul walked up behind me.

"What are you listening to?"

Chapter 6. Autopsy

Imagine for a moment, if you will, being in the morgue, at night, with a dead man right under your hands, and someone you forgot was there walks up behind you. It was exactly like you imagined, except I had to pretend to feel the fear. I was startled, of course, but without fear, my reactions were all a beat too slow.

I spun, realizing mid-turn that it was Paul. I turned the scowl on my face into a quizzical smile. With the backs of my wrists, I tugged the earbuds out. "Oh, hi, Paul. It's a podcast." I took a step forward and raised a hand as if to forestall him coming closer, but he wasn't moving. "Are you sure you wouldn't be more comfortable in the office?" I glanced over my shoulder to indicate the gory nature of my work. "It's technically against the rules for you to be in the room during an autopsy."

"I don't want to get you in trouble." He stepped back. "The coffee is ready."

I thought about it. The cameras in the place were focused on the exam table. The footage wasn't really about security, but more about the evidence found during the investigation. "I can't have anything to drink in here during an exam either, but I will come in there when I'm done."

He shuffled from foot to foot, looking toward the dead man behind me. "What happened to him?"

'An opening for my pitch?' I hesitated a moment more before jerking my head toward the table. "He died in a hotel room. From the way he was dressed, I'd say he was probably just passing through. His I.D. says he's from Vermont."

"How did he die?"

"That's what I'm about to find out." He stepped up beside me and studied the body while I studied him. "If you want to sit on the other side," I gestured to a stool beside a wall-mounted, metal work surface, "you can stay. I have to be able to move freely, and it gets very gory." I reached to one side and lifted an end of a pair of heavy-duty limb cutters.

Paul shrugged and slumped to the stool. "I'll leave if it gets to be more than I can handle." He seemed to kind of melt onto the stool, sitting hunched over in a lump. "To be honest, I am enjoying your company and would rather not be all by myself in there." He seemed less skittish and more like he expected me to run him off. After breakfast and dinner and all that coffee, he was afraid I was about to stop being kind.

I cleared my throat and nodded, pulling my gloves off. I pulled my phone from my back pocket and turned it off, stowing it and the ear buds, before donning a new pair of gloves. "Have you ever seen an autopsy before?"

Paul shook his head. I nodded and began to explain what I was doing. "First, I have to check the level of autopsy ordered." I gestured to the clipboard hanging on the side of the instrument cart. "Mr. Hotel Room here is from out of town. The police don't suspect foul play, but the insurance or police from his hometown might have questions, so he gets a full autopsy." Paul nodded and I continued.

"I've already cleaned and examined the outside of the body, taken samples, and gotten scans of everything intact. Now for the internal exam." I lifted a scalpel and located my incision point at the corpse's collarbone. "The infamous Y incision comes first." I talked him through the stages of opening and examining the chest cavity, making my verbal notes at the same time. He looked on the verge of leaving me to it when I lifted the big limb cutters to remove the ribcage, but he stayed. He seemed to become very interested when I exposed the liver.

"The medics all tell me my liver is going to fail on me if I keep drinking." Paul's voice was passive, like it was rolling downhill rather than being pushed out. He looked down at his feet, or maybe his hands.

"What do you think about that?"

He looked up, only half lifting his head, and didn't meet my eyes. "I don't know. I gave up the drink. Haven't seen a medic since. Don't know if it helped or not."

I nodded and focused on the work before me. *'If he, as an alcoholic, had given up drinking for the benefit of his health, he didn't want to die. Good. A healthy sense of self-preservation is the foundation of rationalizing killing someone else.'* "How do you feel?" A trigger question for me, it was generally benign to others, causing momentary introspection rather than panic.

Paul sighed heavily and straightened somewhat on his stool. "At first, it was horrible. I've never been so sick. But a few days into it, I started feeling my joints loosen up and I slept better. I started having more energy." He lifted a hand to rub his forehead and temples, finally running his palm down the front of his face. "It left a lot of space and energy in my head for thinking."

I finished weighing the organs and double checked that I had taken all the samples before replacing them in the body cavity. I removed my gloves and picked up the chart to inventory the samples. "What do you think about?"

Paul didn't answer but watched me as I moved on to the head and brain examination. Maybe he wasn't watching. He didn't flinch at all, just sat staring in my direction. To be honest, he was quiet so long, I forgot I had asked him a question. When I'd finished the brain exam, he finally spoke again.

"What do you think it means to succeed in this life?"

"Pardon?"

"That's what I think about. People talk about success at money or their job. Some people talk about being important or famous and that makes them a success."

'This is new and different.' "I suppose so. What do you think?"

Paul met my eyes then. "I think you can't be a success if you aren't happy."

I pursed my lips and drew down my eyebrows. "That's very interesting." Actually, it sounded like a massive oversimplification. Still, it was a valid measure of success. I made my final notes and prepped Mr. Hotel Room for transfer. Removing my gloves, face shield and apron, I said, "All done. How about some of that coffee?"

Paul followed me back to the office. I sat at the desk in front of the computer, and he poured two mugs. He took a seat beside the desk and sat one cup in front of me. "Thank you." I sipped once and opened Mr. Hotel Room's file to transcribe my notes.

Paul sipped half his coffee away before speaking again. "Do you think all of these people were successful?"

I looked up and followed his gaze through the observation window and cold room, into the autopsy room and came up short at the closed storage vault door on the other side. "I hope so." I offered him a smile. "Especially if you're right about happiness being success."

Paul grunted, a hoarse sound in his chest. "Yeah. I've never been successful. I thought I might be in the army. I was wrong. Training was okay but the first day I saw combat, I saw the blood and pain..." He trailed off and buried his face in his coffee.

The sound of my fingers tapping on the keyboard seemed harsh with him fending off unwanted memories beside me. I stopped. "I think, if you're right, then happiness is something it only takes a second to have. Once you have it, it isn't something you can lose. And I think, if happiness is the measure of success, and achieving your goal, whatever it is, will make you happy, then you are successful. As long as you are still trying, you haven't failed."

Paul nodded. "I like that."

He left after his second cup, the two takeout burgers swinging in their bag from one of his hands. I saw him out without trying to make any arrangements to meet again. He was a creature of habit and, if I didn't run into him naturally, Crow could always track him down. I spent the rest of the night scrambling to make up for the time I'd lost explaining things and easing the client. I didn't mind too much. I liked Paul. He was surprisingly thoughtful.

The transportation crew that served all the local mortuaries came in just before 2:00 and I stood, watching from the hall, as Mr. Hotel Room followed Ms. Shellfish Allergy out the door. Pete and Donna brought in a teenager at about 2:30 and stayed for coffee. They were the closest thing I had to friends, so I pulled a day shift move and, after initial intake, left the teen for the next coroner.

"How'd the date go, Pete?" I was oddly invested in his relationship with this woman I'd never met.

Pete's grin split his face. "Oh, Denise?" He chuckled. "Oh, that went very well. The concert was shit, so I took her to an after-party. She really let her hair down after a couple of bumps."

I hung my head and let it swing on the end of my neck. "So, this isn't true love, then?"

Donna howled with laughter. "Oh, sweetie. That's a good one."

Pete snorted. "True love's less real than a fairy's tail."

"Fairytale." I closed my eyes.

"That's what I said, isn't it?" Pete turned a confused look to Donna. She nodded.

"Nevermind." I was about to nudge Donna about her sex life when the lights flickered. Pete and Donna shot to their feet, hastily divesting themselves of their coffee mugs.

Crow stepped out of the shadow of the open door and grinned, toothy and creepy. "Good morning, everyone."

I cocked my head to one side. "What are you doing here?"

"You wound me, Little Bird. Am I not welcome?" He sauntered with his hands clasped behind his back to his stool in the corner. Turning back to look at us, he altered his smile to a calmer and more inviting level of tooth.

"Don't bother bandying words. I can't be annoyed right now." I didn't have to try hard to affect smugness on my features.

Crow nodded acquiescence and lowered himself to the stool. "Right. Of course. I, um..."

'Crow is about to lie to me.'

He crossed his knees and hooked his hands around them. "I'm just checking in to get more details about our client's needs."

I squinted at him. "I don't know if I have anything more for you yet."

Pete and Donna, both still standing at attention, squirmed and began to leak nervous brimstone. I grunted and waved my hand in front of my face. "Crow. Let them go." Crow waved a hand and the two demons disappeared. The CCTV monitor showed them scrambling into their ambulance outside. I turned back to Crow. "Now, why are you really here? You know, you only say 'um' when you're lying."

Crow narrowed his eyes at me, and his expression took on a sinister quality. "I don't lie." His voice carried and reverberated from the walls of the office. I sighed and he rolled his eyes with a little flick of his head. "I might occasionally prevaricate."

I sighed again and turned my back on him. "I still have a little paperwork to complete before the end of the shift. You know I'm always happy to accept a ride home, but this is unusual for you. What brings you here, really?"

I could hear Crow shuffling behind me. Finally, he said, "There is something wrong with Paul."

The clock said it was still barely past 3:00. I sighed and turned to face him properly. "Other than the fact he's dying?"

Crow hummed and stood. He poured the last of the hot coffee into his cup, and I queued up a sigh, preparing to brew a fresh pot. Crow surprised me with a snap of his fingers, and the pot started brewing on its own. "His imminent demise is not a problem. No, his death date changed."

I froze in the middle of reaching for my own coffee cup. "Does that ever happen?"

Crow paced with his cup held delicately between both hands. "No. It never has before."

"But he's still dying?"

One corner of Crow's mouth lifted in a sinister smile. "Yes. Oh, yes. He is still dying."

Chapter 7. Bliss

Crow did his best to irritate me for the rest of my shift. Like a bored puppy who keeps trying to chew the shoes off your feet, he could be sort of cute when he got like that. When I learned to think of him as a cute moron, his terror strategies lost most of their edge. Still, he usually tried to put some effort in. I don't think his heart was really in it. Besides making a fresh pot of coffee, he cleaned the exam room floor, restocked the consumables, and danced a short waltz with the teenager. It might be a little morbid but at least he wasn't doing something more grotesquely demon-like.

When 4:00 finally came, he held my coat for me and spun me around to catch me in his arms. Less ignorable than the puppy act, his debonaire beau routine always managed to put me off balance. "Hold on tightly, Little Bird. The night is cold."

With that, we flew. It wasn't the astral projection type of flight. Somehow, he was both the bird and the man flying through the icy night sky. He held me close to his chest and I burrowed my face into his shirt. He radiated heat and I breathed in the hot, spicy scent of him. I don't know why he never seemed to leak sulfur or brimstone. Instead, he seemed to exude a musky aroma that was both intoxicating and alarming, given that he's a certifiable demon.

The trip took less than a minute. Just long enough to make my nose go frosty. He deposited me in the middle of my living room and stood holding me until he was certain I had gained my feet. I pressed my face against his chest again for a moment to warm my nose and skip the drippy thawing process. "Thanks, Crow."

"My pleasure. What do you have planned for the rest of your night?" He turned his back on me and wandered toward my bookcase. A pathetic thing, it had only four shelves less than three feet wide and rising only as tall as my chest. The inner shelves were tightly packed with well-loved books, evidenced by the unreadable state of the spines on the paperbacks. The top held a file accordion for stray but important documents and a stack of three books for which I hadn't yet found a place.

"I haven't thought about it. Don't touch my books, please." I walked into my bathroom and gave my teeth a quick swish of mouthwash. The coffee would eventually win the war, but I was still trying to maintain at least an off-white enamel color. "Do you want to eat?"

Crow snorted. "I almost always want to eat. Are you going to cook for me?"

I cut my eyes at him as I walked past him into my tiny galley kitchen. "I'll cook for myself and make a little extra." He grinned, truly amused, and I set about following instructions on the back of a box. Nothing in my apartment had changed since his last visit, or since I'd moved in, really. Still, he always walked the perimeter.

He poked his head into the bedroom and bathroom, off to one side, and traced the edges of the open area that encompassed the living room on one end and the kitchen on the other. Between the two spaces stood a café table barely big enough for two plates, demarcating the dining area. Being a basement, the four small, rectangular, bedroom windows were high in the top of one wall. The top of the same wall in the living room contained its own set of four tiny, matching windows and the door leading out into the alley. It was all I needed and more.

Crow stopped at one end of the couch and peered into the small terrarium glowing on the end table. "When are you going to put an animal in this box?"

"When I feel like it has a chance of survival." I spooned out the crumb topping and slid the prepared pan into the oven. I had already turned away when I remembered to turn the thing on. "That will be ready in a bit." I reached into a cabinet and pulled out two glasses with a bottle of cheap, sweet, red labelled wine. "I really don't know if I have any more useful information for you on Paul."

Crow took the bottle from me, grunted at the label, and opened it. As he poured, he said, "You have atrocious taste in wine."

I took a glass from him and noticed the bottle label was now black and gold. "What did you do?" I sniffed the wine, my nose hanging over the edge of the glass like a climber hanging onto a cliff. The pungent aroma made my eyes water, and I pulled my face back. "Crow, I really like the sweet stuff."

"Just give it a try, Bird."

With a glare at him, I lifted the glass and sipped. I loved it. Of course, I did. He was always right about things like that. It had the same sweetness of my cheap stuff, but with a rich flavor and the kick of high alcohol content. "It's delicious. Is my bottle in the cabinet?"

Crow grinned, his smarmy told-you-so grin. "It can be, I suppose." He rolled his eyes toward the cabinet and back to me. "Snug in your stash."

We sat, quietly sipping our pretentious booze until dinner was ready. Crow retrieved the dish from the oven while I set out paper plates and forks. Sitting once again at the table with our plates full of something claiming to be food, Crow refilled our glasses for the third time and lifted his fork. "What, may I ask, is this?"

I shrugged. "There's chicken in it." I lifted a bite and looked at it. "And, peas, I think." I stuck the bite in my mouth and was grateful for the alcohol content of the wine.

Crow tried his and lifted his eyebrows, appreciatively. "Oh, I can see why this is such a popular type of food."

I snorted and nearly choked on, presumably, an errant pea. "Are you really just here to hang out with me and snub my food choices?"

"I didn't snub the food. I snubbed the wine." He took another bite and I waited. He went so far as to drain his glass and refill it again before deigning to say anything more useful. "You spent much of the night with the client. Are you sure you didn't learn anything new and helpful?"

I took another bite and returned the smug smile he had given me while making me wait.

"That's just petty, Bird."

I shrugged as I sipped to clear my mouth. "I learned it from you." He surprised me with a little nod of agreement. "The client misses his family, but he's also got this interesting preoccupation with success and failure in life. His theory is that success is equivalent to happiness." I elaborated the best I could with the wine making my head and tongue go fuzzy. "Is that helpful?"

Crow, refilling his glass again, gave a noncommittal shrugging nod. "It's something." He didn't go on, but sat quietly staring at his glass, twisting it by the stem, and watching the dim light sparkle on the surface.

I'd never seen him quite so preoccupied. "Are you okay, Crow?" With him, I could relax. I didn't have to scrunch my forehead to show concern or soften my voice or any of that. I just asked in the flat, emotionless voice of the day after a purge. He never failed to read the correct intention, at least, not when it was important.

He, however, had the most expressive and readable face of anyone I'd ever known. He could tell an entire, convincing lie just with his facial expressions. The almost liquid way his features morphed into a reassuring smile, full of openness, earned a snort from me. A less observant person might have missed the flicker of a confused crease trying to land between his eyebrows, it was gone so fast.

"I'm sure it's nothing to worry about. The powers that be sometimes do make exceptions and changes to various schedules of Creation. Once, the sun stood stock still in the sky for almost an entire day because of one of those exceptions. Still, if we just do the job, everything will work out."

"I don't believe you."

"I know."

He wasn't going to tell me why, but he was worried. I shrugged and stood to clean up our little mess. He refilled his glass and watched. "Bird, explain more about his preoccupation with happiness as success."

I turned the water off and dried the forks, thinking about the way Paul had talked about it. I turned and leaned my backside against the sink counter. "It's not that hard to understand. He had a decent childhood that didn't prepare him for his adulthood. He was given happiness as a kid, and he misses it. For him, that innocence and security of being surrounded by a family made him happy but without the benefit of working for it himself. The gift he was given wasn't his, and it was taken away."

Crow's eyes glimmered with the internal spark of understanding. "Ahh, so he wants to earn his happiness. He has a proprietary notion that, once earned, it can't be taken."

I nodded and moved to one side, reaching into a drawer. "Yeah, let's go with that." My chocolate habit had been out of control when I was a teenager. Thanks to the post-purge numbness, I could sate a craving with just a piece or two after dinner.

Crow had refilled his glass and mine and carried both to the extra-long sofa. The sofa and the bed were the two best pieces of furniture I had ever owned. When shopping for them, my only requirement had been that both be equally comfortable for sleeping. Crow perched on one end, and I pulled my feet up under me on the other. "Do you think you have a handle on how to use this information? Can you find him a swap that will let him feel like he earned his happiness?"

"Perhaps." His narrowed eyes focused on something far away. "The next time you talk to him, it would be helpful to know what he thinks qualifies." He turned his suddenly very present focus on me and released his toothiest grin. "What about you, Bird?"

"What about me?" Nibbles of chocolate melted on my tongue to mix pleasantly with the wine, and I squinted toward the bottle, trying to read the label.

"It's Black Label DuGienne. There is a special place in Hell reserved for the last few casks in existence." Smugness laced his voice. "What about your definition of happiness? What qualifies, in your unique perspective?"

I rolled my eyes away from the wine label and tried to pin him with my gaze. My eyes chose that moment to itch. I began blinking in such a way, he may have thought I was batting my eyelashes at him. "Happiness is overrated." I held up my remaining nibblet of chocolate. "This is bliss."

If I'd thought about it, if I had understood where I was in that moment, would I have answered differently?

Chapter 8. Job Satisfaction

An icy, January cold front moved in while I was sleeping that day. When I got to the dining room upstairs, I glanced out the window, looking for Paul. He wasn't there. I didn't see him again for weeks, and then, only in passing. Crow assured me he was fine more than once during that time. I had no choice but to believe him, but his unconcern and lack of irritation leant credit to his assurances.

Donna and Pete brought in more bodies and shared more coffee. Pete's dalliance with Denise escalated into all-nighters where he introduced her to new and exciting drugs. A binger put her in the hospital less than a month after their first date. He was giddy as he sat in the office, regaling us with the story. "I promised to be there to pick her up when they released her. Her face was priceless." He hooted and shared a celebratory fist bump with Donna. "Heh, yeah. I know exactly where to take her, too."

I split a withering look between them. "I'm judging you both."

Donna cackled. "As long as we both score over a nine."

I closed my eyes and shook my head as I turned away from them. I stared at the computer screen, clicking here and there, to mask the sudden, intrusive memory of the day I'd gotten out of the bin. *'Was my ex-husband a demon?'* It was the first time the thought had ever occurred to me, but it seemed like such an obvious connection. *'I could ask. They might tell me.'* I turned back to them and changed my mind at the last moment. I wasn't sure I wanted to know.

Instead, I asked, "Donna, we spend all this time congratulating Pete over his conquests. What about you? What personal assignments have you been working on?"

Donna rolled her eyes and slid off her seat to her feet. "I'm on-call with the domestics right now." She slumped to the coffee pot and refilled her cup. "I don't know what I did to piss him off, but Crow loaned me temporarily to the homewreckers."

I frowned and Pete chuckled. He lifted a hand toward her, a quick gesture, and said, "Donna's got kind of a knack for causing marital dissention." His face turned slightly more serious as he turned to Donna. "Why haven't you taken any of the transfer offers? It would be a promotion."

Donna shrugged and slumped back atop her seat on the file cabinet. "It doesn't fulfill me like this job. There is all this hands-on mess and then I can't even be there most of the time to enjoy the fallout of my efforts."

Pete reached out to pat her thigh. "Yeah. I get that. At least Crow lets us participate in the collection. Even if he is... you know." Donna nodded and they both sank into their coffee mugs with introspective looks.

'Demons are strange.'

The lights flickered and Crow stepped out from behind the door. "No, Pete, I do not know. Even if I am... what?" Pete and Donna spluttered, standing, and wiping coffee from their faces and shirts.

"Good evening, Boss." Donna always seemed to be the most genteel of the two.

Pete cleared his throat. "Yeah. Hey, Boss. Can I pour you a cup of coffee?"

Crow lowered his chin to stare at them over the bridge of his nose. With a flourish, he twisted his hand in the air and a steaming mug appeared in his hand. "No. Thank you." He stared, unblinking for a moment, watching them squirm as he sipped. "Relax. Have a seat and tell me..." a small smile struggled to lift the edge of his mouth, "how, exactly, am I?"

I glanced between the three of them and snorted. "If you didn't actually have the power to disintegrate them..."

"Ah, but I do, Bird, and that makes all the difference."

I shrugged and turned my back on him. "Not for me." I worked passively on the files in front of me while they bantered and blustered for almost an hour. Crow didn't seem to be concerned with moving the discussion to anything specific, and their conversation meandered, finally, into their plans for the Ides of March. I turned around again, my foot propped on the lower desk drawer, and listened.

Donna scooted back against the wall and crisscrossed her legs atop the file cabinet. "Brandon has recruited eighty-four more Murphy demons for the job."

Crow rubbed his hands together, with his coffee cup between them, and pulled a smirky, narrow-eyed face; like a cat who'd stolen cream from a kitten. "Marvelous. That should be more than enough fire power for our little fief." His eyes sprang open to normal width. "Pete, will you be able to get a few full shipments of Marchides to the street suppliers before then?"

"That won't be the problem, Boss." He sighed. "The street guys don't want to push it because they hate the name."

Crow scoffed. "But it's perfect!"

I rolled my eyes. "None of them get the joke, Crow."

"What if we just call it Ides?" Donna said it looking into her mug, as if she didn't actually care.

"Hey! That's not a bad thought. Right?" Pete looked at me, deliberately avoiding the wounded ire showing on Crow's face.

I looked at Crow and lifted one hand to gesture toward Pete and Donna. "Really? You want your evil plan to succeed but you won't listen to your PR people? Crow, change the name."

Crow lost his angry façade and let his shoulders and cheeks slump. "Bird, you can take the fun right out of torture. Fine. Let them call it whatever they want, as long as it is out and flooding the market by the fifteenth." Pete and Donna grinned at me between sycophantic bows and murmurs praising Crow's bossiness.

"Hey, what's a Murphy demon?" I'd heard of them before but was fairly certain I'd never met one. I sipped my coffee and hoped my attempt to divert them worked.

Donna giggled and shifted around, fidgety, like she had an impolite itch. "You ever heard of Murphy's Law?"

"Anything that can go wrong, will?"

"That's the one. Most of the vortexes of small inconveniences and the last-minute problems that arise for folks are a direct result of the efforts of Murphy demons." Donna paused to make sure I was following her explanation. When I nodded, she continued. "People have a vast store of patience and kindness and brain power. Murphy demons help to drain that supply. So, say, a mom spends all day dealing with a Murphy, then comes home and has nothing left to deal with a child or spouse. Bad things happen in those moments."

Pete grinned wildly. "I applied to be a Murphy once. I got to the work sample part and couldn't cut it." He glanced at Crow. "Before I got this job."

"Really? Did you get too overwhelmed with the human suffering?" I didn't believe it for one second.

He guffawed. "No way! It was the level of fast creativity involved. I'm a very creative guy; I'm just not very fast. Finding ways to take advantage of the circumstances of the mark requires speed."

Donna saluted him with her coffee mug. "Yeah, those Murphys are talented."

"So, wait, I don't understand. What's the plan?"

Crow laughed, soft and whispery. "It's complicated, Bird. However," he leaned forward, catching me with a serious look, "it might be a good idea for you to request that night off. I suspect it will be quite busy." His smile invited Donna and Pete to grin along.

I turned back to my work. "My break has been over for hours. I really have to get back to it." It was a slow night, but I was getting tired of the barbed humor. I flipped open a case folder and navigated to the corresponding file on the computer. Behind me, Crow continued to hold his impromptu staff meeting a while longer before dismissing the pair.

He glided around the office behind me, in an effort, I'm sure, to be distracting. I kind of appreciated that about him. He always made me feel a little like I worked in company rather than always alone. When the transportation crew took the night's passengers away, Crow followed me around as I did my cleanup and stock chores.

"I may have found a potential swap for Paul." He reached out and picked up a box of gloves, flipped them over a few times in his hands and put them back.

"Yeah? Why'd you wait so long to tell me?"

Crow blinked, taken aback. "I only just now received the information."

I squinted at him for a moment before shaking my head with a sigh. "What did you find?"

"She is a home maker and expecting her second child."

I held up a hand to stop him. "Crow, the gender swap is a hard sell if they don't already have those tendencies. What else do you have?"

"You should really try to challenge yourself, Bird." I didn't turn around, but I could feel him grinning.

"Next."

He sighed so heavily the temperature rose a whole degree, and immediately spoiled the effect with a quiet chuckle. "There is this carpenter, newlywed. He's quite young and doesn't have many complications, yet. His demons are overconfidence and impatience, both of which may invite anger on occasion. He has been assigned two more, inadequacy and stimulant addiction, for after he becomes a father."

"What about his wife?"

"She is married to him. What about her?"

"Same questions as last time, Crow. What are her demons? Does she have some extra credit to use against her husband's demons or what? You know... I'm not explaining it to you again." Even after all our years together, Crow still forgot how significant relationships often changed the resources available for a person to fight off their demons.

I could see him bobbing his head out of the corner of my eye. "Right. Of course. She is somewhat sheltered and has been under the strict guidance of her parents most of her life. Her personal demons are insecurity and lack of self-confidence, which she doesn't seem to have ever had to deal with directly. She has been assigned post-partem depression, shopping addiction, and lying after her children are born. For all intents and purposes, she is not currently beset."

I nodded. "That might work. Healthy and energetic new body with a perky and childless young wife. It sounds like something he'd go for. How are the relationships between the couple and their parents?"

Crow stepped up beside me at the workstation. "He has a strong relationship with his own parents and his mother-in-law. His father-in-law is still a bit businesslike and brusque with him. She is still treated like a child by her parents, and she talks to both daily. She has developed a close relationship with both of his parents as well." He peered over my shoulder at the little tool and equipment packages I was prepping for the autoclave.

"Do they eat ice cream?"

"What?"

"Nothing." I loaded all my little packets into an autoclave bag and carried them down the hall, Crow heeling me. "Of his expressed interests, that mother-son relationship and the dream of passing that on to his own child are a priority. I still don't know what he would say qualifies as a success of happiness for him, but I'm pretty sure it involves feeling rooted in his family situation." I hung the bag in the sterilization chamber and closed the door. "Does the mark have any nieces and nephews?" I pushed the button to start the machine and led the way back to the office.

"Two nephews through his sister and an infant niece through his wife's sister. The two grandmothers have recently started taking the children out on Friday afternoons."

"Oh! That's good. If Paul can see the grandmothers in action, it will help him think of his own mother and fantasy son." It was strange. I was always of two minds during these little briefing meetings. On the one brain, my soul squirmed and protested at the manipulation of the little details that were needed to sell a person on a swap. On the other brain, it was a dispassionate review of the facts of the job.

"Are you prepared for a home visit today?" Crow lifted one eyebrow and the corresponding corner of his mouth.

I checked the time and my tiredness. "As long as I can get a little sleep first."

Crow arrived sometime after I had showered and fallen asleep on the couch, again. He simply appeared in my awareness between two dreams. "Little Bird?" The smooth contralto of his voice wrapped itself around my awareness like a down comforter. "Are you ready?"

"Can't we just lie here a while?" The awareness that was me snuggled into that warm comfort.

"No, Bird. We need to make a successful swap. I'm afraid we may be running out of time."

Chapter 9. Home Visit

I didn't have to actually wake up or move or anything. Crow magically hijacked my next dream state and accompanied me, like two ghosts drifting through the details of the life we were viewing. A dreaming body formed around my awareness, shockingly similar to the body I'd worn in college, with slightly longer hair, fuller hips, and sharper features than reality had been. I smoothed my hands down the front of my shirt, feeling the taut muscle of my dream abs beneath. I sighed and took Crow's arm.

With our first step, bright daylight overwhelmed the scene. I didn't recognize the area, but that wasn't unusual. We walked down a sidewalk between a dirt parking lot and a construction jobsite behind a slightly shorter than average young man; the mark. His thick, black hair was cut in a short, crisp style under a hard hat. A thin, loose flannel shirt hung unbuttoned over a white t-shirt tucked into the waistband of thick blue denim jeans. With only a denim jacket to insulate him from the wind, I wondered idly if the tidy little man was cold.

We followed him into a small, portable office already occupied by two crewmen and a secretary. He passed out a beaming smile and friendly greetings to each by name. I noted the bland expressions they returned without a hint of recognition. He punched a card through a wall-mounted timeclock and leaned forward to wave through an open office door. "Good morning, Boss."

A tanned face beneath a close cropped and tidy haircut squinted up at the greeting. "Oh. Good morning. Is there any coffee out there?"

"Yes, sir. It looks like a full pot, but I already have a cup. Thanks for asking, sir." The mark's smile broadened as he turned away.

I wasn't sure if he had meant to provoke that confused look on his boss' face, or if he had sincerely misunderstood, and lifted an eyebrow at Crow. He gave me a wan smile and ushered me out behind the man, onto the jobsite, where he walked briskly across the dirt lot. We followed him through his workday, long stretches of tedium flashing past us like some kind of movie montage without the benefit of theme music. Instead, a running stream of his conscious thoughts played like sound bites. *'Little hammer, in my hand, hit that nail, right on the head... Measure twice? Third time's the charm... Stupid board... Board straight does not account for curving walls...'* He was funny, sort of.

In between, he thought-sang in Spanish. *'Hmm-mm-mm-mmm, te traigo en mis pensamientos... hmm-mm, a donde se hayan, mm-mm-mmm.'*

"Crow?"

"Yes, Bird?"

"Why does he sing in Spanish?"

Crow pursed his lips and cocked his head to one side. "Ah. Because he is second generation, Mexican-American."

I blinked and nodded. It had occurred to me, regularly, to wonder why Crow needed me in this business at all. Then, he would need little things like the importance of ethnicity and personal relationship dynamics explained to him. Of course, our clients would be provided with the knowledge necessary to do any job or speak any language required. Still, little things like this, or like religious holiday observances, might influence the client's decision.

I sighed. "I don't think that'll be a problem."

At lunchtime, we followed the mark to a picnic table with a few coworkers. He brought only a canned soda to the table and seemed to be readily included in the banter. After a while, one of the others offered him half of his sandwich. The mark waved it away. "No, thanks, man. I have a nice pair of tamales waiting for me, but it's a little early." I nodded. *'Late lunch eater or doesn't want to knock the wife's cooking?'*

At the end of the day, we followed the mark back to the dirt parking lot. He, in turn, followed close behind a group of three other men, scurrying to keep up. I winced, listening to him call to the men ahead of him. He asked them about soccer matches, their families, and local events they might attend. They weren't exactly rude but none of them seemed interested in slowing to talk.

I was bored. I might have yawned if my dream body did that kind of thing. "Crow. There is nothing to sell here."

"Are you certain, Bird?"

I considered trying to fake a yawn. "So far, his life looks extremely boring. Average. Nothing to scare off the client."

Crow smiled. "It was work. What do you expect? They can't all be stunt men."

"Oh, yeah. That was a fun one. Is that an option for Paul?" Crow gave me a withering look without answering. I grinned and turned back to the show.

We hitched a ride in the passenger seat of the mark's old, creaky truck, endured some truly horrid mariachi music, and watched him in traffic. He wasn't a rude driver, but his attempts to sing along with the radio dwindled and were completely replaced with flavorful curses by the third red traffic light. Just before a fourth, he turned sharply off the main road and laid on the gas. A few minutes later, he was singing, loud and off-key, once more.

The contrast between pre-traffic, mid-traffic, and post-traffic driver was notable. "I see what you mean about an impatience demon."

Crow nodded and, not long after, pointed out the front window. "That is their house."

I turned my head and watched as the truck approached the small, square home. One story and perched in the middle of a small, but immaculately manicured yard, the white wooden siding gleamed in the sun as we passed it entirely. "Where is he going?"

We turned a corner, and Crow shrugged his eyebrows as he gestured to another house. "Ah. His in-law's house."

The truck pulled into the yard, and we followed the mark to the front door. An older man, slightly shorter with a wizened face, greeted him and, instead of inviting him inside, stepped out. "I wondered if you remembered." The older man said as he led the mark around the side of the house.

"I didn't mean to keep you waiting. I wouldn't want to let you down." The mark's voice had lost some quality I was sure had been there before. "Should I get my gloves?"

The older man heaved a sigh. "Yes, Benigno, you will need your gloves." He reached around to pull his own from his back pocket.

I nodded. "I understand now. His voice is so obsequious compared to earlier. It lost its depth and strength."

"He's trying to curry his father-in-law's favor."

"It's not working. Is the old man just an ass?"

Crow shrugged.

The older man wanted help moving a fence post, and I shot Crow a skeptical look as the two walked past with long-handled digging tools. Crow skipped ahead for me. The two men put away the tools they had used and walked back around to the front door. An older woman, aged with grace, met them on the porch. She shared a kiss with the older man. When he looked at her, his hard jawline softened and his whole face gained a distinguished and solid aspect.

The mark smiled wistfully at that transformation from the bottom of the steps. The woman swung around under her husband's arm and smiled warmly. "Bonnie called. She's home and, when I invited the two of you to have dinner with us tonight, she said I had to ask you. She has a roast in the oven, but she said it will make good sandwiches if you want to stay for pozole."

The mark's thoughts scrambled in patchy phrases. *Better than pot roast... shower... damned old man...*' Finally, he said, "That sounds wonderful, but I've had a very long day. Can we plan to have dinner together tomorrow night?"

At the woman's nod, and the mark's mental sigh, I snorted. Crow chuckled and nodded. We rode back to the mark's house and followed him inside. A much younger version of the older woman, dressed in a smart, charcoal-colored skirt suit, rushed from the kitchen to greet him. He tangled his fingers in her long, ebony locks as they embraced and shared a passionate kiss.

With light back and forth conversation shuffled between kisses, him admonishing her for making him refuse her mother's invitation, and her responding, "You know I can't tell them no myself," the pair undressed each other. They, sort of, bounced off walls until they made it to the shower. Things got steamy from there.

I plopped onto their sofa and looked up at Crow. "Really?"

"It is simply one day in his life, Bird. I will move us along."

He advanced us by about an hour and a half, and the couple had dressed and taken seats at their small dining table when we re-entered the narrative. It was definitely a pot roast. It smelled lightly spicy with an aroma that can only be carried by juiciness evaporating into the air. I listened intently as the mark described various scenes from his day. I remembered the bit about the boss and the coffee, but I didn't remember any smiles or winks. The guy at lunch had not offered to buy him lunch, and he had not been leading the guys off the jobsite. I shook my head and listened to an equally shining report of the woman's day.

"Unless there is major drama after dinner, I think I've seen enough." I turned my back on the dining room scene and reached out to take Crow's arm.

The scene around us shifted and my eyes fluttered open. The rectangular boxes of light from my windows were slanted across the bottom of the far corner of the kitchen. In late February, that meant it was around five in the afternoon. Crow had awakened me early on my night off. He stepped forward from the shadows of my dark bathroom doorway.

I stood, stretched, and glared at him as I walked into the kitchen. "I didn't see any real problem points, Crow." I opened the refrigerator and bent to retrieve a chilled can of soda.

He ambled across the room and sat on the couch. "What did you see?"

I shrugged, yawned, and opened the can as I walked back to the sofa. "Normal, a little boring. Basic life." Sitting beside Crow, I tilted the can back and swallowed half its contents.

"Is that all Paul wants? Have I found the perfect match once again?" He grinned that smarmy smirk that, I was sure, was intended to convey teasing.

I ignored him and, setting the soda aside, swiveled around to lie flat again. With my feet lifted to Crow's lap and my head resting against the arm of the couch, I let my eyes wander over the textured, acoustic ceiling tiles. "Probably. Can you tell me that her children will be her husband's? Will they have a son?"

Crow nodded and began running his hands over my bare feet and legs. It was like he had heat therapy built straight into his palms. I considered and, finally, shook my head. "I'm not ready to make the pitch yet. I haven't talked to Paul in over three weeks. I've barely seen him. Where has he been?"

"I've been keeping an eye on him. The cold weather sent him and a few of his friends into a hotel room for a while. He teamed up with a traveler for a time, but the traveler has now traveled on. He's been around a few times during the day. Actually, Ms. Genia wants to talk to you about him tonight." Crow cut wide eyes at me.

I groaned. "Really? Why? Am I in trouble?" Crow chuckled and I pulled my feet off his lap. I sat up and was momentarily paralyzed by a deep yawn and stretch. Crow reached over and ran his hand down my back. I felt the muscles relax and smooth beneath his touch.

He stood with me. "Shall I meet you up there?"

I turned and dropped my chin onto his warm chest, tilting my head back and making the best puppy dog eyes I could. Playing up the huskiness of sleep still in my voice, I asked, "Wouldn't you rather give me a massage in the shower?"

There is a certain burning intensity in a man's eyes when you offer him an unexpected erotic experience. It's disturbingly similar to the look a child's face gets on Halloween. Alas, Crow was not a man. While Pete and Donna, and maybe my ex, were human demons with all the little foibles of humanity, Crow never was. Crow was one of the first demons, previously an angel, cast out with the rest of his ilk.

That isn't to say he didn't indulge in the occasional erotic encounter with me. It was kind of nice. He was like a toy that didn't need batteries. Equally, he was like a heating pad or massager, food warmer and transporter, and a personal chauffeur, none of which required me to stockpile batteries, gasoline, or cords.

Even the day after a purge, I could never have actual sex with Crow, much less during the in-between state when my emotions were slowly returning. That was a giant step too far. But having him soap me down in a devilishly hot shower and rub my muscles into submission was a frequent treat. I don't know what he gained from it, but he almost never refused and almost always did an excellent job.

Chapter 10. Night Off

The day shift had a rotating schedule where they split up the weekend night shifts to cover my days off. Night's off? Either way, I had the night off. I dressed the same as every night; jeans, blouse, and low-heeled boots under my pee-coat. The evening was a little warmer than I had expected so I left my coat undone for the walk up the alley to the diner's front door.

Crow pulled the door open and bowed me in. Genia, standing at the register, looked up and a broad smile broke out on her face. "Star? What brings you in the front door?" Then she saw Crow step in behind me. "Ah. Mr. Corvus." Her smile clung to her face as she picked up menus and cutlery.

Crow asked in a low voice, "Can we sit in a booth?"

I nodded and waved Genia toward a booth against the windows. I tossed my coat onto the seat and slid in beside it with Crow taking the seat across from me. "Hey, Genia. What's the soup tonight?"

She set the menus and cutlery down for us and pulled that ever present pen from her hair. "The usual, chowder and chicken noodle, but I have a new creamy portobella and basil tomato soup, too. It's pretty popular."

"Oo, that sounds pretty good. I'd love a bowl of that and a nice melty grilled cheese."

"Coffee, black?"

"Mhmm, yes please."

"You got it, Sugar. Mr. Corvus?"

"I think I'll have the same, Ms. Genia." He handed his menu back to her. "Black coffee as well."

Genia gave us her hostess smile and nodded, took my menu and bustled away. I watched her meander around the tables to the kitchen and smiled. I tapped the table to get Crow's attention. "She's not mad."

"I didn't say she was mad. I said she wants to talk to you." Crow twisted his head slowly from side to side, stretching his neck.

I grinned. "Do you need one of those shower massages?"

Crow snorted. "No, thank you, Little Bird. I don't think you could produce or withstand the required intensity to achieve the same effect."

Genia returned with coffee. "Star, Honey, can I have a little chat with you?"

I looked at my coffee, looked up to catch Crow's eye and pulled it back down to the coffee. "Crow?"

He nodded. "I'll wait here."

I took that as a promise to keep my coffee hot and followed Genia to another table. We sat and she leaned in. "That homeless man you brought in the other night has been around a couple of times. He never stays inside and doesn't cause any problems, but I was wondering something. Do you think he'd like a job?"

I blinked. "Oh, I don't really know. I mean, we can ask him. What kind of job?"

Genia lowered her thick eyelashes and cocked her head to one side. "Well, it won't be anything much really. We need a bus boy overnight. Someone to gather dishes, wash them, sweep and mop, you know. It wouldn't be the best pay, but it might put a few dollars in his pocket for getting out of the weather. I'd give him a, let's call it a uniform allowance, too. We can't have him working in a diner in filthy old rags."

I leaned in a bit and smiled. "I think he'd very much appreciate that. May I ask what precipitated the thought?"

Genia scrunched her brow for a moment and shrugged. "The job needs a body and he's a body that seems to need the job."

"I think it's a good idea. Do you want me to make the offer when I see him?"

She waved a hand and began to stand. "If you can just let him know I want to offer him a job, I will make the offer." I stood with her, and we clasped hands before she hurried off.

When I sat back down with Crow, my coffee was waiting, little tendrils of steam climbing each other as they rose into the air. I took a sip and hummed. "I think it may have actually gotten warmer in your charge. Thanks!"

Crow rolled his eyes in conjunction with a sideways grin. The flirt. "I couldn't help but overhear, Bird." He ignored my snort. "Ms. Genia wants to give the client a job?"

I nodded while sipping my coffee, a master level skill. "Seems like it. Just a bus boy gig."

Crow hummed and held his coffee mug on the tips of his fingers. The steam drifting up thickened. "I do not approve."

I paused in the act of setting down my coffee. I had paused in swallowing, too, and had to slurp a little to finish getting it down. "Why?"

"It could jeopardize the contract." Crow sipped the now boiling liquid in his mug and gave a curt shake of his head. "No. It's too risky."

I frowned and sighed. "We can't stop her from offering him the job. Maybe it will help sell our case. There is something to be said for the feeling a man gets from earning his way, even at a crap job. It can't hurt to have the comparison once the dreams start, either."

Crow cocked his head and met my eyes. "How so?"

"Well, staying alive isn't an option for him, but if it were, it would be a long way from bus boy to contract carpenter. Not having the option to work for it in this life will make skipping all that effort in a new life look like an even better deal."

Crow stared at me, completely expressionless. I'm not sure he breathed. When he finally inhaled to speak, I might have squeaked in surprise if my last purge hadn't been so recent. "That is absurd."

'Yeah, this is definitely why he needs me.'

"It's a human thing. Just trust me. It'll be fine."

Genia sent Ellie to bring our food and wait on us for the rest of the night. I wondered if that was Crow's fault or if this was just Ellie's section. I liked Ellie, but she would never win any Intelligence Stars. She had a good heart, though, as my grandfather would have said. I ordered a slice of pie after the sandwich and caught Genia's eye when she handed the plate to Ellie. She grinned and waved, so I waved back and decided it must just be Ellie's section.

Crow's fork whipped out and back so fast I wasn't sure I'd seen it. Looking up at his face confirmed I had. "Did you just steal a bite of my pie?"

"Of course not, Bird. I stole crust." He shivered ostentatiously and waggled his fork at the plate. "What is that stuff in the middle claiming to be?"

I cut a thick bite with the side of my fork and made sultry eyes at it. "Chocolate Silk."

Crow broke off another piece of the edge crust. "That is not a thing that exists."

I solemnly lifted the bite on my fork and pointed at it with my other hand. Locking him in my gaze, I said, "Oh, yeah? Right there, buddy."

He dipped his chin and grinned at me. "I concede and rephrase. That is not a thing that exists in nature."

I stuck the fork in my mouth and slowly drew it out, analyzing the texture and flavor in a way I can't accomplish on a truly feeling day. There was no savor, only the pure experience. I washed it all down with the bitter contrast of hot coffee and nodded. "Thank God He invented inventions."

Crow's lips curled in disgust, and he dropped the remainder of the crust back onto my plate. "That was rude, Bird. I conceded."

"I apologize. But I also win." I stuck another bite of pie in my mouth and grinned around the fork.

Crow rolled his eyes again, this time without the half smile. "Paul is sleeping in an alley tonight. I recommend waiting to see him till morning."

I raised an eyebrow at him. "You don't think you can keep me safe?"

"You are always completely safe with me, Little Bird." His voice had turned tersely serious for a moment. After a pause, the terseness was gone. "It is not your safety that concerns me." He sighed. "As I trust you in human things, trust me in this."

I shrugged and nodded as I scraped the pudding-like filling off of the remainder of the crust. "That's fine with me. Is there anything you'd like to do? It's my night off. I'm all carb-loaded. You want to take me dancing, don't you?"

These were the best times. In the middle of a case, before the pitch and after the swap match was found, there was usually a night or three of these kinds of outings. Long enough since my last purge not to be completely flat and short enough that I could shrug off anything that wouldn't have felt good. During those nights, I was in the best relationship I'd ever had. I knew he wouldn't betray my expectations, and he never expected anything I wasn't ready for. I could give or take as needed without any further obligation to him.

I call this, The Delusion.

Chapter 11. The Delusion

I don't think anyone should have to feel ashamed of past relationships. I mean, by all means, if you feel that you should be ashamed of yourself for whatever reason, go for it. I'm just saying, we all make stupid decisions. I can't be ashamed of being normal. But, maybe I should make it clear that I'm not proud of it, either.

Crow had eclectic tastes. He loved to take me out on the town, but I never knew what we might end up doing. It was kind of a side deal between us. He took me out on an all expenses paid, all plans made evening. In return, I didn't ask too many questions or give him a hard time about his clothing choices for me, and I was required to try to enjoy it. Some of the more memorable outings had been the funeral festivities of a Satanist, a cowboy bar complete with mechanical bull, and a live space-opera, opera. My favorite had been a private, midnight lake cruise. On that cruise, a beautiful voice had recited poetry accompanied by a soft cello and guitar duo. We had just floated along, sipping champagne and watching the stars while we listened.

I thought about those more pleasant outings as I walked back to my basement, a spring in my step. I had about thirty minutes to prepare for anything while Crow was off clearing his calendar of one demonly thing or other. I hoped he wasn't planning something ultimately gross, like the time he'd arranged to have me collect my own fresh escargot. He hadn't made me cook them, thankfully. They had been delicious but not worth the mud bath involved.

When the doorbell announced his return, I fairly glided across the room to let him in. He wore a suit vest with long tuxedo jacket tails and long pants all made of patchwork brown leather. The image was so odd, I couldn't immediately decide if I liked it or not. I was still undecided when he said, "Aster blossoms for my Star in bloom." He waggled a cluster of three oversized flowers on unusually long stems.

I took them and offered a genuinely warm smile in return. "Would you like to come in while I put these in water?"

He always came to the door on date-night, always with flowers, and came in while I put them away. It was like he was following some kind of date protocol manual. The expected interactions were relatively superficial until there was something going on to generate genuine conversation. It was comfortable and sweet, and a little weird. I loved it.

He paced around the perimeter of the apartment while I arranged the flowers in a squat and tubby vase. Once they were placed just so in the center of the table, I turned to Crow with a grin and bounced on my toes once. "All set."

He grinned back at me and conjured a full-length mirror as part of the outfitting process. I stepped forward and watched the transformation. Sometimes the results were beautiful, like the night at the opera. Usually, they were okay but not something I'd choose for myself. This time, he demon-magicked me into a one-piece, dark brown leather thing with zippers. It was skintight and showed off a pair of shapely legs I wasn't familiar with. Weird, but okay, I guess.

Except, there were suggestive cutouts in this thing, some of which were extremely close to displaying more than I wanted to offer. My face, along with the rest of my head, was completely covered in a matching leather mask. I lifted my chin and heard the leather creak where it wrinkled at the base of my skull. "This feels a little hot."

Crow grinned and nodded toward the mirror. "It also hides your lovely face. Let's see..."

First, my hair fell over my shoulders in thick, chunky curls. The spiked heels on my feet morphed into low, block-heel, knee-boots. The bodysuit shrank and re-formed. On my arms, it left behind a pair of elbow-length gloves with all the fingers cut back to the second knuckle. The rest became a scandalously short romper, no shoulders or sleeves, but with a high collar in front and back. Two cutouts in the front showed off my nether-navel area through one and twice my normally available cleavage through the other. One in the back exposed everything from my shoulder blades to the slope of my butt. A tiara perched in my hair, reminding me of an old-fashioned nurse's cap, and did a good job of holding my hair neatly in place. The entire costume was still made from the same patchwork brown leather.

Crow hummed. "Is this more comfortable?"

"As long as it stays on over the important bits." I frowned my best dubious frown at him and took his arm. "I think I'm ready."

Crow handed me from one arm into the other and pulled me close. With one hand on my hip, his arm wrapped around my waist, he picked up my other hand and guided me in the beginning steps of a dance. Before I could wrangle my confusion into a question, he said, "You did request I take you dancing, did you not?" The light faded around us and we flew.

Crow led me through the slow, gliding steps of something like a rumba. It's really hard to tell when you're flying horizontally through the air in the arms of a giant bird man. I was amused that he'd chosen to take my flippant request as a serious wish. At least I know he's listening to me. I placed the toes of my boots atop his shoes and let his steps move my feet and legs. Well, I tried to. I kept thinking I knew how he'd move next, and my feet would slide off of his. Things went much better when I closed my eyes and relaxed in his arms.

We flew for several minutes. He sometimes chose a local outing, but we usually crossed time zones. I was ready for it when the sky brightened around us. I picked up the tangy scent of salt air and inhaled more deeply. There was a hint of the unpleasant, decaying smell of sulfur, and I buried my nose in Crow's chest. His arm tightened around me.

Our dizzying flight ended with a slow, rotating descent until our feet connected solidly with the ground. Crow released me and stepped away, giving a token tug to the bottom of his weird tuxedo vest. As I slowly merged back into reality, the sound of lively music and a laughing crowd drifted to us along with the sound of crashing waves from the same direction.

I tossed a grin at Crow and began to pick my way over the uneven ground. Enormous black stones of irregular size and shape, most of them with a shallow dip in the exposed surface, lay neatly fitted together. Fine grains of coarse black sand, pebbles, and fist-sized rocks lay in the seams and cracks. I paused for a closer inspection and discovered they weren't individual boulders after all. Those cracks were only a few inches deep. The heard but not seen ocean must have carved them this way.

The source of the rotten smell stood some few miles in the opposite direction of the music. The volcano wasn't very tall; rather, it was very wide. With its streamers of billowing smoke, it resembled a pipe's rough-carved, wooden bowl happily puffing away. It was probably just the tip top of an underwater mountain, and I was probably standing on an island. At the time, I just tried to soak it all in.

The sun hovered above the horizon beside the happy little volcano. "How sweet. You made it a literal evening out." I glanced back at Crow and sighed. He was walking along, an inch or so above the uneven ground, hands behind his back and a wistful expression on his face. I grumbled. "That's not fair and should be against the rules." There was no heat in it, though. I was too distracted choosing where to place my feet.

We ran into a sheer drop-off with a black sand beach at the bottom. Crow offered his hand and, after I placed my hand in his, floated us down the thirty or so feet. Thick stripes of black obsidian and thin stripes of reddish-brown stone alternated down the rock wall. Both seemed to radiate a glow of their own. It was quite beautiful.

Crow noticed whatever tell-tale sign I gave and lifted one hand, palm up. A wide cuff bracelet, like part of the cliff face had been molded into jewelry, appeared there. "I believe the colors suit your ensemble."

I reached for the bracelet and froze, my hand clutching nothing as the bracelet fitted itself halfway up my upper arm. A wide, stone collar fit itself snuggly around my throat. Even the tiara hat in my hair felt like it got heavier. I let my hand fall back to my side. "These come off, right?"

Crow chuckled. "Of course, Bird."

I studied the changes in the reflective surface of the obsidian wall. The hat had, in fact, gotten heavier. The thing was now studded in jewels cut from the same obsidian. It was kind of cute. Our feet again on the ground, I followed Crow down the beach. The black sand was surprisingly supportive beneath my boots. Not far from where we'd descended, the cliff face opened in a gaping gash almost all the way to the top. The gash widened into a cavern containing the source of the music accompanied by pulsing lights. I slowed my steps and Crow stepped up beside me, offering his arm. I took it and studied the festivities.

The first thing I noticed was the full bar, complete with barstools and gleaming neon signs hanging between bottles of booze. I started walking vaguely in that direction and scanned the crowd around us. Our outfits were almost streetwear compared to what some others wore. One woman's outfit was composed entirely of two white, patent leather strips, about two inches wide, each. Several men wore full-body paint and not a stitch more. Beyond them, past the bar, flashing lights spun around the interior of the cavern.

I may have tried to tow Crow past the bar at that point. We'll never know because I failed to budge him. I aimed a pouty lip up at him. He was staring to one side with a smirk at Donna and Pete and a couple of others I didn't know. I cranked up the irritation on my face to Pouty Lip Level II. "Nah-ah, Crow! It's my night off. You aren't supposed to work on my night off, either."

Crow shushed me. He shushed me and patted me on the head! I switched Pouty Lip to Gaze of Fury and aimed it at Pete and Donna. Donna's smile slipped sideways, and Pete stumbled mid-step. Beside me, Crow tsked and said, "It isn't work, Bird. They have the night off as well. I think you will be interested in their companions."

By the last, Pete and Donna had arrived to stand in front of us, their friends between them. Donna nodded with slightly widened eyes, and Pete said, "Hey, Star. Do you remember us talking about Murphys?" He gestured to the woman beside him. "Meet Nadia."

Donna lifted one hand to her escort's shoulder. "And this is Brandon."

I blinked and looked back and forth between them a few times. Nadia was a couple of inches taller than me with four-inch heels. That put her around five feet with nothing left over. Her own long, straight, black hair probably covered more than her costume of black fur. Fluffy cuffs at her wrists and ankles made a dramatic contrast with the pale, bare skin of her hands and feet.

By contrast, the man approached seven feet tall. I checked his shoes and confirmed he wasn't wearing any, either. I was beginning to feel over-dressed. From what I could tell from ground-level, the auburn locks atop his head were a mussy nest. With that height, his broad shoulders looked just about proportionately correct. His costume was similar in concept to Crow's. The biggest difference was Brandon wore silk and lace instead of leather, and it covered far less.

"Murphys?" I narrowed my eyes at the pair. "Which one of you is assigned to me all the time?"

They shared a look and chuckled politely. Brandon casually laid an arm around Nadia's bare shoulders. The lace from his detached cuff spilled several inches down her arm. "No one since Job has had their very own personal Murphy."

Nadia leaned her head back to look up at Brandon. "Well, there was that one guy..."

Brandon tapped Nadia's forehead with one fingertip. "That doesn't count, Goose. He wasn't the Murphy's only case at the time." He turned back to me with a smile. "He was just the most active."

Nadia nodded and sighed, accepting the correction.

I grunted a laugh and waved one hand, fast and stiff. "Nice to meet you." A thought occurred to me, and I stepped in conspiratorially. "Do you guys take requests?" I still owed my ex some emotional trauma.

They must have thought I was kidding. The two laughed like a couple of lobbyists, loud and from the diaphragm, so it carried. Nadia leaned back into Pete. "I like her. But," she aimed a quizzical smile at me, "how did you get here?"

Crow stepped up behind me and rested a hand on each of my shoulders. "She is mine."

Chapter 12. Dancing Demons

There is a visceral response most women have when hearing themselves referred to as possessed, like property. Most women fall into one of two camps on the topic, but we pretty much all get that same gut feeling. Camp one feels objectified and de-valued. Camp two gets warm fuzzies on top of the gut feeling. I maintain dual citizenship in both camps.

I can freely admit I want to be able to associate being possessed with being cared for and safe as well as adored and admired. The problem is I have never felt truly safe with any man. Well, maybe my grandfather, but not my father and never my ex. No human man had ever stuck to the deal. So, as messed up as it sounds, even to me, I had only ever experienced that Camp Two feeling when Crow claimed me. I experienced it then and felt my pulse quicken as he squeezed my shoulders.

I batted away my first impulse to preen and looked from Nadia to the lumbering giant, Brandon, and back again. "'His' is less accurate than to say, I'm with him. We're business partners."

Nadia snorted and winged an elbow up at me. "You must be special."

Crow squeezed my shoulders, a little extra firmly. "She is incredibly special. And she wants to dance."

I shot a twisted grimace-flavored glance up at him but didn't actually turn to look at Crow. It was all bluster and show for the under-demons. I looked back to Nadia and shrugged. "I do, actually."

"Wonderful! So do I." Nadia giggled and grabbed Pete's arm peremptorily.

I held up one hand. "Wait. If you don't mind, can I get a demo of you two in action?"

Nadia and Brandon exchanged a look and unfurled twin smiles. Brandon turned his head slowly, scanning the room. Nadia did likewise, looking in the opposite direction. After a moment, Brandon jutted his chin toward the bar and said, "Blue sequins."

Nadia followed his gaze and lifted a hand, gesturing for him to take the lead. Brandon nodded his head toward her and re-focused on his mark. The man, or man-shaped demon; I still don't know; wore a tight, blue-sequined vest straining over his thickly muscled, and otherwise bare, chest over a pair of loose, white linen pants. He stood leaning on the bar, talking with a woman near him when the bartender placed his glass on a flimsy napkin in front of him.

I don't know if he saw the drink and was reaching for it or if he just made an unfortunate sweep of his hand. The back of Blue Sequins' fingers knocked into the glass tumbler, giving him a start. Somehow, his fingers tangled over the top edge of the tumbler and knocked it up onto its bottom edge.

Brandon lifted an eyebrow at me, and I lifted one back. He held up one finger, and Nadia giggled.

Sequins stepped back with one foot to square off against the imminent spill and knocked into another group of partygoers. All three dropped their drinks, jumping back a step, and turned angry stares on Sequins. Their drinks had managed to stack themselves, the glasses anchored one inside the other, creating a stumbling stack about a foot tall. The irritated group tried to step forward, tripped over the glasses, and fell into a heap atop each other. The glasses shattered and spilled their contents in an expanding puddle beneath the pile of people.

Blue Sequins leaned back hard against the bar, his jaw hanging loose, and watched the people pile. They writhed in an attempt to regain their feet, slipped in the puddle, and fell again. They banged their heads together and lay motionless, trickles of blood joining the drink puddle beneath them. Sequins relaxed, his whole body visibly losing rigidity as his knees unbuckled. He lowered himself slowly atop a barstool and turned to reach behind him for his drink.

The tumbler had been sitting there, patiently holding itself balanced on its bottom edge, during the whole kerfuffle. However, as soon as his fingers touched it, it fell completely over, splashing some of its contents into Sequins' eyes.

Nadia and Donna hooted with stuttered laughter. Pete shared a fist bump with Brandon. I clapped, politely, while Crow squeezed my shoulders.

"You think that was impressive?" Clearing her throat, Nadia said, "Let me give it a try." She jerked her head toward an area behind her and to one side. "Do you see the blondie in the minks?"

I wasn't the only one to crane my neck around to see her. Nadia's mark wore about two dozen long white minks, each one swinging loosely from its anchor point at her shoulders, unattached anywhere else. Her platinum blond hair was piled impressively atop her head like a silken beehive. Her glitter enhanced features sparkled as she danced alone at her table of friends.

One of her minks slipped its anchor. The dragging tail caught between her two spiked heels, and she stumbled as the fur fell. Between the spinning woman and the pulsating lights, I couldn't see Minks' expression, but she momentarily stilled her dance and checked what remained of her costume.

I met eyes with Donna before we both turned to give Nadia two-handed thumbs-down signs. "Boo!" Nadia chuckled and pointed one finger at Minks.

Apparently satisfied that the remainder of her carcasses were still firmly attached, Minks bent to pick up the escapee. Somehow, when she tried to straighten, several more minks were yanked free to slide down her body to the ground. An improbable but very possible series of drops, trips, slips, and snags slowly removed every mink from her shoulders. Completely bare beneath, of course, she began trying to tie them around herself about the time she was half-way de-minked. This met with mixed success. By the end, the costume had been reshaped into a furry bikini of sorts.

Nadia held up one finger, her mouth poised in expectation.

The woman, her chest heaving, stood with her arms and legs splayed at the ready. When no more furs fell, she slowly straightened and began to smooth the furs where they were. She twisted and turned and cultivated a huge smile, apparently pleased with the outcome. She turned back to her table of friends, all goggling at her, and began to gyrate to the music once more. One hippy wiggle later, she slipped and lay sprawled on the ground.

Nadia gave a curt nod and smiled. "You may applaud now." We all did, except Crow, whose hands remained firmly on my shoulders. Nadia beamed. "Thank you. Thank you. I do what I can."

Donna nudged Brandon in the short ribs, actually producing a deep grunt. She chuckled. "Yeah, yeah. You guys are very impressive. Why don't you show me what you've got on the dance floor?" Nadia and I clamored our enthusiastic support of this idea, and Crow finally exchanged his grip on my shoulders for a more delicate touch to my waist.

My pulse leapt, and I was grateful not to have a blushing emotional display flood my cheeks. I lowered my eyes, as if watching for stumbling stones, and let Crow draw me through the crowd toward the lights and music. Pete and Donna shared quips with their dates as they followed along behind us. Nadia's high and rolling laughter almost harmonized with Brandon's deep throaty bass.

Crow, chin up and eyes narrowed like laser beams, quietly scanned the writhing mob on the dance floor. To me, he looked like a general entering the field of victory, expecting to be greeted by awe and adulation. He was probably actually looking for higher-ranking monsters. Whatever the motivation, he escorted me forward under an ever-increasing audience of onlookers. Minor demons, minions, and a surprising number of pets, as indicated by their leashes and collars, stepped back, en masse, as we approached. That phantom blush that I couldn't quite accomplish might have blazed from my hairline down to my generously exposed cleavage, on a feeling day.

The music pulsed through me, three distinct but intertwined rhythms building alone between synchronized beats. Some of the dancers swayed to a slower interpretation. Others flailed wildly, trying to catch every beat from every rhythm. The majority fell somewhere on the spectrum between. I let Crow lead.

He started us off with a quick-step, full of twirls and fast changes of direction. Over the course of several, lengthy songs, he gradually slowed our pace, and the music seemed to slow with him. He held me close, one hand pressed against the small of my back, right in that cutout, and his other snaked under my arm so his fingers rested on my shoulder. His grip felt solid and safe as I leaned my head back, eyes closed, and let his hips against mine guide me.

I was hot and thirsty when Crow steered me off the dance floor. He assumed that hip and elbow escort grip on me and led the way up a wide staircase carved out of the cavern wall. It spiraled so that the light from above and below faded into a diagonal slash of pitch blackness in the back curve. At the top, it opened out onto a narrow balcony. The edge had been carved to form a low rock wall and bench, upon which sat our four demon companions.

Crow handed me down to sit on one end of the bench and sat beside me. The bench was long and curved to allow conversation or privacy equally. Donna grinned at me from the other side and held up a tall glass of clear liquid on ice. "You look hot, honey."

I took the glass and waved one hand over its top. "Is that water?" All four under-demons snorted and laughed. One whiff and my nostrils shriveled closed against the fumes. I still don't know what was in the glass. I handed it back to Donna. "No, thanks. I may not know my limits but I'm pretty sure demon hooch isn't within them."

Crow produced a bottle of water. I thanked him and tried not to gulp. Crow gathered my hair in his hands and played with it, holding it up off my neck and creating a light breeze across my skin. Between the breeze and the cold rock leeching warmth from me, small shivers accompanied goosebumps on my arms even as I was still covered in a sheen of sweat.

I turned my head, still sucking on the water bottle, as two waiters stepped out of the staircase and bowed. Both wore classical wait staff uniforms; crisp white shirt, black pants, shiny shoes; as well as flat, white masks. They each carried a laden tray impossibly balanced on one hand. "Shall we set up a table?"

Crow didn't miss a beat in his casual flipping of my hair as he inclined his head. I pulled the bottle away from my face and watched as the waiters shifted to face each other. With their free hands held palm down and fingers splayed, they paused unmoving for a moment. When they turned their hands and lifted, the stone beneath them rose.

I squeaked. Even after all my time with Crow, I never failed to be impressed when faced with a little unexpected magic. That's one of the things I actually miss.

One waiter plucked an apparent napkin from his pocket. He gave it a little whip and let go. As it fluttered down, it spread perfectly and stretched to cover the tabletop. I put the bottle back against my lips to stifle any errant, delighted noises. They deposited the things from their trays and left before I felt safe to remove the obstruction from my mouth.

The snacks and drinks generously heaped on the table slowly disappeared as we chatted and rested. The music echoed and swirled in the cavern, but not as much as you might think. Either there were acoustic mufflers in the high ceiling or some demon trick or other kept the sound down. Literally down. It was almost faint from our balcony, but the volume rose quickly on approaching the bottom of the staircase.

I leaned my head back against Crow's shoulder, his arm around me, insulating me from the cold rock bench. I was relaxed and watched the various demon costumes on the dance floor. A random move of my eye spied Brandon watching me. I furrowed my brow at him. "I have another question for you."

His shoulders twitched, like he'd been caught at something. "I will do my best to answer."

"Can you Murphys make anything that can go right, um... do? Or, go? Whatever. You know what I'm asking."

Pete and Donna looked straight at Crow. I glanced over at him, but he just looked like himself. *'Paranoid demons.'*

Nadia and Brandon shared a deep sigh and Brandon turned back to me. "Well, yeah, we could, but that's not really the job description."

I considered my next words carefully. Surely, I hadn't thought of something they hadn't already tried millennia ago. With a mental nod, I decided there was no harm in asking. "So, you never hand out a streak of good luck? Not even to make it feel even worse when their luck turns bad?" Crow's laughter echoed in his chest and rolled out of his throat. I turned to appraise Crow's far too pleased expression. "I probably shouldn't have suggested that, huh?"

"That gives me all sorts of ideas for the Ides event." Brandon exchanged nods with Nadia and turned his attention to Donna. I caught him studying me several more times before the evening was through. I was sure Crow caught it and, if it was anything to worry about, he would let me know or just handle it for me. Still, the tall demon's stares made me squirm.

Chapter 13. Creepy Do-Gooder

By the time Crow gathered me up and ushered me out of the party at the Sea Cave, I was exhausted. I dozed in the warm comfort of Crow's embrace as he flew us back to my little suburban city. The pitch-black sky of very early morning seemed like a sea of ink. Lacking even the glowing light from the windows of homes and shops, the city was even darker so early in the morning than very late at night.

Crow flew us straight to the alley. As our feet touched down, the costumes we both wore morphed into our normal clothing; jeans and blouse for me and dark slacks and suit jacket for him. I brushed my hands down my shirt and the butt of my pants, feeling everything back in place and familiar. One hand went to my throat, confirming the stone collar had been removed. I flicked my eyes up to see an amused cast on Crow's face. "Just checking."

Crow blinked as if changing the channel and lifted a hand toward the dark alley. "He is alone. I am with you." With that, he faded. I could have walked right through him, but he was still there in that parallel, adjacent dimension of reality.

I sighed and cranked my eyelids open against fatigue. Turning toward the alley, I tried to distinguish the various lumpy shadows one from the other. From the odor, most of them would be trash bags and crates of something old and gross. A long, squelchy fart sounded from one of the heaps near the back of the alley. *'Ah, that would be my client.'*

I picked my way slowly through the muck and almost fell into the piled trash more than once. I muttered half-hearted curses and imprecations. *'Where is this place? What business in the city actually maintains a pile of trash in the alley without racking up fines?'* The thought caught my imagination for a moment. Something more substantial caught my toes, pitching me off balance, and I almost landed on my face.

I must have yelped. The target mound stirred and grunted. "Who's there?" The groggy demand was followed by more grunting as Paul got to his feet.

"Paul? Is that you?" I called out and squinted forward. I wasn't sure how much he could see from his vantage. Crow would save me if Paul tried to throw something or otherwise lashed out, but I needed Paul to not panic. It was hard to make panicky people pay attention to the pitch. Why couldn't Crow pick a time when it would be easier to get to the man?

Paul took a couple of steps forward and grunted sourly. "Ms. Star? What the devil are you doing here?"

I stifled a chuckle. "I was told you were sleeping out here and wanted to check on you." I stopped trying to pick my way through and stood with my fists pushed into my lower back. I twisted and bent a little, playing into the stretch. "This is much less scenic than the park."

Paul grunted again, bending a few times to pick things up around him. When he straightened and began walking toward me, I heard his grumpy mutters. The only thing that came through clearly was 'crazy do-gooder.' It took him a minute to reach me, and when he did, he pulled up beside me and leaned in. That close, I could make out more of his features. The face peering at me over his hulking frame was not happy to see me.

"I was asleep. I didn't care about the scenery." He turned and stomped off toward the street.

I paused, waving the stench cloud from in front of my face. It didn't work, one stench co-mingling with the next as it moved. I followed Paul. "You have a good point there." He wasn't moving fast but he wasn't waiting for me either. I quickened my pace as I reached the sidewalk. "Hang on! Wait. I'm sorry for waking you. Can I make it up to you?" He kept walking. "I'm sorry!"

He stopped and turned his head slightly in my direction. The streetlights, dim and dingy as they were, provided enough light to see his face. His cheeks glistened with the faint trace of tears. "It's a little creepy that you keep showing up like this."

I hustled to catch up and snorted. Big mistake, as the alley was still in my nose. Maybe it was still on Paul. "Creepy? I thought I was being nice."

Paul shot me a sideways look, walking again. "It's creepy."

"Noted. 'Crazy do-gooder activities are creepy.' Got it."

He half-turned his head to look at me again. The use of his own term softened him, and he grunted, the barest hint of a laugh, as he swiped his cheeks with the backs of his hands. "How did you find me this time?"

Any given moment since he woke up could have been an opening to make the pitch. Why I chose this route, I can't say. "My spirit guide told me where you were."

Paul stopped in his tracks and turned to me; both of his eyebrows drawn so close together they formed one continuous bushy line above widened eyes. "Like a guardian angel?"

"Um, sort of." I wasn't expecting that.

Paul glanced up and down the empty street. He sighed, lowered his eyes, and crossed his arms. "I have one of those. Calls himself Damien." He grunted a chuckle.

I got the reference and groaned. "Really?" This was a new one. I glanced over my shoulder. Crow was still invisible, so I carried on. "And the alley was the best sleeping arrangements he could suggest?"

Paul gave a small shrug and shuffled from one foot to the other. "He's probably just a hallucination. Cut him some slack."

I paid his joke a little chuckle. "Okay, fair point." We walked a little way further and I realized I had no idea where I was. A faint glow in the sky behind us told me our direction and I kept an eye out for a street sign or shop that I recognized. "Where are we going?"

Paul frowned. "You said you wanted to make it up to me."

I nodded. When he didn't say anything else, I nudged. "And you have decided how I can do that?"

His step faltered. "I thought you meant coffee and food."

Ah, he was leading us to the Holy Grounds diner. Or, at least, a diner. "I can do coffee and food." I picked up my step a bit and nodded to myself as he kept pace beside me. I was going to have to talk to Crow about transient clients. I longed for the days when I had casually bumped into Madelyn while shoe shopping.

Another half a block later, a thought occurred to me. "How did you meet Damien?"

Paul frowned and chewed the inside of his cheek. "He's been there since the week before my mother died." He kicked at a withered little patch of weeds in the cracks of the sidewalk. "I had a hard time hearing him at first. I thought I was just hearing things."

"Why? Do you hear things a lot?" I shot him a surreptitious glance, just trying to gauge if he really believed his own story. I caught him in the middle of his own surreptitious glance.

He looked uncertain. "The doctors were afraid I would. I had bad flashbacks and sometimes the thoughts in my head were so loud, I started arguing with them out loud, without knowing it." He shrugged, his shoulders slumping farther forward. "They had me on some pretty heavy meds; kept me asleep even when I was awake."

I nodded, remembering my own short stretch of that when I was in the bin. There had been others there with even heavier doses. It kept them calm, but I never understood how they were supposed to work through anything to get better if they walked around like stupefied zombies all the time. "So, how did you find out he was real?"

"Mom died. Damien had tried to prepare me for it, talking about appreciating her while I had the chance, and helping me talk with her." He looked at me. "I wasn't always so chatty."

I smirked. "I can't imagine."

He chuckled, almost a real laugh. "Anyway, when she died, Damien showed up and just kind of stayed."

"What does he do? Is he here now?" I'd never met an angel. Well, not one that was still divine, anyway.

Paul nodded. "He says he's always here, but I can't see him most of the time." He shivered, a full body shudder. "He kind of shows up like you do, just not as creepy." I grinned, wondering if guardian angels had caseloads like Murphys. Paul continued. "He talks to me about the things that still mess with my head. He asks questions that make me think about things in different ways. He listens. He suggested the soup kitchen and got me out of a situation with some of the guys a little while ago."

"A situation? Like what?"

He shrugged, uncrossed his arms, and shoved his hands into his pockets. "Some guys I was staying with weren't quite right. Damien convinced me to leave two nights before they set the hotel on fire."

I swung my head around to goggle at him. "Wow! So, he's like a real guardian angel?" Paul grunted and nodded. I licked my lips. "Does he have any insight about me?"

Paul lifted his eyebrows at me. "Yeah. He said you're okay." That was apparently all I was going to get on that.

The tension in Paul's shoulders had subsided somewhat as he loped along beside me, his longer legs easily keeping up with mine. I hooked my thumbs into my coat pockets and inhaled, filling my lungs with cold, damp morning air. "I haven't been completely honest with you. My spirit guide sent me to you. He's the reason I showed up at the park that morning."

Paul snorted. "You mean you weren't immediately attracted to my expensive suits and all the paparazzi?"

Good. If his first reaction was a joke, he probably wasn't offended by my initial lies. I gave him a smile and continued. "No. It happens now and then; I am asked to get to know someone with a special attribute."

He turned his head and studied me as we walked. "You mean, because I'm dying?"

I tripped. A warm cushion of air caught me a second before Paul's hands gripped my shoulders. I flicked a glance behind me, but Crow was still invisible. I don't think Paul noticed the firmer air or its warmth. "Thank you." My thoughts whirled around like fog. I stood for a moment, taking stock. My ankle was unhappy, but I hadn't injured myself too badly.

Paul steadied me until he was sure I wouldn't fall and let go. He stepped back and hummed. "Are you okay?"

I sighed and smiled at him again. "I'm fine. I tripped over my own feet."

He faced forward again. "That can happen." I fell in beside him, wondering how to proceed after that. Luckily, Paul decided to volunteer more information. "Anyway, Damien told me a few weeks ago that my time was coming. He won't tell me exactly when or how or any of that. All he'll say is, soon." He paused and glanced at me. "What does your guide want with a dying man?"

There I was, all set to inform him he was dying, usher him through the initial disbelief, then make the pitch, and someone had beaten me to the punch. I managed to say, "Huh." It wasn't my most articulate moment. We followed the sidewalk around a corner at the top of a low hill and, all of a sudden, I recognized where we were. Glancing around to find other landmarks, I relaxed. We were still several blocks from the diner and the sun was coming up behind us. I yawned.

Paul grinned at me. "You look like you could use some coffee yourself."

"You buying?" For a split second, I was afraid he would take that wrong. His chuckle allayed my fears, and I sighed. "I've had a busy night and now I'm not sure how to keep talking with you. Should I be distraught?"

Paul pursed his lips and shook his head. "I'm not. I don't think about it too much. That dead guy's liver did make me wonder about it some the other night, though."

I frowned at him before remembering his visit to the morgue. "Oh, yeah, that must have been right after Damien told you."

He nodded. "I don't suppose it matters much how I die. I think he only told me so I'd make better use of the time I have left."

Bingo! "What if you have more time than you think?"

He shook his head. "I don't know what to think. Damien said it would be no more than four months, but it could be sooner."

I nodded. *'Whoever this Damien guy is, he apparently uses the same list as Crow.'* "That's exactly why I was sent to you. I want to offer you a chance to live a whole new life."

"A chance?" Paul smirked, his suspension of disbelief running a little low. "What are the odds?"

I smirked back. "All you have to do is accept it."

Paul's hands went deeper in his pockets and his shoulders hunched forward. This was when I had to wait. Sometimes, the client changed the subject. Sometimes, they took a short moment to think before turning around and pelting me with questions. I kept the silence as we walked and let my thoughts wander.

I wondered if Crow knew this Damien guy. Was he really a guardian angel or was this another rank of demon with an interest in this contract? A yawn cracked my whole face open, and my eyes watered, stinging. I was in the middle of rubbing them vigorously when I realized what I was feeling.

Other sensations lined up to be recognized. One ankle pulsed with burning throbs where I had twisted it when I tripped earlier. Both feet and my lower back were sore from all the dancing, and my tired leg muscles burned. I pulled my coat closer around me, noticing the iciness of the wind.

Taking a mental hold on the panic welling up in my gut, I tried to silently throttle it. The panic began to turn to dread. I could hear the litany beginning in my head and tried to think of something else; anything at all. What songs had I heard while dancing? Nothing familiar, but the memory of Crow's warm embrace and steady, strong guidance through the night stoked a longing for that warmth and comfort again. Of course, that led to sorrowful thoughts of the songs I had last danced to with my ex. The litany grew louder.

The struggle consumed my attention the rest of the way to the diner.

Chapter 14. The Pitch

The bright light of the diner's front wall of windows looked warm and inviting as we approached. Genia's offer sprang to mind, and I mentally lunged for it, using it to smother the dread. "I completely forgot. Paul, Genia wants to talk to you about a job."

"Who?" He looked down at me as if I had interrupted some convoluted train of thought of his own. He turned back toward the diner and squinted. "You mean that nice waitress?"

"Owner, but yes. She mentioned it yesterday, and I was supposed to let you know." My voice sounded flat, distracted as I was by the clamor in my head. I sighed, twice, the second turning into a yawn, and donned a small smile. "You're right, I'm getting tired. I'm looking forward to that coffee."

Paul hummed and let his head slump, his steps slowing. "She seemed like a real nice lady."

I nodded but I wasn't listening. If I hadn't been so tired, I might have finished out the night still tipsy from dancing. Instead, the dread slithered around every desperate thought. *"It will be okay. With a little rest, I'll probably feel nothing again by sunset. This is just a little surge in the feelings building up in me. It will pass."* Consoling oneself is like wrapping one's own presents. Still, I kept at it.

Paul reached the door first and held it open for me. Adrya greeted us with a grin from the counter and met us at the corner booth with two mugs and a steaming pot of coffee. She poured as we settled in. "Good morning, Star, Paul."

Paul jerked with surprise. She'd surprised me too. "Good morning, Adrya. I didn't know you two had met."

Adrya cocked her hips to one side and put one fist on her hip. "Oh, we haven't, but Genia pointed him out." She held out one hand. "I'm Adrya. It's nice to meet you properly."

I met Paul's eyes and saw skepticism mirrored back. He took her hand, though, and shook it. "It's good to meet you, too, Adrya." With a little bounce and a giant smile, she turned and left us to decide what to eat.

I picked up the coffee and sipped. The hot bitterness felt wonderful, warming me as it slid down my throat. I almost cried. "Hey, Paul, I need to visit the ladies. I'll be right back. Are you good here?"

He nodded even as his eyes darted from side to side. "Yup."

I nodded and hurried into the women's toilet. Turning the catch on the lock and running the cold water, I threw myself into the far corner and let my knees fold beneath me. I slid down the wall into a huddled heap and stuffed my forearm into my mouth. There was a walk-in freezer on the other side of one wall, and a broom closet behind the other, but I didn't want to take any chances that someone might hear me. I could probably have slid down to my apartment, but that would mean leaving Paul alone longer than I wanted to. It was a crap time for a meltdown but it's hard to schedule those for convenience.

I sat there for a time, minutes slipping by, coughing raggedly into my arm. I wasn't in real pain. I wasn't even actually sad. But I was filled with dread and panic. All those little sensations and the small emotions attached to them were a warning. I knew it. I could remember those feelings. I could almost feel it then, being lonely and lost. I remembered that I was the remnant of something good. I was the wrapping that had come with something desirable, and now, I was what was left. I remembered that I was trash.

The sharp feeling of teeth in my flesh accompanied the tang of blood on my tongue. I can't say I intended to bite into myself, but it did the trick. Surreal fluorescent bulb brightness and the muffled sound of water rushing into the sink basin flooded my senses. As if I had cornered each of the roiling thoughts of panic, like little hysterical women running around my skull, and soundly slapped them all at once, they shut up. Only the lingering echoes of the chaos remained, and the exhaustion.

I sat a moment more catching my breath before I called in a tiny, ragged whimper that only a demon, or an angel, could have heard. "Help me, please."

"I'm here, Bird." He appeared beside me, kneeling, and gathered me in his arms.

Maybe it's crazy, knowing what he was and what he wanted from me, but I felt safe there. I pressed my cheek to his chest and strained to hear his heartbeat. I honestly don't know if he had a heart or if it beat, but I could hear his voice rumble in his chest as he cooed at me. The vibration and the heat worked its magic and my breaths slowed. My heart slowed. My mind quieted. I breathed deeply, inhaling the spicy scent of him. I'm sure I spent more time panicking alone than I did in his arms, but it was enough.

When I was breathing normally again, he lifted me to my feet and coaxed me over to the sink. He adjusted the water and used a handful of damp paper towels to wash my face. With a fresh wad of paper towels, he began to clean the bite on my arm. I had only broken the skin in a couple of places, but the few drops of blood had mingled with the slobber around the bite to create a nasty looking wound.

I watched him dabbing away the mess and felt the warm sensation of him healing the area. "It pains me to see you hurt yourself like this."

I grunted and sucked in a lungful of air as I lifted one eyebrow at him. "I was careful not to scare the client. Besides, by the time you're done with me, no one will be able to tell anything happened." Cynicism and snark were all I had left after a meltdown.

Crow met my eyes with a flat look. "There is that." He turned off the water and pulled me into another embrace. "You should have called for me sooner, Bird."

He sounded almost hurt. I shook my head at the thought and lowered my eyes. Thinking like that could quickly turn into more intimate thoughts that would only disappoint me and irritate him. There was a line in our relationship, and I wasn't sure what would happen if I crossed it. I let him pull my sleeve back down over the last faint marks. "Thank you. It came out of nowhere."

"Hm. Early as well." He lifted my chin with one finger and peered into my eyes.

I nodded and sucked in a fortifying breath. "Early by a couple of weeks, I think."

He rested his hands on my shoulders and dipped his chin to lock my eyes on his own. "How are you now?"

"I'm okay. I need to get back out there before Paul gets squirrelly." I was an exposed live wire of frayed nerves.

Crow lifted a hand to my face, pushed back a lock of hair, and caressed my cheek with his thumb. He nodded and said, "You look beautiful." He was so tender.

I pushed back and turned to unlock the door. When I looked back, intending to say goodbye or thank him again or something, he'd already faded away. Another deep breath and I walked back into the dining room. Paul was still sitting there, sipping coffee, and browsing the menu. I slid back into the booth and smiled at the warmth when I picked up my cup. I must not have taken as long as I thought I had, or Crow had done a time thing. Either way, my time-out had gone unnoticed.

We ordered some food and were quietly munching when Genia appeared from the kitchen, still tying on her apron. She saw us and smiled. I returned the smile and was alarmed to feel genuinely glad to see her. A new litany threatened in the back of my overtaxed mind. *It's a trap. You are just a customer. She is not your friend.*

Genia made her way over to us, stopping at a few tables on her way to greet her regulars, and snagged a chair from a neighboring table. Placing it at the end of our booth, she grinned. "May I join you?"

Paul nodded, reserved and wary. I wrapped my knuckles on the tabletop, perhaps with a bit too much enthusiasm, and said, "Absolutely. How is your morning so far?"

Genia let out one of those sighs that older ladies seem to have perfected. No matter the time of day or what they've been doing, that sigh says clearly that they will never get enough rest. "It's good, thanks! Well, there was a little tension over a delayed delivery but that's handled. How about you? Did you and Mr. Corvus have a good evening?"

Paul looked at me, curiosity plain on his face. I snorted around a mouthful of coffee and swallowed. "Are you spying on us now?" She chuckled, and I felt my soul reach for that light-hearted sound. My eyes searched the depths of my coffee, and I said, "It was a good night. I haven't quite made it to sleep yet."

"Oh, well, you're up late then, huh?"

I nodded and shrugged. "A bit."

She turned to Paul. "I'm glad to see you, Paul. Did Star tell you I wanted to talk to you?"

I looked up, curiosity briefly taking precedence over my morose mood.

Paul's face remained impassive, "She mentioned it," but his eyes had a tiny twinkle.

"Good. Good. Well, we need someone to do a little part-time work here. Just a little sweeping and mopping, bussing some tables, and maybe a few other odds and ends. It's not much but we really could use the help." Genia tilted her head to one side.

Paul glanced around, taking in the immaculate floor and tables, the full napkin dispensers and condiments bottles. "Really?"

Genia nodded, bouncing her cap of curls forward and back. I lingered on the sudden image of her with longer hair in a mosh pit; collecting amusing thoughts to combat the isolating dread threatening to return. I had a whole big mental chest of such thoughts. I'm not sure why I bothered. It was impossible to remember it was there in the middle of a meltdown.

Genia stood. "Yup. Well, you don't have to answer now. Enjoy your breakfast." She moved to stand behind the chair and gripped it under her hands. "I'll send Adrya over with more coffee. You just come talk to me before you leave if you're interested."

Paul dipped his head and saluted her with his coffee cup. "Thank you."

Genia took that as agreement and, replacing her chair, wandered away. I watched her go and idly rolled a cold, green grape over my lips. The smooth, almost wet surface felt silky against the warmth of my skin. I squeezed my eyes shut, leaned back in my seat, and pushed the grape through my lips. The chill skin of the grape against my tongue triggered a flood of saliva and my cheeks tingled from the sudden stimulation.

I sucked in my breath. "Paul?" I opened my eyes and met his. "I still want to talk to you about that other thing."

He blinked a couple of times, finally lifting his chin when he recalled the topic. "The dying thing?"

I shook my head. "The living thing."

He frowned. "What do you mean?"

I had developed a kind of sixth sense about this part of the process over the years. Tired and drained as I was, I could tell. He was ready. "My spirit guide wants to give you a new body and a new life. At the moment of your death, all you have to do is decide to take the offer and it will happen."

Paul snorted, almost spraying the table with coffee. "You're a real nice creepy lady, but I think you might be crazy too."

I gave him a smug smile, lowering my eyes and suppressing a sigh. "You'll see. Now that we've talked, you will start having dreams, pretty soon, about the life you are being offered, the man living it now, and the people in his life."

"Have you met him?"

I nodded a half shrug. "I've seen one of the dreams."

"If there's a man living that life already..." He trailed off.

"The soul of that man will pass on and you will take over from that point."

Paul pursed his lips and frowned at his cup. After a minute, he lifted only his eyes to meet mine. "So, he would die instead?"

I nodded. Paul sipped his coffee.

I waited for more questions, but Paul seemed deep in thought. He leaned back and slouched, holding his coffee cup between his hands on the table, and staring at nothing in particular.

They did that sometimes, the clients. The ones who weren't completely sure it was just a weird joke. It was a lot to consider. I occasionally wondered if some demon magic or other helped them to accept the pitch. It always struck me as a little easier than it should be to convince folks they could swap fates with some stranger. Still, it did take a little finesse, so I never bothered to ask.

My own thoughts began to roil, and I looked up into the glaring lights in the ceiling, instigating a yawn. Deep and wide, it scrunched all my features, squeezed my eyes closed, and offered an excuse for the tears. When I popped my eyes open, Paul didn't seem to have noticed. I leaned forward. "Hey, I'm going to let you think about it a while. If you want to talk, I'm in here every night before sunset and you know where I work. Just come see me." He barely flicked a glance at me.

I cleared my throat, covering the sob trying to escape. *'Not even a dying man being offered life is interested in me.'* I was losing the battle in my mind.

I nodded and slid out of the seat. My legs felt like overcooked noodles beneath me. Sheer force of will alone kept me upright and walking. I barely made it out and to the edge of the building before I sagged and called out. "Crow!"

His strong, warm arms enveloped me, and the world faded around us. He settled me gingerly onto the couch, sitting on the coffee table in front of me and holding my hands. "You're home now, Bird."

The tattered remnants of my energy and will slipped from my body. I was home. I was safe. I relaxed. I completely passed out.

Chapter 15. Rain

March rolled in a little warmer and the air held so much humidity, I felt like I was wrapped in a wet, woolen blanket while I walked to work. Snowbanks that had turned grey or dirty brown over the weeks since it had fallen began to melt and dwindle under sporadic but heavy rain showers. The phenomenon left the streets a little cleaner but also more treacherous when dark fell, freezing the rain into slick sheets of ice. At least, that was the excuse I used when I started making Crow take me home in the mornings.

It had only been a few days since the pitch and my meltdown. I hadn't seen Paul since, but that was fine with me. I had slept through most of the next night and was still reeling and exhausted. Settling back into the rhythm of work helped.

Pete and Donna had come and gone earlier in the night. They had delivered three bodies and four more had come in from other agencies. It kept me busy and granted a sense of accomplishment when I had completed everyone's exams and paperwork before 3:00. The door buzzer sounded just as I stood to begin my restock and cleaning procedures.

I checked the CCTV in the office and saw a county driver playing with his phone beside a gurney. With a sigh, I went into the hall and let him in. He only had one body to drop off and, when he had gone, I stowed the gurney and took the paperwork into the office to get at least the initial intake started.

I was about half-way through the process when Crow arrived. "Good morning, Bird."

His voice behind me made me jump and I banged my knee on the underside of the desk. "Ow! Damn it!" I pushed back and turned to glare at him. "I have repeatedly asked you not to do that." Rubbing my knee and casting accusatory glances at him, I tried to impress upon him that this pain was all his fault.

He performed a mollifying look of remorseful sympathy and stepped closer. He knelt beside me and placed a soothing hand on my knee. "I apologize. I wasn't trying to hurt you."

Pain gone, I harumphed and turned back to the screen. "I know. I'm fine. Thank you for coming. I just need to finish this lady's intake." I scrolled back to the top of the form and read off the name. "Sonya Melville Berkowitz." I frowned.

Crow nodded and walked out into the cold room. I could see him through the office window as he stood beside the new corpse. He just stood there, hands clasped behind his back and lips pursed, staring down at the place in the HRB where the face would be. I rolled my eyes and turned back to the screen.

Once I had finished the chart, I walked out to get the photos and scans. Crow hadn't moved. Well, what I could see of him hadn't moved. For all I knew, he could be astral projecting or mentally bossing around his minions. Either way, I had to nudge him out of the way to get to the body. "Help or go sit in the office." I checked the time. "I only have about a half hour to get this finished and do the restocks."

Crow looked down at me, hands still behind his back, and seemed to make a decision. "How can I help, Bird?"

I met his eyes with a narrowing of my own. "Really?" At his nod, I rattled off a few cleaning and stocking tasks that needed to be completed. He turned to get started. "Oh, and if you would please, take that bag to the autoclave?"

I turned back to the HRB and pulled the zipper open. "Hello, Sonya. I'll be your hostess this morning. Let's get you..." Sonya Melville Berkowitz. I stared down into the face of the body Madelyn had swapped into. "Oh, Madelyn." Her chart had said overdose. I hadn't made the connection. A great gaping chasm of sorrow welled up inside my ribcage.

I shook myself and finished opening the bag. I talked while I prepped her and walked her down to imaging. "Madelyn, what happened? Was it the Christmas thing? Why didn't you try to reach out to us? They think you overdosed yourself. You know, if you did, they're probably not going to pay out your insurance. I don't know if you had time to get attached to what's his name or the kids but..."

A tap on the door frame was followed by Crow's voice. "Bird?" Crow leaned there, looking at me curiously.

I sniffed and blinked, checking for tears; all clear. "It's Madelyn. Her chart says she OD'ed. Did she? Do you know what happened?"

Crow nodded and stepped back as I stepped out of the imaging room. He followed me to the control console. "She lost against Sonya's demons. It was a little quicker than I had expected. Donna won that pool."

I programmed the x-ray shots and the other scans that had been ordered and started the machine before turning to him. "A pool? You bet on how long it will take them to die?"

Crow nodded, amusement shading his features. "For some time now."

I stepped back. I felt like this should have been something I realized sooner. For several days, I had been dealing with emotional threats and I wasn't good at it. I turned to the console and began programming the camera angles. I felt like I wanted to cry for Madelyn but, at the same time, I wanted to yell at Crow. *'Betting on how long it takes a client to screw up their new life or lose it entirely? I mean, yeah, they're demons, but come on.'*

I turned back to him and shook my head. "I can't say I'm surprised but that's just awful. And poor Madelyn. What really happened, Crow?" The images began to render on the screen, and I looked them over to make sure they all came out well as he talked.

"She was, shall we say, disappointed by the reality of her new life. I don't think she ever truly embraced the *new* of it all." He shifted to stand in his at-ease pose, hands behind his back, chin up a bit and lips pursed between sentences. "She discovered that her new husband is bisexual and in a relationship with another man. While Sonya knew and was happy enough with their arrangement, Madelyn found it untenable. She became distraught and fixated. She was unable to keep up with the demands of Sonya's job with the same skill. It wasn't long after that, she was asked to take a sabbatical and never return."

My eyes began to sting as I listened and surveyed the images. The images began to blur, and I reached for the toggle to adjust the focus. Tears spilled from my eyes. I gasped and turned to Crow. He looked so smug. "Stop. Just... Did she really kill herself?"

"Oh, yes. She went to see her sister, Madelyn's sister. The woman didn't recognize her, of course. It did not go well."

The insufferable thing kept staring through the doorway at the corpse. "That's awful, Crow! How can you talk so happily about so much tragedy?" It was a stupid question.

He turned to me then and frowned, tilting his head to one side. "Bird? Did you just raise your voice to me?"

"Yes! This is not a happy thing, Crow."

"I am a demon, Star. Nothing delights me more than a two for one deal in a contract." He waved one hand toward the imaging room, toward the husk that used to house two human souls. He took one step toward me. "You should be happy too."

'Happy? Why would he say that to me?' My teeth made gritty sounds as I ground them together, biting back nonsensical retorts. I turned back to the images, my face going hot, and I tried to slow my shallow breaths. "Why should I be happy?"

Crow's hot, steamy breath curled around my earlobe as his whisper crept inside my head. "Because, Ms. Nightcastle, Madelyn and Sonya have left a new vessel to purge those nasty feelings into."

I turned my head sharply and gasped to find him still standing beside the door. I hated that particular demon trick. A small smile played on his lips. I sat, stunned and overwhelmed, silent for long minutes. The imaging machine beeped, indicating the conclusion of the programmed series.

The clock on the computer said I still had just under twenty minutes left in my shift. I moved mechanically, adjusted the body and took another round of images, tucked her back into her HRB and wheeled her back to the cold room. I managed to finish the intake, all the while fighting to ignore the roiling, mixed emotions and thoughts trying to cripple me with pain and fear and dread.

Crow had already set the coffee pot and put the note on top. All the bins were clean, and the autoclave was running. There was nothing left to do. I clocked out and walked back out to the cold room. He was standing beside Sonya/Madelyn and held his hand out to me as I approached. "Shall we?"

I glanced down at Sonya/Madelyn. I shuddered and nodded, and Crow opened the HRB. I placed my hand on her forehead, closed my eyes, and inhaled deeply. Crow placed his hand over mine and I relaxed as it all flowed away.

It wasn't the first time I had received a client after a swap, but it was different this time. In the moment, with the lightness and thoughtful post-purge quiet, I had no idea why it had been so different. I chalked it up to the emotions coming back so much sooner than expected and with such a vengeance and zipped up the corpse. "Thank you, Crow."

"You are welcome. Ms. Nightcastle." He took both of my hands between his. "Is there anything else you would like to say to me?"

I grimaced, looking up through my lashes. "I'm sorry I raised my voice to you."

He chuckled and wrapped his arms around me. "Of course, you are, Little Bird." The world faded around us as I snuggled in.

Chapter 16. Damien

I rested better than I had in days and woke up the next night full of energy, with an urge to do something different. I thought about it as I walked up the stairs and leaned against the big, heavy door. The thing was a death trap. There I was, standing atop a skinny board at the top of steep, narrow stairs and struggling against a door that weighed ten times what I did. One slip, and I'd be a goner. I tucked the thought away as a last resort on a feeling day.

The weight of the door shifted past the tipping point, and it swung wide enough to let me squeeze out. I managed to snag a cup and pour some coffee without challenge. I took a sip and looked over to the sizzling, steaming grill. Jacob was missing. I sipped again and let my eyes scan the area. The freezer door was open and I mentally nodded. Turning to head out into the dining room, I almost ran into Paul as he stepped around the end of the dish racks.

"Oh, hey, Ms. Star. Um, you aren't supposed to be back here." Paul held a broom in one hand and lifted the other to tug his forelock, like a salute, and shifted from foot to foot.

"I know. Where's Genia?" I stepped around him toward the door.

"She's out there with the customers." He reached up to hang the broom on the wall mount. He followed me out of the kitchen and waited for me to choose a place at the counter before placing a menu-placemat in front of me with utensils and a napkin. "Do you know what you want to order?"

I set my cup down and shook my head. "I was thinking it would be nice to change it up a little bit but ..."

"Would you trust Jake to experiment for you?"

"Jacob, and no. I think I'll just have a quick spinach and mushroom omelet with some bacon."

Genia stepped up beside me and laid a soft hand on my shoulder. "Hello! You're looking better. I was getting worried about you."

"Hey, Genia. Yeah, I think I just needed some rest."

"Well, I'm glad you're better. I'll go put in that order."

"Thanks." I mirrored her smile and lifted my coffee back to my mouth as she turned to go. Looking back up at Paul, I said, "You took the job, I see. How are you liking it?"

Paul had pulled a pristine white dish towel from somewhere with a bottle of cleanser. He half turned away, sprayed a little cleanser on the towel, and began wiping down the bar, placemats, napkin dispensers, and anything else he could reach. "I didn't realize how good it feels to just have a reason to move."

I frowned. I don't think I had ever heard it said like that before. "Yeah, a purpose, meaning for your effort."

Paul nodded still cleaning. "Ms. Genia took me to the uniform place and got me three. And two pairs of shoes." He paused in his new-found purpose and tugged at the top of one, khaki-colored pant leg.

I leaned forward, obligingly, and peered down at his shoe. "No socks?"

Paul's scruffy cheeks colored, and he averted his eyes. "I didn't want to ask her for socks, too."

I sipped my coffee. "So, what are your hours? Will I see you every night?"

"I'm not sure." His shoulders sagged and he picked up another something and cleaned it. "They didn't assign a shift to me, just told me to come in when I can. There is a shower in the locker room, and Ms. Genia lets me keep my uniforms here. I don't want to wear out my welcome, though." He shrugged.

When he began mumbling too quietly for me to make out what he was saying, I knocked on the countertop. "Hey, just volunteer to come in for a set shift and tell them what it is. If they need different hours from you, they'll tell you." He leaned forward, as if he would protest.

Genia came bustling out of the kitchen with my food and a full pot of coffee. "Here you go!" A rich and buttery scent, carried on thick tendrils of steam, rose from the omelet.

My eyes widened as my nostrils strained to drag in more of that scent. "Oh, wow. Genia, that smells amazing. What happened to Jacob?"

Her high, ringing laughter, not contained by the demure hand over her mouth, spurred an exchange of glances between me and Paul. "He has been taking night classes at the annex. He suddenly got a wild hair and decided doing okay wasn't good enough." She chuckled again and plucked the towel from Paul's hands. "To hear him talk, he intends to turn this little diner into a five-star restaurant."

I shrugged my eyebrows up and the corners of my mouth down in a 'well then' expression. Lifting a forkful of omelet, I sniffed. The deliciousness was definitely coming from in there. I put it in my mouth and let the flavor sit on my tongue for a moment. When I'd cleared my mouth again, I lifted wide eyes to Genia. "You tell Jacob for me, if this omelet is any indicator, five stars is completely possible."

Genia beamed and tossed the towel over her shoulder. "I will!" She topped off my mostly full cup and left us there; me, my food, and Paul.

Paul chuckled and shook his head, watching her go. "She's something. And Jake's a great guy."

"Jacob," I said around a mouthful of omelet. I had one arm wrapped around my plate and my fork was in bunny mode.

"Slow down, Ms. Star." Paul shook his head at me as I looked up.

I screened my mouth with one hand. "Sorry."

He left me to finish eating and do whatever it was that Genia paid him to do. He came back when the omelet had disappeared and refilled my coffee. "Can I get you anything else?"

"No, thank you." I nibbled the end of a strip of bacon, playing with it like a toothpick more than eating.

He turned and sat his coffee pot on a warmer behind him. "Do you mind if I walk with you to work?"

"That would be very nice. Any reason you want to make an unnecessary walk in the yuck outside?"

He shrugged. I sipped my coffee and tilted my head to aim a suspicious look up at him. He shrugged again, darted a squirrely glance at me, and shuffled off to the back. By the time he came back, my coffee cup was empty and only crumbs remained of my bacon. He had changed into his usual untidy jogging pants, t-shirt, flannel and long coat layers, but they appeared to have been laundered.

I stood and slipped on my own coat. "Ready?" He gestured for me to take the lead and followed me outside.

The wind that whipped my hair around in fitful gusts, carried a scent like frozen ozone. I studied the darkening sky and frowned at the roiling clouds coming in from the south. "Ugh, looks like more rain coming."

Paul, hands in his pockets and eyes downcast, grunted as he shuffled along beside me. I was content to let him brood until he was ready to put words to his thoughts. The morgue was in sight before he finally spoke. "I had one of those dreams you told me about."

"Yeah? What did you think?"

"Honestly, I think I must be making up dreams because you told me I would have them." He shrugged. "I didn't know my imagination was that good."

I chuckled. "They're real. I'm not sure where the couple lives."

"They live outside Cheyenne. I saw a piece of mail." He glanced at me and rolled his eyes at my smirk. "Weirdest dream I've ever had. But, Benny seems like a nice guy. Young, though. His wife is really pretty and very sweet."

"They're very affectionate."

He grunted. "And loud."

At the morgue, Paul volunteered to make the coffee while I surveyed my night's workload. With the pot burbling away as it brewed, he sat in a chair to one side of the desk and cleared his throat. "I talked to Damien about the dream."

'Ah.' "Was he upset?"

"No. He said he isn't here to judge. It's up to me, but he wanted me to ask some questions."

I opened a case file and frowned at the screen. "I'll answer anything you ask to the best of my ability."

Paul shuffled on his chair. "When Benny's soul is displaced, what happens to it?"

"He dies."

"Just, dies? He doesn't get... I don't know, recycled to start his own new life?"

I turned my head and frowned at Paul. "Like reincarnated?" At Paul's nod, I turned back to my screen. "I don't think so. A reaper comes and collects the soul. As far as I know, that's it. No do-overs."

Paul leaned back in his chair and hummed. The chair creaked beneath him, soft groaning noises, as he rocked gently with his thoughts. The coffee pot made a steamy, hissing gurgle to announce it was ready, and Paul sprang into action. When he'd placed a steaming cup on my desk coaster, he sat back again with his own. "Have you ever made a swap?"

I clicked save, closed out the case file I had just finished, and turned to sit sideways. I pulled out the bottom drawer and lifted my foot to its edge as I picked up my coffee and sipped. "Mm, thank you." I looked up then and asked, "What now?"

He cleared his throat again and made a tiny gesture with one finger, meant to indicate the whole morgue or maybe my life. "How did you end up doing this life swap thing? Did you take a swap to get you here?"

I grunted and felt my mouth curve upward of its own volition. "No. Ha. That's funny."

Paul's eyes lowered and his head drooped. "I told Damien it was a stupid question."

"No, I'm sorry." *He told Damien?* "I didn't mean to laugh at you. No one has ever asked me anything like that before. No, I have never been offered a swap." I watched him relax and sip his coffee. "Why would Damien care if I've ever had a swap?"

Paul shrugged. "He just wondered, I guess."

"Shouldn't he just know with, like, special angel knowledge?"

He shrugged again. "He's probably just a hallucination, remember?"

'Right.' "Did he get nosey about anything else?"

"He asked about your hobbies and if you're dating anyone. He was real curious about your spirit guide. I am too, really. Do you think I can meet it?"

"Him. My spirit guide is a him. Why was Damien asking about my love life? Does he want to take me out on the town?" I waggled my eyebrows at him.

Paul laughed, relaxing, finally. "I doubt it. He's got the emotional range of a brick wall."

The analogy distracted me for a moment, and I went through a series of options. *'Given my own emotional ups and downs, I suppose I'd be likened to a swinging door. Or maybe a boomerang?'* "Well, for your and Damien's information, I don't date. I was married a long time ago and it isn't something I plan to suffer through ever again." I turned back to my screen and pulled up the next file.

"That's too bad. I haven't ever been married, but Benny and Bonnie make it look nice." He leaned back again and sipped his coffee. "Does your spirit guide have a name?"

"Mhmm. Crow Corvus. It fits. He's very birdlike sometimes." This new file was a mess. I squinted at the pages trying to make out the tiny, scribbled notes.

"How did you meet him?"

'Is that a number nine?' "Hmm? Oh, ah... He just kind of showed up. I was lost and very hurt at the time, and he helped me."

"And now he recruits dying people to swap lives?"

"Yeah." I gave up on the scribbles and guessed the best I could. I would just have to scan the whole page and attach it to the file later. Wondering who had such horrid handwriting, I glanced at the signature. *'Nelle V-something? Never heard of her.'*

I closed the file and frowned at Paul. "It's really not that interesting. You are already part of the most interesting bits." I opened the next file.

"Do you like helping him, Crow, with these swaps?"

'Why is he asking all these questions about me? Why does it matter?' The tippy-tappy of my keystrokes and the soft swish of turning pages filled the air. "I've never been asked that. Never considered it like that. I guess it's not about liking it." I shrugged, still staring at my screen. "It's a fair deal."

"What's the deal?"

I turned to him and sighed. Ready to tell him it was none of his or Damien's business, I met his eyes and realized I couldn't just blow him off like that. *'Thank you, Madelyn, for the unscheduled purge.'* "It's a little personal. I have a disorder of the amygdala that makes living a normal life difficult. Crow helps me with that, and I help him with swaps." I drained the last of my coffee and turned back to my screen.

"Would you like some more?" Paul reached for the coffee pot and, at my nod, refilled my cup.

"You're a natural at that." I shot him a half-smile and hoped he'd change the subject.

He put the pot back and sighed. "We were just curious. Damien doesn't have any questions about Benny, really, just about the process and why you do it."

"And you? Do you have any questions about Benny?"

"Yeah, what's up with his father-in-law?"

I shrugged, thinking of things I'd heard people say when speculating about a television show. "Watch and find out, I guess." Paul stared blankly at my teasing grin, and I cleared my throat. "I think it's just a matter of him not having proved himself to the old man, yet."

Paul sat, quietly contemplative. When he'd finished off the coffee in the pot, he set it to brew another. I enjoyed his silent company, distracted as I was by my files and data entry task. When he stood to leave, I walked him to the door. "If you have any Benny-specific questions for me, I'm here."

Paul nodded, shoulders slouched and hands in his pockets, as he peered out into the drizzly dark of the night. "I'll keep that in mind. Goodnight, Ms. Star."

I watched him shuffle off, unsure what to make of the encounter. None of our clients had ever taken that kind of interest in me or the mechanics of the swaps before. Of course, none of them had guardian angel hallucinations before, either. I sighed, shut the door, and went back to the office. When I'd finished the last of the paperwork the day shift had left for me, I walked out to the cold room. Sonya/Madelyn was gone, of course, but there were a few other corpses needing my attention. I turned on a podcast about recent publications in the field and got lost in the process.

The work went by quickly, and I was already half finished with my end of shift routine when my phone buzzed to tell me to start it. I don't know if you can relate, but a work shift with little to do is worse, in my opinion, than one that is too full. I found myself sitting at the computer, reading, and deleting, the inter-office emails that I usually ignored. As usual, the majority of them simply didn't apply to me. Two caught my eye.

One announced the recent hire of additional staff. I squinted at the names under the photos and glanced at the file cabinet. *Is it worth digging through it just to check that unreadable signature against these names? Probably not.'* The second email cited a new state law on chain of custody in suspicious death cases. That one I printed and tacked to the wall above the computer. *'Those day shift shits probably haven't read it either.'*

Crow leaned in through the door. "Bird? What are you doing?"

I stood atop the swiveling, rolling, desk chair, one knee on the desktop, carefully highlighting the individual steps outlined in the email. I didn't turn around. "Hi, Crow. Just working."

"Yes, well, let's get you down from there."

I surveyed my work and snapped the cap back onto the highlighting marker. "There. They can't miss that." I stood and turned, and so did the chair.

Crow, crossing the room in a burst of demon speed, caught me in his arms before my head crashed on the concrete floor. "I meant for you to step down, Bird." He smirked down at me, held as I was in both of his arms and upside down.

I swatted his shoulder. "Thank you."

He hummed and set me back on my feet. "Just protecting my asset."

"Of course." I looked at the clock and groaned. "It's not even 3:30 yet?" I sagged into the desk chair.

Crow straightened and came to stand with one hand on the small of my back. He looked from the clock to me and snapped his fingers. "I believe you misread that, Bird."

The room around us fuzzed as the clock ticked rapidly through the seconds and minutes until the hands read 4:00. The rest of the room came back into focus, and I smiled as I turned to clock out. "Lovely, thank you. I am more than ready to be home."

Crow took my hand as I stood, my pee-coat already over his arm. "May I make you dinner?"

I wrapped my arm around him, nuzzling my face into his neck and shoulder. "What kind of dinner?" The world faded around us.

He deposited me in the middle of my living room and held me until I was steady on my feet again. Handing my coat to me, he began his walking circuit of my apartment. "I have a treat in mind. I promise to fetch a pizza for you if you don't like it." He peered into my dark bedroom, nodded to himself, and moved on to the bathroom.

I walked to my bedroom door and threw my coat in the general direction of the bed. "That's a pretty good guarantee. I'll take it."

Crow completed his inspection, or whatever he was doing, and turned a toothy smile on me. "Excellent." He strode toward the kitchen, tapping the tiny table as he passed. A bottle of chilled white wine appeared, beside two filled glasses. He snagged one and carried it into the kitchen. Ingredients materialized and covered the countertop. He traded his suit jacket for a white and frilly apron covered in bouquets of yellow, heart-shaped flowers.

I snorted. He shot a look at me, and I held up a defensive hand. "Sorry. It's a lovely apron."

He twitched an eyebrow and turned his back on me. "You seemed quite bored this morning. Tell me about your night."

I sighed and stretched my legs out in front of me. "Paul walked me to work. He had his first dream and chatted up his guardian angel about it. I told you about him, right?"

"Yes, Damien. How did that go?"

"He's remarkably un-judgey for an angel. He seems to be leaving Paul to make his own decision about the swap." I sipped the wine. It was surprisingly delicate. I squinted toward the ingredients on the counter, wondering what he could possibly serve that wouldn't overpower it.

"They're first rule is to protect the free will of their charges." I could almost hear the words, "the fools," at the end.

"It was strange. Paul said Damien had almost no questions about the swap, but he's very curious about me and you."

"Oh?" Crow shot a glance over his shoulder.

I hummed and gave him the broad strokes. "It was a little creepy, honestly."

Crow had mixed a bunch of chopped and seasoned things into a skillet and tossed it around in one of those fancy show-chef moves. "What does this Damien look like?"

"I really don't know. I've never seen him."

He turned the stove off and deposited the sauté onto two plates. He took off the apron and carried the plates to the table. "Bon appetit."

I leaned in and sniffed the plate. Several different types of flakey meats were mixed with strips of peppers and onions and a strange little red thing that looked like a tiny beet root. "Very colorful." Crow had already shoveled a forkful into his mouth. I took a skeptical taste. It was delicious, and with the first burst of flavor, I could taste the lingering notes of the wine being pulled through it. "No pizza required. Well done, Crow."

His satisfaction beamed from his broad grin. He sipped his wine and said, "I'd like for you to try to get a look at this guardian angel."

I grunted. "Paul wants to meet you, too. I'll ask for a trade." At Crow's frown, I shrugged. "As Paul keeps reminding me, Damien is probably just a hallucination. I mean, you'd think we'd have run into guardian angels before if they were real, right?"

Crow pursed his lips and shoved food around on his plate. "Angels are real, Bird. I'm technically an angel."

"But, *guardian* angels?"

He picked up his wine cup and toyed with it between his fingers. "Oh, yes. They are as real as Murphys."

I set down my fork and used a napkin to clear the gravy from my lips. "Are you mine?" I smirked, already dismissing my silly question, and tossed my napkin onto the table.

He stared at the glimmering surface of the wine in his glass. In a quiet and tentative voice, he asked, "Do I act like your guardian angel?" He lifted his eyes to mine, smoky and smoldering with an introspection I wasn't familiar with from him. Before I could decide how to answer, he lifted his eyebrows and, with a noisy inhalation to inflate his chest, said, "No."

I squirmed and tossed my head. Whatever kind of close he and I were, this felt truly intimate. With the most nonchalant smile I could muster, I asked, "Are you sure?"

He stood and, with startling agility, gently pulled me to my feet by one hand. He pulled me close and snapped his fingers. The lights dimmed and softened. Music, at once discordant and soothing, floated through the air. He pulled me into the slow and sweeping steps of a dance. "I'm a demon, Little Bird."

He guided me into my bedroom, coming to rest beside the bed. "I made my choice." He lifted his hands to my neck and slowly drew them down my shoulders, across my upper arms, around to my back. "And, I am very good at what I do." My clothes evaporated away from my skin under his hands. Thick, warm air cushioned my exposed skin, pulsing and massaging knots I didn't realize were there.

As he tucked me into bed, lulled and groggy, I whispered, "You sure are."

He slid under the blanket, cuddling me close to him, and held me as I drifted off to sleep.

Chapter 17. Ides

The next night, I awoke alone and unsurprised. I wandered through my routine, fighting to keep my eyes open, until I had that first cup of coffee under my nose, ready to sip. Jacob waved his spatula and grumbled his loud greeting and banishment as I stumbled toward the dining room. A sound drew me to turn my head as I passed the end of the dish racks.

I caught the sight of Paul's back disappearing into the alley and turned to follow him. At the door, left propped open with a mop bucket, I peeked around the edge. Paul threw a full garbage bag into the dumpster and turned to face a man standing on his other side.

The new guy looked a little like Crow, in that, he was tall and lean, dressed in a smart executive business suit. He looked completely different, in that, where Crow's features were all pudgy or sharp where they should be the opposite, this guy had perfectly defined and proportioned features. I sipped my coffee and leaned a shoulder against the door frame.

Paul wasn't talking loud enough to make out the words, but the one I assumed was Damien had obligingly turned so I could read his lips. "She's right. The swap will kill Benny. Still, it is up to you." The angel lifted his eyes to stare right at me.

I ducked back and frowned before walking swiftly to the dining room. I gave Genia my order and sat down my coffee. Slipping into the ladies' room, I bolted the door and called for Crow.

"Good evening, Bird." He appeared behind me, his reflection in the mirror a moment before he spoke. Maybe he was actually making an effort not to startle me anymore.

I spun. "Crow. I saw Damien." He widened his eyes and made a 'go on' gesture. I shook my head, trying to order my rampant thoughts. "Well, he looks like a really attractive version of you." At his, 'excuse me,' look, I clucked and rolled my eyes. "Come on. You know what I mean. He's tall, has dark hair, and his face looks like something a sculptor would create and name Adonis."

Crow smiled at my discomfort. "Hmm, yes, I think I've seen him."

I swallowed and twitched my eyes at the locked door. "He looked right at me. I was hiding, spying around the door, and he looked right at me. It was unsettling."

Crow frowned. "He's an angel. He saw you whether he looked at you or not."

"That's not less unsettling."

Crow patted my shoulder. "He won't hurt you, but stay away from him. If Paul asks to meet me again, just call for me." He looked upward and sighed heavily. "I need to check on a few things." With that, he was gone.

"Thanks." I poured all the sarcasm I could into the word and went back out to my breakfast.

Paul was busy with his work tasks, but we got a chance to talk when he walked me to the morgue again. "I took your advice."

"Which advice was that?"

"I offered a set schedule to Genia."

"Yeah? What'd she say?" I punched in the security code for the door, and Paul pulled it open, holding it for me to enter first.

"She said it would work out well." He followed me into the office and set a pot of coffee to brew. When we'd settled in with a cup apiece, he said, "I had another dream. Am I going to get one every night?"

I nodded. "Yep. Right up until the day..." I trailed off, realizing I sounded excited about the event of his death.

He nodded, letting his eyes roam over the walls. "It looks like an easy life. Mine probably looked easy when I was Benny's age too." He tapped his fingers on his cup. "He's so full of spunk." A small smile played at the corners of his mouth.

I sipped my coffee and studied him. "Are you still considering it?"

Paul lowered his eyes and nodded. "They speak Spanish at home, a lot. How am I going to do that?"

'Finally.' "You will learn everything you need to know when you become Benny. See, the skills you need and the memories are all part of the structure of the brain you will take over."

"Does that mean I'll forget everything that makes me, me?"

"Nope." I set down my cup to make better use of my hands to explain. "So, the best I can tell, the skills and memories and personality that make you, you, are in two places. One physical copy and one soul-based copy." I held up one hand for each copy, referring to them as I spoke.

Paul watched my hands. "So, like a printed copy of a letter and one stored in the cloud?"

I fucking love technology. Everything complicated can be boiled down to a computer analogy. "Exactly. So, when you take over in the hard copy, the framework, you'll have the structure to guide you on how to fill Benny's shoes, while still being yourself under it all."

Paul lifted one hand to rub his eyes and dragged it down his face. He looked at me and seemed like he was about to speak. After a moment, he turned away. He picked up the coffee pot and topped off our cups. He replaced the pot and sipped before he spoke again. "So, I'd be walking through his life, pretending to be him, and really being me, but not allowed to act like me?"

I frowned and hummed. "When you put it like that, it sounds awful." He nodded, eyes wide and sincere. I shook my head and sighed. "At first, it might be best to mimic Benny as best you can. You have to remember, though, the challenges Benny deals with will be less challenging for you. There are parts of his life where you can succeed more easily than he can. You can start making different choices to grow and change in that life until it fits the real you better."

Paul peered silently at me from beneath a furrowed brow. After a moment of his silent observation, I offered a small shrug and turned to my computer screen. I was acutely aware of him staring into my ear, silent and broody, but my attempts to suggest questions to brooders in the past had never gone well. It was best to wait out the quiet until they thought of another question.

There were only two case files that needed to be transcribed into the computer, and I was half-way through the first when Donna and Pete showed up. I said, "I need to let them in. Wait here?" Paul nodded and I hurried to the door.

Looking over the files of the two bodies they wheeled in, I turned a quizzical expression on the demons. "What does, 'unknown drug suspected,' mean?"

Pete unzipped one of the HRBs and grinned down at what lay within. "Ides."

Donna patted the middle of the other HRB. "Both of them."

I stepped up beside Pete, looked down, and cringed at the twisted face that stared up at me. Mouth and eyes all locked open as wide as they would go, the eyeballs had shriveled, and thin trails of blood-tinged aqueous humor still leaked slowly from the corners of both. Deep furrows ran down both cheeks as if the person had raked them with their nails.

"This is from the drug?" I looked from one demon to the other.

They exchanged looks of their own and Donna shook her head. "No. Ides just makes it easier. The Murphys take care of the damage."

"I thought we were still a couple of weeks out from that."

"Oh, we are." Donna patted her corpse's middle again.

Pete said, "This is preliminary trials. You know. Ironing out the details for the event. The real surge is going to happen on the fifteenth."

I took another look at the corpse I could see and turned to unzip the other. It wasn't in better shape but at least it wasn't leaking anything from its eyes. "Right. I'm going to need to get the intake scans on that one now." I pointed at the first corpse. That eye leak needed to be documented. "You two can wait in the office and have some coffee if you want."

I led the way, dropping the intake files into the incoming basket. Paul eyed the two demons uncomfortably as Pete and Donna shuffled in behind me. I left them to introduce themselves as they would and pulled up the timeclock program. A few keystrokes later, I had requested the nights of March fourteenth through sixteenth off.

Paul followed me out to perform the scans on Mr. Leaky. His face twisted, looking sad and disgusted. "I knew that guy."

"Really? Are you sure? I mean, his face probably didn't look like that on a regular basis."

Paul made a small noise. "Yeah, but I recognize the graffiti on his jacket. Decent guy. Played really good guitar. What happened to him?"

I started the scans and turned. "Have you ever heard of Ides? The new drug?" He nodded, and I said, "Yeah. That stuff will literally get you killed. Stay away from it."

"Maybe that's how I die."

'Hmm, maybe.' "I would hope not."

"I wonder what happened to his guitar. It was a really nice old twelve-string. He kept it in a waterproof case and everything."

I flipped through the file. "It isn't mentioned here."

"Maybe one of the guys picked it up." He shoved his hands into his pockets and turned toward the door. "I'm gonna' go find out. You have a good night, Ms. Star."

"I'll walk you out."

He waved me back into my seat. "It's okay. I'll see you tomorrow."

He walked out, and I turned back to Mr. Leaky. *'Weird.'* I finished up the initial scans and measurements on the dear, departed guitarist before rejoining the EM demons in the office. "Hey, did you two know Mr. Leaky was a friend of Paul's?" Putting a dead friend in front of Paul would be in character for them.

"Was he?" Donna asked, examining a cookie.

"Where did you get cookies from?"

Pete pulled a drawer open under the coffee pot. A bag of gingersnaps lay there, the top rolled down and pinned closed with a chips clip. A sticky note had been taped to the bag with the initials, "N.V." in large print. I snagged two cookies for myself and drew a question mark beneath the initials before replacing the bag.

"Don't sneak anymore snacks. I don't need day shift drama." I dunked a gingersnap and nibbled.

Donna giggled and Pete gave me a salute. "You got it." I shared a little banter and a pot of coffee with the EM demons before they left and I was, once again, alone with the dead.

I worked through Mr. Leaky first. The eye leaks had been caused by some kind of head trauma. Both Ides bodies had numerous contusions and broken bones, and the second corpse had somehow ruptured its stomach. It wasn't the worst damage I had ever seen, but it was bad enough.

They got progressively more mangled as the fifteenth approached. Paul stopped walking me to work after his second encounter with more Ides bodies. I couldn't really blame him, and I still saw him at the diner. Before I left work on the thirteenth, I set my work email to auto-respond with, 'I will be unavailable until the seventeenth. If this is an emergency, please call the main office number.' I gave the number and the business hours and made a cackling imitation of an evil laugh as I clicked the button to confirm.

When I woke up on the fourteenth, I was half-way through my waking routine before I remembered I was on vacation. Coffee dependency is sometimes a problem. I threw on a pair of jeans with a baggy t-shirt and called Crow.

"Good evening, Bird. Do you have plans for your nights off?"

"Nope. Not a thing." I slowly turned in place to face him as he walked the perimeter. "I was hoping you had a fun surprise for me." He came to stand before me, and I batted my eyelashes up at him. "I have three whole nights off in a row. We could do something really spectacular." I locked my hands behind my back and rocked on my feet. "Oo, like a cruise!"

He narrowed his eyes at me and smiled, one of those smoldering grins. "I may have just the thing. Let's get you some coffee and breakfast first, eh?" He offered his elbow and led me out of the apartment.

The night was unusually warm, humid and still. Gravel crunched beneath my sneakers as we strolled up the alley. He inhaled deeply, drawing my attention. "Has Paul committed to the swap, yet?"

I shook my head. "Not yet."

He made an irritated noise. "We need to close this deal, Bird. What does he need to get him to commit?"

I squinted up at him. The fluffy, dark clouds still illuminated by the late evening sun made a purple and blue backdrop to his shadowed face. "Why is this case so much more important to you than others?"

"It isn't."

"Uh, seems like it is. You've never micro-managed me before."

"I'm not micro-managing, Bird. I'm expressing interest." He patted my hand on his arm.

I swatted his patting hand. "Cut the shit. You've been shadowing me and looking over my shoulder every step of the way."

A low rumbling growl rolled from his chest and up his throat. "Fine. There are... oddities, with this case. His death date has changed three times, perhaps due to some manipulation by Damien. I should be able to access his guardian angel assignment details, and I can't. Someone deliberately banned me from them." He growled again.

It was my turn to pat him. "It doesn't seem odd for an angel not to want to share client details with a demon. You are kind of in opposing departments."

He grunted as we turned the corner onto the sidewalk in front of the diner. When he didn't say more, I stepped in front of him, making him stop and look at me. "Are you telling me everything?"

His entire demeanor shifted, his posture and features morphing into casual and relaxed openness. He smiled, big and toothy. "Of course, I am, Bird."

'Yeah. Right.' I aimed a skeptical frown at his head as he stepped around me, reached for the door and pulled it open. I whispered, "I know there's more." I didn't wait for a response as I slipped past him. I led the way to the counter, not even bothering to make sure Crow was following. In that moment, I had the cool knowledge of facts not adding up. I might have been properly angry, but the post-purge effect was holding on better than the last time.

I returned a wave and smile to Ellie and slid onto a stool. Crow took the one beside me a moment later. "Bird..."

"Hey, Ms. Star. Would you like a menu?" Ellie's practiced motions as she laid out napkins and flatware were only slightly hampered by the pen and order pad clutched in one hand.

"Yes please, Ellie. Is there anything Jacob has been experimenting with recently?"

"He's been on a burger kick for a few days. I had one yesterday that he stuffed with cheese on the inside." She half-turned her head and widened her eyes. "It was so good."

I grinned and accepted the menus from her. "I might have to try one. Just black coffee for the moment though."

She nodded and turned to Crow, whom I had yet to face since we'd been seated. "Same, please." She nodded and took a moment to actually write down the coffees on the order pad, the tip of her tongue making an appearance between her teeth. Once she'd placed two mugs of coffee in front of us, she shuffled off to check on her other customers, and I finally turned to Crow.

He was staring at me, something he did when he wanted me to know he was being patient. I sighed. "Whatever is going on with the client, it could affect the contract; especially if I don't know about it."

His face remained as blank as marble for a moment. Then, he pursed his lips and heaved a sigh. "I honestly do not know anything else for certain." He straightened on the stool and sipped his coffee. "But I think you are correct. There is more going on."

I swiveled my stool and faced him properly, my mug between my hands. "You're worried."

"I am not worried. I have an appropriate level of concern and I'm keeping alert for more information."

"And you're snippy."

He growled into his coffee.

Paul came bustling out of the back with a big round serving tray resting on one palm, balanced at his shoulder. A smile cracked his face as he saw us, and I waved. "Hola! Give me a minute and I'll be right back."

I nodded and watched him shuffle off to one of the tables on the other side of the dining room. "He's in a good mood."

"Hmm." Crow grunted and turned back to his coffee. "Do you know what you are going to order yet, Bird?"

I faced my menu and frowned. "No. Are you in a hurry?"

"Of course not." He tapped an item on my menu. "I happen to know Jacob recently changed his recipe for this one and is very happy with the result."

Chicken parma-sagna, one of Jacob's first original recipes and known to cause intestinal pain. "Uh-huh. I'll take your word for that. Actually, I think I just want a little fruit salad and maybe one of those cinnamon pull-aparts. Will you help me eat..." I looked at Crow and realized who I was talking to. "Oh, right, nevermind." I ignored his chuckle.

Paul came back, big tray empty, and pulled a coffee pot off a warmer to top off our cups. "I hope your evening is going well, Ms. Star. Aren't you running a little late?"

I slid my cup back toward me and shook my head. "Thank you, and nope! I'm off tonight. I'm off for three nights in a row, actually. Crow, here, and I are going on a cruise."

Crow held up a finger and I rolled my eyes. "Actually, Bird, I never agreed to a cruise."

"Crow? Crow Corvus?" Paul frowned at Crow. At Crow's nod, Paul stuck out his hand. "Hi. I'm Paul. I've been hoping to meet you."

Crow eyed Paul's hand. He looked at it so long I thought he was going to refuse it. Finally, he clasped Paul's hand and gave it one solid pump. "Call me Crow. It is a pleasure to make your acquaintance."

Paul turned his freed hand over and inspected his palm. "Yeah, um..." He shook his head and re-upped his smile. "Ms. Star has been answering a bunch of questions for me, but I'm real curious about you."

"Oh?"

"Yeah. Do you think we can arrange to sit and chat one evening soon?"

Crow gave him one of those beaming, charming smiles. "Why don't you join us this evening?"

I turned my head so fast, a nerve in my neck twinged. "What?" I shot a glance up at Paul. "Crow, I thought..."

Crow took one of my hands between both of his and patted it. "We are still going out. We will simply be three instead of two."

I yanked my hand from his and gave him a squinty-eyed glare. Something in his expression as he looked back at me, or maybe one of his demon tricks, stalled all my arguments. Turning to Paul, I gave him a sideways grin. "It would probably be more fun than just hanging out with Crow."

Paul chuckled. "I'll think about it. Meanwhile, are you two ready to order? Jake's got a new meatloaf dinner that's pretty good."

"Jacob." I corrected him without thinking about it.

"You want to try it?" Paul raised his eyebrows at me.

Crow said, "I'll give it a try."

I shook my head and ordered the fruit and pastry. I waited for Paul to toddle away with our orders before turning to meet Crow's eyes. "Just so you know, entertaining clients does not count as a date night."

Crow smirked and turned to face the wall separating us from the kitchen. He reached out to pat my knee with one hand. "Of course not, Bird." His eyes moved slowly, back and forth across the wall, following Paul's movements on the other side.

Chapter 18. Sports

There I was, a lidded, insulated coffee cup in one hand and a bag of most of a cinnamon pull-apart pastry in the other, tagging along behind Crow and Paul as they chatted and meandered up a sidewalk in the post-twilight murk. *'What the hell?'* Acutely aware of the date on the calendar, I stewed in silence as we walked. Crow was supposed to be taking me out for fun in a safe and remote part of the world. Somewhere untouched by the havoc that was ramping up to explode the next day.

I cast furtive glances down every alleyway and side street we passed, catching glimpses of scurrying rats, feral cats, and dark human forms, all equally suspicious of anything not themselves. Two crusty men in one alley, with a barrel fire between them, turned toward us as we passed. I accidentally met one's eyes. His face twisted as he looked away, turning his back to me and facing the fire. The frenzied flames leapt upward, licking at their hands and casting lurid shadows on the brick walls to either side. It was creepy, even for me, and I hang out with demons.

Crow led us in a winding path at an unhurried pace in the general direction of the newer housing developments on the south side of town. The first several of those lots had been snapped up and built up over a year ago, but it was still sparsely populated with manicured medians and molded curbs. It was almost like parkland with randomly situated buildings here and there.

I, myself, have never had any interest in being a homeowner. Between neighbors and maintenance and interest rates on a mortgage, not to mention being utterly alone in the world, it just doesn't seem like a good plan.

Ahead of me, Crow met Paul's questions with his own brand of tedious wit and humor. Paul, like so many others, had trouble pinning down his answers. "But why, Mr. Corvus?"

"Please call me Crow, or Mr. Crow if it makes you more comfortable." Crow's voice carried a hint of frustration.

"I still don't understand why you would want to help me live on. What makes me more worthy than Benny?" Paul trudged, his shoulders hunched forward and his hands in his pockets, one solidly placed foot after the other, but his eyes took in everything. His head turned constantly, streetlamps glinting off his too wide eyes.

"It isn't a question of worthiness, so much as a question of will. Benny does not have the opportunity that you do to make this choice. If he were dying, perhaps he would." Crow, his head tilted at that odd, birdlike angle, gave a terse nod to punctuate his answer.

Paul's shoulders heaved with a disgruntled sigh. "Will? Like free will?"

"Precisely."

"What about Benny's free will? Isn't it the same as stealing for me to choose to exert my will to take something from him that he wants to keep?"

"No." Crow drew out the word just enough to tell me he was lying. It sounded almost exactly like when he said 'um.' "In point of fact, it is definitely not in the category of theft."

Paul glanced back at me. I shrugged and sipped my coffee. He sighed again. "What if, just out of curiosity, I was able to talk to Benny and ask him what he thinks?"

'Interesting. I wouldn't have expected Paul, our homeless, drug-addled-but-in-recovery, vet to be the one to come up with all the new questions.' From the dark aura amassing around Crow, he hadn't expected it either.

"Firstly, I sincerely doubt he would believe you or take the conversation seriously. Secondly, you are getting to know him. What do you think he would say?"

Paul became thoughtful, and the gritty sound of our feet on the sidewalk took on a steady cadence, like a heartbeat, as our steps began to synchronize in the otherwise quiet evening. The amber and white lights of a neighborhood park with a small baseball field to one side came into view, a welcoming beacon, as we topped a rise. A loud crack echoed off of trees and light poles from the game, complete with spectators, being played on the field. Paul paused in his trudge to watch and listen to the cheers.

I reached into my bag for a piece of pastry; the uncrumpling of paper loud in the lack of conversation. Crow and Paul both turned to stare at me. Crow blinked once, flicked his eyes to the bag in my hand and back, and blinked once more.

One cheek stuffed with pastry, like a squirrel with a stash, I frowned. "What? You want some?"

Paul chuckled and stepped toward me with his hand up. "I'll take a pinch, Ms. Star."

Crow continued to stare flatly. "No. Thank you." He turned toward the game and began walking one slow step at a time toward it. Paul and I followed, of course, but he stayed at my side, sharing my treat. Crow's sonorous voice drifted back to us. "Have you ever played a team sport with friends, just for fun?"

Paul looked at me and I gestured to him, as if passing the question back. "He knows I don't do sports, team or otherwise."

"When I was a boy. I played flag football with my school. In the service, the guys and I sometimes played basketball, you know, over there." He cleared his throat and looked down at his feet. "That court is a pile of rubble now."

Crow's steps picked up and his dark aura diminished as we approached the ball field. "Did you enjoy it?"

Paul nodded. The nod turned into an almost rocking motion as he walked. I held out the open bag to offer him another piece of pastry. He declined and sighed.

Crow didn't have to turn around to see the nod and nodded as well. "Why don't you play anymore?"

Paul pulled a wadded piece of tissue from his pocket and wrapped the rest of his pastry in it before shoving the whole thing back into his pocket. He lifted his chin and sniffled. The light, coming from everywhere now, glistened on the tears pooling in his eyes.

Crow led us toward the ball field, past the line of women waiting for the restrooms, past the line of men waiting for a beer, past the bleachers sparsely filled with friends and family of the people on the field. We stopped on the far side of the visiting team's dugout, Crow peering through the fence toward the coach's box. I hung back, letting Paul step closer. Crow was watching him, even if his eyes were trained on the pitcher. Whatever he saw, he liked. He straightened and put back his shoulders, clasping his hands behind his back.

The batter swung. A loud crack rang out, through us and over our heads. Paul flinched, then stepped forward to place a hand on the fence as the ball sailed toward the outfield and the batter hurtled himself toward first base. Even in the harsh glare of the floodlights, the pink tinged flush of his damp cheeks was evident.

'What emotion does this evoke for him? Is he sad? Happy? Nostalgic?'

I popped another two pieces of my pastry into my mouth, one for each cheek, and turned to find somewhere to sit. The ground was dewy, and the bleachers were way over there. I sighed. Under my breath, I muttered, "Crow, would a picnic table be too much to ask for?"

Apparently, yes. A blue, tubular bag appeared, resting against my knee. I yelped and jumped, knocking the bag over with a clatter and thunk.

Paul turned to look at me, as did a couple of passing strangers. I promised myself I would scold Crow later and almost dropped my nearly empty coffee cup as I shifted the things in my hands and bent to pick up the folding camp chair. "I'm fine, just clutsy." I shot Paul a wry smile as I tugged on the bag's drawstring.

Paul stepped over and took the chair from my hands. "Let me help you, Ms. Star." He set up the chair beside me, facing the field, and patted the seat. "Where were you hiding this?" He quirked an eyebrow up at me.

"Thank you, kindly, sir." I grinned at the back of Crow's head and plopped into the chair. "Crow brought it."

Paul frowned. "But..." He turned to look at Crow.

Crow turned with one of his toothy grins to show two more chairs in his arms. "I'm generally well-prepared." He handed one to Paul and opened the other for himself.

With Crow on one side of me and Paul on the other, the sense of being constantly under observation robbed some of the enjoyment from my pastry nibbles. I sipped my coffee and cleared my throat. "Do we have any idea who's playing tonight?" I didn't care at all, but I really wanted them to look somewhere else.

Paul squinted at the uniforms on the players. "Looks like the Morris Tires team and the High Hill, City Mobile team visiting." He lifted a hand to gesture indistinctly and nodded to himself.

"Would you like a cup of coffee, Paul?" Crow held a tray with three cups out in front of me. I traded my cold dregs for a fresh cup and pulled the lid off. I breathed in the steam and wiggled down in my chair.

Paul stared, uncomprehendingly at the proffered cups before finally taking one. "Uh, thanks."

Crow shot me a toothy, creepy grin as he took the third cup and made the tray and my old cup vanish. I narrowed my eyes at him and wished, not for the first time but for the first time in a while, that Crow could read my thoughts. I was going to have many words for him later.

Paul, after a sip of his own hot beverage, settled back and focused on the game. For a time, the cheers and jeers of the crowd, the crack of the bat against the ball, and the brazen calls on plays filled the silence. Finally, Crow repeated his question. "Paul, I am still curious, why don't you play anymore?"

"Who would I play for?" The big man leaned forward in his chair, elbows on his knees, rolling his still-lidded cup between his hands. "I lost track of all my service buddies. None of them were from around here anyway. Family's gone."

'I've felt that.' I laid a hand on his arm. "You could play for yourself."

He glanced at me and sat back, turning his cup to find the sipping hole in the lid. He took a long pull from the cup and looked back out over the playing field. I shook my head. I love my coffee, but I'll never understand how anyone can guzzle it like that while it's so hot.

"Have you ever tried bowling?" Crow tilted his head back and poured an equally impressive amount of hot coffee down his gullet. Well, impressive if he were a human man.

Paul shook his head.

"Benny is a bowler." Crow shifted in his chair and crossed one leg over the other.

Paul glanced at him and back to the game. "Is he any good?"

"He has potential."

I grunted at the smugness in Crow's response. "Does he enjoy it, Crow? Or, is it something he does because someone else said he should?"

Crow turned a disapproving frown on me. "I believe his father-in-law is the team captain."

Paul grunted, a wry chuckle, and shook his head. "He needs to stop sucking up to that old man. I think he'd get more respect from him if he stood up to him, showed him who he really is, instead of trying to be who he thinks the guy wants to see."

I nodded, and Crow said, "Quite likely. You could make that happen. If you chose to make the swap."

Paul nodded and lifted his cup to his lips. He held it there, as if on pause, without sipping. He lowered it again to speak. "You never said, can I just have a talk with Benny?"

Crow sighed. Loud and growly, it startled me. He wasn't usually this impatient and never this obviously disgruntled in front of a client. He turned to Paul, his face an intense mask of determination. "If you could, what would you ask him that you can't glean from watching how he comports himself in his life? What answers would you accept? Might you find that he couldn't answer you satisfactorily? Would you then want to also speak to Bonnie, or her parents, or his?"

Paul, not obviously affected by the outburst, hummed, lifting his coffee and sipping. "I'd just ask him if he wants to live."

Crow blinked. He looked at me, as if I was somehow responsible for this conversation. I looked back and shrugged my shoulders as well as my eyebrows over widened eyes. He blinked again and turned back to the game. I couldn't tell you who was winning or by how much. I didn't really care, but another crack of bat against ball brought a wave of cheers and stamping feet from the bleachers.

Paul chuckled. "I'd probably tell him to stand up to the old man, too. Bonnie would probably thank me."

Chapter 19. On a Cruise

Paul left us once he'd reached the bottom of his coffee cup, and Crow insisted we stay and watch the rest of the game. It was only a few minutes but, between the rickety chair making my back twinge and Crow being deep in thought and refusing to speak, it seemed like it took forever. He was in a mood.

I'd only seen him this way a couple of times. He wasn't angry, only quiet and pensive. I waggled my cup at him, and he waved his hand to refill it. I wouldn't say I was content, but close enough. I sipped and watched the players scurry about on the field, as if any of their frenetic effort would amount to anything. There is a show on TV that describes itself as a game where the rules are made up and the points don't mean anything. Isn't that all games?

Eventually, the people began shuffling away, a few arguing, many laughing. As I stood, preparing to leave, one group of couples began arguing loudly over who was to drive. A man in a ballcap yelled, "It's my goddamn truck!" and shoved another man dressed in jeans and a white t-shirt like a fifty's mechanic.

"You're drunk as Granny at a Bridge game, Buddy. Let Henny drive." Said a third man. He had his arm around a petite woman huddled against his side, chewing her lip.

"I'm not drunk, you idiot. I had one beer." Baseball cap guy scoffed and shook his head. He staggered a couple of steps backward and tripped. He landed hard on his ass in the grass and immediately began screeching. His whole friend group rushed forward, surrounding him.

I looked up at Crow. He had dismissed the chairs and the refuse of our picnic and stood in his at-ease posture, hands behind his back, passively waiting for me to be ready to leave. "Is that Ides? Here? At a yuppy ball game?"

He lifted his eyebrows at me and hummed. I gestured toward the small group, and he made an 'ah' noise. "Yes, actually. Donna did a very good job on the marketing for the event. Ides has now saturated most of the area within a two-hundred-mile radius." He winged out an arm. "Come. I believe you asked for a cruise."

I perked up and grinned, taking his arm. "I did indeed."

He walked me toward a tree line in the opposite direction of the parking lot. Once we were shadowed enough not to draw any attention, he pulled me close, and we flew. Settling me on my feet in my living room, Crow released me to walk the perimeter.

I shook my head at him and walked into my bedroom. "If you see any spiders in your inspection, please, don't tell me. Just get them out." Crow grunted from somewhere near the kitchen as I stripped and tossed my clothes into a hamper. I had climbed into the shower, adjusted the temperature of the water, and was mid-gargle by the time he stepped up to the doorway. "A shower, Bird?"

"Not a real one. I feel muggy from walking in the night air." I shrugged as I stood and slid the frosted glass door closed. "I'm just going to rinse off."

I let the hot water cascade over my head and shoulders, breathed in the steam and coughed as the moisture tickled the soft tissue in my throat and lungs. When I was thoroughly drenched, I picked up a shower poof and put a dab of soap gel on one side. As I scrubbed my pits and other warm bits, I thought about the weird evening with Crow and Paul. "How do you think your meeting with Paul went?"

Crow's form was a vaguely darker shadow in the dim rectangle of the doorway. As he moved, leaning further to one side, the swirls and dips in the frosting of the shower door fractured his outline. It was odd, but I thought I could almost see black wings and enormous curling horns. I rolled my eyes at myself and tilted my head back under the water.

"He is a strange one. Damien does not seem to have marked him, but mine slid off; rubbed away." Crow trailed off.

My eyes still closed, I paused in splashing water around. "Mark? What are you talking about?"

Crow was silent so long, I looked to see if he was still there. Finally, he said, "An angel mark. Or demon, depending on the individual's address."

There was no hesitation or drawn-out word in his speech. He wasn't lying, so why had that taken so long? I turned off the water and slid the door open. Steamy mist curled up from my skin in the comparatively chill air. "Am I marked?" I reached for a towel as my skin prickled with tiny chill bumps.

Crow stepped forward and laid a hand on the towel rack, holding my towel hostage. "Oh, yes. I marked you the day we met."

I grunted and stamped my feet. "Crow! It's cold. Gimme it."

He grinned, a sultry smile. Offering me a hand, he helped me out of the shower and pushed my hair back over one ear. Still damp, but no longer dripping, surrounded by the heat rolling off of his body, I looked down and a sideways grin slid over my face. A bright yellow, string bikini with inconsistently sized white polka dots barely covered the important bits. A thick beach towel, one they call a sheet, hung over one of my shoulders. "Is this the whole outfit?"

He pulled a pair of sandals from behind his back and let them swing from his fingers. "Yes."

Some time later, I lay face down on the deck of a large boat, or small yacht, in the middle of a body of salt water. The sun, several inches off the horizon, beamed down on my exposed skin, warm and relaxing. It had been a long night and, after stuffing myself at the seafood buffet on board, the gentle rocking of the boat on the waves lulled me into a contented doze.

Crow flitted to and fro, occasionally stopping to sit on a cushioned bench nearby. From there, he asked inane questions just often enough to keep me from falling asleep entirely. We weren't completely alone, but the people-shaped minions steering the ship and doing all the necessary tasks to keep us afloat in the right direction weren't really people. They didn't make extra noise or speak at all as they went about their assigned tasks.

Crow plopped onto the cushioned bench with that squelchy squeak of water-resistant material and leaned forward, elbows on knees. "Is this really all you want to do, Bird?"

I lifted up on my elbows and squinted toward him. He still wore his customary black suit and looked like nothing less than a blackhole void sucking in the brilliant light around him. I lifted a hand to shade my eyes. "Aren't you hot in that?"

"No." He sighed and leaned back. "I don't get hot or cold. You know that."

I heaved a sigh as I heaved myself up to my knees. "It makes me hot to look at you like that." I reached for the tube of sunscreen on the deck beside my towel. Spreading the thick lotion over my shoulders, chest, neck and face, I eye-balled him through my lashes. "Do you want to help me out here?"

Crow appraised me for a moment before rolling his eyes and standing. His clothing changed as he stood. A thin blue polo shirt hung loose from his shoulders over baggy, knee-length cargo shorts and sockless deck shoes. He knelt beside me as he slid on a pair of dark sunglasses. "Is this better for you?"

I gave him a tiny smile. "Hm, much, thank you." He took the sunscreen from me and motioned for me to lie down. The moment I did, the intensity of the sun brought tears to my eyes. "Can I have some sunglasses or a hat, too?" He waved, backhanded, and a floppy canvas hat appeared upside down beside me with a pair of large sunglasses nested inside. "Thanks!"

He nodded and began slathering my legs with sunscreen. "Bird, are you happy?"

Propped on one elbow, I stared at him from behind my shades. "What? Why?"

He focused on my legs. "I asked you first. Answer me, then I will answer you."

I bent my other elbow and leaned back. I let my head fall back and gazed, upside down, out over the edge of the boat, across the expanse of rolling waves, nothing but us and water and sunlight in any direction all the way to the horizon. "Right now, in this moment? I am deeply contented." I lifted my head, thrilling in a moment of vertigo. "Generally, though, no. Of course not. I'm a profoundly broken person who relies on a deal with a demon to purge painful thoughts and feelings on a regular basis. It's a safe assumption that I gave up on working through my shit and earning some happiness a long time ago."

Crow pushed my legs apart and moved to kneel between them. With a firm grip on my hips, he scooted my butt closer to his knees and continued to spread sunscreen over the exposed skin of my hips and stomach. The slow massage across my skin distracted me from his silence and I lay flat, eyes closed behind my shades, lulled into another languid doze.

"What can I do to help you be happy?" His voice was strange. Deeper and more sonorous than usual, but quietly intimate, it rousted me from my doze. His hands had made their way up to my abdomen, tracing my ribs and edging under the bikini top loosely covering my breasts.

I frowned and sighed. "Crow, you're being weird. Why would you ask me that?" I paused and cracked my eyes open to look at him. "In fact, you still owe me the answer to that question."

Crow grumbled and sat up, removing his hands from my skin. "I've been giving Paul's success theory some thought."

"Ahh, and now you're worried I'm going to quit on you in favor of seeking my own happiness?" If I'd thought I had a chance, I would have quit Crow's deal long ago.

He nodded and moved to sit beside me. "Something like that."

The tilt of his head, the fidget of his fingers, the lack of eye contact all leant credibility to his air of worry. I didn't believe it for a second. "You can't make me happier. You already do everything you can." That was true as far as it went. He gave me all the support and attention he had to offer. He gave me the only kind of reliable and consistent companionship he could.

It would take a real human person to give me a chance for real happiness. Just one. One I could depend on and trust. Someone who needed me, who needed to be needed in return. A smile played with the corners of my mouth. Basically, it would take Crow, but human, and that didn't exist either.

A bead of sweat dripped from a strand of my hair into my ear. I sat up and vigorously rubbed a knuckle at the tickle. "Ugh. I just got slathered but I'd like to cool off. Can I get back on board if I jump over the side?"

Crow grinned. "Yes." He stood and offered me a hand up. "I will join you."

We stepped up on the bench and dove into the water, Crow's shirt and shorts becoming swim trunks on the way. At first, I just dove and swam and splashed on the surface. Crow swam backstroke laps around me, grinning. In the middle of one dive, as I examined the hull of the boat, Crow rocketed down to my side, trapped my hand in his, and began to pull me deeper.

My breath began to run out, my lungs tightening while my diaphragm spasmed. I needed air. I tugged against his grip on my hand, going so far as to try to swing my feet between us and kick him loose. He turned a creepy, toothy smile on me and pulled back.

I began to panic as the need for air became painful.

Crow pulled me into an embrace and forced my lips to his. Sweet air filled my lungs, and I froze, momentarily dizzy with oxygen rushing to my brain. When he pulled back, his creepy grin had turned mischievous. "Just breathe normally, Bird."

He spoke, clear as a bell, under water and startled me so badly, I yelped. He laughed and I tentatively sucked in a tiny gasp of the sea. An odd sensation of water being compressed, and air extracted from it centered somewhere in the middle of my throat. Crow laughed again at whatever face I made and reached up to brush the place behind my ear.

"What the..." The words escaped me in my startlement, and I lifted a hand to the place he had touched. Gills. Checking both sides, I confirmed, I had gills. I turned a grin on Crow and aimed a swat at his shoulder. The water resisted, not allowing my hand to gain any force of momentum, but it was only an ineffective, token gesture anyway. "You could have said instead of scaring the piss out of me." My voice gurgled like an air bubbler in a fish tank.

Crow took my hand again and pulled me with him as he swam for the seabed. "Where's the fun in that?"

It wasn't as deep as I expected. Coarse white and grey sand covered the area, bright white lines of refracted light making the ground look like some Dali-esque jigsaw puzzle. Darker shadows drifted by, and I looked up. Fish of varying shades of orange and red or blue and green swam past, the smaller ones in schools for safety against the larger but solitary predators.

Something with a long and pointed snout charged through the middle of one cluster of shiny yellow bodies. I gasped. "Is that a swordfish?"

Crow shook his head, his thick hair waving around his head. "I believe that is a blue marlin. Swordfish are smaller and they don't typically range in this area."

I twisted around to float on my back and stared up at the surface. "Where are we? I thought we were in the middle of the ocean. Why is it so shallow?"

Crow laughed. He undulated to propel himself and used his arms to steer as he swam rings around me, over and under. "We are. This is what happens after a volcanic upwelling has moved on and time and the ocean have worn the land back down."

I flipped over and stroked away toward the shadowed edge of the sandy plateau. Something solid glistened like twinkling stars through the gloom. The craggy edges of a wall of coral became clear as I approached. The twinkles resolved into small, even more colorful fish. Watching the waving ends of tubeworms and flowery coral protrusions, I began to notice the little shrimp and crabs and eels picking their way through, like little commuters on the streets of a strange city.

"This is beautiful," I breathed.

"You are beautiful." Crow cast the whispered words into my ear from where I had left him.

I shot him a look before whipping off toward the coral. I glided down, nearly scrubbing the tender flesh of my stomach against the sand. Kicking idly with my feet, I crawled with my hands along the bottom, startling myself as much as the starfish and an octopus hiding there. A big, dumb grin broke across my face as I twirled to watch them hurry away.

As I got closer to the coral, I noticed it had a brown and grey, rocky base under the colorful and waving garden on top. I also realized how much bigger it was than I had assumed from a distance. Broad and branching types looked like enormous elk antlers sticking up out of the sand. Rumply surfaced round corals on the bottom ranged from the size of a basketball to some with diameters longer than I am tall. I reached out and gingerly touched one of the balls.

I thought maybe it would feel like a puffball mushroom. I was wrong. It felt more like a rough bone. I climbed the side of the reef, like scaling a cliff, only weightless. The first time I touched one of the soft corals on top, I yanked my hand back, prepared to be revolted. The plantlike animal was apparently equally startled. It yanked its frilly orange edge back into a crevice, looking for all the world like a clam sticking its tongue out at me.

Crow swimming around behind me, watching me, laughed and came to my side. "Be careful, Bird. Some of these can give you a serious chemical burn."

"More serious than you can cure?" I teased him and continued to pull my way up the side of the reef.

"No, but I believe the experience would be unpleasant for you, nonetheless." He glided upward beside me, smug and self-satisfied as usual.

I was glad he was beginning to act like himself again. The weird questions of my happiness made me uncomfortable. This I was familiar with. This I knew how to respond to. I could have flipped and glided my way up the reef-side, too, but I enjoyed feeling the textures. A hole opened in the side of the reef, inviting me to climb through.

I shot a glance at Crow. He tilted his head down at me. "Are you sure you want to do that?"

I chewed my lip and narrowed my eyes before nodding. "I trust you." I wrinkled my nose and turned back to the mystery tunnel.

It widened almost immediately after I squeezed past the shoulder-width opening. I lifted my hands to either side, palms out, and touched everything. Velvety on the left and lacey on the right gave way to feathery and fanned. All snatched themselves back from my touch, exposing the harder rocky corals on which they grew.

The tunnel branched twice but maintained a steep upward incline. The refracted lines of light coming down from the surface filtered through the soft corals, providing enough light while lending an almost late evening atmosphere. I kicked and spun to look up as I moved forward. A branch of hard coral ripped my shoulder.

I slapped a hand over the wound and squealed. My knees curled up toward my chest, almost in a fetal position, as my momentum continued to carry me past the booby trap. A trail of blood, surprisingly dark and distinct in the water, swirled in my wake. Crow pulled me into his arms and rubbed his hand over the wound.

The bleeding stopped immediately, the flesh knitting back together without so much as a faint scar. "Little Bird, you need to be more careful."

I chuckled as I examined the healed area. "Every rose has its thorns, huh?"

A deep shadow from above us darkened the quizzical look forming on his face. We both looked up to see an enormous shark swimming through the tendrils of blood in the water. I sucked in a mouthful of water and felt a forced jet of the stuff coming out of the gills behind each ear. That would have been a gasp topside.

Crow frowned and said, "Wait here." Without waiting for me to agree, he shot straight up and barreled into the shark. Up and up they went until Crow broke the surface, carrying the shark with him.

I grunted and said, under my breath, "Excessive, but effective." I was still waiting to see them come back down when two more shadows drew my attention. More sharks were following the blood trail on the current toward me.

Crow appeared beside me again and took my hand. "Are you ready to go or should I evict these fellows as well?"

I grimaced at the oncoming sharks and nodded. "Let's go." I looked around us again, trying to take in the magic and memorize it before it faded away.

Crow settled us on the deck once more. He didn't let go as soon as our feet touched down and I tried to ask why. I couldn't pull any air into my lungs. Crow's hand came up to cover my nose and mouth. My eyes went wide, ready to fight, and the pressure began to build in the space behind my gills. The feeling of compression intensified, and trickles of cool water leaked down my neck. A moment later, Crow brushed his thumbs over where my gills had been, smooth skin once more, and let me go.

I opened my mouth and sucked air into my lungs, pinning Crow with Gaze of Fury. "Again, Crow, you could have warned a body." A minion handed me a big, fluffy towel and a frozen, fruity beverage infused with liquor. I was grateful for both.

Crow grinned. "Again, Bird, where's the fun in that?" He lifted one hand, now holding his sunglasses, and fitted them onto his face. With a final grin, he turned and walked toward the double-stacked tower section of the boat where the bridge deck was located. "I have another event planned for dinner this evening. Relax. I'll be back."

I stuck the straw of my beverage between my teeth and sipped, tiny bursts of flavor spurting over my tongue. *'What is he up to?'* I lay back down on my deck towel, shades over my eyes, and considered what Crow's motivation might possibly be. A rough thud vibrated through the ship and jostled me awake. My skin was dry and tender as I moved, and I kept expecting to feel it crack open. The sun kissed the horizon in the west and a sparse field of palm and coconut trees waved in the breeze off the starboard bow. "Crow!"

He appeared from around the bridge deck tower, carrying a bottle of water in one hand and a filmy length of cloth in the other. "I'm here, Little Bird." He smiled, an unfamiliar, sideways smile. I'd say it was genuine, if I didn't know better. "I imagine you are parched." He handed me the water bottle and waited with that patient and weird smile as I opened the bottle and downed half of it. He helped me to my feet and offered the length of material in his other hand. "The wind is going to pick up. We don't want you to catch a chill."

I traded the water bottle for the cloth and shook it open. "Thank you." I settled the knee-length, thin, brushed cotton robe over my shoulders and pushed my arms through the sleeves. I winced at the tenderness of my skin and groaned. "You let me get a sunburn."

He chuckled at my petulant pout and took one of my hands in his. A tingle accompanied the soothing sensation that traveled across me as he healed my skin and urged me to follow him. "Would you like to join me on the beach?" We walked to the side of the ship, and I grinned at the tiny island sprawled out beside us.

A fire, low flames licking across an enormous bed of coals, lay a few feet up the beach with something large and meaty roasting on a grate above it. Minions moved here and there, setting up lanterns and a table with chairs. Crow indulged me with a slow, manual lowering of a dinghy over the side and paddled me to shore. It was only a few dozen feet or so, but it was a nice spice to the experience.

On the beach, Crow introduced me to our dinner. The unfortunate shark he'd propelled out of the water earlier smelled fabulous. He turned me toward the table situated atop a thick, woven mat, and let me tour the inside of a small, three-sided pavilion behind it. Maybe he was just showing off, but the full lavatory with a soaking tub and plumbed toilet was a delightful find. The entire island was smaller than a typical Walmart store, but the ups and downs in the terrain limited our exploration to the beach area in the failing light.

After dinner, I took the opportunity to soak in the tub while Crow washed my back and kept my banana daiquiri filled. He provided me with a light, linen pants suit for the evening, and we sat between the rebuilt fire and the crashing ocean surf, watching the stars. It was peaceful and calm, and I had time to think.

"Crow?"

"Hmm?"

"Are you feeling okay?"

He cast a surprised look at me. "Of course. Why do you ask?"

I shrugged, considering. "You were acting odd earlier. Even for you, it was odd. You haven't asked about my happiness before."

"Haven't I?"

"No." I studied him; the set of his shoulders, the lift of his chin, but his features were indistinguishable in the night. "I would appreciate it greatly if you would share with me what made you ask now."

A shooting star trailed across the sky followed by two others, moving faster, burning hotter. "Make a wish, Bird."

I shifted to face him more fully. "I wish you would be honest with me."

He grunted and fidgeted. Finally, he shook his head and said, "It's the case. Um, this client. I am becoming frustrated and annoyed with it. I wanted to make sure that it wasn't causing you to be discontented. I did not mean to concern you."

'*Liar.*'

I nodded. "I see. Are you reassured?"

"Not entirely. It should have been a simple yes or no answer. What I received was an essay on why happiness is an unobtainable, theoretical concept." He huffed and rested his head on the back of his chair.

I straightened and gazed out over the water again. Something huge, possibly a whale, jumped in the distance. A bioluminescent glow twinkled in the spray and splash. I smiled and considered the question. '*Am I happy? Well, no, absolutely not. But, why?*'

"No. I am not happy, Crow." He turned so fast I could almost hear the snap of his neck. "But think about it. I'm not unhappy either. I'm not anything."

He rested a hand on my shoulder. "You are definitely something."

I snickered. His shallow understanding of the complicated meanings behind emotions was almost naïve. "Well, yes, I'm a human woman, a professional and a demon's sidekick. But I don't feel anything. Not happiness or sadness or anything in between, most of the time." I patted the hand he still rested on my shoulder. "I don't think you need to worry about Paul turning me into a disgruntled employee."

He smiled, exposing enough teeth to be seen in the dark. "That is good to know, Bird. Thank you."

It was enough to satisfy his concerns, but the key phrase was still there. I had said, 'most of the time,' and he hadn't picked up on it. It tickled the back of my mind. *'What about the rest of the time?'* The thought poked at the tender memories of pre-purge meltdowns. *'I hated it. Why? Why, in my most raw emotional state did I feel disgust and revulsion toward Crow and our deal?'*

I closed my eyes and tried to call to mind the fantastical images I had seen on the reef. Blood in the water overlayed the glittering landscape in my mind. My eyes popped open again and I scanned the sky for shooting stars. Tiny pinpricks of light against the enfolding blackness stubbornly refused to fall. My gaze fell down to the equally dark surface of the sea, unevenly broken only by the lighter, frothy lines of breaking waves, but nothing magical glowed to distract me.

I looked inward and remembered Paul's smile as he accepted a piece of pastry, and the glisten of tears on his cheeks. I didn't want him to make this choice. I didn't want him to kill Benny. I shivered and glanced at Crow, my first instinct being to reach for him. For an instant, that horned outline seemed to overlay his silhouette. Only for an instant. It resolved into the familiar shape so quickly, I dismissed it as my imagination. But it was enough to halt my tongue before I said his name.

I felt something. Not the familiar panic and dread, but something equally unpleasant. I flicked my tongue out to wet my lips and prodded that unpleasant thing encroaching on my thoughts. What was that? I gingerly turned and twisted the feeling in my thoughts, becoming bolder as I found familiar facets here and there. I took hold of it and braced myself against the recognition. It was guilt. I felt guilt and I felt remorse, all wrapped up in the certainty that I was helpless to do anything about it.

After I drifted to sleep on the beach to the sound of the surf crashing a dozen paces from my feet, I had fitful dreams of sharks attacking homeless men. The one part I remember well was a line of about a dozen Pauls, arms linked, doing some kind of Rockettes-style, running dance to mariachi accompaniment. Crow woke me with a big plate of breakfast shark and magically conjured coffee. By the time I had finished it and made use of the lavatory facilities in the pavilion, I had managed to dismiss the dream and the thoughts of the night before.

We spent the day wandering around the island, exploring craggy ravines, fabulous waterfalls, and taking in the view from the summit of the tallest point as the sun set. It was the evening of the sixteenth, and Crow transported me back to the ship for the return trip. We cruised along over the ocean, the sun fading on the horizon behind us until I fell asleep on the deck.

Chapter 20. Home

I awoke lying in my bed, blankets tucked under my chin, late evening sunlight casting rectangular boxes onto the walls of my room. I stumbled through a shower and frowned at the distinct tan lines running across my collarbones as I settled a loose cotton blouse over my shoulders. Choosing the smallest shoulder bag I owned, I transferred my wallet, keys, and other needful things from the pockets of my coat and tossed the coat onto a closet hook. Upstairs, Paul ushered me out to a seat with my breakfast before I saw Genia.

She appeared before my first coffee refill. With a deep sigh, she sat on the counter stool beside me and grinned. A flick of her dish towel made a playful swat at my arm. "Looks like someone had a tropical vacation!" She eyed my face and hands, all the exposed skin in evidence.

"Hey, Genia." I, with the ever-present rim of a coffee cup pressed against my lips, slurped and grunted. "Yeah. Crow took me on a cruise. I had a great time. Saw some tropical fish and a reef and even some sharks."

Her nose wrinkled at Crow's name, and she rolled her eyes toward the wall. "Well, the tan looks great, honey, and I'm glad you had a good time. You deserve nice vacations."

I grinned and stabbed a sausage with my fork. "How is Paul working out in the job?"

Genia beamed. "Oh, he's so good. I'm so glad you brought him to us. You may have noticed, I have him helping wait tables now. He even takes orders here at the counter sometimes."

I nodded to my mostly empty plate. "I did! I'm so glad it's working out for you both."

"Me too! Actually, he's taken over so many of the muscle jobs, Jacob has had too much time on his hands." The grin on her face matched the twinkle in her eye. "He's talking about making a *special* menu and asking trusted customers to try things on it to decide if he should make them regular menu items."

I drew my eyebrows down and gave her the side-eye. "Trusted customers or brave ones?" I smiled immediately, not wanting to hurt anyone's feelings by accident.

Genia laughed, the beautiful, ringing, and genuine laughter that seemed to be simply a part of her natural makeup. "Oh, honey, you tickle me sometimes. No, really. Trusted customers. And friends, like you."

I sputtered, coffee threatening to come out my nose.

Genia patted me on the back. "You okay?"

I nodded, squinting my eyes as they teared up. "Wrong pipe. I'm fine."

I was not fine. *'Did this amazing woman just call me a friend?'* She had never done that before, and I was immediately seized by the dread; that if I believed she was my friend, someone with more than a fiduciary interest in me, she would hurt me or betray me. I shivered.

With a last, concerned look at me, Genia stood and began to edge her way toward the opening in the counter. "Well, slow down or something. We don't want to lose you to a half ounce of black coffee in your lungs." She sidled around the counter, picked up a pot of coffee off the warmer and hovered it above my cup. "Promise or no refills."

I chuckled, still holding a napkin to my face. "I'll be more careful, I promise."

She tilted the pot and topped off my cup. "Good. Anyway, consider this your formal invitation to be an official taste tester. I'll let you know when Jacob's ready to share his creations." She winked at me, returned the pot to the warmer, and walked into the kitchen.

Paul came out a half a moment later, laughing and looking back at something over his shoulder. I stared. I don't think I had ever seen him fully laugh before. When he turned around, still grinning and shaking his head, he noticed me and walked over. He stood on the other side of the counter, and his eyes flicked to my cup, noted it was still full, and rolled up to meet mine. "Ms. Star, did you enjoy your vacation?"

"I did, thank you." It was almost like talking to a different man. There was a looseness to his shoulders and a straightness to his back that hadn't been there just a few short weeks earlier. He looked happy and engaged, clear-eyed and light-hearted. *'Hmm, maybe a certain birdman had been right to worry about the client taking this job.'*

"What have you been up to?"

He found a clean towel and began polishing things close at hand. "Oh, not much. Jake helped me find a room to rent from a friend of his."

"Jacob."

"Yeah, Jake. Anyways, I moved myself and the clothes on my back in there about a week ago. A few days ago, I got a microwave oven and a real bed with one of those square frames under it to lift it off the floor and everything. I've actually been sleeping an awful lot." His grin exposed a gap to one side of his upper teeth I hadn't known was there before. "I've had so many dreams about, ... um, certain people, I'd like to talk to you. About them, I mean."

"Yeah? Alright. I need to go soon, but..."

"Hang on. Let me clock out and I'll walk with you."

He had turned and was half-way to the kitchen door before I could process what he said, much less answer. When Paul returned, he had changed into an apparently new pair of jeans, sneakers, and shirt. I looked him over appraisingly as I followed him to the door. "Nice duds."

He chuckled and pushed the door open for me. Standing against the door as I passed, he lifted one ankle to the front of his other thigh and tugged on the hem of his pants. "Yeah. I got socks, too." The grin he aimed at me resembled nothing so much as a very happy Saint Bernard.

I had a moment of disconcerted angst as I felt myself being swept up in his energy. Atop all my trepidation, a grin spread across my face, his merriment infectious. I shouldn't have been able to feel that, not yet, but there it was. My steps were light, and my hair bounced around my shoulders as I loped along beside the big guy. At least, if I was mirroring his expression, I was probably not acting suspiciously. That voice of caution in my head receded with a grumble and a final, *'Just keep it under control.'*

Paul ambled, fingers anchoring his hands into his pockets and shoulders thrown back. The jaunty twist of his whole body with each long stride said more than any of his words about the change that had come over him since the baseball game. "And that's when Benny finally stood up to the old man."

"Really? Coming out of church? For the whole world to see?" I tried to imagine choosing such a public and important forum to confront anyone.

"I know! I almost couldn't believe it myself." He chuckled and shook his head.

I smirked. "I guess if the old man had killed him, you'd be less enthusiastic about it."

"Ha. Yeah. I probably would." He winged an elbow in my direction, not quite connecting with my arm. "Nah, actually, the old man gathered up his wife and looked over at Bonnie and said something like, 'Mija, dinner will be served at six'." Paul's voice took on a lower timbre and a passable accent before returning to his own normal tones. "I thought Bonnie was going to have a conniption once she got Benny back to the truck."

"A whole conniption?" I remembered my mother talking about having conniption fits. Well, about other people having them. She used to spend whole Saturday breakfasts talking about my grandmother's temper. Before she died.

Paul laughed, letting the mirth roll from his chest until it dwindled away naturally, like an overturned soda can pulsing fizzy liquid out in spurts. "Oh, boy. Well, Benny and Bonnie got real quiet and, once they got home, she made them a couple of sandwiches. I think that might be the first time I've ever seen her wear a nightgown."

I widened my eyes at him. "Oh, shit."

"Yeah. Benny's in the doghouse."

"But she didn't go have dinner with her parents?"

"Nah-ah. She stayed by her husband. You wanna' know what I think?" Paul's eyes twinkled.

"Absolutely." I tossed my hair over my shoulder and sniffed as we turned a corner. A light breeze, still warm with the late evening sun, carried a refreshing hint of crisper, night air. It struck me square in the face and momentarily stole my breath. I blinked and expanded my lungs against it.

"I think, Bonnie was actually proud of Benny. I mean, she was scared of pushing away her parents, but I think she really wants Benny to take her father's place as the strongest man in her life. She wants to see him demand respect from the old man for himself. I think she spends so much time defending him to them, it's wearing down her respect for him." His gaze unfocused, he seemed to be looking at something far away. Probably remembering some scene or other from the dream.

"You don't think she'll side with her parents?"

He shook his head, small tufts of hair coming loose from the tidy, combed pattern he'd begun to favor. "No way. Not after she missed Sunday dinner to stand by her husband. Nah, she's mad at him but more proud than mad."

I studied his face for a few steps. "Have you gotten attached to them?" This was always a good sign. I used to think getting a client to become emotionally invested in the mark was a bad idea. You would think that would make a person less likely to take the swap, right? Turns out, no. At the point a client feels some emotional attachment to what they view as characters in a show, they are only a scary moment away from accepting the swap.

"Who wouldn't? Bonnie's adorable. Have you seen her with her nieces and nephews?" I shook my head. "She's a natural. She's going to make a great mom one day. I know she doubts it but, I know she wants at least one of her own. And I can see it." His wistful smile was like a palpable down-shift of his enthusiasm. Even his shoulders seemed to sigh.

"What?" I lifted a hand toward him but didn't touch. "What's wrong?"

Paul flicked his eyes at me. When he'd faced forward and firmly fixed his attention on the street ahead of us, oncoming headlights glinting in his eyes through the twilight, he said, "Nothing's wrong. I was just thinking about the names they picked a while back while they were..." He flicked his eyes at me again. "Well, they were dreaming about a baby."

The familiar anticipation of a choice forthcoming sent a chill little spike into the base of my skull. "Yeah?"

He grinned. "One of the names they liked was Paul."

The anticipation spike pulsed, and I covered a shiver with a chuckle. "That seems a little like fate, right?"

Paul huffed through his nose and frowned. "It felt..." He took three more steps during the pause. "It felt nice. Warm and gratifying, but a little uncomfortable, too." Furrows settled across his brow, taking their time to draw together and deepen.

'What? Dammit, Paul.'

"It made me think of my mom and how she will never get to play with a grandson. I wish I had taken the time to live and enjoy what I could while she was here." He shook his head. "Ms. Star, I have so many regrets. I wrapped myself up in the things that hurt so much I didn't let myself even see the things that were good."

A knot formed in my throat. It reminded me, forcibly, of the choking knot I had experienced the day I'd been diagnosed. I cleared my throat, and the memory. "That's part of the reason we're offering you a chance to try again."

He nodded and we passed another block in silence. The morgue was in sight, and I slowed my pace. "We're a little early." As we turned into the driveway, I saw three unfamiliar vehicles parked in the lower lot. "There are people here."

Paul lifted his head and followed my gaze. "Who?"

I frowned and started to shake my head. Then it dawned on me. "Oh, I bet those are day shift folks. They were short-handed while I was on vacation. We're probably swamped." I stood at the top of the driveway and turned to face Paul. "I don't know if you should come in tonight. I wasn't really thinking about it until just now, but it might be a nasty, morbid mess in there, and I don't know those people."

Paul nodded and gave me a wide-eyed look of understanding. "That's okay. I have a microwave dinner waiting for me at home."

The statement had all the elements of a sad little lonely person talking about eating a pathetic dinner alone, but the tone of his voice said it was something he was looking forward to. He imbued the word 'home' with reverent happiness even I could pick up on. "That sounds lovely."

"It has been so far. I've been working my way through different brands. So far, the Richoletta brand has the best meatloaf." He laughed. His shoulders and stomach shook as it rolled out of him. He punctuated the laughter with a clap of his hands and was suddenly upon me. I froze. He had both arms wrapped around me and had managed to tuck my head back over his shoulder. Then he lifted.

There I was, feet dangling off the ground, the breath startled out of me, and the scent of Old Spice and soap invading my sinuses as I sucked in more. The crazy client was hugging me. A giant bear hug that squeezed me in all the wrong places. I relaxed. It was kind of nice. I guess.

Just as I had almost talked myself into lifting my arms to give a polite squeeze back, he let my feet fall back to the ground and steadied me with his hands on my shoulders. "I just want you to know, no matter what, I am so glad I met you."

I cleared my throat and tried to smile at him. It was awkward. I readjusted the strap of my bag and tugged at my clothes as I shifted from foot to foot. There was nothing in his eyes except sincerity, and they drew me in, calming me. "Well, I'm glad, too." An easier smile curved my lips.

He stepped back and studied me, rubbing his palms on his jeans. He licked his lips and bobbed his head. "Well, you have a good night, Ms. Star."

"You, too. Be careful getting home."

That beatific smile sprang to life on his face again. "I promise." With that, he turned and loped back the way we'd come.

Chapter 21. Day Shift Invaders

Inside, the chaos was more than I'd bargained for. The shelving gurneys had been dragged out of storage and rows of bodies, stacked five shelves high, filled the cold room. A tiny path from the hall, through the cold room, led into the office. Lights blazed, seeming brighter than normal with so much less space to fill. Music came from an autopsy room, positioned like an airlock between the cold room and the larger, longer-term storage freezer, and I saw the back of a man in a lab coat bobbing his knees as he performed an autopsy. I glimpsed another lab-coated person moving between the racks as I made my way toward the office to clock in.

A third person sat in the desk chair, apparently filing her nails, with her feet up and ankles crossed on the desk. She sneered up at me as I entered. Not missing a stroke of the file against her nails, she asked, "Who are you?"

I rolled my eyes and hung my bag on the wall hook beside the door. "I'm Star, Sherika. We've worked together for almost six years and met at least a dozen times."

"Oh, right. Morticia from the nightshift."

'Morticia?' Several unkind nicknames for the other woman sprang to my mind. As if she had room to talk. Sherika's dismissive and bored voice made me want to shake her. In my experience, only her laugh was worse. When I thought of the day shift, this human-shaped irritant was what came to mind.

I approached the desk, and she didn't move. "May I use the computer, please? I need to clock in."

She heaved a sigh, excessive on its own, and locked eyes with me before rolling hers and letting her feet fall to the floor. It wasn't like I was responsible for the lack of any additional computers. I resisted the urge to shove her aside and waited as patiently as a saint for her to stomp out of the way.

I clocked in and checked my email, carefully reading each before deleting it. There were only a handful, and none of them were worth my time normally, but anything I could do to passive-aggressively ignore Sherika was more than worth it. Too soon, I turned off my autoresponder and found myself out of reasonable excuses to stay in her way and swiveled in the chair. I almost bumped my knees into the woman. "Jesus! What are you doing?"

Sherika rolled her eyes again and stepped around my knees to rest a possessive hand on the back of the chair. "Waiting for you to move so I can get back to work."

'Fucking day shift asshole. I bet, if I slap her hard enough, her eyes will roll like that on their own.'

I stood and walked into the cold room. My personal lab coat, the one I had claimed as my own, was still where I'd hidden it, hanging inside the supply closet on the back of the door. I ran my eyes over the shelves as I tugged it on and adjusted my sleeves inside the coat. The boxes of gloves and masks and other personal protective equipment and sanitary supplies were disheveled and sparse. That could mean they had kept the cold room and autopsy rooms well-stocked. More likely, it meant there was nothing stocked out there, as well as running low in here.

I sighed and grabbed two boxes of gloves and a few other things I knew I would need. I turned to walk out and shoved the door closed with my foot. My phone chirped just as the door latch clicked and I lifted my chin to grumble at the ceiling. *'I should never have turned off the autoresponder.'* My phone chirped again before I had managed to empty my hands, and again as I pulled my phone from my pocket.

Two of the emails were obviously day shift junk. The third, from the department head, Mr. Pisani, was more interesting.

"*Ms. Nightcastle.*

I hope this email finds you well-rested and fresh after your vacation. The region experienced a surge in accidental deaths and the case load indicates a need for more man hours to process the deaths in a timely fashion. Several additional technicians have been assigned to assist you overnight. As this is your shift, and you have seniority, it has been decided that you will take the lead and run the department during your regularly scheduled shift. Additionally, you have been approved for mandatory overtime until the current influx has ended and all cases have been cleared."

It went on to list the people who would be invading my domain and detailing the additional hours I had been assigned. The important bit, though, was that I was in charge. Sherika was about to be very uncomfortable. I hoped the terrible woman didn't make it impossible to refrain from killing her with my own two hands. If only Crow hadn't decided to have a Murphy Party locally, I wouldn't be in this mess. A fact of which I would remind him if I had to call him to help me cover up a murder.

I tucked my phone away and situated my pile of supplies more securely atop a rolling cart before pushing it toward the autopsy rooms. The first was still occupied by the dancer. The second was lit up but empty. I wheeled my cart into it and groaned. *'Why the hell can't anyone have the decency and professionalism to reset the room after a procedure?'* For a moment too long, I stood there, head bowed, and eyes closed, simply trying to regain my internal composure.

The voices of the dead, an imagined cacophony in my mind, distracted me with reminders that every moment I took on myself, on fighting with coworkers, and on menial tasks robbed the dead of details that might be important in laying them to rest.

"Dammit." The muttered curse shouldn't have been loud enough for anyone to hear, and I yelped when a throat cleared behind me. Spinning like an ice skater doing a change of direction move, I faced the intruder.

"Hi there! You must be Starling. I'm Neville." The man stepped forward, a big smile exposing teeth too white to belong to a coffee drinker and held out a hand.

I frowned at the hand, big and empty with sparse little dark hairs peeking out from the edge of his lab coat sleeves and spilling over the back. His nails were very clean but chipped here and there. One had a red and angry cuticle where he'd picked off a hangnail. I shook his hand. It was soft but firm, and a little clammy. "Yeah. I think I saw the announcement when you were hired. Just call me Star."

"Great. It's nice to meet you, Star. I'm sorry you had to come back to this mess. You always leave everything so tidy and well-stocked for us. I feel bad about all this." He swiveled at the waist and glanced around the exam room and over his shoulder into the cold room. A tiny furrow made a brief appearance on the stage of his forehead and was gone before he turned back to me. "It's your house. How can I help?"

I narrowed my eyes. Behind him, Sherika was crossing the cold room to the hall. "I'm going out for a smoke!" She called in a breathy voice that might not have carried without all the inventory for the sound to bounce off. I stifled a growl and shook my head.

"Yeah, she's a challenge." Neville rolled his eyes with a grin.

I wanted to ask if he was for real. "You just finished an autopsy?" At his nod, I continued. "So, you're qualified to handle a case from start to finish?"

"Absolutely. Fully certified and ready to work."

I nodded and took a step forward. The man stepped lithely back out of the doorway and turned to the side to let me pass. "Good, then I need you to be my second. Sherika is a glorified file clerk and can't be trusted with evidentiary materials. Is Gail here?"

He accompanied me, at my elbow as I moved toward the hall. "Yeah, I think so. I'm not sure where, though. She's been darting back and forth all evening."

I nodded, my thoughts reorganizing and assigning tasks to names. "Good. She's a great tech, but a little sloppy with autopsy work. Can you go herd Sherika back in here? We'll have a quick meeting here in the hall in five." He turned to head for the door. "If she gives you any trouble, tell her she'll be clocked out for this unscheduled break if she doesn't get in here."

He snorted without turning back and I walked toward the scan room. I found Gail using the scanning network computer to play solitaire. "Hey, Gail. Shift meeting in five in the hallway." She jumped at my voice, and I turned away, only mildly amused and even more mildly ashamed.

I walked back to the office, quick-stepping to make it there and back before the meeting I had called. Sliding to a stop inside the office doorway, I looked down at the coffee maker and couldn't find it. A pile of case folders lay atop it, another pile beside it, another on the chair and more on the desk. The incoming basket, however, was empty save for two sheets of yellow memo paper. If I kept sighing, I was going to dry out my lungs.

"Crow. I need a hand." I darted a glance out the door; still all clear.

"How can I help, Bird?" Crow, stepping out from behind the door, smiled at me with that weird new smile.

"Don't do that."

"What? Did I startle you again? You called me, Bird."

"No, nevermind. Look, can you stack these case folders neatly and in order of arrival, oldest on top over there?" I pointed at the desk. "Also, if you can, sort out the JDs to come first in a sub-sort with the rest, alphabetically by name."

Crow raised an eyebrow. "JD. John or Jane Doe?"

"Yeah, sorry. Habit." He was still smiling so I went on. "Then, can you brew a pot of coffee? It's going to be a long night and these day shift *people* are slobs."

Crow's smile deepened and he lifted a steaming cup of coffee toward me. I breathed a grateful hum and accepted the cup. He turned his head to the piles, and I turned to look with him, holding the cup up where the steam could warm my nose. The files shifted and the coffee maker, now clean and sparkling, began to burble as it brewed.

"Thank you. I'll call again later. I have to go have a meeting now." His eyes twitched toward the door, and he disappeared without a word. I turned to see Neville poking his head into the cold room from the hall doorway. He met my eyes and nodded before ducking back out.

I sipped my coffee down to a level that probably wouldn't slosh and hurried toward the hall, cup in hand. I stopped and rested a shoulder against the doorframe. Three pairs of eyes met my own as I sipped my coffee, making a point to keep my cup held well into the hall. If I was going to be the boss, I had to follow the rules when anyone was looking, right?

Sherika frowned at me, obviously wondering where the coffee had come from. I smiled at her over the rim and reveled in anticipation of her reaction to my instructions. "I hope you have all had a pleasant evening as far as possible given the small village of dead people in our care."

Neville chuckled and Gail looked from one face to the other, as if unsure of what mood to adopt. I straightened where I stood. "You should have all read the email from the boss instructing me to direct our efforts. To that end, Gail, I want you on weights, measures, and scans." The woman nodded. "Sherika, you're on sanitization and supplies."

She groaned. "I don't think so. I'm nobody's maid."

I smiled, as broad as I could, and imitated the posture I'd seen Crow use so often with Donna and Pete. "That's a very unprofessional attitude. I hope I misunderstood you." I hooked a thumb over my shoulder. "This room is full of individuals who deserve our best efforts. If you don't feel you can perform your duty for them, you are free to go. I will let Mr. Pisani know we need another tech."

Sherika huffed and made to shove past me into the room. I shifted to block her path. "The meeting isn't over."

She quivered, the pale skin atop her cheekbones flushed as she looked up at me. In less than a heartbeat, she had backed down and backed up, but it seemed longer at the time.

"Does this mean you understand and accept your assignment?" I willed myself not to blink as I continued to meet her eyes.

She turned her head to look at the outside door and, all in a quiet rush, said, "Yeah, fine. I get it."

'Close enough.'

"Good. Neville and I will perform the autopsies. For tonight, I am going to split the work." I went on detailing the next stage of organization, assigning data entry to Gail when she wasn't doing scans and piling on the sanitization tasks for Sherika. Given her attitude, I went so far as to have the woman write down the list to keep her from skipping things.

Sherika fumed as she pulled a broom and mop bucket from the hall closet. *'Whatever. She could curse my name if she felt like it, as long as she did it while doing her job and out of my way.'* I refilled my cup in the office and picked up the first few case folders in the stack. "Crow?" I called him while I browsed the names and dates on the folders.

"Yes, Bird?"

I turned a smile on him. "Thank you so much. Now, I need to ask for a couple more favors. I mean, we are in the middle of this mess because of you and your schemes."

He inclined his head in a bow. "Conceded."

I jerked my head toward the window through which the inventory overflowing into the cold room could be seen. "Can you organize those bodies the same as the folders?"

With Crow's help and, I'll admit, Neville's backup, the night got smoother. With a podcast in my ears, the hours, and mangled bodies, ticked by until suddenly it was midnight and Sherika and Gail were getting ready to leave. I waited to call a break for Neville and myself until I confirmed Sherika had clocked out. I wasn't authorizing her to be paid to hang out for another fifteen minutes just so she could ruin my break.

When the clatter of Sherika's street shoes ended with the thunk of the outer door, an involuntary sigh escaped me. Neville's tiny chuckle reminded me I still wasn't entirely alone. I turned in the desk chair to find him rummaging in a small, soft-sided cooler. "When does your shift end, Neville?"

"I'm here till three." He didn't look up from his rummaging.

I frowned and reached for a napkin to wipe the old coffee film from the inside of my mug. "So, you only got here an hour before me?"

"Hm?" He finally looked at me, still not having found what he was looking for. "Oh, no. I just volunteered for the extra OT."

"OT? Aren't you a coroner, too? We're salaried. We don't get overtime." I thought he must have been more than just distracted to make such an obvious mistake, and it caused my internal lie detector to hum.

"Yeah." He turned from his cooler and crossed to the coffee pot table. He pulled out the top drawer, lifted a bag of gingersnaps, and shot me a grin. "I need the hours filled. OT means Occupied Time." The sticky note on the outside still said "N.V." with my question mark beneath. Now it also had, in distinct block letters, "NEVILLE VIVANTI," printed neatly across the very bottom edge. He found a place to lean against and continued. "Not that I'd turn down a fluffed-out paycheck." He winked at me and laughed.

I eyeballed the note on the bag, then studied his face. It was hard to glean anything from it with his smile getting all crinkled as he chowed down on two cookies at a time. My eyes drifted back to the note. "Neville. That's a very formal name. Do you have a nickname?"

He bobbed his head and ambled back toward his cooler. "My friends call me NV."

"Envy?" I scoffed, and a dozen or so half-formed punchlines offered themselves up in my mind. "Yeah. I'm not calling you that."

He snorted, coughed on cookie crumbs, and cleared his throat. "My mom calls me Nevvy, but I prefer no one else does. What do you want to call me?"

I shook my head. "I'll think about it." I lifted the coffee pot from the burner and filled my cup. "You want some coffee?"

He dipped a hand into his cooler and pulled out a water bottle. "No, thanks. I don't drink coffee."

'I knew it.'

"What? You don't like coffee?" I replaced the pot on the burner and watched the sloshing surface as it settled to indicate it still had roughly four cups left.

Neville gulped half of his water and chuckled again. "Oh, no. I love the stuff. I'm just allergic to it."

I goggled. My whole life would be over if I developed a coffee allergy. "Is that something a person can be? Are you even human? What kind of monster is allergic to coffee?"

Cookie crumbs flew in a disgusting spatter as a deep belly-laugh forced air from his lungs. As he lifted the hand with the water bottle to cover his mouth, he inhaled. Apparently, he managed to suck some crumbs into his trachea and began to cough in choking fits. A little water sloshed from the bottle and spattered in the cookie debris on the floor.

"You're cleaning that up." I was fairly certain he wasn't dying, even if it did look like an uncomfortable, Murphy-level, series of events. "You monster."

He finally got himself under control. Still gruffly clearing his throat, he snagged a wad of paper napkins from beside the coffee maker and bent to clean up his mess. I turned back to the computer and checked the time left in our break. It was nearly over, so I reviewed the data entry Gail had completed and noted where she'd left off. She'd done a good job of keeping up with us over the hours and I made a mental note to commend her for it. Maybe she could do some of the intake prep tomorrow night and help us speed things up.

I hadn't seen Donna and Pete all night, nor any other body deliveries. I wasn't complaining. The last thing we needed was another influx before we had made a dent in the cases we had on hand. I turned and said as much to Neville. "Do you think the crisis is over?"

Neville had regained his perch atop the corner stool with a pudding cup and a spoon. A small, slightly-cleaner-than-the-rest, circle gleamed in front of him where the cookie crumb puddle had been. He shook his head, looking intently into his pudding as he swirled it with a spoon. "No, I doubt it. All new cases are being re-routed for triage intake at the temp state site."

'If he'd found a pudding cup in that cooler, what treat had he been unable to find earlier?' I lifted a quizzical brow at him but didn't ask. With a shake of my head, I dismissed the thought and frowned. "There's a temp state site?"

"Yeah." He looked up at me, pudding-sign dark on his lips. "How did you not hear about it?"

An unscheduled laugh burbled up from my chest. "I had a fortunately timed cruise. I've been away from any news or screens for a few days."

"Lucky you. You should have seen the chaos when it first started." He hung the spoon on his tongue and dragged it languorously downward.

I averted my eyes. "I'm glad I missed it. That must have had the boss about to rupture an artery."

Pudding gone, he dropped the cup and the spoon back into his cooler. With a small sigh, he bobbed his head softly and let his eyes trail over the walls of the office. "It seems like this area was the epicenter, so he was fighting for help over the phone constantly until the first wave crashed in High Hill."

High Hill. I hummed. Crow had admitted there was Ides at that game. I wondered idly if the yuppy with the baseball cap or any of his friends were going to end up on one of our slabs. I hummed again.

Neville nodded and chuckled, wry and soft this time. "Yeah, well, once the deep pockets started laying down, they got the state site up. Now, an SBI task force is running down leads on manufacturers and distributors. I think they even have a forensic coroner team working the intakes. We probably won't see any cases where we need to worry about evidentiary procedure unless one pops up in this crowd." He jutted his chin toward the cold room.

I squinted at him. "Why do you sound like a cop?"

He sighed and hopped to his feet from the stool. He turned to close his cooler and said, "Family conditioning. Just about everyone in my family is in law enforcement in some way." He gave an unconvincing smile.

I stood and picked up another handful of case folders. Splitting them with Neville, I said, "I guess we'd better see about it then."

Chapter 22. Workflow

Working through the in-house case load from Ides took longer than I'd hoped but not as long as I'd expected. There were a few contributing factors, most of them problems, that began cropping up almost the moment I arrived the second night. Neville was in an autopsy room with more music, 80s pop this time, spilling out of his phone. He bobbed and shook his head like a wet dog with palsy. He didn't seem to be in pain or distress of any kind, so I assumed he was just an enthusiastically bad dancer.

Gail was in my desk chair, not lounging or filing her nails, thankfully. The screen showed a half-complete restock order. I peered at it over her shoulder as I hung my bag on the wall hook. "Hey! Where's Sherika?"

Gail shrugged and finished tapping on the keyboard before turning. "Hey, Boss. I haven't seen her." She stood.

"I'm not the boss. Ew." My tongue curled on itself as if it tasted something gross. I cringed with the brief impression of trying on an angry, balding, Italian American man's life. "Just call me Star."

Gail didn't show any sign of having noticed. "Can you check this requisition? I ran out of several things while restocking. Nothing we should miss for a couple of days, I hope, but..."

I nodded and moved toward the chair. "I got you." I slid into the seat and scrolled to the top of the form. Gail's handwritten list lay beside the keyboard, and I scanned it, checking to see everything had made it onto the requisition. Gail left me to it, so she wasn't on hand to receive the praise I had to offer when I'd approved the requisition and sent it in. I used her discarded shopping list to jot a note to her on the bottom. I'd either remember to give her an atta' girl or she'd see it here later. I do try to be a good supervisor.

With a sigh, more to refocus my thoughts than anything else, I opened my email and checked for anything regarding Sherika's whereabouts. My eyes widened with anticipation when I saw one from Mr. Pisani with the subject line, "S. Jones removed from assignment."

"Ms. Nightcastle,

Due to an unfortunate incident earlier today, Sherika Jones has been placed on administrative leave and removed from the night shift assignment. Unfortunately, that leaves us short-handed. Believe me, I would not have taken these steps if there had been any other option.

You will be assigned another technician as soon as one can be hired. Until then, please do the best you can. I appreciate your dedication and all your efforts to meet the challenges facing us...blah, blah, blah."

'Unbelievable.' I didn't know what the woman had done but it must have been bad to deserve administrative leave during a flood of death. It was like being suspended from school during exam week. Except, there wouldn't be a make-up week. I shook my head. The important thing was she wouldn't be there to make me tense.

I looked out the window into the cold room. The other important thing still filled the room. We had worked through ten cases the night before, from start to finish. It didn't look like we'd made any progress at all. I squinted and walked out, checking tags on the stacks. "Hey! Did more bodies arrive? I thought they were all being diverted."

The music from Neville's autopsy room stopped and he poked his head out. "I thought so too." He frowned, holding his gory, gloved hands up in front of his chest. With a shrug, he dipped back into the room. A moment later, his music picked up where it had left off.

'How'd he do that with bloody gloves on?'

Gail appeared from the hall, heading toward the supply closet with a spray bottle in hand. I intercepted her and asked about the apparently new bodies. She blew hair away from her eyes and looked toward the racks. "I'm not sure. I can do a quick search and see if anything comes up in the computer."

I offered her a thankful, but decidedly small smile. "It's okay, I'll check it out myself. It's almost half past now. Can you tell Neville to let you know when he's done with his current case and both of you meet me in the office for a quick meeting? New bodies aren't the only news we need to talk about."

Gail nodded and scurried off, doing what Gails do best. I needed coffee. I got the pot brewing and settled in to dig up clues about what exactly administration was doing and why it was wrong. When Neville and Gail finally joined me, I was on my second coffee refill and ignoring an itch in the back of my mind. I was sure that, with the slightest encouragement or attention, that itch would blossom into a magnificent headache.

I sighed, turned in the chair to face them and crossed my knees. I felt exactly like a supervillain, so I donned my best supervillain accent and said, "Hello, team." The ridiculous greeting had the desired effect.

Neville chuckled and rested one hip atop the corner stool. Gail rolled her eyes above a wry but humor-filled smile and settled atop the short file cabinet. "Did you find Sherika?"

I snorted. "Sort of. That's one of the reasons we need another team meeting. Sherika won't be rejoining us. I don't know what happened and I don't care, but she's off for a while. There are no extra hands to fill her place right now, so it's just the three of us for the duration."

Gail's jaw slackened and let out a whiney, "What?"

Neville, right atop her, said, "Sheesh! I'm not sure if that's actually a loss."

I tried to keep a straight face and didn't share my own opinion. That would have been very unprofessional and downright self-incriminating. "The three of us seem to work well enough together. Here's what I propose." I managed to slide in a few atta' boys to Neville and remembered all of Gail's atta' girls, too, as I detailed my new workflow plan.

Gail picked up all of Sherika's restocking duties without batting an eye. I also assigned her to the initial intake procedures, from verification of identity through all the scans. She beamed with pride, realizing the reward of being trusted with so much responsibility. Neville grinned, sharing Gail's proud moment.

I met each of their eyes and noted their nods and lack of questions. "Good. Now, about the new inventory." I twisted to reach behind me. A printout of an SBI memo in hand, I turned back to them and relayed the bullet points. I went a little off script at the end. "Basically, the state site is running out of room and resources to hold onto so many bodies. They made the executive decision to release all non-event-related cases back to their home coroners."

I handed the paper to Gail and continued. "For now, they're still handling the initial intake for all new cases, and only releasing the ones that drug test negative a handful at the time. That means we can probably expect a half dozen or so new cases each day. Don't count on them to be worked before our shift."

Neville groaned and lifted his face to the ceiling. Gail was still frowning at the printout.

I stood and stretched. "Don't stress it. The ones they're sending are our regular customers and the intake checklist online looks thorough." It took far too long to get through that meeting, but it was worth it. The frontend planning steamrolled upcoming challenges before they got to us, and the next several nights ticked by almost without incident.

*****

By night four, little precursor headaches had popped up three more times without ever quite becoming painful, and Neville's music had started to get on my nerves. At our first scheduled break, I asked him if he could wear earbuds or headphones.

"Sorry, can't. Earbuds give me an ear infection and headphones give me a headache." He twisted the lid off a water bottle and tossed back several big gulps.

I considered the long-term ramifications of punching the bottle while he held it tilted up like that. "How about a compromise? I'll turn my earbuds up a notch if you turn your music down a couple."

Gail laughed. "Or we could take turns picking what we all have to listen to."

I hummed under my frown, considering it. "That's a good threat." Neville snorted and pinched his nose to keep water from streaming out. I shook my head at him. "You might want to consider giving up eating and drinking in company."

Gail giggled and pushed off the wall. "I'm going away for the rest of break. Back in a bit."

I nodded, absently. That was her way of saying she had to use the facilities. It was cute, in a faux snark kind of way, and I filed it away, possibly for my own personal future use.

Neville, airway clear once more, rocked on the corner stool. "What do you listen to on your earbuds?"

"Podcasts, mostly. Industry stuff like forensics, new lab procedures, testing techniques and case studies, generally. I tried learning to speak French from a podcast once, but that was completely useless."

He chuckled and stood, walking toward me. "How are we doing meeting quotas on Deadman's Village?"

"On what?"

He snorted. "You said it first." He gestured to the cold room. "The small village of dead people?"

I looked out the window and vaguely recalled the meeting on the first night. "Oh, right. Not bad. We're clearing about a dozen cases a night, including the incoming." I shook my head. "It looks like the two day shift teams are each covering about the same, so we should be through the thick of it by the end of next week."

Neville sat his water bottle on the table beside the coffee pot and bent to lift the neat stack of case folders from the chair to the floor beneath it. As he settled into the chair, the scent of something spicy and warm wafted off him with the flutter of his lab coat. "I think we should have a little party when we get word we're getting to the end."

I frowned, still trying to place that scent. "Why?"

"Because it's an excuse to have a party? Duh."

I furrowed my brow and stared at him.

He cleared his throat. "I mean, um, I was thinking of a luau. You know? With leis and grass skirts and ukulele music."

"Grass skirts may be a bit much." I didn't know how seriously to take this conversation. I had a vague recollection of other places I'd worked where coworkers seemed to revel in any chance to eat to a theme.

Taking my statement for agreement, Neville grinned. "Gotcha'. No grass skirts. Don't worry about it. I'll take care of everything."

'What did that mean?'

I turned back to the computer and glanced at the clock. Gail rejoined us just as I said, "Break's over. I'll sweep." Neville rolled his eyes and stood. He made to follow Gail out, and I stopped him. "Put the files pile back on the chair please."

His mouth formed a little O as he spun on his heel and dropped into a squat. "Right." He grunted out the word as he lifted the stack back into the chair.

As a team, we did a collective cleanup after our breaks. By this point, we had the cleanup phase down. Gail pushed the cleaning cart, emptying waste bins into one side and gathering biohazards into the other. I pushed the wide-headed broom in long, ground eating sweeps. Neville came behind me with the mop bucket, painting broad semi-circular arcs over the tiles. In under ten minutes, we were each back on task, serving the citizens of Deadman's Village.

Neville had the unfortunate habit of hanging out after he'd clocked out each night. As helpful as he was, picking up the restocking and sanitization tasks I normally did at the end of my shift, it meant I couldn't call on Crow until right before time for me to clock out and leave. I complained as much to Crow that morning. "I don't mind him, but it's hard to wind down if I can't relax before we go home."

"Would you like my help convincing him to leave earlier?"

I studied him across the autopsy table and the remains of the woman on it. "Why are you grinning?"

"Am I?"

I grimaced and bent back to sewing up the Y incision in front of me. "Yes, I think you might be." I sighed, momentarily fogging my face shield. "No, I don't want you to do anything. Well, not yet. I'll see if he can be reasoned with, first." I glanced up. "I'll reserve you for plan B."

"As you wish." He hovered while I finished my task and returned the woman's case folder to the stack to be transcribed into the computer. We'd separated the desk area into three separate shift assignment spaces. Keeping track of the cases, start to finish, was easier when they didn't change hands too many times. Gail would start her next shift by clearing the data entry on these cases before I arrived.

When I was ready to leave, my purse on my shoulder, lab coat hanging behind the door in the supply closet, and the coffee pot set to brew for the next folks, I turned to Crow and held out my arms. "Home, please."

He chuckled and stepped closer, allowing my arms to slide beneath his coat as he wrapped his around me. Upon rematerializing in my living room, he said, "The weather isn't icy or dangerous anymore. Would you like to begin walking again?"

"Honestly, not until Ides is over." I gave his ribs a squeeze and disentangled myself. He began to walk a circuit around the apartment as I ambled toward my bedroom. Stripping out of my clothes, my jeans got momentarily hung up on my shoes. I dropped onto the foot of my bed and squinted down at my trapped feet.

Crow frowned as he came out of my bathroom and paused in the doorway. "Does it look like it's going to be over soon?" He crossed the carpet to kneel at my feet and tugged my shoes from the ends of my pants legs.

"Thank you." I fell backward on the bed as he pulled my pants and underwear free. "I mean, I guess I hope it will be over soon." I lifted my head and met his eyes. "Why? What did you do?"

"Nothing, Bird. Nothing you don't already know about, anyway." His clothing faded away, and I squeezed my eyes closed, letting my head drop back on the pillow.

He lifted his knees to the foot of the bed on either side of me and crawled up my body until he sat above my hips. "I, um…" He was about to lie to me, but first, he lifted his heated massage hands to my abdomen and began to caress away my give-a-shit. "I miss you. You need more time off."

"Truer words…" I mumbled and closed my eyes. If he said anything else, it was lost to my unconscious perception.

*****

By night six, I had dialed in my routine to ensure I got plenty of rest and food between morgue shifts. I didn't expect to get a single night off until the Ides case load had been processed. My physical needs were being met, but those distracting precursor headaches persisted. I realized, after waking with one on the fifth night, they never developed into full-blown headaches. Rather, they remained dull and nestled like an odd itch in the back of my brain.

That evening, I noticed another oddity. The brain-itch faded when Genia and Jacob greeted me and was almost gone entirely as Paul walked me to work. I chalked it up to the level of coffee-borne caffeine in my system at any given point and shrugged the thought away.

We were halfway to the morgue, with him happily chatting away about his new coffee maker and matching coffee table, when I realized I was smiling. My smile began to fade as all the possible implications listed themselves out in my mind. I didn't feel the familiar dread or panic, or even the new and unexplored guilt. It wasn't another emotional surge. I crossed off each possible explanation as quickly as I thought of them. When my imagination ran dry, I was left still wondering what was happening to me.

Paul noticed. "Is something wrong, Ms. Star?"

I shook my head and shoulders, an over-powered shiver, and aimed a reassuring smile at him. "I'm fine. I think the pace at work is starting to catch up with me."

Paul nodded. "I wouldn't doubt it. When's the last time you did something fun?"

I snorted, then considered it. "The cruise. My life has been eat, sleep, work, repeat since then."

"That's rough. You should try to do something fun during your off hours in the morning."

"Do you have any suggestions?"

Paul pursed his lips. All his features pulled forward in support of a beak-shaped, thoughtful frown. It caught me by surprise, and I chuckled. That surprised me too, and the chuckle caught in my throat, turning into a cough. Paul tapped my back as I caught my breath. He was still tapping as I got myself under control, and I flapped my hands toward him. "Quit it. I'm fine."

Paul held up his hands defensively and skittered to one side. A step too far and he toppled off the sidewalk. I caught the hand he flailed toward me and yanked him back just as the headlights of an oncoming car lit up his startled expression. The whole thing seemed so ludicrous, I opened my mouth to ask if he was okay and rolling giggles came out instead.

Paul, having regained his balance, stood half bent with his hands on his knees, catching his breath. He trained his wide eyes on me before flicking them to follow the taillights of his would-be killer.

I slapped both hands over my mouth and tried to stuff the giggles back inside while trying to push out the words, "Are you okay?"

Paul turned a grin on me and joined my giggles with his own relieved chuckles. I don't know how long we stood there, our hysterical fit precluding walking, talking or anything else. When we finally sucked in deep calming breaths, both holding our sides, I moved to stand against the side of a building and closed my eyes.

'What was that! Where is my fear and dread and panic? I get free laughs now without paying for it in tears? What the fuck is happening?' I was on the verge of talking myself into a panic.

Paul moved over beside me and leaned down. "Ms. Star? How are you feeling?"

I turned to face him so fast my hair whipped up, making a slapping noise on the bricks of the wall behind me. *'Why would you ask me that, you asshole!?'*

My jaw went slack as I realized, I was okay. "I, uh..." I straightened and gazed up into the sky. "I'm okay."

It wasn't quite full dark, yet. Even if it had been, here amongst the lights of the city, I wouldn't be able to see many stars shining up there. Not nearly as many as had been over the little island. What I could see twinkled along the eastern horizon just as beautifully.

Paul nodded and sighed, a happy noise. "Yeah, sometimes a good belly laugh is what you need."

I caught myself staring at him. He had no way of knowing how decidedly wrong this was in my life. But there was still a smile on my lips. It was tiny but there was a decided upturn to the corners. "I guess so."

We pushed off the wall and began walking again. Paul glanced at me several times as we trudged up the next hill, but by the time we had gone another block, he was happily chatting away once more. "Juice said a guy named Will took the guitar from there. I'm gonna' try to meet up with that guy and see if he's willing to trade."

I frowned. "What guitar?"

"Remember, a couple weeks ago? There was a guy in the morgue I knew and..."

"Right! Right, sorry." I offered an apologetic grimace. "There has been some stuff since then."

Paul chuckled. "Yeah." We turned the last corner and Paul reached out to tap my shoulder. "If I can offer an observation?"

I nodded, tilting my head to one side. "Sure. What's up?"

He took a deep, steadying breath. "Well, I know you've been busy and all, but if you needed a laugh that bad, maybe you can find another way to relieve some stress until you can take a night off?"

He wasn't wrong. We parted ways and I tried not to give myself a panic attack thinking about the encounter. It was no wonder I was stressed into hysteria. Paul fed me breakfast and escorted me to work each evening. At work, Neville and Gail were constantly cutting up and tossing greetings and banter every which way. Crow escorted me home each morning and fed me dinner if I stayed awake that long.

It was a nightmare. I felt like I hadn't had a single moment to myself since the cruise. There was a reason I usually worked alone on the night shift. I thought that must explain that new little itch in the back of my mind, growing in intensity again as I punched in the access code on the morgue door. So, it probably wasn't the caffeine after all. I probably just needed my me-time.

As I walked into the office to clock in, Neville's music drifted through the open doors between us. He had eclectic tastes and today he was playing do-wop. It was a song I had heard from him a couple of times before and I hummed along. That little itch in the back of my mind faded as Neville's clear voice lifted on the chorus, and Gail's high, lilting soprano drifted in on the harmony.

As I opened my email and turned my mind to work, a mechanical click to one side drew my attention. Full of steaming liquid vitality, the coffee pot timer had switched from brew to warm. I was shocked I hadn't smelled the deliciousness in the air as I breathed in the comforting scent. I must have been more pre-occupied than I realized.

Gail and Neville both came in just as I reached to pour a cup. "Good evening, Boss. Anything new from the powers that be?" Neville took his seat on the stool and pulled out his personal cooler.

Gail snorted at him. "He just wants to see your face since he remembered to set the coffee pot for you."

I sipped the shimmering elixir in my hands and hummed. It was surprisingly good, particularly since it was made by someone who didn't drink it. "You did that for me?"

Neville, having found and unwrapped a candy bar, said, "Only if you're happy about it."

I hummed again. Something in the scent and flavor, deep and heady, transported me back to childhood. My eyelids drooped under the weight of the decadent flavor as my mind snuggled into the warm memory of a soft blanket under my grandfather's arm, watching cartoon animals chasing each other through cartoon forests.

I pried my eyes open, tucking the memory away, and looked up to wink at Gail. With another sip, I turned back to the computer. "Nothing new tonight. But it looks like our supplies finally got here."

Gail nodded. "I already got them stowed and distributed."

"Great! Good job. And Neville? How have you been a productive leader in the Village tonight?" I hid my grin behind the rim of my cup.

He returned my grin anyway. "It's good, isn't it?" He stuck his candy bar between his teeth and tore off a hunk.

I narrowed my eyes above a wry smile. "What did you do?"

He bounced in his seat, one-third of a candy bar hanging from the side of his mouth, leaving his hands free to rummage in his cooler. He discarded the cooler and pulled the candy bar from his mouth with one hand as he lifted a small, clear bag with the other. "It's called Ranier Red. My, uh, friend in Washington State grows it. Columbian and Ecuadorian hybrid beans." He sighed with that bobbing nod. "I love the smell. I figured you might appreciate it, too."

I closed my eyes and sipped again. The memory of a bean grinder whirring while this scent permeated the air beckoned my cares away. "Hm, yeah. It's very good." I opened my eyes and met his, twinkling and dark. "Living vicariously through your boss? I'll allow it."

Neville grinned and let his eyes roll up with a delighted waggle of his head. When he'd straightened in his seat, he sat the little bag on the table beside him and cleared his throat. "My friend will be delighted to know you approve."

Gail groaned through a wide smile. "Can I try a cup?"

"Absolutely. A treat like this should be shared." A relaxed smile lifted the corners of my mouth. "Thanks, Neville." With coffee infusing my sinuses, the little brain-itch faded away and put the caffeine theory back on the board.

Chapter 23. Luau

The email came the next Wednesday evening.

"*Ms. Nightcastle,*

The state sent word they are clearing the SBI holding site and shutting it down. We will be receiving the last of the diverted cases tomorrow and all new cases, as of noon today, will be processed as usual. I am asking all department heads to send a report on when the mandatory overtime can be reasonably discontinued.

Please take a moment to assess the status in your department and send me your appraisal ..."

I leaned back in the desk chair and sighed. *'My department? I don't have a department. I have a shift. With one person. Myself. Whatever.'* I continued to scan the email and grunted at the last paragraph. He'd awarded me an unscheduled night off, just one, but I could take it any time after I had cleared my department and signed off on ending overtime.

I had a pretty good handle on where we were in the case load. Just to be certain, I pulled up the inventory Gail had been keeping for us. If we cleared another dozen or more cases that night and another the following night, assuming the day shifts didn't slow down, that would leave us only two or three cases in addition to the normal, daily customers by Friday night. I hit the reply button, confirming three more nights to finalize the case files, and chose the following Monday to take off. I hit the send button and grinned at my clever acquisition of a three-night weekend.

I informed Neville and Gail at our first break. Gail began texting friends to line up her weekend plans even before she excused herself from our company. Neville had promised a luau for the final night and pulled a pocket-sized notepad from the outer pocket of his cooler. "Here's the plan so far. What do you think?"

I turned from the computer screen, where I had been emptying my email inbox, to find the little notepad far too close to actually read. I plucked the thing from his fingers and gave him a stern look. His boyish grin took the brunt of my look without so much as blinking.

In block letters, a neat little outline described the food, drink, music and decorations as categories. The details listed under each were illegible. I frowned, then squinted, turning the notepad this way and that. "I've only ever seen such horrible handwriting once before in my life." I shoved the notepad back at Neville. "It was at my grandfather's house as a kid, on the ground in the chicken coop."

The confused little tilt to his head, adorned with a single lifted eyebrow, gave the wrinkles on his furrowed brow the impression of sliding off to one side.

I chuckled and clarified. "It's chicken scratch."

His boyish grin returned. "Yeah, I'm dyslexic, so I'm probably lucky I can read and write at all."

I wasn't sure what to do with that information. Based on his handwriting, I was pretty sure it was true. The humor at his expense felt a little awkward, then. "Oh, well, I guess that's pretty impressive. I mean, becoming a coroner with dyslexia."

"It's fine. I didn't mean to make you uncomfortable. I always feel compelled to give an excuse for my handwriting. I wouldn't have handed you the notebook if I hadn't been so excited with my stupid party. I apologize." He lifted one hand to scrub the back of his head as he peered down at the open page of the notepad in his other hand.

I closed my eyes and sighed. He had been vulnerable with me. If I'd learned anything from mine and Crow's clients, it was that reciprocal vulnerability was the expected response. However, he was not a client. "Why don't you read it to me?"

The little details that fleshed out his party plan elicited a queue of groans in my throat that eventually began to sound like a growl to my own ears. "That sounds good, Neville. If you promise not to ask me about it anymore, I approve your plan."

His unconfoundable joy produced another wide grin and he bounded the short distance to the other side of the office, tucking his notepad away. With a solid clap of his hands, he said, "Well, I'd better step on it if I want to be done in time to luau!"

*****

When I awoke Friday night, I was full of verve and vigor. I hadn't realized how much I had been looking forward to the end of the Ides mess. I poured myself a cup of coffee and gave it a sniff, then grimaced. It was still good for diner coffee, but it just hadn't been the same since Neville had introduced me to Ranier Red.

Jacob raised his spatula and the volume of his unintelligible grumbles. One corner of my mouth hooked upward. "Good evening, Jacob. I'm going."

Paul came through the swinging doors carrying a deep plastic tub full of post-meal debris. "Hey, Star. Do you know what you want to order tonight, or do you need to study a menu?"

I hummed into my coffee cup. "I think I'll take a look at the menu."

He nodded and stepped around me. "Okay. Ms. Genia's in there. I'm on dish duty tonight." From anyone else, that would have been a complaint.

I returned a fraction of his smile and stepped into the dining room. Genia was busy clearing another table, so I snagged a menu from under the register as I made my way around to my customary seat at the counter. I placed the menu on the surface in front of me and browsed until Genia made her way over.

"Well, hello! You look perky tonight." She had one of the dish tubs tucked under one arm and resting on her hip like a baby.

"Do I?" I took a moment to study her round face, the rosy blush to her cheeks, and the ever-present pink tint on her eyelids. I suppose I was looking for anything that had changed in her features in the past couple of weeks. Maybe her hair was a little longer. It was hard to tell with all the short, springy curls. She looked the same. That was oddly comforting.

She turned and settled the dish tub onto the counter against the kitchen wall. "You do. You must have rested well." She pulled the pen from her hair and an order pad from her apron. "What sounds good?"

With a brief thought toward Neville's luau, I located the sandwich section of the menu and pointed randomly. "Can I have a..." I lifted the menu to read what I'd chosen. "Are these new?" In all my years living under the diner and eating there nearly every day, I had never seen the Deli Deluxe Panini as an option.

Genia grunted a chuckle. "About a month old. You don't spend a lot of time with the menu. That's a good seller, though. Do you want just the sandwich or do you feel like fries or salad or soup..."

"Oh, right, uh... How about a cup of that tomato one?" I laid the menu aside and tugged my coffee cup closer.

Genia jotted the order down and reached for the coffee pot behind her. She trained a studious gaze on me and topped off my cup. Genia asked, "How are you holding up?"

I shrugged my eyebrows over a fortifying sigh. "I think if the ceaseless work without a night off had gone on much longer, I might have cracked."

"Oh, does that mean you've finally gotten to the end of your big work project?" Genia replaced the pot and leaned back to rest her hips against the counter.

I nodded and reproduced the grin Paul had given me about doing dishes. "Looks that way. I'll have three nights off starting tomorrow."

"Good for you. You deserve a little extra break. Does that mean you will be available for the taste-test dinner?"

I had completely forgotten about Jacob's special menu. "Really? Are you sure you want me as a taste-tester?"

She laughed softly and lowered her eyes. With a shake of her head, she stood upright and said, "Star, Honey," she looked up, "it wouldn't be right without you." She paused and tilted her head to one side. "Please come?"

A lump formed right atop my vocal cords, and I cleared my throat. "I'd love to."

Genia smiled, warm and inviting. "Good." She side-stepped, picked up the dish tub, spun on her heel, and bustled into the kitchen.

I grinned at the door swinging behind her. In my head, I argued with myself.

'It's dangerous to believe Genia thinks of me as a friend.'

'It can't hurt to enjoy the concept for a little while.'

'She just needs something from me.'

'Would kind and motherly Genia, really lure me in just to betray my trust?'

A list of names and examples sprang to mind, and I buried it in my coffee cup. *'Enough of that.'*

I picked up the newspaper and browsed the ads. A picture of a can of Spam sparked a vague recollection of Neville saying something about Spam sandwiches. In the interest of coworker peace, I intended to try Neville's party food, but I was hedging my bets.

Ellie brought my panini and soup out and placed them in front of me. "There you go! Enjoy, Ms. Star." She topped off my coffee before she dropped my check beside my plate and hurried off. My sandwich was delicious, especially dipped in the soup, but I only ate half. Remembering the threat of Spam, I flagged down Ellie and had the other half of my panini wrapped to-go.

Paul was still on dish duty in the kitchen, and I hadn't seen him even once by the time I had my leftovers tucked into my purse. I looked around the dining room, really seeing it for the first time that night. Almost every table was full. My cozy little diner buzzed with conversation and the clink of forks and knives against plates. It wasn't overly loud but, now that I'd acknowledged it, the noise seemed to thicken in the air, surrounding me.

I needed to get out. It was time to leave anyway. I didn't have to wait for Paul. Just as I stood and dropped money on the counter to pay for my meal, he came barreling out of the kitchen, still tugging a loose windbreaker on over his shirt. "Wait for me, Ms. Star."

I paused where I stood and watched him scurry around the counter. "Did you get the dishes finished?"

He darted a glance at me, caught my smile, and grunted. "No way." He led the way out and set a relaxed pace beside me. The sun was low, mostly hidden by the city skyline, but not quite on the horizon. A chill breeze ruffled Paul's hair and I inhaled, deeply, tasting the scent of exhaust fumes from the passing cars.

Paul winged an elbow up as if to jostle me but didn't quite make contact. He said, "Thanks for waiting for me. I know you can take care of yourself, but it gives me peace of mind knowing you made it to work safely."

"Yeah? What about you? What if I worry about you walking home after you drop me off?"

He snorted. "No reason to worry about me. Nobody's gonna' think I have anything worth taking."

"If you say so. Still, there is a certain event still outstanding..."

"The taste-test dinner?" He grinned.

'That is not what I meant.'

"Ms. Genia said you were coming. I've gotten a sneak peek at a few of the things Jake is cooking. Sneak smells, too."

"Jacob."

"What?" He gave me a confused look.

I repeated myself, "Jacob, his name is Jacob."

"That's what I said, isn't it?" He frowned at my shaking head. "What did I say?"

"Jake."

"Yeah. That's what I said." He gave me a quizzical look, as if he truly didn't understand.

I gave up. Eventually Jacob would catch him and make him use his proper name. "So, are any of his creations promising?"

"They all smelled great, but I think he's still working on presentation." Paul lifted his chin and cut his eyes sideways at me.

I chuckled and sighed as we started up an incline, the first of many hills on our path to the morgue. At the top, the first intersection we needed to cross was also the most heavily trafficked. The street we were on crossed one of the four main thoroughfares in Chester City. A right turn there was a straight shot north about thirty miles to Lincoln. Paul reached the crosswalk signal first and pushed the button.

As I looked down the street, watching the oncoming lights of traffic, a dark, smudged something caught my eye. In the sky and moving fast, a black, white, and grey blurred mass streaked toward us. There was no change in the flow of traffic, nothing to indicate any drivers had seen it as whatever *it* was drew closer.

The blob lost altitude quickly as it neared. Full tilt, it fell from the sky and crashed in the middle of the intersection. It made no sound. Not a single car swerved. There was no impact crater or dust cloud or anything you would expect from a crashed something on pavement. Instead, the air around the something rippled, like the surface of a soap bubble.

Headlights shone through the scene as the traffic continued to flow through the intersection. The shimmer faded and the something resolved into Crow and Damien. They each had the other by the neck with one hand, their free hands each balled into fists. They pummeled each other, raining down blows that would have destroyed a human opponent.

I stepped to the edge of the curb. "Crow?"

Paul stepped up beside me. "Damien?"

Neither celestial being acknowledged us as cars continued to zip through them. I looked up at Paul. He stared, squinting into the flashing lights of traffic, concerned but silent and still. The traffic signal turned yellow.

I asked, "Should we try to get to them?" A Chester Electric Company truck made a left turn. The driver covered a yawn with one hand as he steered the truck with the heel of his other, right through the fight.

Paul shook his head. "They're in the middle of the intersection." The traffic signal turned red, stilling car headlights to illuminate the angry pair still locked in the grip of a physical disagreement.

The cross-street signal turned green. A few cars eased into motion. The two man-shaped figures pushed off each other, glaring. I could see their lips moving but couldn't hear a thing.

The angry face-off between Crow and Damien ended abruptly as each rocketed away in opposite directions. Paul turned to watch Damien fade from view. "I've never seen Damien angry. Not even disgruntled."

"Yeah. I don't understand what we just saw either." I shook my head, still watching the speck that was Crow flying away.

"Should we be worried?" We had missed our chance to cross the street and Paul pushed the crosswalk button again.

"I don't know." I offered Paul a shrug.

He shrugged in return.

We waited out the round of stop and go signals in silence. When the signal changed, I kept pace beside him as we hurried across and noticed the lip-chewing frown on his face. "I don't know if worrying is going to help without knowing why they were fighting."

He glanced over his shoulder. "I think I'm gonna' worry anyway. At least until we find out more. Could you hear them?"

I shook my head. "I saw their lips moving but I couldn't hear anything."

A couple of silent blocks passed before Paul groaned and touched my elbow, stopping me. "Maybe it's a dumb idea but I have to try to call Damien."

I shook my head. "We should both try." I didn't think it would work, but I felt as helpless as Paul did. It was the equivalent of trying someone's cell and was the least we would do for a human friend.

He nodded and we stepped apart. "Crow?"

"Yes, Bird?" Crow's irritable voice caressed my ear, like warm breath.

I turned to see Paul standing several feet from me, holding a hand up to the side of his face as if cradling a cell phone. *'Good thinking.'*

I pulled my phone from my pocket and held it up to my ear. "Crow, are you okay?"

"Of course, Bird. Why would you ask such a thing?"

"Uh, because you and Damien just had a streetfight? What happened?"

A long pause preceded a temperamental huff. "We were unaware we were being observed."

"How is that possible?"

"Bird, if you only called to ask about a personal issue between myself and another celestial, I really must insist that you respect my privacy."

I don't think I had ever been confronted with evidence that Crow was hiding something from me before. "So, you're okay?"

"I am well."

"Okay. I'll see you after work?"

"Yes."

The abrupt silence accompanied by a chill bump-inducing breeze against my ear let me know he had disconnected. I lowered the phone and stared at the screen. The time glowed up at me. I sighed. Turning to Paul, I found him equally confounded. We resumed walking, discussing the terse conversations we had both managed to have.

"Neither of them knew we were watching?" I stopped at the top of the driveway to the morgue.

Paul shook his head. "Real odd."

We said goodbye, and I tried to put the incident out of my mind as I entered the morgue. A weird and meaty smell drifting through the halls helped distract me. Neville had really thrown a luau. I hoped he hadn't tried anything as ridiculous as bringing in a whole pig to roast. With visions of Bunsen burners lined up across a gurney, I didn't want to think about where he might attempt such a thing.

I followed the sound of ukulele music and found Neville and Gail in the office; him stringing pineapple-shaped lights over everything, and her busily typing away at data entry. I cleared my throat, extra loud, to be heard over the festiveness filling the room.

Neville darted a startled glance over his shoulder and tried to shift the strings of lights in his hands. Presumably, he was attempting to empty one of them. The lights were uncooperative. I followed the bend of his body, the way it was focused in one direction. His phone was the only thing I could see to draw him. He'd hooked it up to a set of small speakers, for a richer and louder musical experience.

I reached past him and turned down the volume knob on one speaker. "Is our body count smaller than anticipated?"

"Thanks, and yes, actually." Neville resumed hanging lights. "I've already finished the last three cases in the backlog."

Gail turned her head and smiled as she briefly met my eyes. "Hey, Boss."

I hung my purse on the wall hook, patted the lump of my leftover sandwich, and spared a moment to steel myself. I copied Gail's small, rational smile and turned. "That's great. So, how many new customers are still waiting?"

Neville began to chuckle. "None!" He gave his head and shoulders a little sideways wiggle; left, right, left, from the hip. "Except for cleanup and restock and filing, our night is clear. Well, barring any deliveries." Tossing the remainder of the lights atop the short file cabinet, he retrieved a long, bright yellow Hawaiian shirt. With a self-satisfied expression giving his face a square-jawed, blocky aspect, he presented the shirt to me.

It appeared I had no way to avoid a party. I took the garment in both hands and gave it a little shake. Printed atop the blinding yellow background were big, red blossoms with inappropriately large stamens. Equally large green leaves in wide vertical stripes underlay the plethora of randomly placed flowers. I looked up, hoping to see a "gotcha" grin on Neville's face.

No such luck. Under his lab coat, Neville wore his own festive shirt in orange, red, green, and too many other colors over a black background. Gail, still tippy-tapping at high velocity, wore one with a red background unobscured by a lab coat. Since Gail had obligingly donned hers, I felt compelled to wear mine as well. I sighed and slid into the thing.

It was enormous. It fell almost to my knees. I felt like I'd been swallowed by a cotton garden. Neville, his shirt only reaching the top of his thighs, laughed and said, "You two could almost use those as lab coats." I frowned at him, and he shrugged. "I said almost."

Gail closed out the file she'd been working on and turned in the chair. "Looking good, Boss!" She held up two thumbs and winked.

I shooed her out of my chair and clocked in. I caught the flash of movement behind me in the reflection of the monitor and tried to dodge a lei being tossed over my head. I was too slow. "Really, guys?"

I turned around to find Neville handing out paper cups filled with bright red fruit punch. Gail sipped hers and began to bob to the music. I accepted a cup with a wistful gaze at the coffee pot, but I refused to dance. The Hawaiian-themed ukulele playlist didn't seem to have any other consistent thread. The only thing I vaguely recognized was a jaunty version of "Over the Rainbow."

After a few songs, Neville turned to the long folding table against the office wall, over which he'd spread a plastic tablecloth. I was mildly impressed. He'd made use of the tablecloth-covered piles of various files and documents which normally resided on said table as platter pedestals for his buffet spread. He made a plate for himself and retreated to the corner stool. Gail followed his lead, taking the chair beside the desk.

The weird meaty smell turned out to belong to the promised grilled Spam sandwiches. After one bite, I wrapped up the remainder of mine to save for later. I had no intention of eating anymore of it, but I thought Crow might like to try it even with the pineapples to make it sweet. The thought reminded me of the altercation in traffic with Damien. With a significant effort of will, I pushed the worrisome thought aside and tried to join in the banter.

"What do you have lined up for the weekend?" Neville shoved a corner of his sandwich into his mouth.

Gail raised one hand to cover her mouth as she chewed her bite over to one side. "My cousin is coming in from Renn and we're headed into Lincoln to see what kind of trouble we can cause." Her smile was lopsided with one cheek stuffed with sandwich.

I said, "Oh, fun." Banter was always an elusive thing for me when I tried to actively engage in it. I became awkward and was usually a beat too slow with my contributions. It put people off and wasn't pleasant for me, either. Still, I listened and offered a few inane, generic remarks often enough to be considered participatory.

"Where's Renn?" Neville stole my only relevant question.

It wasn't all bad, though. Along with a black and white ice cream he claimed was made of dragon fruit, Neville had made a pineapple upside down cake. I ate two slices. It was good cake.

When the food was mostly demolished and the second round of dancing had petered out, they surprised me with a gift. "Guys? What did you do?"

Gail gave herself a little hug and bounced on her toes. Neville shook his head. "Just open it."

The paper was Hawaiian themed as well, and I took quiet delight in shredding the ugly flowers. Lifting the lid of the box inside, the scent of freshly ground coffee beans wafted out. A goofy grin slid over my features, and I glanced up to see both of their faces. Gail fairly vibrated as she nibbled her lower lip, and Neville bobbed his head encouragingly.

Nestled inside the box was an extra-large, ceramic coffee mug filled with a bag of Ranier Red. The horrid Hawaiian theme had landed on the mug in the form of two large flowers like the ones on my shirt. They looked like they'd been drawn by children, complete with thumbprints marking the end of each stamen. The flowers, each labeled on one petal with Gail and Neville's names, bracketed a hand-lettered message. "#1 Boss."

"Guys." My voice cracked and I covered my mouth with my hand. In that moment, I was happy, ecstatic even, but I was going to cry. It was going to be ugly and messy, and I wasn't sure if I would be able to stop. In that moment, I was also stunned. There was no panic or dread. For the second time in under a week, I was feeling something amazing without the obligatory pain.

I carefully sat the mug beside the coffee pot and stood. Holding my arms out wide, I scooped both of them into a group hug. I stepped back before I made them as uncomfortable as I already was. "Thank you, both. That's probably the best present I've received since I was a child."

I was keenly aware that Crow had given me much more elaborate gifts, but he didn't count. He wasn't a real person. These two real people had spontaneously gotten me a gift, made it, with no expectations attached. Without doubt, there would be ramifications later. But in that moment, all I could do was smile.

Chapter 24. Reunion

The luau-themed party eventually wound down and Neville began clearing away the mess. Once he'd exposed the work surface of the table upon which he'd spread our buffet, Gail began sorting case folders for filing. I wandered out, through the cold room, to the larger, colder, long-term storage room. I just called it the freezer.

Each autopsy room had its own entry into the freezer for obvious reasons. The main entry from the hall was a set of heavy, insulated, double doors. I shoved my way inside and groped for the light switch. Light flooded the room. Twice as big as the cold room staging area, it seemed cavernous with only the empty stacking shelves and shredded bits of soiled and torn plastic sheeting left in a scattered mess. The concrete freezer floor was tiled from one insulated metal wall to the other. Sloped, shallow wells leading to floor drains were spaced out every ten feet or so. Smudges and lumps of things I wasn't interested in identifying made black, brown, and red splotches here and there.

I donned a new pair of gloves and a face shield. Thinking of my preferred lab coat still hanging in the supply closet, I decided not to retrieve it. Instead, since the ugly Hawaiian shirt I was still wearing had already proved itself to be an adequate insulator against the cold, I decided to test its other lab coat qualities. I flicked the switch to open the floor drains and got to work.

Once I'd folded down the shelves and shoved them into one corner, my thoughts drifted back to the street fight between Damien and Crow. There was more than one oddity there and I intended to have all my questions prepared and ready to light like charcoal when I grilled Crow about it later. I planned to confront him as soon as he arrived to take me home. The more I thought about it, the more I wished I could send Neville and Gail home early.

With the shelves out of the way, I used the broad-headed broom to gather all the debris and bagged it up while my mind tried to tease out the problem. What could provoke Crow into a physical confrontation. It didn't make any sense with what I thought I knew about him and the way his world worked. The more I pondered that thought, the more convinced I became that Crow was hiding more than a personal disagreement.

I mixed a cleanser solution and hosed down the open floor, grateful for the pressure washing wand which precluded the need to scrub. My thoughts had run into a wall. I couldn't think of anything to ask Crow past, "What are you trying to hide from me?" Everything else in the conversation would depend on his answer.

I used the broom to encourage the filthy, sudsy water to find the drains in the floor and moved the shelves to their permanent storage corner. My mind gnawed on the Crow problem while I gave the corner that had temporarily housed the shelves another quick cleaning. There really wasn't anything else I could do about him until I had him in front of me. So much for preparing the grill.

I looked around the freezer and grunted. There wasn't anything else I could do in there either. I disposed of my gloves and face shield and shivered. Sweaty patches around my collar and under my armpits had soaked into the Hawaiian lab coat as I cleaned. Splashes of the cleaning water had dampened it further, and the freezer was turning the moisture to ice. I shed the failed experiment as I walked back into the office. Gail sat at the computer, playing solitaire, and Neville gave hints over her shoulder.

"Hey, if you two want to get out of here, I don't mind." I pulled the basket from the coffee maker and set it up with Ranier Red from my present.

Neville grinned, "I don't have anywhere to be. I can go fiddle with the scanning system for a while..."

"No." I cast a scornful glare at him as I pulled the pot from the coffee maker. "Never ever fiddle with that set-up. I don't know if it's easy to break, but the guy comes in once a month to calibrate it and I don't want to explain how it got broken."

Gail laughed and closed the solitaire window. "Well, I'll take you up on it. I could use the extra sleep time before tomorrow night."

Neville said, "Oh, right. You have big plans."

"Yep." She had clocked out and stood as I headed out to the hallway water fountain. She followed, with Neville on her heels. "Have a good weekend, Boss. I'll see you Tuesday."

"Wait, what?" I paused, pot hovering above the water fountain, and frowned at her.

Neville chuckled. "Oh, yeah. You should have gotten a memo."

"Mhmm." Gail reached up and flicked a chunk of thick and wavy dark hair out of her eyes. "You really need to read your email more carefully, Boss." She grinned and shoved her way out the door.

I watched the door close behind her and shook my head. Turning back to the fountain, I filled the pot. "So, what should I have gotten a memo about?"

Neville leaned against the wall with one shoulder. "The powers that be decided the three-shift system worked well and, with a few adjustments, decided to make it permanent. You are now officially our boss."

I frowned heavily at the water rising in the pot, willing it to go faster. I needed my coffee if I was going to deal with this. Back in the office, I started the pot and opened my email, searching for this memo, and found it. It had been shunted into some kind of 'really important' subcategory of the inbox. After a shallow rabbit hole to figure out how to turn that off, I opened the memo.

Ms. Nightcastle...

I skipped ahead. The first paragraph told me what a great job I had done. The second paragraph told me my new title and how much money I was getting in my salary bump. The third paragraph listed my punishments.

To that end, you are being given permanent supervision of the third shift. You will be responsible for a four-person crew, including yourself. Gail Shephard and Neville Vivanti will remain part of that crew as well as an additional tech.

"But I don't want to be a boss." I whined as the coffee pot burbled. I imagined it was trying to console me. I rested my elbows on the desk in front of me and laid my face in my hands.

Neville walked up behind me, crooning a sympathetic noise. "But you're a great boss, ... Boss."

His chuckle made me groan. The coffee pot burbled, a loud, hissing noise that fitted my sentiments exactly, to indicate it was ready, finally, to dispense bitter warmth. I inhaled a deep and fortifying breath before turning with a bossly smile. "I know. I have a mug that says so." He grinned at me as I picked up my present and poured for myself.

Neville laughed and sauntered over to his stool and cooler. "Do you ever drink herbal tea?"

"Coffee."

"Yes, but you drink other things too, right?"

The smug look on his face made me want to smack him. With a sigh, I refrained and nodded. I sipped the coffee and regained some of my tattered patience. "Of course, I do. I just prefer my coffee."

That smarmy smirk spread over his face again. "I think you mean you prefer *my* coffee." He nodded at the small bag of Ranier Red and waggled his eyebrows at me.

I grunted. "It was a gift. Its mine now." Another thought came to me, knocking my head off tilt as it landed. "Hey, speaking of which, does your friend produce enough to be a restaurant supplier?"

Neville had unwrapped another grilled Spam and pineapple sandwich. He took a large bite and nodded. Still chewing out of one side of his mouth, he said, "I should think so. They have a whole shipping department on site."

I averted my eyes, burying my attention back in my cup. Two thoughts fought for supremacy. The first, Neville had the table manners of a wolf boy. The second, maybe I could convince Genia and Jacob to make Ranier Red the new Holy Grounds house brew.

The CCTV monitor flared to life showing Pete and Donna in their ambulance. "Looks like we have a customer." I felt a little lift at the corners of my mouth as I watched Donna and Pete exiting the bus. I think I might have missed them.

Neville squinted past me at the computer clock. "Does that say 11-something?"

"Yeah, 11:38. Your shift is almost over, huh?" I frowned, thinking about how Pete and Donna might behave around Neville; or Gail for that matter. A list of concerns with these two parts of my life mixing began to populate in my mind. I topped off my cup and stood, heading toward the hall.

Neville followed, like a curious cat. "Yeah." He sighed. "I'm technically off at midnight. I can stay and help with the incoming."

I slapped the palm-sized button on the wall to open the double doors. "I think you've earned the right to go home." I slouched against the wall, feeling only half-dressed without my lab coat at work.

Donna led the way in once the doors were fully open. She pushed one gurney herself with Pete following behind her with a second. Donna grinned as her eyes met mine. "Hey there, sweet cheeks. I see you survived the Ides of March."

"Hey, Donna. I see you two did as well." I lifted my mug in salute to Pete. "What do we have here?"

Pete blew out a sigh and leaned against the end of his gurney. "Boring old couple appear to have died in their sleep."

Neville grunted beside me. He stepped forward and waved. "Hi. I'm Neville. Let me get the door for you." He gave me a look as he turned for the cold room door.

I knew that look. I'd been rude, apparently. "Sorry. Neville, this is Donna and Pete." They shoved their gurneys through the door, each giving Neville a nod as they passed him. Following them in, I said, "Guys, this is Neville. He's another coroner here, my second in command on the night shift from now on."

Donna locked the wheels of her gurney and shoved the case folder at me as she turned to Neville. "It's very nice to meet you." She swayed closer to him with her first couple of steps toward the office. She patted his shoulder and lifted her nose to sniff distractedly. "What is that fabulous smell? You know, a morgue isn't supposed to make a body hungry."

Neville turned that, 'how rude,' look on Donna. I could always count on the demons to be more socially awkward than me. Pete stuck out a hand to Neville. "Hey. Were you here long before the recent event?"

Neville took the proffered hand automatically and gave his head a little shake. "Hmm? Oh, no. Only a couple of weeks."

Pete nodded and followed Donna who had already disappeared into the office. Neville lifted his eyebrows at me in one of those questioning expressions that invited me to be on his 'us' team. That would make the demons members of the 'them' team. That was new for me, and I wasn't sure what to make of it. I gave an expedient shrug and followed Pete.

Donna found the spare mugs and poured two cups of coffee. Handing off one mug to Pete, she turned to her customary low filing cabinet to sit. There she paused, staring at the coiled end of the still gleaming pineapple-shaped lights. "Um. What is this?" She lifted the coil on a hooked finger and spun on her heel to hold it out to me.

Neville chuckled and managed a passable flush to his cheeks as he stepped past me and took the lights from her. "Pardon that. We were just celebrating the end of that recent mess. The boss here let me throw a luau." He offered a grin to the room and scrambled to clear things out of the way.

I rolled my eyes and walked over to my desk chair. "Relax you two. Have a seat and catch me up on all your nefarious deeds during the event." I wasn't sure how else to proceed. Pete and Donna weren't likely to blow their own covers, much less mine, but if I didn't take the lead, Neville and the two demons were likely to keep making uncomfortable overtures.

Pete took his seat beside the desk and sipped his coffee. "Hot shit! That's good coffee."

Donna giggled, a skeptical wryness flavoring the look she gave him as she scooted back onto the cabinet. She sipped. "Damn. That is pretty tasty. What is it?"

Neville, having found a temporary place to shove the light coil on the floor beside the filing cabinet, straightened and cleared his throat. I waited for him to explain the coffee, but he only slumped over to his corner stool and pulled his cooler up to his lap.

I frowned at him and explained it myself. "It's called Ranier Red, and Neville here is the generous man responsible for the treat. Oh, and look at this awesome mug my minions made for me." I held up my mug, still half full, and nodded patiently at their noises of admiration. I took another long pull from my mug and topped it off again. The thing held twice what a normal coffee cup could.

The coffee had probably earned Neville plenty of points in their books, but when Pete and Donna turned to express their appreciation to him, he asked, "Would either of you like a grilled Spam and pineapple sandwich?" He pulled one out of his cooler with each of his hands.

Pete hummed and half-stood, one foot stepping far out, to lean across the floor and take one. "I haven't had one of these in years."

Donna accepted one as well and sniffed it. "You've had this before?"

Pete unwrapped his sandwich and grinned while nodding rapidly. "Back in my island-hopping days." He shoved a corner of the sandwich into his mouth and chomped down. His eyes rolled up and his eyelids fluttered down. "Mm! Good."

Donna smirked at me and nibbled hers. "Oh, that's really good."

"You two; your tastes are as bad as Neville's." I held my mug up at my chin, effectively hiding behind the thing.

Neville had pulled another sandwich from the cooler with a bottle of chilled tea. "It isn't our fault your uncultured palate can't appreciate the finer things."

That was better. By siding against those nasty sandwiches, I had ushered Pete and Donna into Neville's 'us' team. That left me as the solitary member of the 'them' team. That was more squarely in my comfort zone. "Whatever. The cake was good, though."

"There was cake?" Donna looked hopefully at Neville.

"There was. It was well-received." Neville grinned around his sandwich. Donna grinned back, a devilish gleam in her eyes.

Pete shoved the last bite of his sandwich into his mouth. With bites three times the size of my own, his cheeks puffed out as he chewed. "Mm." He grunted and sipped his coffee, managing to squish the bite to one side before he tried again to speak. "You're alright, man. Where did you come from?"

I repressed a shudder and turned away from the masticatory display. Neville, talking with his mouth equally full, replied. "I grew up in a little town in the Florida panhandle. I went to college in Gainesville and headed back north to Florida State for my doctorate. I did my post-doc work outside Seattle. I worked in a large clinic retreat on the coast there for almost ten years before deciding I needed a change. That's when I came here."

In that moment, I felt like a horrible person. Why hadn't I asked about any of that? It wasn't that I didn't care. I just hadn't thought about it. It wasn't relevant to the business that brought us together. Still, it was that sort of expression of interest in your co-workers that made it such a good idea for me not to have any.

"Wow, you don't look old enough to be ten years out of a post-doc." Donna had somehow managed to lean back against the wall with coffee in one hand and half a sandwich in the other. She looked not only comfortable, but almost seductive as she crossed her legs toward Neville.

Neville coughed, as if a crumb had caught in his throat. "Well, thanks! It's genetic. My dad looked like he was twelve every time he shaved until he was in his thirties."

I turned to the computer and the two new case folders. The clock on the computer said 11:46. I opened the top folder. Mrs. Laura Landon, DOA, asleep in her bed. I opened the other atop the first. Mr. Benson Landon, DOA, asleep in his bed. Husband and wife. There were a few scene photos in the file, and the chatter around me faded away as I was drawn into one. The late Mr. and Mrs. Landon had been found spooned together, her head resting on one of his arms and his other arm reaching around to cup his wife's breast. 'What a way to go.' I couldn't imagine it.

Neville's voice intruded on my thoughts. "What's it look like, Boss? Should I stay and help out?"

I shook myself and closed the folders. "No, you should go home. You're going to be here covering for me all by yourself for the next two nights."

Neville gave a perfunctory nod of agreement. "Good point." He began packing up his cooler with the luau décor. "Well, it was nice to meet you both." He shook hands with Pete, and when he offered his hand to Donna, she used it to pull herself to her feet.

She, having divested herself of her refreshments, stood close, her upturned face sharing breathing room with Neville's. His face flushed prettily again as she inhaled, her bosom swelling to brush his chest. "It has been a delight to meet you. Perhaps some tragedy or other will cross our paths again."

Neville skipped a couple of steps back and teetered to one side as he pulled the strap of his cooler up over one shoulder. "I'm sure it will." His weak smile slid away as he turned widened eyes to me and cleared his throat.

"I'll walk you out." I stood, taking pity on him. "You two help yourselves to another cup of coffee. I'll be right back." I steered Neville by one elbow through the door.

In the hall, Neville glanced back over his shoulder and grunted. "She's a little forceful. Is she always like that?"

"Only when her mark is unsettled by it." I pulled open the door, held it for Neville, and stepped out behind him. The chill night air was heavy with humidity carried in on the warmer daytime breezes. The cold dampness lay in thick sheets of glowing fog from somewhere around our ankles up to the level of the streetlights. "If you act like you like it, she'll lose interest."

"Ah." He up-nodded, a quick lift of his chin. "I've known a few women like that before." He sighed as we stepped around the ambulance parked directly in front of the door. He turned and looked as if he was about to speak when his eyebrows drew together above a frown.

I followed his gaze to the other side of the parking lot. A figure sat atop the front hood of a car, a dark silhouette against the glowing greyness of the fog. A red glow intensified as the figure pulled a deep drag from a cigarette. A faint sweet scent perfusing the fog begged the question, what kind of cigarette?

I squinted and took a few steps closer. "Crow?"

The long, lanky figure unfolded itself and stood, flicking the cigarette off to one side. "Hello, Bird."

"Do you know this person?" Neville, the concerned furrows of his brow shading the contours of his hard jawline, kept pace beside me as I crossed the parking lot.

I flicked a glance up at Neville. *'Had he always been that tall? And broad?'* The man was becoming a distraction. I turned back to Crow. "Yep. He's my..." I wasn't sure what to call him. I studied him, standing there with his hands clasped behind his back and feet set comfortably but squarely beneath him. "His name is Crow. We are kind of friends, I guess."

Neville looked confused and as if he might ask questions. I quickened my pace to forestall him. "Crow? I wasn't expecting you this early."

Crow leaned down as I approached and laid a chaste and warm kiss on my cheek. As he straightened, he laid a hand on my shoulder and pulled me to his side. "I know, but I thought you might like my company at your break." He turned to Neville and offered his hand. "Crow Corvus. You must be the Neville I have heard so much of this last couple of weeks."

Neville narrowed his eyes at Crow's face, then his hand, and then me. He shook Crow's hand, standing at his full height and lifting his chin. "That's me. You have me at something of a disadvantage, Mr. Corvus."

"Please, call me Crow." I squinted from one of them to the other, not sure which one was behaving more strangely.

"Sure." Neville jutted his chin toward the car behind Crow. "This one's mine. I was just leaving."

Crow bowed and side-stepped, maneuvering me along with him. "By all means, don't let us keep you. I understand from Star here that you have all been under a great deal of stress. I hope you have a restful evening."

Neville nodded, looked at me, and paused. Lips parted, I was certain he was going to say something about work or coffee or something. He only nodded once more, said, "Goodnight," and got in his car.

I disentangled Crow's arm from my shoulders and ushered him back toward the morgue door. I punched in the security code and Crow opened the door for me. Behind us, the engine of Neville's car growled to life, and the transmission settled into gear as we stepped into the bright warmth of the hall. "What are you doing here so early?"

"Am I not welcome, Bird?"

I sighed and trudged ahead toward the office. "Of course, but neither of the folks on the slab were clients. I still have four hours left in my shift, and what was all that smoking on his car about?" I tossed an accusing glare over my shoulder. "You have to admit, it's a little odd for you to show up for no reason."

Crow glided along behind me, affecting obliviousness. "I do sometimes indulge in various smokable herbs, Bird. You, yourself, have asked me before not to do so inside the morgue."

I dropped the subject as I stepped into the office. He wasn't likely to become less intentionally obtuse with Pete and Donna there. Those two had started another pot of coffee and were both chortling over a joke I had missed. Crow stepped in behind me, and they stood, their humor evaporating.

"Sit, please. It has been some time since we were all able to gather here. Relax and let's enjoy our reunion." Crow perched on Neville's stool and Pete brought him a cup of coffee.

Donna wriggled back into her spot and smiled. "How did your thing go, Boss?" I grunted inwardly at the stark contrast between Donna addressing Crow as "Boss" and Gail addressing me.

"It went well. The correct messages were sent and received." Crow held his coffee on his fingertips, that smarmy, self-satisfied look spreading over his features.

I left them there, drinking up my new coffee and being demonically annoying. I retrieved my lab coat, started a podcast through my ear buds, and settled into the solitary work. By the time Pete and Donna left, I had already taken the Mister to run his scans.

Crow joined me. "How are you doing, Bird?"

I sighed and flicked a small smile at him, feeling the faint edges of fatigue beginning to cloud my thoughts. I was still going to grill him, but dead bodies took precedence. "I'm feeling the fatigue of the last few weeks, but otherwise, I'm fine. What "thing" was it Donna asked about?"

"Oh, you know. A little manipulation of events here, some insinuation there..." Crow slid up behind my chair and laid his hands on my shoulders. Warmth and massaging pressure relaxed deeply embedded knots of tension.

My eyes closed, and my head lolled back. With a moan, I forced my eyes open and looked up into Crow's smiling face. "I really need to work efficiently to get these two taken care of. Please don't relax me too much."

He lifted his hands in surrender and stepped away. I checked the scan sequence and stood, heading back to the cold room to begin the intake on the Missus. "Oh, I almost forgot, I saved some of the luau food for you." Crow veered off toward the office. I called after him, "It's in the middle desk drawer."

Crow leaned in the office doorframe to nibble, knowing the rules against travelling with food, and sent his voice into my ear as I worked. "This is quite good, Bird. "It is unfortunate you are unable to enjoy it, but I am happy to be the beneficiary of your misfortune."

"It's really gross." I grimaced at the remembered flavor and texture. "I have another sandwich in my purse. You can have that too if you like." Crow found the other sandwich and smiled as he chewed, one sandwich in each hand. Whatever, as long as he didn't get underfoot while I was working, he could eat it all.

As I wheeled the Mister back from scans, the Missus taking her turn there, Crow joined me in the cold room. "How can I help, Bird?"

I frowned at him and this new and apparently persistent helpfulness. "Restock the consumables?"

The Landons had no markers to indicate a suspicious death, and I finished both before 3:00. Staging them to one side, ready for pick-up, I returned to the office with their folders and noticed Crow had emptied waste bins and even swept, unprompted. As I opened the data entry program, I wondered if I trusted him to make suture packs and prepare other small tools for the autoclave. I glanced into the cold room where he danced a waltz with the mop. *'Probably not.'*

As I finished up my shift, I grimaced at the return of that little itch in the back of my mind, clocked out, and flicked the office lights off. It didn't get dark enough. Neville had left the pineapples on, and I grinned at them. It really had been a fun little celebration. I turned away, leaving the glowing pineapples to make the day shift shits wish they had been invited to the cool kids' party.

Crow gathered me in his arms half-way across the cold room floor. He nuzzled his cheek against mine. "Shall we?" I had barely wrapped my arms around him when we flew.

Chapter 25. Dinner Plans

My feet touched down on the carpet of my living room before I even considered protesting. Crow stepped back, ready to release me, and paused looking into my face. "Little Bird. Are you well? You look unsteady."

As my awareness returned to the reality of my physical body, I realized I was in fact bone weary. That wasn't fair. I still had demon grilling to do that night. I looked into Crow's concerned face and nodded. "I'm okay, just so exhausted." I made a move toward the couch and Crow supported me with one arm around my waist.

Settling me onto the couch, he left me there to walk his circuit around my apartment. I lost track of him until he sat and lifted my feet into his lap. With slow movements, he unlaced my shoes and pulled them off, followed by my socks, and began to delicately massage my feet and ankles. "Are you hungry? Would you like a shower? Or, do you just want to crawl into bed?"

My head lolled to one side, my eyes closed and my mind beginning to buzz with oncoming unconsciousness. I grunted and shoved myself into a more upright, sitting position. "No. None of that, yet. I want some answers about that street fight."

Crow inhaled deeply and sighed, a long and extended hiss deep in his throat. "I thought we agreed that it was a personal matter."

I stood and aimed myself at the kitchen. "You said it was. I don't have anything to base that on. It looked pretty spectacular." I made it as far as the little café table and stopped. "What could possibly bring you and our client's guardian angel to blows?"

Crow stood and stumped up behind me. He pulled a chair out and settled me into it. "Sit down before you fall. I will make something for you to eat."

I found myself leaning forward, elbows on the tabletop and my face in my hands. "I may be getting a headache." The itch was back.

Crow touched my forehead, like a mother checking a child for fever. The itch subsided and a little of the fatigue-induced brain fog cleared. I straightened. "Thank you."

Crow nodded and turned toward the kitchen. "I have expressed my perspective. It is personal. However, I have nothing to hide from you. What would you like to know?" He began bustling around, resulting in intermittent sounds of chopping, stirring, and sizzling.

"What happened?"

"We had a disagreement."

"About what?"

"Our jobs."

I sighed. "How did it start?"

Crow poured something into a sizzling skillet and a new kind of sizzle started. "I went to see him. I asked him what the parameters of his assignment were."

"What did he say?" I slouched in my chair with my arms crossed loosely over my abdomen.

Crow turned off the stove eye with an indelicate flick of his wrist. "He said what they always say. He was assigned to be Paul's guardian angel. He isn't required to give me any details if he doesn't want to. He didn't want to." He tossed a plate in front of me on the table with a fork and a chilled can of soda. The plate bounced a little, spiraling down on its bottom rim like a coin at the end of a spin. Crow raised a hand and halted the plate wobbles. He lowered it more delicately with the lowering of his hand and sighed. "I apologize, Bird. Damien is a frustrating opponent."

I nodded and opened the soda. "I see." I drank a deep gulp from the can and hovered my face above the plate, inhaling the scent. "Smells good." I lifted a forkful to my mouth. I was so incredibly tired, I seriously considered letting Crow completely off the hook just so I could get to sleep sooner.

I dismissed the temptation as I swallowed and cleared my mouth with another gulp of soda. "How did it come to blows?"

Crow took the seat opposite mine and materialized a bottle of something in front of him. He hovered his fingers above the bottle cap and snapped. The cap spun loose, flipped off the top of the bottle, and landed in his waiting hand. "I asked too forcefully. He rebuffed me with equal force."

I began to perk up a bit with a few more bites of food. "Mm, so, basically, you fought over secrets he wanted to keep?"

Crow hummed and lifted his bottle to his lips. Swallowing a deep guzzle, he smacked his lips and frowned at the bottle cap in his hand. "What I don't understand, is how you and Paul saw us. I am certain neither Damien nor I are responsible."

I shrugged, stabbing something meaty with my fork. "We don't know either. The two of you just appeared out of the sky, landed in the intersection and proceeded to tussle as cars zipped right through you. You were both a little fuzzy, kind of washed out, and we couldn't hear a thing."

A dark mask crawled slowly across his features as he stared down at the bottlecap. Something had sparked a thought. I put another forkful of food in my mouth and watched him. Watching the play of reactions to his internal dialogue reminded me of how I felt watching the fight. I could see things were happening, but I had no frame of reference to define what I was seeing.

Finally, he shrugged and turned a small smile toward me. "I can see you are too tired to have any fun tonight. How about tomorrow? Would you like a date night?"

I frowned into my mostly empty plate. "I can't tomorrow. At least, not until later. Genia is hosting a dinner party. She's expecting me."

"How fun for you." I thought I could hear one of the snarky undertones of a person being insincere, but nothing about the way he smiled at me seemed insincere. "That will be a nice change of pace from work."

"Yeah, Paul is very excited about it. Apparently, Jacob has been busily testing recipes and plating options for a while now." I leaned back in my chair, abandoning the scattered remains of my meal. "That was good. Thanks."

Crow smiled and reached under the table to lay a warm hand on my knee. "Would you like a shower?"

I closed my eyes and imagined standing that long. "Only if you hold me up."

He chuckled and stood, holding up a hand. I placed my hand in his and he tugged me to my feet, then bent and scooped me up in his arms. I yelped as my feet left the ground and threw my arms around his shoulders. Our clothing melted away as he carried me into the bathroom. He handled me like an infant as he magically adjusted the water temperature and ran a bath.

I nestled into his embrace, relaxing and allowing him to shift me into his lap as he sat with me in the steamy water. I laid my head back against his shoulder and squinted. "My tub isn't this big."

"It is tonight, Bird." He gently poured water over my head and worked shampoo into a lather. "Tell me about Neville and the other one. Gail? How do you like working with them?"

The shampooing flowed into an all over soap-down. "They're pretty okay. Neville is a giant child but he's an efficient coroner. Gail really rose to the challenge. I'm going to have to put her up for a raise at evaluation time if she keeps progressing."

"So, you work well together?"

"Yeah, surprisingly well. Oh, and," I giggled, my eyes still closed, "they got me a present." Crow's warm hands worked soapy lather into the creases and folds between my legs. I lost track of what I was saying as he coaxed my nether regions into shuddering alertness. As the climax passed, leaving me nestled into sweet contentment, his hands moved farther down my thighs.

I sighed. "That was very nice, but I've completely lost track of what I was saying."

"Your minions gave you a gift?" Crow's deep rumbling murmur drew me in like a lodestone to a magnet.

I shifted to nestle my cheek against his chest and took a moment to remember what I had been talking about. "Neville and Gail, they got me a giant coffee mug." I described the luau inspired design of the mug and my emotional response to the gift.

Crow laughed softly, making his chest jump beneath my head. "Do you think they got enjoyment from surprising you with that gift?" He began to pour hot water over my head and body, rinsing away the soap.

"They seemed to." I wiped water from my eyes and rolled over. He reclined against the back of the magically huge tub so that I floated just above him, my nipples brushing the soft fur of his chest. I crossed my arms on his chest and laid my cheek down. The water lapped at my ear, and I imagined I could hear his heart beating. So faint and distant, it was probably my own heartbeat conducting through the water. "Crow, did you get any answers out of Damien?"

His hands stilled on my back. He heaved a sigh, and his hands began to move again. He traced the line of my spine in small circles, and the water temperature rose a couple of degrees. "This is not something you should worry about. You don't need to know. It doesn't impact your part in client relations."

"I would like to know anyway, please."

"You wouldn't understand, Bird."

"Try me, Crow. I am very understanding." I turned my head, resting my chin on my crossed arms, and looked him in the eyes.

Crow moved his hands to my sides, applying gentle pressure to the bottom of my ribs. That place was like a muscle-relaxing switch for me. My eyes fluttered closed, and I went limp like a kitten being carried by the scruff. "Damien is in what you have aptly described as a competing department."

"Like in a big company?"

"Sure." I could hear the amusement in his voice. "I learned from other sources that he took the assignment to Paul specifically to break our operations; this deal between you and I."

I frowned. "To keep us from making swaps? He can't make us stop." I opened my eyes and studied his. "I thought they were all about free will. He can't make the clients turn us down."

Crow smiled, no teeth, just a curve of his closed lips. "He only has to convince you, Little Bird."

"That's never going to happen."

He leaned in and touched the tip of his nose to mine. "How can you be so sure?"

I closed my eyes and let myself sink back into his watery embrace. "Because I need you and our deal. I'm not giving you up."

His arms tightened around me. "Are you ready to go to bed?"

I nodded and relaxed, letting his arms lift me from the water. He stood me up outside the tub and wrapped a soft, fluffy towel around me. A full body hug managed to wick most of the moisture off of my skin. He ran his hands through my hair a few times, until it was equally dried.

When he led me to the bed, he slid under the blankets with me, continuing the gentle massage while I gave in to the comfort. He was quiet so long; I began to doze. His silky, soothing voice whispered, as if to himself, "Who was responsible for making us visible to you and Paul? It wasn't Damien, me, or another angel or demon. That only leaves one probability."

I tried to turn, to roll onto my back, and ask him who he was talking about. I was too warm, too cozy, and too tired. If he said anything more, it was lost to my sleeping mind.

*****

When I awoke the next night, Crow lay beside me, watching me claw my way up out of sleep. He did that sometimes, and it usually meant he was excited about our plans. I frowned at him. "Hey. I didn't expect you to still be here since I have that dinner party to go to."

He laid a warm kiss atop my forehead and gently caressed the side of my face. As his hand brushed my skin, the sleepy murk subsided from my perceptions. I became aware of the light level in my bedroom and frowned. "Am I up earlier than usual?"

"A bit." His husky whisper felt almost like a blanket itself.

Suddenly too warm, I kicked my covers off and rolled away. I groped for my phone and couldn't find it. "Ugh, where is it?" I stood and ambled into my living room. Finding my phone in my purse, I checked the time and wondered what I was going to do with an extra hour before the dinner.

Crow appeared in my bedroom door, naked as a bird. "Are you interested in a proper, upright shower tonight?"

"Will it come with a cup of coffee at the end?" I plugged my phone in, lay it on the side table beside my terrarium, and slumped across the carpet toward him.

He chuckled and ushered me into the shower. It occurred to me that this was one of our favorite activities and I wasn't complaining. The hot water, the scented soap I used only on special occasions, and the warm massage helped roust me properly. By the time I was dressed and sitting at my table with a cup of demonically conjured coffee, I was also squinting suspiciously at Crow.

"What are you excited about?"

"What do you mean, Bird?"

'Evasive.' That meant he wasn't going to tell me, no matter how much I pried. I cocked my head to one side. "Is Paul okay? Has his time come while I was sleeping?"

He gave me a withering look. "He is busily preparing for dinner upstairs. If his time had come, don't you think we'd be in route to make the swap?"

I grunted. He had a good point but, between the street fight and this mood, I wasn't inspired to trust him. I finished off my coffee and stood. "I should go ahead up and see if I can help."

Crow nodded and dismissed our cups. "I will walk with you. The sooner you begin your dinner party, the sooner we can go on our date."

The open and honest smile on his face made me pause. If he was excited about some event he'd planned, that could explain his presence and attitude. Turning for the bathroom, I shook the thought from my head and sighed. My hair was still damp. A quick brushing under a hair dryer settled the dark brown waves across my shoulders. Good enough.

True to his word, Crow walked me up the alley and to the front door of the diner. A little sign on the door announced the diner was closed to the public for the next few hours for a private party. Inside, the place was milling with people I didn't know, and I almost fled.

Genia saw us through the plate glass windows and hurried to open the door. "Star, honey! And Mr. Corvus. Are you joining us? There's plenty of room for Star's guest."

I blinked and turned to look up at Crow. He smiled back at me, creepy and toothy, and turned to Genia. "Oh, no, unfortunately, I can't stay. I hope you have a lovely evening." He kissed the top of my hair and turned away.

I gave a half smile to Genia and flicked a frown at Crow's quickly retreating back. "He's being so weird tonight."

Genia laughed. "Weirder than normal?" She waved a hand in his direction, dismissing him, and tugged my sleeve. "Don't mind him. Men are all strange sometimes. Come on in!"

I followed her in and saw Paul coming from the back. He carried warming trays to a long table in the center of the dining area. Almost all of the regular tables had been shoved together to make one long one. White tablecloths with charger plates and utensils set out before each chair marked the place settings. Little pint-sized clear vases sat at the top of each place setting holding a single lily in each.

Genia showed me to a seat at the table. As we approached, I saw the vases had been marked with guest names. The ones to either side of mine said "Paul" and "Adrya." I sighed and relaxed a bit as I dropped my purse onto the chair.

Genia said, "I have to go help Jacob now, but help yourself to the drinks." Her glorious smile and twinkling eyes made me smile with a warm and cozy, safe feeling in my gut.

Unsettling as that gut feeling was, I couldn't work up any fear. I moseyed over to the drinks, sinking deeper into relaxation and calm. Adrya stood behind the drink table, shoving bottles of various types of drinks into a large wash bucket of ice. "Hey, Star. There is coffee in the big dispensers on the next table over, but I have water and soda and beer over here."

"Thanks. This works." I took a bottle of water and eyed the coffee dispenser, remembering my intention to talk to Genia about Ranier Red. I twisted the bottle top off and lifted it to my mouth as I turned to survey the other people milling about. "Who are all these people?"

Adrya blew a lock of hair from her eyes and looked around. "Well, most of them are daytime regulars. Well, about half and half customers and other small business owner friends of the Albrights."

Ellie sauntered over arm in arm with an apple-cheeked young man. "Hi, Star, Adrya."

We returned the greeting, and I stuck my hand out at the young man at her side. "Hi. I'm Star."

Ellie giggled. "This is my brother, Evan. He's about to graduate from Wesleyan this spring."

Adrya stepped in with the appropriate response. "Here in Nebraska? That's a good school. What is your degree in?"

Evan began to answer, and Paul waved at me from across the room. I excused myself and wandered over to where he was arranging the warming trays down the center of the table. "Hey, Paul. Are you excited?"

"Hey, Star." He straightened and surveyed his work. With a sigh, he said, "Yeah. It's smelling real good in the kitchen. Jake's been at it since early this morning."

I chuckled and shook my head. Before I could respond, Another couple approached. Paul's face split in a grin. "Star. This is Mr. and Mrs. Popadopoulis. They are the kindly couple that rented my apartment to me."

Mr. Popadopoulis reached for my hand. Clasping it between both of his, he shook it enthusiastically. "Call me Milo."

His wife took her turn giving me a much more reasonable handshake. "I'm Hera." She turned a fond smile on Paul. "It isn't much of an apartment."

"Well, it's perfect for me and I couldn't be more grateful." Paul excused himself, bustling off to help with more preparations.

'Great. Now what do I do with these two strangers?'

"It is really kind of you to make room for Paul." I sipped my water and hoped that was open-ended enough.

"Not at all." Milo's deep baritone rumble carried like an opera singer. "We are grateful to him for staying onsite when we can't be there. Dry cleaning requires a lot of investment in equipment, and we had two break-ins last year."

Hera nodded and patted her husband's shoulder. "The insurance company was about to raise our rates. Once Paul moved in, we were able to claim an on-site caretaker slash security guard." She waved a hand in the air between us and giggled.

I widened my eyes and pushed one corner of my mouth upward. "I bet that was a relief." I looked up and scanned the room. Not finding any distraction or excuse to disengage, I cleared my throat and turned back to the nice couple. "So how long have you known Genia and Jacob?"

Milo hummed a precursor rumble and said, "Oh, many years now. We were in the same small-business class in the early days. Our boy, Vittor, had his first job as a bus boy here in this very diner."

"Oh? Where is he now?"

Hera sighed and glanced down before meeting my eyes again. "He's working in Portland now. I think he may be preparing to ask his girlfriend to marry him."

It was a sweet and motherly tone, but some thread of hurt registered in my ears. I cocked my head to one side and, after a moment's hesitation, shifted slightly to lean in. "Oh, I'm sorry he's so far away. I hope I get to meet him soon, though."

Milo looked like he was about to launch into something else when Genia rescued me. She and Jacob stood just in front of the kitchen door. She lifted her hands and clapped gently a few times. "Welcome, everyone. Thank you for being here with us on this special occasion."

Jacob, one arm around his wife's waist, grunted and cleared his throat. "Yes. Thank you all. I hope you enjoy the dishes I have prepared. Before we get started, Genia is going to describe the score cards. Adrya is passing them out to you now. Excuse me, please. I am so grateful you are all here, but I'm going to go get the food now."

Light applause accompanied his retreat and Genia launched into her explanation of how to give feedback on the various dishes being presented. I took a score card from Adrya and followed along with the instructions. Each dish would have an identification number with it, and we simply had to choose a numerical rating and give any specific feedback on the card.

The room full of guests began to find their seats and the lights were dimmed. Genia and Jacob brought out three or four dishes at a time and laid the trays on the warmers. Each guest was encouraged to try whatever looked and smelled appealing. Safely bookended with Paul on one side and Adrya on the other, I settled back and grinned at the beautiful samples. Paul took one of each and seemed to be taking the scoring very seriously.

I tried something like a puffed pastry stuffed with something creamy and cheesy and tasting of lobster. It was incredible.

Paul chuckled at whatever noise had escaped me. "I told you."

I chuckled back, and we worked our way through a handful of dishes without much chatter. In the lull between dishes being served, I studied Paul. We hadn't had a chance to talk about the street fight or what we'd learned since then, but I wasn't sure this was the best setting to bring it up. The Bonnie and Benny Show didn't seem any more appropriate. Instead, I asked, "Hey, did you ever track down that guitar you were looking for?"

Paul sipped a bottle of soda and nodded. "Yeah! I am supposed to go after dinner to meet the guy who has it. If it's the right one, I'm going to offer to buy it from him."

"Do you know this guy?"

He shook his head. "I've never met him, but my buddy, Juice, vouched for him. It isn't far." He grinned and pulled a small flip phone from his pocket. "I finally got a phone today, too. If you put your number in there, I can give you a call when I have the guitar."

I smiled. "Wow, you're really moving up in the world." I picked up the phone and punched in my digits for him. "Don't be sending me booty calls with that, now."

He laughed. "But, you're the only number I've gotten so far." He laughed and tucked the phone away as the next selection of dishes were deposited in front of us.

Jacob had prepared a dozen savory dishes, four soups, and a half dozen desserts. By the time we'd gotten through them all, I was completely stuffed and having trouble enjoying anything more. I leaned back after taking a bite of a cherry tartlet and tossed my napkin atop my charger. Swallowing, I said, "I can't think of anything to say except, wow."

Paul, leaning back and patting his distended stomach, chuckled. "Yeah. I'm glad I have a little walk to help me work through all that."

Jacob and Genia returned and cleared everything from the table. Applause from the stuffed guests around the table greeted Jacob's arrival. Milo, on the other side of the table, stood and embraced him. "Jacob. Well done, my friend. This is an incredibly delicious menu." I thought I saw a glimmer of tears threatening in Jacob's eyes.

Hera stood and gave Genia a more reserved peck on the cheek. "Completely credible, I think." I was sure I saw a tear from the corner of Genia's eye.

The score cards were collected, and the guests began to mill about again. Most of them carried a steaming mug in their hands and I pursed my lips, wondering if it was a good time to corner Genia about the coffee. Given that she was surrounded by happy guests, I shook my head and decided to save it for another time.

Paul, tugging his wind breaker on as he came out of the back, caught my eye and nodded his head toward the door. I followed and we stepped out into the brisk night. "I wanted to check with you about that fight before I left."

I nodded. "Yeah, me too. I talked to Crow. He said it was just a disagreement between his and Damien's opposing goals. He wanted details of Damien's assignment, and Damien didn't want to answer any questions. It doesn't seem like they should have been fighting over it, but he swore it wasn't really serious."

Paul grunted as he zipped up his jacket. "Not serious but they came to blows in the middle of the street?"

I nodded. "That was my thought too."

"Well, Damien said about the same. He did seem surprised that we could see them."

"Yeah, Crow was distracted by that. He said he wasn't responsible either, but he has an idea about who might be. I kind of fell asleep before I could find out more."

Paul nodded and looked down the street. "I need to take off, now. Benny and Bonnie are supposed to have dinner with her folks, and I don't want to miss how that turns out." He grinned and I laughed.

"Okay, be careful and let me know what happens with guitar man." He nodded and gave me a little salute before turning away. I watched him go. He looked happy, an errant breeze picking up a wispy bit of hair on top of his head as he loped up the sidewalk. The same breeze reached me, and a chill coursed down my spine. I shivered and hoped I'd hear from him again soon.

I turned to look back through the windows and smiled to see the happy faces surrounding Jacob and Genia. The evening seemed to have gone well. *'Good. They deserve it.'* I turned away and let my steps bounce as I loped down the alley. I groaned when I reached my door and raised a hand to my head. The little itch was trying to reemerge. I spoke low, barely louder than the jingle of my keys in the lock. "Crow. I'm home now."

Crow's voice in my ear said, "I'll be there in a half hour. I hope you are feeling energetic."

I smiled and wondered what he had planned for me.

Chapter 27. The Fall

There had been no warning. He'd arrived as usual, with a bouquet of purple, bell-shaped flowers. After dressing me in a long-sleeved, pink coverall and black, steel-toed boots, he'd whisked me away. When we'd landed, it took a moment for my vision to clear and to orient myself. There was no sign of a party or event or anything that might be considered a destination activity. Instead, there was only an empty skyscraper rooftop stretching between me and a long fall.

Clinging to Crow, hating him for everything I was worth, I asked, "Why are we on top of a fourteen-story building, Crow?"

He laughed that insufferable, smug, joy-filled chortle that could only ever come at my expense. "You are perfectly safe with me, Bird." He reached behind his back and, with a flourish, brought out a pink hard hat and safety goggles. "Put these on."

I snatched the goggles with one hand, still holding his arm in a death grip with the other. He chuckled and flipped the hard hat onto my head. "Why, Crow. Why are we up here? Why are we on the very highest part of the roof?"

"We aren't on the very highest part, Bird." He twisted to point behind me.

I growled and risked a quick turn of my head. A creaky click in my neck accompanied a twinge of protest from my muscles. Without seeing whatever was behind me, I snapped my eyes shut and turned more slowly back toward him. "Crow." My voice was so full of patience, it was almost solid.

He laughed again and pulled me closer to his side. "Look, Bird."

I opened my eyes and inhaled deeply. His upward facing palm made a sweeping arc toward the horizon. We were somewhere in the world where the sun was rising. The hazy layer of smog hanging over the city skyline glowed, amber and gold. It captured my attention momentarily, interrupted by a sudden, stiff breeze that rocked me on my feet.

Crow wrapped that errant arm around me. "This is a bustling city in western India. This building is over sixty years old and is slated for demolition to make way for a new condominium development."

"Demolition? Crow? When?" The rule was that I had to at least try to enjoy whatever he planned. I was having trouble finding the fun part.

"Calm down, Bird. We have plenty of time to get you positioned." He laughed and maneuvered me directly in front of the little whatever behind me.

I sighed. *He needs me. He needs me and he wouldn't risk hurting me bad enough to lose me. Letting me get hurt so bad he has to save my life would run me off. Right? I think I would leave if my life was in danger. But if he can heal me, I'm not really in danger. Would I leave if it just hurt really badly?* My thoughts were not helpful.

He chortled, another demonically delighted sound, and asked, "Bird, don't you trust me?"

I looked up at his ecstatic expression. "No!"

He laughed again. "Yes, you do. Come on. Lift one leg like a crane." He had me put one foot up flat against the short wall behind me and magically glued it there. "Good, now, as the building begins to fall, this is going to be the last big piece to go. We are going to surf it down."

I could no longer form verbal protests. I punched him in the short ribs. An explosion sounded, reverberating up my legs, and flights of pigeons exploded from three different areas around me. Several more explosions sounded in quick succession. The far end of the roofline disappeared, followed by two- and three-foot swaths of roof rapidly closing on my position.

The solidity beneath me fell. My breath caught and my hair lifted off my neck. The solidity to which I was attached shifted, and I began to tip backward. Crow sort of hopped, and the thing attached to my foot shifted again, now pulling me downward faster than backward.

Crow beamed as he held me tight against his side. Time, or my perception of it, changed. I felt somehow outside of it, watching it flow past but not flowing with it. I watched like an observer behind my own eyes as each moment passed. With a replay of the moment before and a preview of the moment after, each moment taking too long, somehow, this felt more under control.

I began to catalogue the experience. The heavy piece of building I rode like a surfboard dragged me along with it, my hair streaming behind me. I realized my own body was virtually weightless. If I were loosed, I thought I would float in the air like a helium balloon. A rolling laugh fought its way up my throat, allowing my paralyzed lungs to begin to breathe again.

Crow's arms squeezed me. His laughter no longer seemed spiteful in my ears. Huge waves of roiling dust and debris billowed up and over us. Not yet half-way down, the debris and most of the dust cloud seemed to stop around us. I paid a brief thought to being struck by that debris if that semi-permeable barrier wasn't there to stop it.

The weightlessness extended the stomach dropping sensation, and I released Crow with one hand to place it over my own abdomen. The pressure helped, and I tried to focus on everything at once. Even slower than normal, everything was still moving too fast to take it all in.

The rumbling sound of concrete, glass, and metal landing, breaking, and piling up beneath us filled my ears. I couldn't hear my own laughter, only Crow's wild chortles. With each lung expanding breath, I smelled dry plaster dust and the faint aroma of carpet mildew. The light dust that came through Crow's debris barrier coated both of us. Each time I readjusted my grip, a silky fine layer moved under my fingers like water.

Crow's arm around my waist tightened, lifting me upward slightly as the building shard we rode collided with the bulk of the pile. The jolt of the impact accompanied the return of my body's weight. Every joint in my body, hips, spine, neck, everything, rattled with jarring force. My knees bent instinctively as the building shard changed direction. No longer heading straight down, the shard took a logarithmic turn, sliding down the side of the debris pile, and slowed.

Crow held me steady as the shard slid to a stop and he released the foot holding me there. The shard teetered at the end of its slide, unevenly balanced. Crow pulled the hardhat off my head, my hair dripping building powder in streams. I lifted the goggles over my head and looked at them, extraordinarily clean, and shook my head. More building powder fell out and I sneezed.

Crow grinned down at me and asked, "Do you want to go again?"

I found the fun. Each of the following new demolitions were as exciting as the first. At the end of the last, I grinned and shook my head, raining building dust. "I think I've had enough. My knees are wobbly, I'm filthy," I looked up and met his eyes, "and I'm hungry. I feel the need for funnel cake, caramel apples, and a huge turkey leg."

Crow pulled me close to his side and laughed. I shnuffled into his chest and sneezed at a puff of debris dust, exhilarated and high on adrenaline. As we flew, the grimy feeling of my skin and hair faded away. The coveralls changed, and the heavy boots on my feet lightened as they morphed into sneakers.

A little glow beneath us resolved into a carnival or fair as we drew closer. Squeals and laughter floated up to us with the music and noise from rides and games. Crow set us down in a darkened patch behind a ride and gave me a moment to acquaint myself with the jeans and t-shirt ensemble I wore, the same as his with a different color shirt.

Both of us had a paper bracelet on one wrist, and I frowned at it. "Unlimited rides? After surfing down falling buildings, I think it might be anti-climactic."

He smiled and took my hand. "You requested snacks."

I chuckled and let him pull me into the crowd. We found the funnel cakes first. I got one with too much sugar and cinnamon and followed Crow down the midway. He stopped at a baseball-throwing game and pointed up at the biggest, most pastel-colored stuffed squid I had ever seen. "Shall I win this for you?"

"Can't you just conjure one for me?" I stuffed another piece of sugary treat into my mouth, eyeballing the pastel Kraken.

"Of course, I could, but where is the fun in that?"

I lifted one eyebrow at him. "Okay. But you have to play fair. No demonic cheating."

He placed one hand over where his heart should be and lifted the other, palm out. "You have my word. I will not use any extra-human ability."

I shrugged and looked back at the deliciousness in my hands. "Yeah, alright. Do it."

He chuckled and approached the game counter. "How does this work?"

The bored-looking teenager behind the counter pulled three baseballs from his apron and laid them in front of Crow. "Three balls for a dollar. Just knock over all three bottles and you get a prize."

Crow nodded, placing a dollar bill on the counter, and my jaw dropped. I shook my head and stepped up, snatching the money from beneath the teen's reaching fingers. "Hang on. What size of prize?"

The teenager rolled his eyes and reached into a box at his feet. He lifted a miniature stuffed squid on a key ring. "This is the base size prize."

Crow's confounded look was priceless. I laughed and asked the teen, "How do we get that one?" I pointed a sugary finger up at the Kraken.

The teen glanced up and grunted. "Everybody always asks about that one." He shook his head and sighed. "You have to trade up." The kid went through the rules and established that it would take a perfect, one hundred twenty-six-time winning streak to acquire a single Kraken.

Crow gained an ever-increasingly perplexed expression. At the end of the kid's spiel, he turned to me and said, "It seems like many tosses of the ball but not hard. What's the trick?"

The kid gave Crow an appraising look. "It's just a way to get people to spend more money, man."

Crow turned on him. "Yes, of course it is, but it doesn't seem very crafty. I thought these games were supposed to be harder than they seemed."

I chuckled. "Here, hold my funnel cake." I shoved the mostly empty plate at Crow's chest, dusting him with sugar. I handed Crow's dollar bill to the kid and he stepped back. I picked up the balls, turned, and lined up my pitch. With a slight rocking motion and both elbows up, I unleashed the hardest, fastest pitch I could. To my great surprise, I hit the bottles squarely in the center of the little pyramid. They wobbled but stayed firmly upright.

The kid snorted and Crow let out a long, "Ahh." He stepped up and took the other two balls from me, exchanging them for my plate. "I understand now. I can do this." His first ball missed.

The kid laughed, earning him a tight look from Crow. The kid held up both hands and cleared his throat. "Nah, man. Sorry. No offense. Try your last ball."

Crow bounced the ball on his palm and pursed his lips. Carefully lining up his pitch, Crow threw again. The ball arced and landed atop the bottles before rolling off.

The kid snorted again and stepped forward. "Okay, okay. Here, try again." He laid three more balls atop the counter. "No charge, and I'll give you the next size up if you win."

Crow narrowed his eyes at the teen. "Okay, but how about I pay you for this set, and you give me the next size up from that for every game I win?" That's when I caught on. Five one-dollar bills later, I had a Kraken tucked under one arm and a caramel apple on a stick in the other hand.

We wandered through the noise, lights, and people, eventually finding a turkey leg to share, until my adrenaline high faded, leaving me exhausted. Crow gathered me and the Kraken in his arms for the flight home, and I watched the lights of the world flow past.

As my feet settled onto the carpet of my living room, Crow gave me a quick squeeze before letting go and stepping back. We shared a grin and I spun away, dancing across the floor with my Kraken, around my little table, and back to flop onto my couch. I folded my arms around the Kraken, hugging it close and let my head fall back.

Crow completed his circuit and joined me, sitting close and urging me to cuddle into his side under his arm. "I hope you enjoyed yourself, Bird."

"I did!" I wriggled until I could crane my neck up at him. "I have been getting more and more emotional surges. I think I'm going to need a purge soon."

"Has Paul accepted the offer?" Crow lifted his free hand to stroke my hair.

"Not specifically. He's very invested in the mark, though. I think he really likes that life." A blue flash caught my eye and I struggled free of Crow's embrace. "I can't believe it. You let me leave my phone here?"

Crow chuckled. "I did not know it was my responsibility to tell you to take it. Should packing your phone not be one of the things you do while preparing for a date night?"

I adjusted my grip on the Kraken under my arm and waved at him to shush. "I have a voice mail. It could be work." I pressed a button and held the phone up to listen.

Hello. This is Nurse Hoffner at Chester City Regional Hospital. A man was brought in this evening with no identification. We got this number from his cell phone... I stopped listening.

There I was, flushed with excitement and the happy hangover of too much fun, a pastel-colored, stuffed Kraken under one arm, its tentacles dangling and trailing behind me, as I listened to a message from a hospital. In that moment, I felt like I deserved every bad thing that had ever happened to me.

I turned to Crow and said, "Paul has been taken to the hospital." I dropped the Kraken and put the phone on speaker to replay the message.

Hello. This is nurse Hoffner at Chester City Regional Hospital. A man was brought in this evening with no identification. We got this number from his cell phone and were hoping you could come down. If you can help us identify him, we can discuss his condition and treatment.

The message gave the hospital phone number and the floor number we should go to when we arrived.

I turned to where Crow still sat, passively listening to the message. "Do you know what happened? Is Paul okay?"

Crow stood and clapped his hands together. "Well, I can tell you he is in bad shape, but he isn't dead yet."

My re-surfacing emotions roiled in my stomach, and I wanted to lash out. He was so smug and chipper. But, this was the whole point of our deal. We knew it was coming. As Crow had pointed out when Madelyn had come back with Sonya's body, I should be happy. I was going to be allowed to purge.

I turned away from him and opened my contacts list. I called Genia, woke her, and told her about the call from the hospital. "I don't know what his condition is or anything. They didn't even say it was Paul, but he is the only person I know whose only phone contact is me."

After her initial shock, I could hear her bustling, moving, and waking Jacob. "They left a message? Were you asleep? What time did they call?"

"No, I was out and didn't hear the phone. I don't know." I pulled the phone from my ear and tried to find the date stamp on the missed call. I decided half-way through the process that it wasn't important and pressed the phone back to my ear. "I can be at the hospital in just a few minutes. Meet me there?"

"Yes! Go! I'll call Adrya and Ellie on the way." She hung up abruptly and I blinked at the phone a few times.

Crow stepped closer to me and held out his arms. "Shall we?"

Chapter 28. Life Choices

We arrived at the hospital, Crow materializing us inside an empty elevator, which we rode up and stepped out onto the orthopedic ward. I turned my frazzled gaze back and forth, trying to determine where and how to get answers. Donna pushed upright from the wall she'd been leaning against. "Hey, Boss. Star. He's this way. You can check in with Hoffner at the station."

Crow took me in his ushering grip, one hand under my elbow and the other on my waist. Donna peeled off without a goodbye as we approached the nurses' station. A young man with a charming smile looked up at Crow's approach. "Can I help you?"

I shoved Crow over with my hip. "I'm Starling Nightcastle. I got a call about a friend of mine. Nurse Hoffner..."

An older woman behind the male nurse stood. "Hi, I'm Nurse Hoffner. I wasn't sure we would see you tonight."

I scowled at the implication that I would blow off a call like that. I inhaled deep enough to ensure a good volume could be maintained through the entirety of the tirade I intended to unleash. Crow pulled me back, forcing most of that breath out with an arm around my middle.

He said, "We were traveling and only just got the message. We believe the patient you called about may be our friend, Paul."

Crow handled the nurses and, finally, we were led down the hall to a dark room. The nurse flicked on a single light, and I pushed past her. "That's him. Paul? Can you hear me?" I hoped very much that he could not. A cast covered the lower half of one leg. Another wrapped around his ribs. Even his head was wrapped in gauze and covered with a thin beanie hat device. His eyes and half of his jaw were swollen and purple.

"Is there anyone else we should call on his behalf?" The nurse crossed her hands at her waist with vast and obvious patience.

"I already called them." I gingerly lifted one of Paul's hands in mine and asked, "What happened?"

The nurse sighed and shook her head. "The best we can tell, he got mugged."

"Mugged?" I shook my head and frowned, watching Paul's chest rise and fall slowly. "The mugger didn't take his phone?"

The nurse chuckled softly. "No. They didn't take that, either." She nodded to a far corner.

I glanced where she indicated and saw a large, tatty guitar case. It was black with numerous rips and scars in its surface. An equal number of long bumper stickers were wrapped around its sides, and I thought it was completely conceivable they were the only things holding it together. I grunted a half-hearted chuckle. "He got the guitar."

"What's that?" The nurse was too loud. I flinched and turned Gaze of Fury on her.

Crow stepped forward and touched the nurse's elbow. "Is there paperwork I can fill out for you?"

I gave him a grateful look and turned back to Paul as Crow escorted the wretch out. "Paul, I hope you can't hear me. I hope you're completely oblivious, dreaming about coffee or whatever Benny and Bonnie are up to. Even doing dishes is a better dream than what waits for you out here."

My mind swirled with old emotions and memories from hospital scenes of my past. They pasted themselves like a collage atop all the thoughts and feelings of this hospital scene. Paul's beefy hand encompassed between my own felt too cold.

Crow reappeared at the door. "Bird? What is wrong?"

I glanced at him and realized I was crying. I shook my head and resumed watching Paul breathe. "I don't know. Maybe I got too close to him. Maybe I need a purge." I shrugged.

Crow hummed and found a chair. He sat and laid a clipboard on his crossed knees. "I have Donna watching for the others."

"Thanks." I cringed at the thought of the two EM demons hovering like vultures. The scritch-scritch of a pen on paper made me look at Crow again. "Are you actually manually filling out that stuff?"

Crow hummed again. "Oh, yes. I quite enjoy the feel of making a mark with indelible ink on paper."

'Weird demon.' I lost track of time trying to ignore my thoughts and willing Paul to keep breathing. I heard Genia and Jacob's voices in the hall before I saw them. At first, I thought I might just ignore them and keep concentrating on Paul. Some tiny, irrational part of me argued that, as long as I willed it, he would keep breathing. In my world, where a demon gave me gills, took me demolition surfing, and swapped souls, maybe it was completely rational to think I could magically keep Paul breathing.

When Genia came to stand behind me, chafing my shoulders and crooning her sadness and prayers for Paul's recovery, I couldn't take it. Maybe on the day after a purge I would be able to listen to the sadness and navigate my own. *'Not today.'* I gave Paul's hand one last squeeze, stood, and pulled my fingers from his. I rested his hand at his side and patted it before stepping back.

Genia took my vacated seat on the edge of the mattress as the heart monitor began to beep irregularly. Jacob turned to the door to welcome Adrya and Ellie in. Crow pulled me back beside him against the wall.

The heart monitor flatlined. Genia cried out in a wordless wail. Jacob, Adrya, and Ellie rushed forward like a crashing wave. Crow tugged me out into the hall.

Nurse Hoffner and several others I didn't recognize came barreling down the hall and into Paul's room. Jacob came out a few moments later, herding the sobbing women ahead of him. Genia saw me and grabbed me by the arm. She pulled me in with Adrya and Ellie, their outstretched arms swallowing me into their emotional support structure.

I don't know how long we stood like that. In my mind, my sobs and wails matched anything the other three could produce combined. In reality, I had trouble simply breathing, straining to hear the crash team working. I knew it was over when I saw Donna and Pete hovering a few doors down with a gurney. Hoffner confirmed it when she stormed out of the room and threw her stethoscope at the wall as she disappeared around a corner.

I pulled free of the teary tangle and turned to Crow. I pressed my face into his shoulder and spoke too low to be heard by anyone else. "He's gone?"

"Not quite." He shifted me to see Donna and Pete wheeling the gurney toward Paul's room.

The young male nurse stepped out to speak with us and I buried my face back into Crow's shoulder. I didn't want to listen. Nothing he said would change the bottom line. Paul had died, and sometime in or before that moment, he had taken the deal.

*****

A hurricane of mixed emotions decimated the landscape of my fragile mind all the way back to my apartment. Crow settled me onto the couch, clutching the guitar in my arms like a surrogate for Paul. He sat on the coffee table in front of me, his hands on my knees. "Bird? We need to go soon."

It had taken almost an hour for the on-call doctor to approve the release of Paul's body. When we left, Donna and Pete were busy wrapping him up. I estimated how long it would take them to arrive at the morgue. "I don't want to be there when they drop him off." My voice quavered and broke.

Crow, with remarkable patience, nodded and patted my knees. "It will all feel much better once the swap is complete. We can wait a few more minutes."

I nodded and closed my eyes. Rocking gently with the guitar case upright in my lap, I lost track of time again. I kept replaying my interactions with Paul since that first morning in the park. He'd had so many close calls, and this guitar had been his undoing. I suddenly needed to see the thing.

I shot to my feet and startled Crow. I stepped around him, ignoring his noises, and kicked the Kraken out of my way. I had to kick its tentacles separately. Kneeling between the obscenely happy Kraken and the coffee table, I laid the case on the floor. I knelt there, running my hands along the rim of the lid, until I found and flipped open all of the latches. The lid of the case was sturdier than I had expected, not wobbling or bending at all on its hinges.

Inside, nestled into soft, golden felt lining, a beautiful old acoustic twelve-string gleamed. The body was a soft yellow wood with a natural-looking finish. The pickguard and tuning pegs were a darker wood. The strings gleamed, inviting me to pluck them. I reached toward them and stopped. I didn't want to hear it.

I slammed the lid back down, suddenly angry, and stood, rounding on Crow. "I'm ready."

*****

Neville's favorite 80s pop music blared from the luau speakers in the cold room when we arrived. Pete and Donna were still there, each with a bottle of tea in one hand. Donna rested her free hand too far up Neville's thigh as she traded banter with him. No one gave any hint they saw us. Crow drew me by my hand across the cold room floor to a gurney staged against the far wall. He unzipped the HRB and stepped back.

'Here we go.'

"Wake up, Paul," Crow commanded.

Paul's eyes fluttered open. At first, he only moved his eyes, scanning the ceiling and our faces. With a smile twisted by the swelling in his jaw, he tried to speak.

Crow frowned and touched two fingers to his cheek. The purple swelling subsided, and he said, "That's better. Try again."

I gave Crow a long look. *Did he just heal Paul's corpse?* Paul worked his jaw and winced. *Okay, not healed, just improved.*

Paul sat up. "I wasn't sure it would work. Even after the dreams and Damien telling me it would, I really didn't believe it."

"Have you considered my offer?" Crow asked.

Paul nodded. "Yeah, I guess I'm gonna' take you up on it."

Crow looked to me. I frowned, sighing, and stepped forward. "Paul, we need to be sure that you understand what you are doing."

He smiled. "Hey, Ms. Star. I understand it alright. I'm about to go kill Benny and help Bonnie build their lives up better. I know."

"You are sure you understand his demons and you're ready to stand against them?" A lump formed in my throat. Everything about this felt completely wrong.

"I think I understand Benny better than Bonnie does. His demons aren't nearly as big as mine. He just needs to slow down, see the bad with the good, find what in his life needs some elbow grease, and do the work." He inhaled, straining against the cast over his ribs. He winced. "Yeah, I can do this. Let's go."

I had three and a half minutes left to try to talk him out of it, but this talk had never changed anyone's mind. Crow only gave it to me in the beginning because I couldn't believe it was pointless. Then, there was Paul, a good guy, someone I liked and had rooted for, and I wasn't going to take the whole five minutes with him any more than I had with Madelyn.

Crow was right. It was pointless.

Chapter 29. Change of Plans

We flew in our astral forms through the tarry black of deep night. Crow's winged, bird-shape was an inky splotch between me and the few scattered light sources on the other side of him. Paul's ghost rolled and wiggled as it was carried along beneath us. I almost smiled, thinking how much it looked like he was enjoying even this experience.

The squat little house in its neatly manicured yard took shape beneath us, expanding in our field of vision as Crow lowered us into the bedroom. The darkness was broken by the light of a streetlamp glowing through the window, falling full upon Bonnie's peaceful, blissfully ignorant face. Benny, his pillow curled under his chest, faced almost straight down into the mattress.

'Great. The fool is going to smother himself before we get to make the swap. If he does, can I use Benny's body to purge? Will Paul still be condemned even if he was deprived of the opportunity to follow through?' Benny snorted and rolled over. *'Nevermind. He's fine.'*

Paul's ghost hovered over Benny's sleeping form. A beatific look softened his ghostly features as he studied one, then the other. Crow reached out to make the swap.

Paul pulled back. "Damien!"

Crow snatched his hand back. "What are you doing?"

A bright white flash, so fast it could have been my imagination, announced Damien's arrival. He stood on the other side of the bed and tugged Paul's ghost back beside him. "You called, Paul?"

I should have heard my teeth click together as I snapped my hanging jaw closed. I shook my astral head. "Paul, what's happening?"

Paul frowned sadly. "I'm sorry, Ms. Star. I can't do it. I know it's important to you, but I can't." He looked down at the sleeping couple. "I love them."

Damien laid a hand on Paul's shoulder. "What would you like to do now, Paul?"

"I want to talk to Benny."

Crow took a step forward, the air seeming to vibrate with his fury. "Unacceptable! You can't..."

"Be silent, Demon." Damien didn't raise his voice or move or change his posture. He simply looked into Crow's eyes and told him to shut up. "This is a matter of Free Will."

"He's dead! He doesn't have Free Will anymore." Crow snarled, his man-mouth distorting with the sound.

I almost held up a finger and said, *'Actually.'*

Damien beat me to it. Finger raised, he said, "Actually, you have created an extra-temporal pocket in which Paul is both alive and dead. For as long as he remains in this pocket, he has the right to every advantage of Free Will."

'I knew that. You told me that years ago. Come on, Crow. Get with the program.' I should not have been so amused.

The horrid smirk that slid across Crow's face may have been the least attractive thing I have ever seen. "Then he will need to be ejected."

Damien's finger went up again. "Actually, you may have the power to create and destroy these pockets; however, so do I. I am holding this one, now, as my human client has called for my aid."

I looked to Paul. He was still studying the peacefully sleeping Benny and Bonnie. I might almost have called the look on his face fatherly. "Did you plan this the whole time?"

Paul turned to me. "Oh, no, Ms. Star. Damien had told me that I could call him if I changed my mind, but I really didn't think about it until I was here, looking at them. I promise."

My mouth twitched in a half-smile. "You love them?"

He looked down at them again. "How can I not?" He turned back to Damien. "I just need a minute to talk to Benny."

A tempest of anger spilled off Crow, assaulting my astral skin and hair. I wasn't sure what was happening. I knew Crow was pissed, and if he could find a way to regain control, he would try. At that moment, he had no options. I silently urged Damien and Paul to pick up the pace a little before Crow thought of something.

Damien touched Benny's forehead and made an upward sweeping motion, calling Benny out. Benny's ghost coalesced at the foot of the bed. A glittering silver umbilical of spirit still tethered him to his body. For a long moment after his ghost materialized, Benny stared at his own sleeping form, face implacable and calm. His gaze shifted to his wife and his face began to crumble. "Bonnie, mi amor. ¡Mi amor! No quiero dejarte. Seré mejor, me convertiré en lo que necesitas. No quiero morir. ¡Escúchame!" His ghostly sobs sounded breathy and insubstantial.

Paul stepped nearer and Benny finally saw the rest of us. He jumped, crouching as if to run, as Paul stopped his approach. "Benny. You are not dying. Not right now. I'm here to help you."

Damien narrowed his eyes at Crow and threw one hand up, palm out, toward us. They disappeared from my awareness. Apparently, they disappeared from Crow's as well. He threw his head back and screeched, one long, gritty, guttural cry. The shock wave knocked me back into the dresser. My astral form didn't feel any pain from the impact, nor did it produce any damage to the solid piece of furniture. That didn't make it any less terrifying.

Crow's form wavered, grew, distorted, and finally snapped back into his familiar man-shape. I pushed away from the dresser and took two slow steps toward him. "Crow? Are you okay?"

He rounded on me, meeting my eyes with a furious glare that stopped me in my tracks. "Yes, Star, I'm fine. Don't I look fine?" His voice dripped with contempt and sarcasm. He stepped forward, his demeanor like that of an angry bear. Each slow step seemed to involve the articulation of his whole body.

I skittered backward. "Nope. You look pretty upset."

He stopped. He lowered his head and, as he raised it again, he straightened his spine and put back his shoulders. In a tight, soft monotone, he said, "I apologize, Bird. This is not your fault. None of this is your fault. Come. I will take you home."

I nodded, looking him up and down. He was himself again. I sighed and joined him, letting him fly me back to my apartment. He settled me back into my body, still standing there in my living room. He turned to make his circuit around the perimeter before I had fully regained awareness of my surroundings. I turned in place, looking for him.

His normal, measured glide was like a bird soaring on air currents. That night, as he came out of my bathroom, he rebounded off the door jamb of my bedroom and hurtled through the kitchen. I jumped as he gave the brushed steel door of the refrigerator a thump with the side of his fist. He growled as he slowed and turned toward me.

I swallowed, hard, but held my ground as he approached. "Crow? Do you want to have a shower or something to eat?"

"No! I don't want to play human boyfriend tonight."

"How can I help?"

"You can't. You have one purpose in this arrangement, and that is not useful, now." He turned his back on me. I watched his shoulders and back heave as he, once again, reined himself in. "I have to go."

"Okay." Stinging tears welled up, obscuring my vision. "Is this the end of our deal?" My voice broke and the tears spilled out.

He hung his head and sighed audibly. When he turned back to face me again, he gave me a more tender look, the fury sitting just beneath the surface. "That is not what I want, Bird. I will be back before you wake up tonight. Right now, I must go."

He stepped close and lifted a hand to the back of my neck. Drawing my head closer to him, he kissed my forehead and released me. I spun in place, looking for him, but he had gone.

It took me the better part of half an hour to pack all the roiling emotions away; tucked into a deep, dark box on a high shelf to one side of my mind. I spent another half-hour finding and putting away little bits of those emotions still scattered here and there in my thoughts. Finally, my thoughts cleared enough to line up for observation.

It was the strangest resurgence I had ever experienced. I felt it all, pain, sorrow, regret, joy, gratitude, all of it, old and new, swirled around in my head just like every other time. Except, this time, it only took an hour for me to feel stable and functional.

I walked into the kitchen and set a pot of coffee brewing. I was exhausted but not sleepy. My body felt heavy, and my eyes stung like they should be red and swollen. A look in the bathroom mirror assured me they were neither. I washed my face anyway. It helped some. The sound of the coffee pot's ending burble helped more.

I poured a cup and folded myself onto the end of my couch. The light from my terrarium glowed soft and warm over my shoulder in the otherwise dark space. I lifted my cup in front of my lips and gently blew over the top. As the steam tendrils parted, I froze, locked in the gaze of a pair of pastel-colored eyes.

The Kraken lay curled on its side, its cartoon smile turning predatory at that angle. I followed its imagined gaze to the guitar case on the floor between us. Paul was still dead.

Whatever else had happened that night, good or bad, my friend was gone. I sipped my coffee and felt an upwelling in my chest. He really had been my friend, even if he had never thought of me in the same way. I was going to miss our walks each night. I would miss chatting with him. I was going to miss the inspirational way he enjoyed the most mundane chores. Who was I ever likely to meet again with that beautiful spirit of gratitude?

My phone rang. I groaned and sat my cup on the coffee table. Sniffling and wiping at my face, I answered the phone. "Hullo?" So what if they could tell I was crying. People were supposed to be allowed to cry when their friend died.

"Star?" Neville's voice surprised me.

"Neville? What's wrong?" I pulled the phone away to glance at the time. *'3:00 AM. Nothing good ever comes from a phone call at 3:00 AM'*

"Nothing, Boss. Um, well, sort of." He made a noise something like a chuckle. "It's the damndest thing. I know there are case studies of it happening, but I've never seen it."

"Neville!" I snapped and immediately regretted it. "Neville. What happened?"

"Sorry." I rolled my eyes as he exhaled into the phone. "There's a guy here. He says he knows you."

I reminded myself not to shout again. "And?"

"He's one of the villagers. Stone cold a couple of hours ago, just now, he sat up and asked if you would come get him. His name is Paul."

*****

When I got to the morgue, I stepped through the cold room door and skidded to a halt. Paul was wearing my discarded Hawaiian print shirt, sipping a cup of Ranier Red, and lounging on a gurney with a lab coat over his lap. Neville had rolled the desk chair out and sat nearby, chatting with him.

"Paul!" I gaped. I'm not sure there was a more appropriate response I could have come up with at the time. I stood there far too long, taking in the healthy flush of his cheeks, all signs of the bruising and swelling gone. "Paul?" He laughed and didn't seem to be in pain, so whatever miracle had brought him back and healed his face must have helped those broken ribs too. "You're alive!" I launched myself at him.

Neville stepped between us and caught me, loosely in one arm. "Whoa, down there, Boss. I've been trying to get him to let me take him back for scans; the ones the hospital sent over showed some serious fractures. Maybe let's not rough him up until we can take a look?"

I lowered my eyes to the arm still wrapped around my waist and back up to Neville's face. *There's that pretty little blush.*

"Unhand me."

Neville pulled his arm back like I'd suddenly burst into flame. "Sorry."

"It's fine. Don't do it again. Et cetera." I waved him away and closed the gap between me and Paul. "Can I hug you?"

"You'd better!" He pulled me in with his free arm and I tried to keep too much pressure from any one spot.

When he finally released me, I looked him over again from head to toe. "Paul, we really should get the scans. If there is something else going on, we could lose you before the hospital has a chance to even check."

Neville stepped up and took the coffee cup from Paul's hand. "See? I told you. You said if she said you needed it, you would do it."

Paul gave the most convincing long-suffering sigh I've ever heard but relented. I turned to Neville, "I'll take him. You stay in here and do your normal work things." I didn't sound terribly bossly but I didn't care.

I wheeled Paul down the hall and positioned him the best I could without getting out the sling. "These are pretty intensive scans, so they take a while. I'll just program it for x-rays and maybe a CT."

Paul reached up and laid a hand on my shoulder. "Ms. Star, I'm fine. Damien said I might have some bruises left on my ribs and I'm going to have to just deal with the broken leg healing on its own. Everything else, though, Mr. Crow healed me up when I was dead."

I goggled. Crow was going to shit pitchforks. "Then, I'm hugging you properly." I was never much for hugs. They tend to put one's back in perfect stabbing position. But Paul was getting a hug.

When I straightened, having failed to elicit any cries of pain, I cleared my throat and sniffled. "Okay, I believe you, but I'm still running the scans. Then, I'm going to call us a cab, and we're going back to my apartment. Damien can come get you from there if you want."

Paul grumped at my retreating back. "I really don't need any scans. I'm fine, I swear."

"I know. You have to have them anyway." I punched in a short series of x-rays and one CT aimed at his head.

"Why, though?" Paul continued to protest from inside the room.

"Firstly, I don't know anything about angel medicine. How do we know Damien has any idea what a human body is supposed to look like?" I watched as the first series resolved on the monitor.

"He's an angel. I'm pretty sure they learn the blueprint for humans in angel college."

I chuckled and nodded, pleased with the scan clarity. That was good because I wasn't sure I could argue Paul into letting me start over. I raised my voice. "Okay, say he's right and you're fine," which seemed to be the case, based on the x-rays, "I have to contact the hospital to let them know you are not, in fact, dead. They are going to require scans."

"So, let them do them."

"Our machines are better and faster. Hold still." I waited for the last scan to complete and resolve on the monitor.

"For how long? You know, if I hadn't asked him to call you, I wouldn't be having this argument."

I grinned and walked back into the scan room. "And now you no longer are. Scans done."

He gave me a drop-jawed look of disbelief. "You sneaky little ..."

I unlocked the wheels on his gurney and pushed him toward the cold room. "You are doing great. Everything came back clear except for a little clean fracture in that leg."

"So, I can walk?"

"Nope. Not without crutches."

Neville met me at the office doorway with my mug, full of decadent deliciousness. "Thank you. Given the circumstances, I will overlook the coffee in the cold room, but don't do it again."

Neville chuckled and winked over my head at Paul. "Yes, Boss. Absolutely, special circumstances."

I took a long pull from my mug and set it down on the desk. "I need to go find a set of crutches from the junk closet. Can you call us a cab?"

"I'm off in about ten minutes and everything is finished here. Why don't I just drive you?" Neville shed his lab coat and walked it out to the hooks.

I walked past him toward the scan room. "You don't have to do that. A cab will be fine." I ignored his deep-voiced mutters and kept walking.

At the end of the hall, past the scan room, I pulled open the old, wooden door to the junk room. So-called because everything in it was covered in dust and, even if it were still in good working order, most of it would be obsolete. Old sets of crutches and walkers and such were among the items I knew had been tossed in there years ago.

I stepped inside and flicked on the lights. I spotted the crutches I was looking for right away. I spent another five minutes burrowing a path through the center of the room to reach them. My cheeks began to ache, and I realized I was smiling and had been for some time. After everything I'd been through that night, I didn't care. I would care deeply at some point, but not right then.

I reached the crutches and tugged one free. Twisting at the waist, I hefted the thing in one hand and launched it back toward the still open door like a spear. My aim was true, and it sailed out into the hallway, clattering on the tile floor and skidding several feet. I took a moment to be slightly impressed with myself before turning back to the task of pulling the second crutch free.

Someone, at some point, had made the genius decision to lift an old table of some kind onto the top of the pile. One of the legs had gotten pushed through the frame of the crutch. The crutch itself had been shoved into another hole. It was a slow game of pull-the-peg to release each structural link in the tangle. With a triumphant "A-ha!" I flipped the table onto its side and finally released the crutch. I held it aloft in both hands, eyes closed, face split in a grin, and turned slowly to the imagined roar of a crowd shouting my praise. I was doing well with the imaginary fans that night.

Completing the turn, I lowered the crutch and looked down, preparing to step over the junk. When I looked up, a reaper stood there in the doorway like an ink spill, almost soaking up the light. My whole body spasmed like I'd been tapped with a live wire. The foot hovering in front of me to take another step kicked like it was grinding gears on its way to reverse. I stumbled and, if not for the crutch lending me support, I might have fallen backwards.

Finally overcoming the initial startlement, I pressed a hand to my chest and breathed deeply. I squinted down at the reaper who had, in turn, cocked their head to one side and was squinting back at me. I sucked in a lungful of air and plastered a professional smile on my face. With a wobbly bow, I said, "Master Reaper. To what do I owe the honor?" If Crow had taught me anything, it was to be respectful of the reapers.

The reaper looked me up and down before stepping forward and reaching out toward me. "Hello, Starling. May I give you a hand?"

I frowned but took the offered hand and clambered down the junk pile. "Thanks. So, how can I help you?"

"I am here to offer you aid, in fact." The reaper preceded me through the doorway and turned. It was the first time I had ever seen a reaper smile and I, the demon tool, thought it was creepy.

I flicked off the junk room light, followed them out, and retrieved the other crutch from where it lay a few feet further on. Giving my hair a toss out of my face as I straightened, I turned back to the reaper. "Is there any way we can talk about whatever this is tomorrow? I have to go celebrate and just be happy right now."

"No. This is time sensitive. The reaper schedule takes precedence." Their smile became amused, and even more creepy.

I turned my back on them. "Right." I took one step and came up short. The reaper, no longer smiling, occupied the space my next step needed. "Jesus!" I gave back the step I had taken. "Alright! What do you want?"

The reaper sat, some invisible surface availing itself to catch their bum. "Paul is alive. Crow," the reaper said his name with a sour twist, "healed most of his injuries. Damien reattached the soul to an intact body; therefore, Paul gets to live."

"I'm super happy Paul is okay; joyful even, but Crow is pissed, and finding out he's responsible for healing Paul isn't likely to make him happier. I want to dwell on this joy a little while." I paused there. I remember thinking about how annoying all these extra-human folks were becoming. I had been emotionally yanked one way, then the other, covering the full range, without pause, in the last twelve hours.

The reaper's expression remained flat and neutral, giving nothing away, even as they pushed the hood of their robe back. This one's body appeared to belong to a fan of the Spice Girls. I suppressed an inappropriately timed giggle at the thought of "Reaper Spice" joining the band reunion tour.

I folded my legs beneath me and sat on the floor, laying the crutches down beside me. "Okay, I'm listening. What is so hell fire important that it can't wait until I've had a chance to catch my emotional breath?" My voice was beginning to gain volume by the end.

The reaper returned the small, businesslike smile to their face. "You were deprived a purge by the survival of your friend. Have you considered what this means for you?"

I licked my lips, suddenly very aware of the emotional rapids I had been paddling across all night. "I'm trying not to think about it too hard until I have the chance..." I trailed off.

'Until what?' I had no purge vessel. The only option was letting Crow help me suppress it until we could sign another client.

The reaper leaned toward me. "Tell me, Starling. How do you feel?"

Epilogue 1. Crow

You may call me, Crow Corvus.

I leaned heavily against the side of the stone archway at the top of the stairs. Donna and Pete were handily tied up with their day jobs for some time yet, and the injury would be healed well before they arrived. I called a stone handrail up from the balcony floor and groped my way to the bench seat on the other side. As I settled onto the cool, hard surface, I dismissed the handrail and allowed my aspect to relax.

You may think of it as akin to unbuttoning your trousers after an indulgent meal. Nothing comes out that wasn't already there, it is simply no longer stuffed into a shape of submission. I am not fond of being the submissive in any dynamic. Over the eons, there have, of course, been times when it was appropriate; short times. There and then was not one of them.

I laid supine upon the bench and stretched, keeping one hand over my wound. Positioned just above my left hip, the cretin had gored me all the way to the bone. I'd snapped his horn off and left him bleeding out for the trouble. His minions probably arrived in time to save him. Still, the fool had told me what I needed to know. They hadn't gotten to Star. Not yet.

My Little Bird. When, at first, I'd been assigned as her personal demon, I had not been impressed. She did not seem like much of a challenge. Unable to see her uniqueness for many years afterward, I neglected her, in truth, and had not harbored much hope for her potential as a mark or an asset, until her ninth year in this life. Since then, she had become a treasured prize. One which had gained me great prestige. One I was not prepared to lose, even in death.

I closed my eyes and concentrated on the wound. I couldn't heal myself the way I could heal The Flesh, but, with the relaxation of my aspect, I could send more of my energy to the task. It was a boring half-hour, as convalescing tends to be, for which I compensated with a little indulgent voyeurism.

Donna and Pete arrived just after the climax of the display, stepping out onto the balcony in typical oblivious form. They saw the display models first and made appreciative noises as the models cleaned up their messes and left. When they turned their attention back to me, the ridiculous human-demons both paled and scurried to their seats. Human-demons, while useful tools, are still human and, therefore, easily cowed. As I had not yet re-asserted my usual aspect, the sight of me in something close to my true form was satisfactorily intimidating without a single, overt act on my part.

I sighed and tensed my aspect, conforming to the mediocre, male, human appearance with which they were most functional. "Welcome. First, well done and good work on the Ides of March. I expect suggestions and ideas from each of you for at least four more events before year's end."

"Thanks, Boss. I'm working the kinks out of a couple of ideas now. I should be ready to present at least the first by next month." Pete leaned back on the bench and laid his arms out to either side of him along the top of the back rest.

"I'm hoping to work some kinks into mine." Donna guffawed and sipped some fruity frozen thing that smelled of kerosene.

Pete snorted and narrowed his eyes. "Actually, I was thinking about more holiday inspired events. What do you think about something to do with Mother's Day?"

I donned one of my bossliest, toothy grins. "That is an interesting concept. Let me know when you are ready to present a complete outline."

Donna pursed her lips and looked down into her drink.

Pete said, "You got it, Boss."

I tele-conjured an order for general refreshments from the bar with a flick of my fingers and turned to the next topic. "Now, how is the seduction of the new coroner coming along?"

Donna perked up, her sultry smile brightening her otherwise common aspect. "Neville? It's going well, I think. I began with very forward flirting and made sure he knew I was interested. It's only been a few days, but he seems to enjoy my advances. I think he's going to counter-propose a date soon."

"There haven't been any problems with his interest in my Little Bird to deter him?"

"Of course, there were, but she's oblivious to him. A few well-placed reminders that she is his boss and doesn't see him as a man were enough to hose out that spark." Donna stuck her straw between her teeth and sipped through a toothy grin of her own.

Since her reassignment to my retinue, she had developed necessary new skills quickly, but seduction and beguilement would always be her singular talent. "Wonderful. Keep me updated." She nodded and visibly relaxed.

I turned to Pete. "How is your new trainee working out? It's your first since that unfortunate incident in Hawaii, is it not? Is there any cause for concern with young Gail?"

Pete shook his head and crossed his arms over his chest. "I don't think so, no. She's got good instincts. She's using her family and oldest friends as homework subjects. So far, I'm pleased with her progress."

"You are certain she hasn't slipped up around my Little Bird?"

"Yes, absolutely certain. Gail likes Star. She's glad you have the nondisclosure rule in place. She wants to befriend her."

"A friendship?" I scowled.

"Limited, of course. There will have to be a little distance between them. Boss to subordinate, you know?"

"Make sure of it."

"I'm on it, Boss."

Epilogue 2. Damien

My Name is-Dami'el, but you may call me Damien.

I took Paul home Sunday morning, and he led the way inside, propping the cased guitar in one corner and his crutches against one arm of his second-hand sofa. Taking a seat beside them, he said, "Thanks for the lift home and everything else last night."

I perched rigidly at the other end of the sofa. I'm not generally comfortable making use of human implements, but I do try. "I am pleased. The outcome was better than I could have hoped."

"Good." Paul yawned. "Sorry, man. I know I've been dead or unconscious most of the night, but I'm really tired."

I nodded with a small smile. "Of course. I will get to my points. I'd like to discuss your future."

Paul grinned. "Now that I have one, I would too. How long do I have?"

I gave a short shake of my head. "That is unclear. You have been given a second chance, but just like with your first one, it doesn't come with any guarantees."

"Is there anything I can do to insure myself?"

"Perhaps." I studied Paul through squinted eyes for a moment. "How familiar are you with amygdala enlargement syndrome?"

Paul raised one hand to scrub his eyes and yawned. "I've never heard of it. What is it?" He blinked and met my eyes again.

"It is complex and unpleasant and extremely difficult to treat with modern means. It is the condition Starling lives with. It is the condition that makes her susceptible to Crow's manipulations."

"That's awful. What can we do?"

I nodded and let the corners of my mouth turn upward. "We can offer her an option."

"What kind of option?" Paul turned his head to verify the guitar was still safely propped up.

I said, "She needs a new way to deal with her overwhelming emotions and keep them under control."

"Well, of course, she does, but what kind of option?"

Paul's furrowed mask of confusion grew distracting, with all of the deep ridges and shadows of flesh. I looked away and said, "Crow's deal with her has buffered her from most of the emotional turmoil she would otherwise face. However, it is the goal of the angels to help her to face her emotions and learn to master them."

Paul chuckled. "You know, Damien, what Crow does for Ms. Star is like morphine for her feelings. She's a junkie. You're talking about making her quit and go through withdrawal."

I stood. "That is an apt analogy. One that I sincerely wish you will not share with Starling." I glanced toward Paul out of the corner of my eye.

Paul grinned and waved one hand at me. "Yeah, ye..." His speech cut off in another yawn.

I began to pace the short length of the little apartment. "We believe we can provide a buffer, a flow rate valve, if you will, to allow her to process her emotional chaos internally rather than requiring an external purge."

Paul lifted his chin and frowned. "What? How is that better? Wouldn't an angelic buffer be the same thing as Crow's purges?"

"No. This is vastly different." I suppressed a sigh as I turned to begin my third lap and tried to find the right words to alleviate his fears. "We are not trying to manipulate her or have her manipulate anyone else. This is purely an option for her benefit. We are giving her the opportunity to learn to process her emotional condition on her own. When she completes the course, she will be free of her dependence on Crow."

The sparks of Paul's thought process showed as twitchy cheek muscles on his face. "So, you want to put her into therapy?"

"That, too, is an apt analogy." I allowed myself to sigh and returned to the edge of the sofa. This would be easier if The Flesh weren't so dependent on the rules of their social interactions, or if they were still able to access telepathic language centers. "We shall need a therapist. We would like to offer you the job."

"Wait a minute, now, Damien. I don't know how to do therapy." Paul's protest landed somewhere between whiney and irritable.

"The use of the term was an extension of the analogy. You will not be an actual therapist." I took a calming breath and reasserted my patience. "We have another option in mind. The Master Reapers Division believes our interests in this area have recently come into alignment with theirs. They have asked for a liaison to work directly with them and, on their behalf, with Starling, as well."

Paul lowered his chin and lifted an eyebrow. "What does a reaper liaison to angels do?"

I almost corrected him, but the job title was one of the least important aspects of this arrangement. "Paul, you have distinguished yourself in many ways in the last four months. In addition to the role of liaison to the Reapers, we are prepared to offer you a human-angel assignment. Such an assignment comes with significant perks to enhance the comfort of the average human life." I paused and caught his eye.

"There will also be a training period, of course. In the end, you will be assigned particularly to Starling. You will carry out specific interventions and liaise with Master Reaper representatives in furtherance of her... therapy." I paused and asked, "Do you have any questions thus far?"

Paul bobbed his head, impatiently. "Yeah. How do we get started?"

The End of Book One

PREVIEW OF BOOK 2

AVAILABLE NOW FOR PREORDER!

Starling Nightcastle

Book Two

The Demon On Her Shoulder

Prologue

When I was nineteen, at the end of my sophomore year of college, about six weeks before his high-school graduation, my brother died. He slumped over on the couch one night and fell into a coma. It was the next morning, when my calls were greeted with a full voice mail box and I was beginning to panic, that I finally got my grandmother to answer a call.

By the time I got to the hospital, even second cousins I had only seen at Christmas and funerals were there. He was my brother for God's sake, and I was the last person to find out.

They had him laid out in a bed surrounded by beeping, blinking and otherwise annoying machines shaped like ugly boxes with monitors and wires and hoses coming out of every inch. They had a hose going in one arm and another coming out of his other. Another hose was shoved into his thigh, and another came out from beneath his gown.

My grandmother walked me and Mike, my boyfriend at the time, my ex-husband now, inside. "Don't stay too long. There are more people in the waiting room who want a turn." With that and a nod, she turned and left me and Mike there. I found a stool and rolled it up beside my brother so I could reach out with one hand to hold his. I rested the fingers of my other hand on his shocking red hair, so unlike my own mousy brown. Where his was a thick mat of wispy fine straight locks, mine was thick and coarse, prone to chunky, unruly waves. I glanced up to where Mike leaned on an equipment cart in the corner of the curtained off area. He was distracted with his new flip phone.

I turned back to Nate's face and stroked his hair. His forehead felt too cold. I looked around but couldn't find any blankets to pull up or tuck in. I leaned over and laid my head on his chest with my eyes closed. "Nate? Are you cold? What happened? Why are you in here?" He didn't respond. I guess that's what coma means.

It wasn't a real room with walls and a door. It was just one of eight wedge shapes formed by curtains on two sides and a third halfway from the doctor and nurse's hub in the center. It wasn't fully closed, and the incessant beeping and giggling from the cluster of ice-hearted jerks, gathered there with their coffee and pastries, fanned a spark of righteous indignation in my chest. I tried not to cry as I lay there concentrating on that precious heart beating in his chest. The mechanical echo from the heart monitor sounded like a mocking countdown accompanying my dread.

"Graduation is only six weeks away. You don't want to miss it. I already bought my shoes to go with that dress you helped me pick out. Do you remember? You flirted so hard with the salesgirl. Hailey? Don't you have a date with her planned? She really likes you. I can't believe you found a girl that is as into that game as you are. Don't think I don't know about you and her running quests against that other team."

I felt a giggle at the thought of him and Hailey dressed like two little Rambo cartoons in that game and bit down hard on my cheek to stifle it. This wasn't the time for me to burst into a fit of giggles. The tears were more appropriate, and I let them flow.

An evil nurse in a set of green scrubs threw back the curtain with a screech of metal against metal. He breezed over to the beeping machine and marked a few places on the monitor readout. "You need to stop touching him, Ma'am."

I lifted my head and stared at him. "What?"

"It's too much stimulation." The nurse didn't look at me. "He needs to be asleep."

Fiery rage consumed me, and it poured out in my voice. "He's in a coma. How is he supposed to know we don't want him to leave us if we can't touch him? How are we supposed to make him wake up?"

"Ma'am. That's not how comas work." He reached down and tugged at the stool.

I had the choice of being dragged away from my brother or standing. I stood, and Mike finally noticed. He walked over and put a hand on my arm. "Can she hold his hand?"

The nurse heaved a sigh. "If she must."

I glared ineffectively at the side of his head and turned my attention back to my brother. I laid my hand on his and tried to remember what we had been talking about. Behind me, Mike talked to the nurse.

"Scans show a golf ball-sized tumor on his pituitary gland. His blood sugar is 843 and his blood pressure is 72 over 89. We are giving him fluids and waiting to see if the blood transfusion is going to help his numbers. He's extremely dehydrated and ..."

I stopped listening. Even as a pre-med undergrad, I knew how bad that was. How had my mother let this happen? How had my father let this happen? How did a seventeen-year-old boy with graduation around the corner and a cute new girlfriend become dehydrated and fall into a coma without anyone noticing something was wrong?

My grandmother pulled back the curtain with the ripping sound of one obstinate metal scraping past another. My mother was with her. The nurse held up both hands. "Only two please."

Mike nodded and leaned down to peck my cheek. "I'm going to go wait with your family so you and your mom can sit together a while." I nodded, still reeling with disbelief.

My grandmother huffed. "You really need to let someone else have a turn. Don't be so selfish all the time, Star."

I didn't turn. "I just got here, Granny. I may not get to see him again."

"Oh, pooh. He'll be fine. He deserves to know how many folks are here." The nurse began herding her and Mike out of the little..., not room. Area. My grandmother huffed again and walked out.

My mother moved to sit in a chair opposite me with my brother between us. "Did you hear about my new puppy?"

I looked at her and blinked, as if her words would make more sense if I could see them. "What?"

She pulled her digital camera out of her purse, and I heard the little jingle happily announcing its power-up. She fussed with the device for a while, then made an "ah" noise and lifted it, turning the display screen to me. A photo of her with a fluffy Pomeranian puppy in her lap showed her laughing and the puppy in the middle of bouncing and yipping.

My brother was there in the picture beside her. His smile was wan beneath eyes with a yellowish cast. With his head listed over to one side, I imagined the photo had captured the moment just before his smile slid over the edge of his cheek.

I took the camera and flipped to the next photo. Apparently, it and the several after it had been taken in quick succession. I stopped on a short video and played it. There was Nate, sitting beside my stupid mother, showing all the signs of not being alright. He acted almost drunken in the clip. His head wobbled and he almost dropped a can of soda as he lifted it to his lips.

I looked up at my mother, sitting on the other side of her dying son, grinning, and turned the screen to her. Her eyes flicked toward it and her smile lost its life. It became the shell of the expression as she focused on the display. "A puppy? Your son is right there beside you, dying, and you are playing with a puppy."

She reached out, and I let her take the camera back. I pulled the stool back up to the bedside and scooted closer to Nate's head. I laid my head down on the pillow beside his ear and closed my eyes. I blocked out the beeping and the chatter and my stupid, dissociated, self-centered mother.

"Nate. Please. You have so much to come back for. Please don't leave. You can come live with me. I'll get an apartment and we can be roommates. You and Hailey can teach me and Mike how to play that game and you can whip us, thoroughly, every single day. I still owe you for graduation. Remember? You were the only person at mine. I get the right to go to yours. Please, Nate, don't leave me."

A cousin or someone came in and took my mother's place, taking their "turn," I guess. I ignored them. I wasn't leaving.

I, eventually, did have to leave. Mike took me home, and I sat in the back corner of my shower under the hot water and cried, laughed, giggled with hysterics, and cried some more. It was dark as we opened the front door to head back to the hospital. My phone rang and I began to sob. He was dead. Mike answered the call, but I already knew.

For days afterward, I fought off the tormenting and completely selfish thought that he might still be alive if I hadn't left his side. He must have been fighting to hold on, knowing I was there rooting for him. He must have thought I had given up on him. When I'd left, so had he. Three days later, standing in the bright and cheerful sunlight, listening to some random pastor who got Nate's name wrong twice, I watched the ashes of my brother's body being sealed into a concrete vault.

I never recovered from that loss. I poured through the coroner's report and tried to understand what had happened. I got thrown out of the coroner's office when I went in with questions. I may not have been entirely rational. Mike tried; I think. He just never understood what I was feeling. I didn't really understand it either.

It was one of the biggest influences in my decision to become a coroner. I wanted to be able to answer the questions of the hysterical woman whose brother had died. Mike didn't get that either. We had a fight that should have ended our relationship when I finally told him I wanted to be a coroner.

We'd gone through medical school together, by that point, and he had a very different vision of our future than mine. He eventually convinced me, cajoled and threatened me, to complete a medical residency before making a final choice.

The asshole. He wasted so much of my time.

Chapter 1. Ranier Red

My name is Starling Nightcastle. I often wake from dreams about living someone else's nightmare. For most of my life, I've been stuck in my own nightmare, looking for a way out. One day, I'd find one. Until then, I needed coffee.

In the weeks since Paul's resurrection, I had suffered the house brew at the Holy Grounds diner with heroic patience. Not by choice, mind you. I had brought it up with Genia the very next time I saw her, but between all the new recipes that had to be photographed and finalized for Jacob's new menu and reorganizing the kitchen freezer to accommodate the new ingredients, she wasn't able to give any thought to it.

I understood. Honest! That didn't mean I wasn't persistent. The next time I brought it up, I did so with a tiny baggie of Ranier Red grounds for her to sniff. The aroma of those freshly ground beans, so like the smell of my grandfather's kitchen on the Saturday mornings of my childhood, the safe and cozy snuggle on the couch, my mug of mostly milk and his of steamy coffee; it was my secret weapon. That was enough to get her to agree to a taste test, but she insisted it be scheduled for a time when everyone could participate. Democracy can be so clunky.

So it happened, one fine spring evening, Genia, Jacob, Adrya, Ellie and I all gathered on one end of the service counter while Paul brewed a sample of Ranier Red and poured us each a cup. Ellie was the first to react, pursing her lips around the tiny sip she'd taken. "This is coffee?"

I chuckled and took a more generous pull from my own cup. "Yep. Good, isn't it?"

Adrya hummed. "It has such a strong, bold flavor with almost no bitterness."

Genia nodded. "This is an excellent find, Star, honey. Tell us about it, please."

I shot a glance at Paul, and we exchanged grins. "Well," I turned to catch Jacob's furrow-browed gaze and cleared my throat. "It's called Ranier Red and is produced by a small farm in Washington State. They can supply all your coffee needs; pots, filters, grounds, and all the accessories. The beans are a hybrid of plants from Ecuador and Hawaii, and the farm is completely organic."

I was obsessed with the stuff. I had spent the days before the taste test finding out as much as I could about the company. "My co-worker introduced me to the brand, and it's just so good." I sipped from my cup again, using the steamy liquid to physically make myself stop gushing.

Jacob graced us with one of his infrequent chortles. "You make a fine sales rep, Star. It's a good cup of Joe." He saluted us with his mug and tipped it up to empty it. He set the cup down and leaned in to peck Genia's cheek with a sweet kiss. "I gotta' go cook. It's good coffee, Gee-Gee."

I beamed at his retreating back. It wasn't that Jacob had never talked with me, or around me. It was just so infrequent. For him to approve my suggestion so publicly ignited a warm glow of happiness in my chest. I buried my face in my nearly empty mug and squeezed my eyes shut.

Genia, Adrya and Ellie clucked over their mugs about the pros and cons of switching brands. The sound of dining utensils clinking together and scraping against plates drifted into my ears; sharp like the tinkle of breaking glass. Paul reached out and placed his hand on my arm. I jerked at his touch and almost sloshed the dregs from my cup as I turned.

He stood there, a deeply understanding look in his eyes and a pot in his hand waiting to grant me a refill. He didn't take his hand off my arm as he poured. "I think you've pretty much convinced them." He waggled his eyebrows at me and chafed my arm.

'Damn.' He had developed a sixth sense about when my emotions were giving me trouble. The only real-life person who had ever seemed to understand what I was going through, I was extra glad Paul wasn't dead. I turned and checked on the ladies, confirmed that they were doing a fine job of talking themselves into adopting a new house brew, and turned back to Paul.

He took a long pull from his own mug and hummed. "Have you talked to anyone from the company about becoming our supplier?"

I nodded, still holding the cup in front of the lower half of my face. I tried to focus on contrasting the heat of my mug with the chill of the air around me; the physical sensation like an anchor in the stormy sea of my emotions. They were getting worse.

Paul chuckled and pulled the dish towel from his shoulder. Using the towel like a whisking broom on the counter in front of me, he said, "This is the part where you give me a detailed account of the conversation."

I allowed myself to smile back at him and lowered my cup. I felt as if I were vibrating in my seat as I related the gist of my phone interrogation of the Ranier Red sales office. "They were very nice and put up with my questions longer than I had expected. It's a family business, owned now by the daughter of the founder. This wouldn't be the first commercial supply contract they've gotten but not by much."

"That sounds like right where we'd want to be. Not the first so they don't make all their first mistakes on us, and still not too many others to take all the attention." Paul finished his cup of coffee and gestured at mine.

I huddled over my cup and pulled it closer to me. "I'm not ready to be done." I whined and immediately blushed. "Sorry." I straightened on my stool, then shot a look at the corner booth. It was empty and I turned back to Paul. With a jerk of my head toward the booth, I asked, "Wanna' join me for breakfast before I have to go to work?"

Paul grinned and nodded. I gave him my order and he walked it back to Jacob in the kitchen. I carried my mug and my purse over to the booth and settled in. Ellie was the first to walk over as I waited for Paul. "Ms. Star?"

I smiled up at her and let the smile ratchet up in intensity a notch or two when Ellie returned a wide and genuine smile of her own. "Hey, Ellie. Paul already got my order and I still have a full cup..."

She lifted her hands and waggled them at me. "Oh, good, because that's not why I came over."

I tipped my head to one side and thought, *'Okay. Good to know,'* as I sipped my coffee and waited for her to say more.

"Yeah, I was wondering if you remembered my brother, Evan?" Ellie bit her lip and lifted her eyebrows in a way that caused a crease to furrow between them. Between that and the wringing of her hands I assumed she was hoping for an affirmative.

"Kinda' tall, looks like you, but, you know, a guy?" I guessed as I searched my memory for a male Ellie.

"Oh, good!" Ellie transformed from stiff and hopeful to melted and relieved as she sagged into the booth seat across from mine. "He was afraid you wouldn't remember him, but I told him you were good with people."

I choked on my coffee.

Ellie straightened and looked like she might come around the table to pat me on the back. "Are you okay?"

I waved her off and nodded. "Fine. Just tried to breathe and swallow at the same time. What's going on with your brother, now?"

Ellie settled back and sighed. "Well, he's getting out of school this year and was hoping to get an internship with you at the morgue."

It clicked then. At the dinner party when we'd tried out Jacob's new menu, there had been an apple-cheeked male Ellie. "Mhmm, what was his degree in again?"

Ellie rolled her eyes up and chewed her upper lip. "Um, pathological doctor?" She shook her head and looked back at me. "Something like that. Can I give him your number? He's so smart, and he's worked so hard."

I really thought about it, really hard, looking for a way to say no. I sighed. "Yeah, just warn him to make sure he calls after dark."

Ellie bounced up from the booth seat, rounded the table, and was upon me before I could brace myself. She threw her arms around my neck and squeezed. I wasn't sure if I should worry more about passing out when she cut off my oxygen supply or spilling my coffee when I passed out. Luckily, she let me go with a quick, "Thank you!"

I watched as she bounded off to take care of customers, newly seated in a booth that had been empty when I'd sat down. They must have come in while she and I were talking, but I hadn't noticed. I lifted my coffee to my lips and watched the way Ellie moved and the expressions she made. *'What a little hustler, and good at it, too. She'd played dumb and fooled me.'* It was the first time I had ever questioned Ellie's intelligence. I'd been duped.

Adrya and Genia walked over, interrupting my downward spiral as I questioned my own intelligence, powers of persuasion, and general worthiness as a human. The vinyl seat cover made loud protestations, like a flock of balloon animals being tortured, as Genia and Adrya wriggled into the seat across from me.

"Star, honey, this is amazing coffee."

Adrya nodded. "Mhmm. I think we're all on board for it."

Genia said, "Well, at least as far as checking it out more."

"Right." Adrya gave a punctuating nod.

I scooted down in the booth seat and hunched over my coffee. "Right."

Genia grinned. "Right! So, I'll arrange to call the number you gave me and get the details."

Adrya sipped her coffee again. "Mm. This is a really special find."

Genia reached out and briefly touched my bare forearm with fingers that were coffee-warm. "Very special."

She and Adrya bounced up and out of the booth, almost colliding with Paul as he approached. Paul executed a graceful pirouette with the serving tray and averted the whole thing so smoothly, neither woman seemed to realize the proximity of the call. He sat the tray down on the end of the table and glanced over his shoulder at the two retreating backs.

He snorted and gave his head a tiny shake as he began to empty the tray of its burden, including a fresh, full pot of coffee. "They're excited. I heard Jake say he thought it was a perfect time to switch the house brew. 'This stuff will go better with my delicate new pastries.'" He chuckled and held the empty serving tray out behind him without looking. Ellie strode by and plucked it from his hand as he folded himself into the seat.

When he'd scooted and settled where he wanted to be, he looked back up at me. The hungry visual perusal of his plate was consumed by a solemn gaze of concern as he looked up. That hit me as hilarious. Coming, as it did, atop the other ping-ponging emotions I'd dealt with that night, I did the only reasonable thing. I whimpered.

Paul let his head lean to one side and hummed a gruff and low noise of understanding. He topped off my cup and said, "Emotions acting up again?"

I nodded, a weepy-eyed and grateful affirmative. "I feel like a kite on the beach at sunset."

He double blinked at me, then gave his head a tight shake. "Eat something. Concentrate on the physical sensations, like we practiced."

That was something else I'd been doing since Paul's resurrection. Practicing wrangling my rampant emotions with mindfulness exercises. I didn't know if they were any more effective then, than they had been in the bin, but it meant so much to Paul. I took a deep breath and picked up my fork. "Right. Food." I sniffled and began eating my bad feelings away.

I stared at my plate as salty steam filled the inside of my mouth. I breathed slowly through my nose, letting the fresh breath carry the steam down my throat and cool the food on my tongue. The low buzz of the florescent lights hummed as if sharing my appreciation for the rich and buttery flavors. The soft and warm sensation permeated my entire body and oozed out into the air around me.

Paul reached for his coffee. The movement shattered the moment and I leaned back in my booth seat. I swallowed and, with a deep sigh, closed my eyes. I followed the sensation, real or imagined, of the food I had just swallowed as it traveled down my esophagus and into my stomach. The contents, exclusively coffee up till that point, lodged a protest with my decision-making faculties. I spent the next few seconds reassuring my unsettled stomach that I would take its complaint under advisement. When I opened my eyes again, Paul was quietly nibbling on a link of sausage and watching me.

I turned a narrow-eyed gaze on him. "What?"

Paul let a corner of his mouth twitch upward and grunted around his sausage. When he'd swallowed and cleared his mouth with a sip of coffee, he said, "You know 'what'. Same questions I've had since..."

He trailed off and I let him off the hook with a nod. "Yeah, I know. I mean, Damien has explained it pretty well for you. I trade my services with people who have special qualities to Crow. In exchange, he purges these pesky emotions."

Paul crinkled a paper napkin between his fingertips, wiping grease in reddish, brown streaks on the dull white paper. "How are things between you two?"

I couldn't help it. A full belly laugh rolled up my throat and spilled out across the table between us. I pressed my free hand across my gaping maw and darted a wary glance around the dining room, concerned I had drawn attention. The thought stifled the giggly noise better than my hand and I sucked in a calming breath. My lungs inflated, straightening my back, and I found Paul's calm gaze waiting patiently for me to respond with words.

My cheeks flushed, the heat washing down my neck and chest. "I'm sorry. I'm still a kite, and the wind is picking up." I sighed and dropped both hands to my lap. Food wasn't doing the trick. I began to run the edge of one thumbnail along the hem of my shirt and spoke in time to the stropping rhythm. "I have seen Crow almost every night since..." I cleared my throat. When Paul's only response was an aborted grin, I continued. "but he's been distant. If he's getting any backlash from..., well, he hasn't told me."

"So, he isn't angry anymore?"

I thought about it. The night Paul had changed his mind about taking a swap had been the first time Crow and I had ever experienced a client simply rejecting the deal. Crow had been terrifying in his demonic outrage, but it wasn't directed at me. In fact, he had visibly reined himself in to deal with me alone afterward. But he had been short and clipped with me, that night and ever since. Not inattentive, but he hadn't lingered with me since that night either.

I shook my head. "I don't think so. I think he's just busy, scrambling to get another lead."

Paul pursed his lips and stared into his coffee. I wondered idly if there might be some kind of bug doing the back stroke to provoke that look. The thought became less idle when Paul sipped.

'No choking or sputtering or chewing; must be bug-free.'

He smacked as he swallowed and turned a quizzical look to me. "So, you're still committed to the deal with him?"

I frowned. The massive weight of guilt pulling at me since that day gathered itself and settled more solidly atop my shoulders. "I don't see an option. I appreciate all the effort you have put toward helping me ride the waves, but this is not a long-term solution." He shot a glance to one side and shrugged his eyebrows. "That almost looked like an eyeroll, mister. What?"

He chuckled. "No; well, maybe, but not at you. Damien says this will work, we just have to be patient and persistent." He shrugged properly. "Do you want some more coffee, or should we get your leftovers wrapped up?" He looked at his wrist as if checking an invisible watch.

When my father used to do that, to make a point about the time, he would make a quip. It was grotesque and not at all appropriate for a child in the single digit age range. So, of course, I repeated it then. "Is it a hair past the freckle on a monkey's ass already?"

Paul turned his head to give me a side eye.

I cleared my throat and brought my mostly drained coffee cup back to my lips, muttering from behind the rim, "Nah. You can put it in the donations."

Earlier in the week, he had regaled me with the successful first distribution of reclaimed food to his street friends. I had asked if his friends minded getting other people's leftovers. His response had been a sideways grin and, "You really think homeless guys care who the leftovers belonged to before?"

His face lit up and he stood. Lifting dishes from the table, he said, "Let me just run these into the kitchen." He settled my nearly full plate atop his spotlessly clean one and hurried off.

I lifted the coffee pot and let the last drops trickle into my cup. The coffee was lukewarm and had lost its shimmer, but the scent as it sloshed and the taste as it chilled the tip of my tongue were divine. The tiny cup's worth was one very large mouthful.

There I was, my cheeks puffed out and my eyes squinted, delighting in a bitter, cold, black coffee choking hazard, when Crow's voice landed on my ears. "Careful, Little Bird."

Coffee went everywhere.

Chapter 2. Client Profile

I looked up to see Crow sitting primly in the middle of the booth opposite me. His hands were folded, fingers interlaced, on the table between us, his typical suit jacket over a dress shirt and a pair of distressed, fitted blue jeans. I scowled as coffee dripped from my lip. The smirk on his face was one of the most wonderful things I had ever seen.

"Did you just... appear?" I tugged a couple of napkins from the table dispenser and sopped up the mess, beginning with my face.

"Of course not, Bird. I arrived invisible and waited for the opportunity to announce myself."

"And then, you appeared out of thin air."

"Did it really happen if no one witnessed it?"

I rolled my eyes and squeezed my fists in my lap. Each time I had seen him since Paul's resurrection, I had felt a compulsion in my bones to fawn over him and beg for some overt sign of his good favor. It was embarrassing, and I refused to give in. So, I usually tried to play it cool and exchange quips with him until he got to the point.

That night, Paul rescued me, walking up at that moment and sliding in beside Crow, as if they were best friends, or brothers. "Mr. Crow! We were just talking about you." Paul's genuine happiness at seeing Crow shone through his affable smile.

Crow inhaled, deep and slow. "Yes. I know." He turned back to me. "I apologize if I've seemed terse recently, Bird. I've been somewhat stressed given recent events at work."

I met both sets of unblinking eyes, shaking my head between one and the other, and sighed. "Yeah, okay. What brings you to the diner tonight?"

It felt like a strange, cold, and distant thing to say to someone who literally knew everything about me. As my personal demon, Crow had been around since I'd gained the ability to discern right from wrong. Up until a few weeks before, I had thought I had understood and been comfortable with the rules of our relationship. Then and there, I was deep in the foggy center of uncertainty.

Crow gave no sign of any tender thoughts or feelings, simply sitting primly and casting unkind glances at Paul beside him. "I have found our next client. I will tell you all about her on the way to the morgue, if you would like my company." He turned to meet Paul's grinning stare.

Paul chuckled. "We were just about to head that way. You have good timing, Mr. Crow."

I frowned, drawing my brows so far down and tightly wrinkled, I could see the blurry tufts of my eyebrows overhanging my eyes. "You two..." I huffed and shook my head. Snatching my purse with one hand, I began to shimmy out of the booth seat. "Let's get going if we're going."

Paul stood and adroitly turned to bow Crow out of the booth only to discover the booth seat was empty.

Crow cleared his throat from where he stood at the door several feet away. "Yes. Let's, Bird."

Paul chuckled and shared a glance with me, sweeping one arm before him in a gesture for me to lead. I sighed, shook my head, and lowered my eyes as I took my first step toward the door. Each step was slightly faster until I almost trotted through the door as Crow pushed it open. He swung out behind me, leaving Paul to catch the closing door for himself.

Paul muttered, "Not so gracious as last time. I wonder why."

I snorted and kept walking. If they were going to antagonize each other, I wasn't going to get in the middle of it. I set a relaxed but quick pace up the sidewalk toward work. The sun, setting ahead and a bit to the left of the lay of the street, cast long orange and violet streaks through the clouds on the horizon. What I could see of it through the buildings was stunning.

Crow and Paul each achieved a pace that brought them up on either side of me before I made it to the first intersection. Paul inhaled loudly as I pushed the crosswalk button, and said, "You have a new client prospect? I'm sure Star's relieved to hear that."

Crow lifted his chin and made an odd pursing motion with his lips. The motion pulled the muscles of his neck in a disturbing display beneath his skin. "Indeed. Bird, should we not talk in private? You realize Paul is in collusion with the opposing department?" He waved a hand on a flaccid wrist in Paul's general direction.

I turned my head between them. Crow feigned sincere concern for supernatural corporate espionage, while Paul grinned, met my eyes, and wiggled his fingers at me. Facing forward and letting a groan of frustration burble up from my throat, I shook my head. "No, Crow. I blame you, you know. You always knew this was a possibility. Paul, as a former client, is really the only real human I can share any of this with. You're, well, you and all, but sometimes, it's nice to talk to someone about all this stuff who doesn't have an agenda for me."

I knew it was the wrong thing to say as soon as I said it.

"No agenda? Bird, might I remind you that the only reason they interfered with him was to bring him into their agenda!" Had it been anyone else, I'd have said Crow sounded petulant. His eyes bulged from their sockets and his jaw hung slack as he waved in Paul's direction.

I looked back to Paul. Once again, he grinned, met my eyes, and wiggled his fingers at me. I let my head slump to one side and my shoulders slouch as I gave him the most withering look of disdain I could muster.

Paul spoke over my head to Crow. "I am not here to interfere. My only agenda is to be the best friend I can be to Star. Her decisions are all her own."

I turned to Crow and held up my hand as if to display Paul upon my palm. "See?"

Crow vibrated with tension in his head and shoulders and sighed. "Fine, Bird. Don't say I didn't warn you."

I led the way across the intersection. The tension between them was like a palpable wave driving me forward as they heeled me to either side.

"The client is a devoted wife and mother with an interest in ballet. I thought we could attend a performance she will be attending. Perhaps meet her during intermission?" Crow's voice seemed higher in pitch, a little breathier than usual.

Paul chuckled. "What are you going to do? Buy her popcorn and ask if she wants to trade lives with a ballerina?"

I heard Crow's step falter, then quicken. "As a matter of fact, the client does already come with a suitable swap option. The prima ballerina of the company that will be performing would make a more than suitable swap."

I turned down the street the morgue was on just as a grunt came from Paul. I looked over my shoulder to see Crow looking completely innocent as Paul pushed away from the corner. I stopped and turned to face them. "When, Crow?"

He cast a glance at Paul. "Tomorrow evening."

I nodded and sighed. Meeting Paul's eyes, I saw no reproval or disappointment. "Can we talk in the morning?"

He shook his head. "Nah uh. I'm planning to be thoroughly asleep when you leave work." He grinned down at me. "It's okay. Why don't you come by the diner after the ballet, and you can tell me all about it?"

I gave him a grateful smile and nodded. "Okay. Now, off with you both. I have to get to work."

Crow gave a minute bow and faded away. Paul took a deliberate step in to the space Crow probably still occupied on some dimension. He tugged his forelock with a sideways grin. "Have a good night, Ms. Star." With that, he executed a perfect about face and proceeded back the way we'd come.

I watched him turn the corner and turned myself back toward the morgue. "You're still here, aren't you?"

Crow faded back into view on the other side of me. "Of course. We can't trust that Convert."

Nothing I said was likely to change Crow's opinion. To him, Paul was more than just the one that had gotten away. He was a failure. He was proof that the power of Free Will was stronger than a demon. Crow would never admit it, but I could tell. Paul and whatever else he stood for terrified Crow.

As the closest thing to a friend or lover I'd had in more than fifteen years, that touched a soft spot in me. I reached out and, timidly, wormed my hand into the crook of Crow's elbow. "It's okay Crow. I chose this deal with you. My reasons for it haven't changed."

He turned and graced me with one of the tender smiles I hadn't seen in weeks. He patted my fingers on his arm and said, "Thank you, Bird."

My chest fluttered, either with butterflies escaped from my stomach or my racing heart, I couldn't say. My habitual thought pattern landed straight on how sweet and downright vulnerable he seemed in that moment. Some new and annoying voice drifted out of my mindfulness practice, whispering doubts. I squeezed his arm and held my peace.

When we reached the top of the morgue driveway, I stopped and turned, placing one hand lightly against his chest. I looked up at him through my lashes. "Will you be able to meet me when I get off work tonight?"

He smiled, lascivious wickedness lifting the corners of his eyes to match his grin. "I can't wait." He leaned close, enveloping me in the warm, spicy aroma of his presence. He deposited a soft, chaste kiss on my forehead and vanished.

Chapter 3. 14

Bouncy 90s pop music spilled out of an occupied exam room as I crossed the cold room floor. Neville tapped his foot and bobbed with the rhythm. Gail met me at the office door, coming out as I went in. We each slid to the right and squeezed past.

"Hey, Boss." She tossed the greeting at me with a flip of her hand, not slowing down.

I grunted my response, not yet having a verbal one cued up. I pulled the door around to hang my purse on the back and watched around its edge as Gail hurried across the cold room. She slid to a stop beside a young man still possessed of a few pimply blemishes on his cheeks. I paused there, watching as she animatedly described what he was doing wrong.

Movement behind them caught my eye and the corners of my mouth quirked upward. Neville skirted the duo and approached, carrying my preferred lab coat. He grinned and proffered the coat as he reached the door. "Good evening." His Count Dracula impression sounded more like Count Chocula.

"Hey. What's going on?" I accepted the coat and jutted my chin toward the frenetic scene in the cold room.

Neville tossed a glance over his shoulder and rolled his eyes. "It's his first night. Gail's just tired of going over the intro spiel."

I hummed as I turned to the office computer to clock in and check email. "This isn't the same one from the night before last?"

Neville clicked a button on the coffee pot and settled into a chair beside the desk. "Nope. You're thinking of 13. And that was a woman."

I met his eyes and blinked. "Really?" He nodded, and the coffee pot burbled. "Wow." I shook the confusion from my face and shrugged. "I left you two in charge of interns for a reason. What's the outlook for this one?"

Neville pulled open a drawer beneath the coffee pot and retrieved an eight-pack of miniature donuts. "This is a twenty-six-year-old graduate of the pathology and microbiology program at UNMC. He's waiting for a residency program. We call him 14."

My eyes shifted between Neville and the scene in the cold room. "He's twenty-six?" At Neville's nod, I shook my head and asked, "And the pool?"

Neville shoved a donut into his mouth and worked it to one side. Cheek stuffed, he said, "Gail gave him a week. I'm not sure yet."

I nodded. "Do we have a second intern coming in, or has the administration located a suitable tech?"

Neville shoved another donut into his mouth, effectively packing both cheeks in a way he must have learned from watching squirrels and shrugged.

I crinkled my nose at him and waved my hands in a shooing motion. "Fine, go, get to work." I offered a small smile to soften any abrasiveness the shooing may have contained and turned back to the computer. Neville's presence and activity fled my conscious awareness as he rose and walked toward the door, and I perused the emails in my inbox.

Having been assigned a supervisory position on the night shift, email had taken on a more important if infrequent role in my duties. Therefore, I made dutiful note of a few points of interest and deleted everything else. When the coffee pot gave a long, burbling sigh, I turned to pour a half cup for myself and stifled a scream.

Neville leaned there between the door and the coffee pot, delicately munching the last donut from his pack. His back was to me, and he turned to look over his shoulder when the squeak of the aborted scream reached his ears. "Anything interesting in email?"

"I thought I sent you to work."

He shrugged and held up his empty donut wrapper. "No food outside the office." He leaned over to deposit his wrapper in the trash and brushed the crumbs from his hands as he straightened. "It wasn't insubordination, I promise."

I rolled my eyes but couldn't stop a tiny grin from parking itself on my face. "Fine. Just make more noise next time." I pulled the lower desk drawer out far enough to rest my feet on its edge and sipped my coffee. "There are a couple of new calendar items. I put them on the shared one." I sipped and flicked my gaze to the empty in-box next to the computer. "What does the case load look like in Deadman's Village?"

Neville shoved his hands in his own lab coat pockets and turned to look out the open door. "At the moment, there are four villagers for us to process. Gail's trying to get 14 to take scans after she does the weights, measures, and photos. He's slow." Neville frowned. "I have already put those four in the order they should be worked."

I turned my head and watched Gail herding 14 through the door with a gurney between them. I turned back in time to see Neville shaking his head. I sipped my coffee, closed my eyes to savor it, then stood, shrugged into my lab coat, and clapped my hands. "Let's see if we can help her get things moving."

The work progressed with the speed of chilled molasses. Fortunately, it flowed as smoothly as molasses, as well, at least until Pete and Donna arrived with two new villagers. Gail and 14 met them at the door, and I joined them as the two demons moonlighting as EMTs wheeled the newcomers into the cold room.

Donna gave the brief summary. "One male, thirty-two, car accident, DOA at the ER. One female, eleven, died from injuries in the same accident during life-saving efforts. They had just opened her up when they lost her." The contented smile on her face was a jarring contrast to the report, but not out of character.

Gail thumbed through the files for both and nodded. A moan from 14 caused her to whip her head around to face him. The young man stared at the two human remains bags, or HRBs, looking like he wanted to be sick. Gail rolled her eyes and smacked the two folders into his chest. "Take these to the office and put them in the incoming basket." 14 lifted his hands and caught the folders, nodded without taking his eyes from the HRBs, and swallowed hard before turning away.

Gail turned to me and shook her head with a sigh. "I don't know about that one."

I chuckled and lowered my eyes to the bodies. Neville came sauntering out of an exam room as Gail and I each unzipped a bag for a cursory visual inspection. Donna glided toward him with a sultry curve to her lips. I caught a straightening of Neville's shoulders as he watched Donna approach before my attention was riveted to the body under my hands.

I'd opened the adult male bag, and, besides the expected breaks and blood, there was no evident cause for expeditious action. I shifted my attention to the young girl's body and Gail. Gail had come a long way in the last few weeks. When the perky young woman had first been assigned to the night shift, she was barely skilled enough to be trusted, unsupervised, as a lab tech. Now I watched as she expertly scanned the body for signs of ongoing damage or deterioration. She ignored the tragedy of the mangled mess before her and made a professional assessment for the good of the deceased. When she looked up and met my eyes, she cleared her throat before speaking. "She looks stable."

I could feel the prideful beaming smile glowing on my face and cleared my throat, as well. "Good. Do you want to take your intern through the recording process?"

"Want is a strong word, but sure." Gail met 14 as he was exiting the office, the red rims around his eyes saying he'd taken a moment to have an emotional response. She got him turned around with a few waves of her arms and they both dipped back through the door.

"No. I don't think so. Please, Donna, can we discuss it later?" The pitch of Neville's voice rose like the anguished cry of a cornered mouse.

I zipped up the HRB before me with a loud, ripping sound. "Donna, please don't torture my subordinates."

Donna's high laughter rang like a chime leading into the husky lilting cadence of her voice. "Oh, he's just being coy. If this is torture, it's the most exquisite kind." She shot a glance up and back at Neville, then spun on her heel. "Is there any coffee?"

I turned to Pete, who quietly stood to one side. He had his phone out and frowned with pursed lips over its glowing screen. Before I could speak, he glanced up at Donna's retreating back and turned to follow her.

I sighed and fell in behind him. I heard Neville's steps retreating back toward his exam room and called over my shoulder. "Are you coming?"

Neville shot a quick look at where Donna had just stepped through the office door. Meeting my eyes again, he shook his head, and turned back to his exam room.

I frowned and hoped I wouldn't have to intervene for the sake of workplace serenity. I certainly didn't want to lose Neville's skill now that I'd grown accustomed to having him and Gail there. With a sigh that heaved my shoulders up nearly to my ears, I turned to follow the crowd.

In the office, Donna had taken up a place just over 14's shoulder. "You misspelled that." The young man jerked as her arm flashed out to point at a place on the screen.

"Donna, what's gotten into you?" I gestured for her to take her customary seat on the short filing cabinet. Donna turned to me and made a scrunched face of dissatisfaction before rolling her eyes and sauntering to her seat. I picked up my coffee from where I'd left it beside the pot and noted the squinty-eyed glare Gail aimed at the other woman. I cocked my head and one eyebrow at her as I caught her eye over the rim of my mug. A sip from my cup reminded me how long it had been since I'd poured it. I put it back down as Gail lowered her eyes in an abashed pout and turned to supervise 14's efforts.

The scene sent ripples of giggles overflowing into my sinuses. I tried desperately to swallow before a couple of snorts broke the dam. With my hand clapped over my mouth and nose, both air accessways were effectively, if temporarily, blocked. A roomful of curious eyes turned on me. I raised one finger, my other hand still securely affixed to my face, lowered my eyes and backed out of the office door.

Once I'd made it halfway across the cold room floor, the lack of oxygen had dampened my desire to giggle. My gasping breath seemed to amplify as I removed my hand from my face. It was the creepiest sound I'd ever heard in the morgue. There I stood, with spittle still covering my hand and drool leaking from the corner of my mouth, when Neville popped out of his exam room casting about with his eyes.

His survey landed on me, and a series of transient expressions morphed across his features. Startlement flowed into confusion, followed by curiosity and amusement, before landing on mild concern as he took a few steps closer. "I thought I heard something strange. Are you okay?"

I turned my frozen expression away from him and glared down at the slobber on my hand. A quick step to the end of a gurney put me in easy reach of disinfectant wipes. I busied myself with cleaning up and said, "I tried to laugh and sneeze at the same time..."

"That happens. What was that noise, though?"

At that, I looked up and realized, he was completely sincere. I should have guessed, with his table manners, worse than this had happened to him in my presence. I half-snorted again before catching myself and turned it into a hum. With a small shake of my head, I threw the wipe into the trash and reached up to pull my hair out of the drool left on my face.

A white paper towel appeared before my eyes, fluttering from the tips of Neville's fingers. He waggled it at me. I accepted the sacrifice and rubbed the towel over the entirety of the lower half of my face until I was satisfied. That too went into the trash, and I felt more emotionally stable. I was measurably irked and delighted by the freeness of that particular emotion in comparison to the rapid bouncing from happy to sad to panicked that had become my norm. Pleasantly irked was a state I thought I might be able to maintain for an extended period.

Gently amused beneath my irkedness, I finally turned fully to face Neville. He was on his phone and had wandered off a few feet in the interim. The heel hadn't even been paying attention to my embarrassing moment of weakness and exposure.

"Who do you think you are that everyone would be watching you? Folks have got more important things to do than watch some conceited child." My grandmother's voice floated to me from the depths of memory.

"I wasn't conceited, Granny. I'm still not."

I felt her judgy gaze like a bouncy house landing on my head and shoulders and slowly deflating. It surrounded me and pushed me down, confronting me with the ineffectiveness of my defenses. It is a heaviness that lays on a person's heart and lungs, making it hard to breathe. The state of helpless despair that voice typically evoked in me frayed at the edges of my thoroughly irked temper. I felt every ounce of it, but, at the same time, I was solidly irked.

Oh yeah. This could definitely work.

I frowned at Neville and cleared my throat. "That better be something inappropriate that I can growl about." I closed most of the space between us as Neville grunted a weak laugh.

He still didn't look up. He did take a step or two closer as an explanatory rumble emanated from his mouth. It sounded something like, "Ask'n m'ex sump'n."

"Did you say, 'your ex'?" I closed the remaining distance in one great stride. "Did you?" Irked was sliding down in favor of curious excitement. I quickly reminded myself that he was a heel, and that I wasn't surprised he had an ex. I stopped my logical rationalizations short of reminding myself that I too had an ex.

Neville hummed and poked a button on his screen with his thumb and snared me in his gaze as I attempted to slide close enough to read over, or under, his arm. "Yeah. It's been some years but we're still friends." He thumbed the side of his phone, and the screen went dark before I could see any details. He dropped the phone into his shirt pocket beneath his lab coat and smiled down at me. "How is 14 taking to Pete and Donna?"

I tossed a glance toward the office. Through the window and open door, I could see Donna making catty faces in Gail's direction. I shrugged as I turned back to Neville. "I think Gail's already made him cry."

Neville chuckled and grinned down at me. "If gatherings of this size are becoming the standard, you're going to have to convince management to allocate resources for a proper breakroom."

I rolled my eyes and took a step to lead the way back to the others. "You mean a proper office? This is the only breakroom without going up a floor." Neville made amused noises as he followed me, and I had to cling to the irk.

The office was in fact too small for that size of crowd. 14 had rightfully commandeered my seat at the desk as he was actually working. Gail was snugged up beside him in the corner chair. The two EM demons relaxed in the opposite corner; Pete atop the corner stool, and Donna perched upon her file cabinet throne. I looked over the remaining options, discarding each as too uncomfortable or too undignified.

Neville stood idly beside me for a breath before jumping forward with a startled, "Oh, right! I thought we might run short on seating." He crouched beside a long, all-purpose table and pulled out a folding camp chair. It looked like a miniature or child's chair when it was all folded up. I watched avidly as Neville flicked and unfolded until it was a full-sized, if oddly shaped, chair.

When he'd placed the plastic and aluminum booby trap on the floor before me, he swept his hand out and beamed at me. "Boss?"

I studied the chair, my gaze directed down my nose to better scoff. "Oh, no. I really couldn't take your seat."

Neville began moving before I finished speaking and pulled another chair from beneath the table. "You aren't. That one is all yours." With a quick series of flicks, a moment later, he was sitting sprawled in the second chair.

Gail chuckled from her sturdy wooden chair. "Another present? Look out, Boss."

Neville frowned at her, and I said, "That's dangerously close to HR talk."

Gail cleared her throat and turned back to supervising 14 at the same time Donna quietly sniggered. Something was not right between those two. Neville dropped into his own chair and reached out to pat the seat of the other. "It's perfectly safe. Sturdy." He gripped the empty chair and clattered it against the floor.

A hiccupping whimper escaped my throat and I turned it into a throat-clearing cough as I stepped up to the waiting seat. I shot a quick look around the room, ineffectively looking for Murphys.

Pete said, "It's safe. I'm sure it won't just fold up on you."

I responded with a withering gaze of wry unamusement and turned away from the seat. "I haven't gotten a cup of coffee yet." I almost resisted the urge to stick my tongue out at him.

Neville joined me at the coffee pot, rummaging in his snack drawer. "You don't have to sit in the chair if you don't want to."

"Really?" I almost rolled my eyes at myself and the way my relief came pouring out in that one knee-jerk response.

Donna giggled and hopped down from her perch. "Hey!" She skipped up to us and slid in between me and Neville. "I have the best idea. We should all go out drinking this weekend!"

"That's a horrible idea," I said, right atop three other voices, each expressing various levels of excitement for the outing.

"Aww, come on, Boss." Gail whined.

I frowned at her and shook my head. "What? Why?"

Pete dismounted the corner stool and stepped close, pinning me between him and Donna in the line-up. "Star, even the intern wants to go."

14 whipped his head around with a protest bumbling its way out of his mouth. Gail nudged his shoulder. "He's joking. You aren't even invited."

"No one is invited. I can't be the only one to already have plans." I raised my mug above my head with both hands and sidled out of the demon sandwich. "Break is over in five. Donna, Pete, if you are finished with your coffee..." I gave them each a warning gaze.

Pete widened his eyes and turned away, lifting his cup. Donna pouted and turned to Neville just in time to watch him wander away, back to his chair with a banana and a squeeze pack of almond butter. She watched him for a moment, her face a mask of confusion. She caught my eye and the expression dissolved into boredom. I took advantage of the break in our gazes when Gail and 14 stood and walked between us, following the pair with my eyes.

Gail pointed and explained and led 14 through the initial clean up processes for the body of the young girl. It began almost immediately. 14's face paled and his eyelids drooped as soon as the HRB was removed. When Gail made him begin removing and cataloguing the clothing fragments still on the body, his mouth went tight.

I eased back and sat in the chair beside Neville. "This is painful to watch." The demons came to stand behind us, watching the trainwreck in progress.

By the time Gail instructed 14 to begin cleaning the body, sweat had broken out on his brow, and his face was flushed. When his cheeks started to puff with a heroic effort not to be sick, I'd seen enough.

I stood and stepped up to the doorway. "Gail. He's going to..." Gail looked over at 14 and lunged toward a waste basin. Too late.

Fortunately, the intern had the sense to turn away from the body. Unfortunately, he didn't have the sense to recuse himself before he vomited all over the floor. 14 sank to his knees, still heaving over his mess.

Gail huffed so loudly that I could feel the sound wave as it rolled through me. She unlocked the wheels of the gurney, kicking them with her toes, and pushed it out of the way. When she came back to 14, she pushed a mop and bucket in front of her.

I turned to Neville. "Are you sure this guy graduated med school? Did anyone check his references?"

Starling Nightcastle
Book Two
The Demon On Her Shoulder
COMING **May 7, 2023**!
AVAILABLE <u>NOW</u> FOR PREORDER!

A Note from the Author

Thank you for reading *Starling Nightcastle, Book One: Deals With Demons*. I hope you have enjoyed it! I always appreciate feedback; please leave a review wherever you bought this book.

Look for more Starling Nightcastle stories and other tales at www.UbrielBryneBooks.com[1].

For a full list of available titles or to join my newsletter mailing list, visit www.ubrielbrynebooks.com.

---

1. http://www.UbrielBryneBooks.com

About the Author

Amy Norton has been a professional legal code editor since 2015. She writes under her own name as well as Ubriel Bryne and Jami Lee Montgomery and publishes all three under www.UbrielBryneBooks.com[1].

Amy lives in the tropical hell that is the panhandle of North Florida with Zacharyn Norton, two loud-mouthed dogs, and two cats, one lanky, the other a chunk. When she isn't braving the wild waters of her local area in her kayak, crossing swords with mosquitoes and competing in water acrobatics against colossal alligators, she is hiking and camping or taking road trips to hike and camp in new and less nightmarish climates.

Ubriel Bryne's writing is sometimes whimsical and sometimes flippant but always full of creative imagery. She has been writing for two decades and released a few shorter works here and there. Her debut science fiction novel series, The Ports of Surset, was released in 2020. The Starling Nightcastle series is Ubriel's urban fantasy debut.

Contact the Author

Website www.ubrielbrynebooks.com
Twitter @ubrielbryne20
Instagram ubrielbryne20
Reddit r/ubrielbrynebooks
Facebook /ubrielbrynebooks/
I love to talk about my books! Contact me anytime.

Lightning Source UK Ltd.
Milton Keynes UK
UKHW021850120123
415233UK00015B/865